MINE TO SHIELD

PROTECTION SERIES
BOOK 9

KENNEDY L. MITCHELL

© 2024 Kennedy L. Mitchell

All rights reserved. This book or any portion thereof may not be reproduced or used in any manner whatsoever without the express written permission of the publisher except for the use of brief quotations in a book review.

This book is a work of fiction. Any references to historical events, real people, or real places are used fictitiously. Other names, characters, places and events are products of the author's imagination, and any resemblances to actual events or places or persons, living or dead, is entirely coincidental.

Cover Design: Bookin It Designs

Editing: The Ryter's Proof

Proofreading: All Encompassing Books

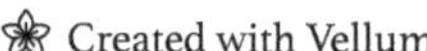 Created with Vellum

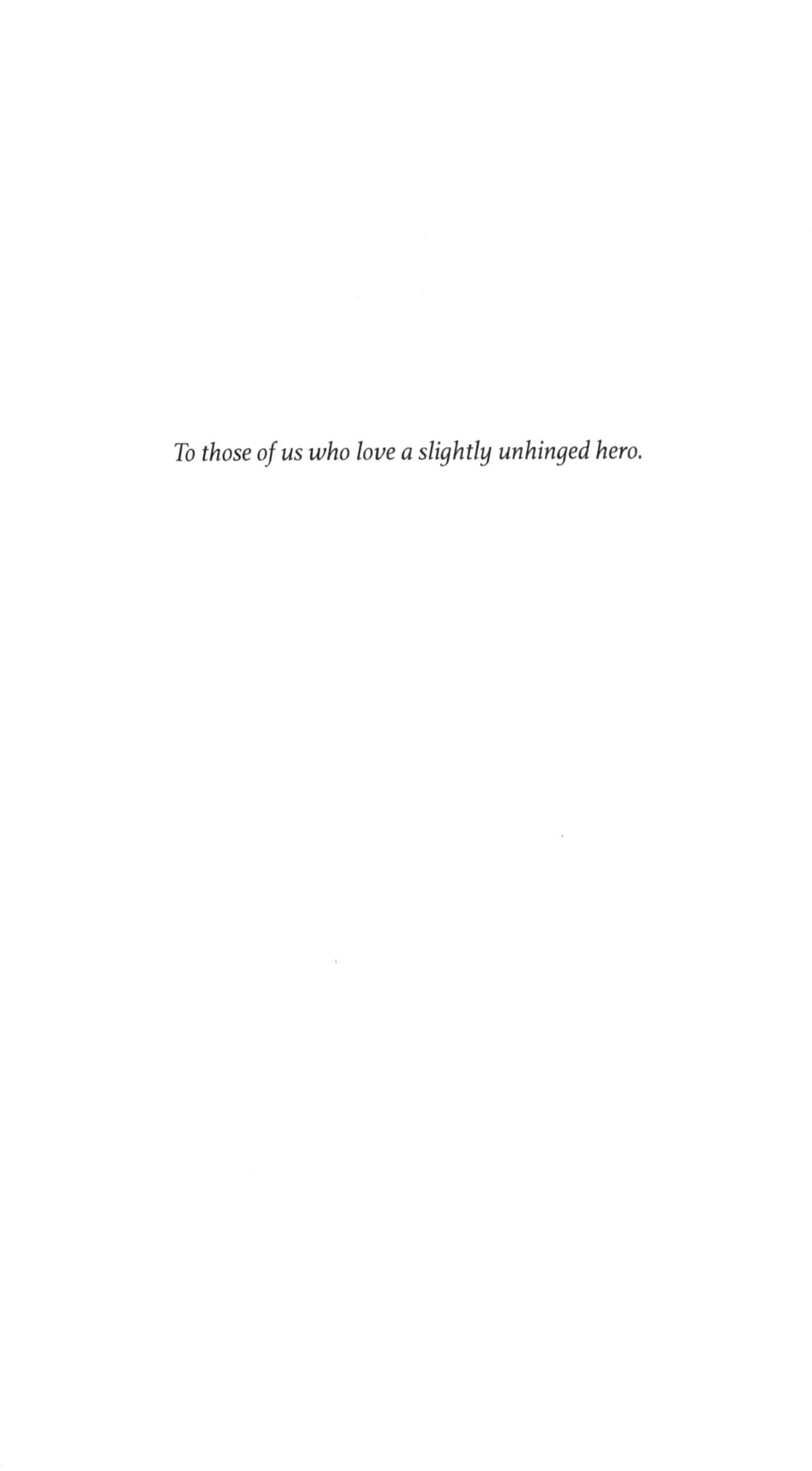

To those of us who love a slightly unhinged hero.

PROLOGUE

The soft white lights draped around the Christmas tree blinked, reflecting off the darkened dining room window. Normally, the sight offered a rush of excitement and anticipation, a reminder of the upcoming holiday. Not tonight, though. Not even the tiny snowflakes fluttering outside the bay window could distract me from the uneasy feeling churning in my gut.

Something wasn't right. The building tension in the room thickened the air, clogging my throat. My nervous gaze darted between my parents as they silently pretended to eat their dinner, neither one glancing up from their plates to meet my questioning stare. Hands tucked beneath the mahogany table, my anxious fingers picked and peeled at the dark blue nail polish, the uncomfortable quiet amping up my already strung-out nerves.

Even though tense family dinners had become the norm the last few months, tonight felt different. It felt more. As if we balanced on the edge of a cliff, mere centimeters from falling off and plummeting to our death.

Finally, after minutes passed of me silently begging for

anyone to look my way, Mom's dark brown eyes flicked up from her full plate and landed on me. The way she pushed the lemon pepper chicken and rice around instead of eating it wasn't fooling anyone. The corners of her lips curled upward, but there was a slight tremble in the forced smile.

My heart raced, and I curled my fingers into my palms until blunt nails dug into the skin.

What the hell was going on?

Dad cleared his throat, snapping my attention to the other end of the table. He slid the white cloth napkin over his lips, wiping away nothing since his food was also untouched, and tossed it onto the plate. Both lean forearms pressed to the edge of the table, his chest swelling with a large inhale right before meeting my gaze. His light eyes held my stare for a few heartbeats, lips pressed in a tight line.

"What's going on?" I asked, unable to take another second of whatever this was. I had my suspicions, but I didn't dare voice them. Not when I was almost certain the walls in our house had ears.

Paranoid? Maybe, but it was warranted, considering who my parents were connected with.

Two years ago, our lives changed. Initially, I thought for the better, but after several months of being in Georgia, I slowly realized the truth. The Union of Blessed Souls promised to help my parents through a rough patch in their marriage. The local church was praised for not only strengthening marriages but also bringing families back together in a happy union.

And, for a while, it worked.

Dad didn't work late nights anymore, Mom was happier, and that made me happy. Then things shifted after both were promoted to teachers at the compound, helping other couples like themselves. Soon, their free time was committed to various church functions, and their circle of friends dwindled to other followers only. From the outside looking in, everyone considered the ten thousand-plus congregation of followers, both online and locally, a megachurch.

I considered it the foundation of a cult.

The first time I uttered those concerns, my mother grounded me for a week and took away all electronics and connection to anyone outside the church. For a then fifteen-year-old, it was devastating enough not to voice my concerns again. Staying connected to the outside world kept me sane as my parents slowly became less and less like themselves and more and more like those who followed Pastor Paul.

I studied my father, fingers once again nervously picking and scratching at the chipped nail polish.

Within the last three months, he'd lost a significant amount of weight, almost to the point I worried he was sick. A defeated aura engulfed him, following him around like a shadow, which was the opposite of the successful and bois- terous seven-figure executive he was before we moved from Texas. Same with Mom. Her clothes hung off her thin frame, bones jutting out in places that used to be curvy. I couldn't even remember the last time I heard her laugh. The same aura that seemed to suffocate Dad had its death hold on Mom, too.

Defeated.

Worried.

Scared.

Instead of responding to my question, Dad shifted his haunted gaze to Mom and dipped his chin in a subtle nod. I jumped at the intrusive scrape of chair legs along the hardwood floor and shifted to gape at Mom as she stood from her seat, my eyes wide and pleading for answers. With another trembling, forced smile, she plucked my empty milk glass off the table and headed toward the kitchen, disappearing through the swinging door.

I sucked down gulps of air, my heart racing so fast it felt like I just ran a marathon.

"Dad," I pleaded, turning to face him head-on. Hands clasped in front of me, I swallowed down unshed tears. "Please." My voice cracked. "Tell me what's wrong—"

His eyes widened in what seemed like panic. "Nothing is wrong, Kay-Kay." My racing thoughts stumbled on hearing the nickname he called me all my life until recently. The swoosh of the swinging door had me turning toward the noise as Mom walked back into the dining room. My gaze flicked from Mom to Dad, who seemed to track her movement, focus intent on the full glass of milk clutched in her hand. "Don't worry, we're going to fix this. Everything will be okay. I promise."

The heavy glass bottom clunked onto the wood table directly in front of me. Instead of moving back to her empty seat, Mom waited at my side, trembling fingers stroking through my dark hair.

"You should finish your milk," Dad ordered, while picking up his own glass. "It will be good for you."

Not *it's good for you.*

It *will be* good for you.

I swallowed hard, mouth and throat suddenly dry.

Before I could speak, Mom bent at the waist and pressed a soft kiss to my temple.

"Trust us, Kay-Kay," she whispered, the words barely audible. "Please."

It was her tone, the words, the plea, everything, that had

my shaky hand reaching out and wrapping around the Waterford crystal.

Did I trust them? Yes.

My parents loved me. Even with the crazy shit the church had them do, I always knew deep down Mom and Dad loved me. I was their miracle after doctors said pregnancy would never happen for Mom.

The milk almost sloshed over the rim of the glass as I raised it to my lips. With each gulp of the cold liquid, my gaze snapped between the two people I 100 percent trusted to do what was right for me. Halfway through, I lowered the glass, but Mom tipped it back again, forcing me to drink what remained.

As soon as the last drop passed my lips, Mom yanked the glass from my hand and hurried back into the kitchen. The sink water running had me narrowing my eyes at the door as if that would help me understand their odd behavior.

"I love you," Dad said, his voice cracking. Shoving away from the table, he stood and inclined his head toward the foyer. "You should get some sleep."

My jaw went slack. "It's seven thirty." But even as I spoke the words, a heavy blanket seemed to settle over me, thoughts turning sluggish and eyelids growing heavy. I blinked up at Dad in horror as understanding hit me. "What did you—"

"Go upstairs. Now, Karigan," Dad snapped, cutting me off.

Tingling pinpricks raced down my legs, the muscles weak, barely holding up my weight as I pushed off the table to stand. Every second that passed, my mind grew more sluggish, movements slow as if I were wading through dense mud. Halfway to the massive stairwell that led to the bedrooms upstairs, my legs completely gave out. I toppled forward, screaming on the inside as the floor rushed toward me. Before I collided with the sparkling marble two sets of hands caught me beneath my arms. With maximum effort, my head rolled to the left, and I slowly blinked at Dad's ghostly pale face. I didn't have to look to know Mom helped support my now-dead weight based on the familiar, expensive perfume wrapping around me like the hug I desperately needed.

"We can leave her down here while I go grab our bags. How much did you give her?" Dad whispered between heavy breaths as they hauled me in the direction of his office instead of the stairs.

"I don't know. I don't know," Mom said between sobs. "Maybe we should've trusted her, told her the plans. I'm so sorry, baby. We had no other choice."

I wanted to comfort her, tell her that whatever made her cry like her soul was being ripped out of her body, we could fix together.

Their frantic whispers dulled. Words failed to register as my neck muscles gave up supporting my head. Vision hazy, I barely recognized the soft rug that covered the hardwood floor in Dad's office, the only clue to where they dragged me. Butter-soft leather caressed the back of my arms, and well-worn cushions molded around my back and legs as they situated me on the small couch. Unable to move, I stared at the beams crisscrossing the ceiling. I blinked when Mom's worried face appeared, hovering over mine, followed by a feather-soft touch along my cheek, wiping away something wet.

Tears.

My tears.

"I'm so sorry, Kay-Kay. We're so sorry we put you through this, but we will make it right. He can't—" The familiar chime of our doorbell rang through the house, cutting Mom off. Her eyes widened, the spike of fear palpable. With a whimper, she kissed my cheek and disappeared from view.

Their frantic whispers carried through the office, though they grew quieter. The double doors rattled together as they snapped shut, sealing me inside the office alone. I lay on the couch, lids too heavy to keep open any longer, with only the sound of my thundering pulse and quick, shallow breaths filling my ears.

I fought against the heavy pull of darkness, my body and mind slowly succumbing fully to whatever drug Mom put in my drink. Anger at her and Dad sparked just as a female scream pierced through the silence, followed by shouts and the sound of something shattering.

Fighting against the drugs, a frustrated and terrified scream ripped through my mind. I was vulnerable and alone, and that scream. I knew the owner of that scream. Fresh tears leaked from the corners of my closed lids. More shouts had my heart racing only for it to freeze mid-beat at the unmistakable, rattling boom of a gunshot.

I stilled, not breathing as I waited, knowing deep down something terrible had happened. If I wasn't sedated, I would've jumped off the couch when the bang of a second gunshot rang through the office. Inside, I cried and begged, though my body wouldn't respond to my desperate need to expel the grief raging inside me.

Both of my parents were dead. How I knew that, I wasn't sure, but somewhere deep in my soul, I knew. All those happy memories.... No new ones would be created, and the future I pictured with them at my side was ripped away.

And I had no clue why.

Deep male voices filtered through my clogged ears. Too

far gone, knowing nothing was worth fighting for anymore, I sank deeper into the darkness that I now welcomed. Before I sank too deep, the sensation of a presence loomed over me. It felt sick, evil, as if an oily substance coated my skin.

"Don't worry," the evil presence whispered, the calm voice familiar yet not. "You're right where you belong now."

The urge to run, scream, or hide swept through me like a tidal wave just as the last sliver of consciousness faded. But I couldn't even move as two arms hauled me into the air, stealing me from the place I called home.

I had no idea the nightmare that awaited me.

One I had zero hope of escaping.

1
———

MILLIE

10 YEARS AGO

"Shit." I jerked my hand out of the overstuffed backpack and slipped the injured finger between my lips. Pulling it free, I examined the ultra-thin paper cut, a line of blood the only visible sign of the wound.

With a sharp headshake, I turned my focus back to pulling the binder and textbook for class free from the bag, both clasped in a single-handed grip. A loud smack vibrated through the large room when both slammed onto the desk in front of me. Someone two rows down turned at the sound, but I pretended not to notice. I'd grown used to ignoring curious stares and quiet whispers over the years. It didn't bother me anymore. At least that was my favorite lie I liked to tell myself.

Out of the corner of my eye, I watched a student across the room talk with her friend, their blatant stares on me.

With both hands tucked beneath the desk, I slowly released a centering breath while tapping out a familiar sequence along my thighs to distract me from their curious attention. I did what I could to stay invisible and off others' radar, but my petite size and young age seemed to draw unwanted attention no matter what I did or where I went.

And believe me, it was unwanted.

Desperate for a distraction, I flipped through the textbook with one hand, the other nervously twirling the new gel pen along the top of the desk as the classroom's stadium-style setup filled with students and their loud, excited chatter. Every few minutes, I anxiously checked the time, desperate for the class to start. If the professor were up front talking, then the chances of someone filling the empty seat beside me were slim, and I wouldn't be forced to attempt a normal social interaction.

Which meant I wouldn't embarrass myself.

Socially awkward would be a kind label to describe my ability to engage with anything that required air to live. Unfortunately, that wasn't only my perspective, but my parents', as well. They and basically anyone who ever interacted with me assumed something was wrong, all because they couldn't understand why. Why I didn't want to be social, why I preferred books over people, or why I couldn't carry on a normal conversation.

Their ever-growing list of what made me different and awkward was long.

That definitely didn't help with my self-confidence problems. Nothing said love and support like being labeled strange because you didn't behave or want the things society deemed as normal.

After labeling my awkwardness too odd for their very social and public lives, my parents shipped me off to be someone else's problem. I have bounced around the best boarding schools in the United States ever since. With my unusually high IQ, obsession for learning, and all the free time in the world because I had zero friends, I sped through grade after grade after grade at warp speed.

Which all led me here.

Nineteen years old, taking a senior-level psychology class at Stanford University all alone, and I was completely okay with that. I transferred from Harvard after the spring semester, hoping this program would prove more challenging.

Fingers crossed.

Speaking of which, I studied the injured finger, finding a dried slice of blood along the minuscule cut. Distracted, I didn't notice the person squeezing their way down the aisle. My heart sank when the enormous shadow passed over the desk, a presence hovering at my side. Gaze lowered, I held a shallow breath, hoping whoever loomed over me would choose another place to sit. Seconds ticked by, but the person didn't move on. My breathing picked up, and my pulse raced as my nerves skyrocketed.

The person at my back cleared their throat, cutting through the tense silence between us.

"Hey, quick question. Are you—"

Heat flushed under my skin as my irritation swept away the earlier nervousness. Why couldn't people just let me be?

"Yes," I snapped, cutting the male voice off. "I'm in the right classroom," I said without looking up. "Yes, I know this is a senior-level course. Yes, I wear kid-size shoes. No, I do not want—"

"Really?" he asked.

I paused my practiced rant that answered the most popular curious questions tossed my way, finally daring a glance over my shoulder at the student who disrupted my solitude. For the first time ever, I had zero thoughts as I studied the stranger. Exotic aqua eyes filled with humor watched me as a single corner of his lips pulled upward in what the romance books I devoured would label a sexy smirk.

And holy shit, this was my first time to see it in real life. They were right. It was damn sexy. Or maybe it was just him, all of him. Heat pumped through my veins for a very different reason than the earlier irritation of my invaded personal space.

My breath caught and my stomach flipped with his stare locked on me.

What the hell was wrong with me? Was I sick?

Still gawking at the boy—no, this guy was all man—not uttering a single word, I pressed the back of my hand to my forehead, discreetly checking for a fever.

"As intriguing as your tiny feet are," he said, that smirk pulling into a wide smile, "are you saving this seat?"

"Why would I save a seat?" My head tilted to the side in confusion, making my thick, black-framed glasses slip down the bridge of my nose.

"For a friend?" he questioned, clearly as confused as me.

I shifted my attention to the empty seat and frowned. "That wouldn't make sense. I don't have any friends." When I dared a glance back up, his smile had faded, replaced with a look I was not only very familiar with but completely hated, too. "Don't feel sorry for me, I don't. I prefer to be alone."

I did.

Right?

Or was that just all I was used to? Hell, this was the most I'd spoken to a fellow student in... well, ever, and somehow, it made me question all my life choices.

My brows furrowed as I tracked his movements. He slid into the vacant seat without another word and leaned back, still staring like I was a curiosity or a zoo animal. Again, something I was very familiar with. A forlorn sigh escaped, knowing he would dismiss me for someone more interesting or not as socially dysfunctional in three, two—

"I bet you save a ton on shoes."

I blinked at the too-attractive-to-not-be-fictional stranger. Yes, I would definitely call him attractive. Another first. If it weren't for romance books, I wouldn't know what this fluttering feeling was in my lower belly, considering this response hadn't happened with a real-life, not-on-paper male.

"What?" I asked and dipped my head to glance under the desk. "You're asking because my shoes look cheap?" Sure, they were worn, but the Converse held up well. Considering my feet stopped growing years ago, why waste money on new shoes when the ones I had worked just fine?

His brows furrowed. "No. Because they're so small."

Frantic movement across the room had us both glancing toward two girls, both waving their hands with wide smiles on their faces. Having his attention, they pointed at a seat between them and motioned for him to join them.

For some unknown reason, my heart sank, knowing full well he'd go sit with his friends—hell, he'd probably take an opportunity to move by a stranger, anyone less awkward than me.

"It just makes sense that kids' shoes would be cheaper than adult shoes, considering they use less material. Right?"

I flicked a confused look at him, then back to the still-motioning group. "Your friends are waiting."

Lips pressed in a tight line, his aqua eyes scanned my face before looking away. "I don't have any friends."

"That's my line," I responded immediately, like an idiot.

Those exotic eyes locked on me, and for a brief second, everything around us faded.

Holy shit, those romance authors actually knew what they were talking about. Now I felt bad for scoffing at all the descriptions of swooning that I believed were completely made up. Because I was pretty sure whatever was going on with me was, in fact, swooning.

Too soon, the boom of a voice had me breaking our stare off and turning toward the professor down front. The first day of class was always the same, no matter the level or university, but I still hoped we would dive into the first few chapters of the textbook. I read the entire thing front to back and couldn't wait to discuss the areas I had questions about and found intriguing.

"You know we'll just go over the syllabus today, right?" the stranger whispered while leaning into my personal space. Strangely enough, for the first time ever, I didn't mind.

"I like being prepared." I scanned the desk space in front of him that was empty, except for a single pen with chew marks denting the cap. "Apparently, you don't."

Arms folded on the fake wood, he rested his cheek on a single forearm, face turned toward me. I shifted in the seat, squirming under his full attention.

"As long as I hear whatever we're covering, I'll retain it." My lips parted in surprise. A wide smile made his cheeks bunch. "I'm not just a pretty face, and if you're here, in a senior-level class, at the age of...." He trailed off, obviously wanting me to fill in the blank, and arched a brow.

"Nineteen," I whispered, trying my best to ignore him and pay attention to the professor.

"Then I'm betting you aren't either."

"Aren't what?" I reluctantly dragged my focus from the front to him.

"Just a pretty face."

A sharp laugh escaped, and I clapped a hand over my mouth. The few students in front of us turned with scowls on their faces before noticing the guy sitting beside me, their annoyance immediately vanishing.

No friends, my ass. What was this guy up to? It wouldn't be the first time one of the popular kids befriended me to conduct something cruel later on, all for a good laugh from their real friends.

Clearing my throat, I shot him a glare. "What do you want?"

He studied me like he needed a second to debate his answer. "A chance."

"A chance at what?"

"Being your friend."

I blinked, the professor forgotten, as I watched the guy suspiciously. "Why would you want to do that?"

"Do you always ask so many questions, Velma?"

"My name isn't Velma," I huffed. So that was it. He thought I was someone else. Which made sense and explained this whole unprecedented conversation. But what it didn't explain was why I suddenly hated this Velma. Someone I didn't even know yet wanted to throat punch.

"You remind me of her. The dark, reddish hair, thick glasses." He gestured to my face. "All of it."

"Where is she?" I asked before I could stop myself.

His blond brows pulled in tight. "I don't know. Somewhere helping the gang solve a case, probably."

"So she's in law enforcement?"

"The paranormal kind, sure."

I wracked my brain for anything I'd ever read that

suggested the US government had a paranormal law enforcement division.

"I'll have to look that up," I mumbled, not enjoying him knowing about something I didn't.

Another first.

"You do that," he said with a knowing smile. "If you're not Velma brought to life, then who are you?"

I clenched my hands beneath the desk and wiped both sweaty palms along my dark jeans to clean off the layer of sweat. "Millie," I whispered, catching the professor's pointed glare. "Millie Anderson."

That knowing smirk reappeared. "Did you take the blue pill or the red pill, Miss Anderson?" He chuckled under his breath, like that was some kind of inside joke.

"I don't do drugs."

That smile of his grew even wider. "Never seen *The Matrix* either, I take it." He unfolded an arm to slide a hand along the desk; he held out his hand, fingers wiggling in invitation. "Then, as your friend, I demand that you watch it. I'm Killian. Killian Cooper. My friends call me Coop or Cooper."

I blinked at his offered hand. "I'm more of a reader."

"Really?" He laughed. "That, I expected." My cheeks flamed. Was he making fun of me? "Sorry, that sounded bad. I meant it as a compliment."

His fingers continued to wiggle, tempting my hand to slide against his. With a full inhale, I placed my palm on his and squeezed.

"Nice to meet you, Millie," he whispered.

"You don't have to lie," I said, pulling my hand back. "No one wants to meet me."

A hard glint appeared in his aqua eyes. "I do. Now stop

distracting me," he said with a wink. "I'm trying to listen. This is very important stuff."

With that, he turned, chin on his folded arms, gaze locked on the professor.

I blinked several times, trying to understand what the hell had just happened. Turning to look around the space, I noted the others in the room, the chilled air pumping through the vents, brushing along my bare arms, and then, of course, the feel of his skin against mine. So, this wasn't a dream.

Was it?

2

MILLIE

TODAY

"We should take advantage of this situation and go snoop around the house. Check out what the dean hides in his bedside drawer."

The flute of champagne in my hand paused halfway to my lips as I shot Carol, the psychology department's admin and the only person in the crowded room I considered a friend, an incredulous look before taking a small sip of the bubbly liquid. Last year at the university's New Year's Eve party for the staff and professors, she suggested we strip and jump into the dean's enormous pool, so maybe I should be thankful this absurd idea had our clothes staying where they were.

"I actually think I'm going to head home and—"

Carol groaned and rolled her eyes. "Come on, Millie, it's New Year's Eve! You're free to do whatever you want. The divorce is final. Go find a hot colleague to fuck in one of the seventeen bedrooms."

My nose scrunched at the suggestion. After taking another sip, I set the mostly full glass down on the high-top table between us. "You know I won't do that," I muttered.

"Besides, I should go because I have things that need to get done before school starts back."

She arched a perfectly defined brow and drained the rest of her drink before sliding mine closer. With the delicate stem pressed between two fingers, she spun the flute, making the bottom vibrate along the table.

"That new book you've talked nonstop about releases this weekend, doesn't it?"

I faked an incredulous scoff. "No."

It will be released in three days. My exciting plans were to reread the previous six books in the series. Sure, I had a photographic memory, but even though I remembered every word, I still experienced the stories differently every time I read them. There were times, with books that touched a forgotten place in my soul, that I hated my memory. Wished I could forget the story altogether to read it again for the first time, to experience that pulse of excitement with every page turned.

"What about McDonnell?" Carol waggled her brows. "He's a cutie and close to your age."

Close as in being a decade younger than the average professor, which still put him years older than my thirty-year-old self. Sure, the anthropology professor that my chipper and way more outgoing friend pointed out was attractive, but in a bland way.

My breath never caught when our gazes clashed. He didn't make me feel like the most important person in the room, tracking me with a stealthy gaze like one would a precious jewel surrounded by dangerous thieves. Only one male ever did that, and he was gone.

Vanished.

Taking my feeble heart with him.

"You should go for him," I suggested. "He's cute and close to your age."

Carol's laugh was easy and carefree. "You're getting so much better at that."

That being intended humor. Not me misunderstanding a conversation and taking their words too literally.

"Oh!" she exclaimed and smacked me on the shoulder. "Who sent the gorgeous black roses that were delivered on the last day of school? Those had to have cost a fortune."

My lips parted, ready to tell her I didn't know who sent the stunning arrangement of my favorite flower. Every December 17, except for the year Bronson and I were married, a beautiful arrangement found their way to me, and I'd yet to learn who they were from. The only note was a basic type-printed *Happy Birthday*. No signature, ever.

Was it creepy? At first, yes. But now, being back on my own, it made me feel not so alone in the world. My parents didn't care enough to even call me on my birthday, much less send me flowers or a card.

Finding comfort in my flower-sending stalker versus being frightened needed to be added to the very long list of things that made me abnormal compared to the rest of society. Not that I particularly wanted to be like everyone else. It took a few years, and one amazing friend, for me to be proud of my differences. Those oddities that others deemed awkward or unusual are what made me me.

And I was the best me on the planet.

Clearing my throat, I scanned the room, hoping Carol wouldn't pick up on my small lie.

"My parents sent the flowers." My smile was tight as I worked to make my words believable. "They send them every year. Listen, I've got to go. See you on campus next week." I took one step away before looking over my shoulder, my smile genuine this time. "Happy New Year."

"I have a good feeling about this year for you, Millie. It's going to be the best yet," she said, tilting the flute my way. "Just you wait."

"I won't hold my breath," I muttered as I offered a small wave before beelining it toward the exit. Time for comfortable clothes, a roaring fire, and reading until I fell asleep. Now *that* was a New Year's Eve party.

Standing outside the mansion's oversized wooden front door, I wrapped both arms around myself and tilted my face toward the falling snow. Closing my lids, I tried to ignore the growing ache in my chest that bloomed every time I thought about him.

"Happy New Year, Killian," I whispered into the night. "Wherever you are."

***

"Dr. Anderson, you cannot be serious," the young woman huffed from the other side of my desk. Setting the pen down, I turned my full attention to the clearly frustrated student. "You cannot expect us to write this paper over spring break."

I blinked. "Why not? You'll have all the time you need to research the three groups, choose one to assess the leader's mindset, and create a theory about what will happen if the government or local authorities do not shut that group down."

"But it's spring break," she whined while stomping her foot. When I didn't respond, the pout on her face turned into a sneer. "This is why everyone hates taking your class. Learning about cults should be fun, not this."

"Fun is Netflix documentaries," I responded with a sigh. "Not a graduate-level psychology course at Harvard."

Her lips parted, no doubt ready to argue more, but a sharp knock on the doorframe of the classroom drew our attention, stopping her retort. My teaching assistant, Jeremy, and a man in a black suit filled the doorway, a manila folder clutched in the latter's hand. My heart rate spiked as I took in the stranger, and understanding snapped into place. The chair slowly rolled back when I stood. Fingers on the worn desk, I leaned forward and inclined my head toward the hall.

"Sorry, but we have to cut this discussion short. I have another meeting. Good luck with your paper. Hopefully, you put more effort into this one than you did the last."

I shouldn't have said that, but holy hell, I was so tired of these students thinking they could push me around because we were nearly the same age. Maybe I was a little over teaching, too. Becoming bored quickly was a flaw of mine. I needed to keep my brain active, constantly learning new things to stay intrigued.

With a curious stare, she skirted around the man, glancing over her shoulder as she disappeared down the hall. Jeremy cleared his throat, drawing my attention from the stranger to himself. Lips pressed in a tight line, hands balled into fists at his side, he appeared pissed. My dark, straight hair grazed along my chin as I tilted my head, confused about why he would be angry.

"This guy came by our office—"

"My office," I grumbled under my breath, too low for him to hear.

"Demanding to see you. But he wouldn't tell me his name or why he needed to see you. Want me to kick his ass out of here, Millie?"

I bit my tongue until I tasted blood to keep from screaming. Too many times to count, I told him to address me as Dr. Anderson, but he continued to use my first name, thinking we were friends or, worse, that he had a chance at me saying yes to a date.

"It's Dr. Anderson," I gritted out through clenched teeth. His nostrils flared in what seemed like annoyance. "And it's fine, Jeremy." I motioned the stranger forward. "Please close the door behind you. This is a private and confidential meeting."

"But—"

"I'm fine," I hissed, fingernails biting into my palm. "While I appreciate your concern, it's unnecessary. That will be all."

I swallowed a laugh when the man turned and shot Jeremy a cocky smirk, staring him down until the door finally closed with my angry assistant on the other side. With a chuckle, he turned back to me, features settling into that blank mask once again. The squeak of the soles of his dress shoes was the only sound as he drew closer.

"Dr. Anderson. I assume you know why I'm here." He held up the file in his hand, which had the FBI's logo stamped on the front, and inclined his head. "When I was told to drop off the file, they mentioned you've consulted with the local FBI office in previous cases."

I nodded and curled both hands behind my back to keep from making grabby hands at the folder. Excitement thrummed through my veins, making my breathing choppy. As the few prior cases had, consulting on a case for the FBI would bring the challenge I desperately needed. "What group does the FBI need help with this time?" There was no hiding the interest in my tone. Months had passed since they needed my insight regarding the many organizations and groups I studied and documented across the country.

What could I say? I got bored easily. What else was I supposed to do with my free time besides study various cults and high control groups around the country? It was my specialty, after all.

Without a response, he tossed the folder onto the desk. Not caring that I looked overly eager, I pulled the file close and flipped it open, thumbing through the pages, quickly skimming the words but retaining every one.

"Finally," I breathed. "This group is beyond dangerous and has operated in plain sight for too long. Their followers grow by the thousands every year." I shut the folder and tapped the center. "What made the FBI finally deem the group important enough to warrant an investigation?"

"There has been a recent development, and you've been requested to consult on-site, where you'll be debriefed on that new information."

"On-site? That's new." I rapped my fingers along the top of the desk. "Okay, sure. Spring break is next week, so I can take the day to travel to Quantico and—"

"Dallas."

"You said Quantico wrong."

A hint of a grin pulled at his lips before it disappeared. "The Dallas-based supervisory special agent over the behavioral analysis team requested the consult. She is handling the new information and is to determine if this is an FBI matter."

"I can't make that drive to Dallas from Cambridge." The pace of my fingers picked up as my mind filtered through all the things that needed to be done. "Okay, I'll book a flight today—"

"No need. They have a jet."

I gaped at him. "They have a jet." He dipped his chin in acknowledgment before flicking his wrist to check the time. If possible, my jaw dropped even more. "You mean *now*? As in *today*?"

He arched a brow and glanced around the empty classroom. "If the schedule that I pulled before coming here is correct, that was your last class before the break. Unless you have more important plans than helping the FBI?"

Well, he had me there. I didn't have more important plans; in fact, I had zero plans.

Guess I was going to Dallas.

PACKING WAS A WHIRLWIND, but thankfully, I didn't need too much, considering it was only a single overnight stay. Two hours after the agent—who never gave me his name—stepped into my classroom, I was buckling the seat belt, relaxing back into the soft leather seat of the FBI's private jet. Scanning the empty cabin, I didn't hold back the wide grin that spread across my face.

This was new.

I loved a new adventure. There was something about the unknown, about having to prepare yourself for any possibility, that sent a thrum of excitement through my veins. I used to hate change and loved the constant that came with a solid routine. But that was before an aqua-eyed boy disrupted my life, changing the way I viewed everything, and ultimately altered my career path.

Not that it did any good. I still hadn't found him.

Shoving that constant failure aside, I pushed an AirPod into each ear and hit *play* on the audiobook I downloaded on the drive to the airport. With the sexy male narrator's voice pouring through the earbuds, I tapped the iPad, bringing it to life. I frowned at the multiple missed texts that popped up on the screen from Jeremy. The messages started as confused, then escalated to anger, making me snort.

Idiot. His infatuation with me was becoming a nuisance. No matter how many times I told him I wasn't interested, he continued to press the issue. Last semester, he crossed the line, cornering me in my office to spill his unrequited feelings before attempting to kiss me.

That rewarded him with a bruised esophagus from a well-placed throat punch I delivered when my words didn't work. I wasn't a fan of physical violence, but I wouldn't hold back to defend myself. Unfortunately, my clingy teaching assistant still thought he had a chance.

Like the throat punch was some type of love tap.

Rolling my eyes, I cleared the messages without responding and clicked on the document folder that held all my research. If the FBI was ready to investigate The Union of Blessed Souls, then I needed to be prepared. I had a feeling they wanted more than the basic overview of the group. No one would send a private jet for something they could find online. No, they'd want to know the ins and outs that I uncovered through months of research and that one brief trip I made to Georgia. Though no one knew about that.

Actually, they were the FBI, so they probably did know.

I chewed on my lower lip, the words blurring on the screen. This trip would put me in the heart of an FBI office, unlike previous consults that were conducted at my office or on the phone. Maybe while I was there, I could ask someone to look for my missing friend. They had all kinds of technology and agents with skills who could find him easily.

Or maybe help identify the secret flower sender.

My dark hair skimmed along my neck, and I quickly shook my head to dislodge that thought.

Did I really want to know who sent me the flowers? It was fun to fantasize at night that they were from the one person I missed the most. The one I searched for since the day he went missing.

Not knowing added a level of mystery I needed in my boring yet stable life. It wasn't dangerous, or hadn't been in the past, so what was the harm in hoping, knowing that there was someone out there thinking about me?

It was comforting to know maybe, just maybe, I wasn't as alone as I thought.

3

KILLIAN

TODAY

Hands stretched high in the air, I smoothly lowered both arms, following the instructor's calming voice to move into warrior one. Sweat slicked every inch of my skin from the heated air pumping through the vents; steady drops dribbled from my hair onto the towel covering the yoga mat.

Like normal, the teacher's smooth cadence chased away the memories I tried my damnedest to forget, drowning out my father's voice demanding a younger me to do better, be better, and not fail. Which was nearly impossible, considering his high expectations of everyone around him, which were even higher for his only son. Yay me.

"Fuck," I muttered as I stumbled, getting lost in my head and not concentrating on my balance. Knowing I wouldn't fall back into the peaceful headspace needed for the final few minutes of class, I angrily snatched up my water bottle, towel, and mat. Everything stuffed in my arms, I weaved through the others, offering the teacher an apologetic look for leaving early.

Pushing the door open, a burst of cool air immediately

chilled my damp skin, making a shiver bolt down my spine. Not that anyone would notice, even if they were beside me in the hall. The best trained me to smother all physical reactions at all times. Emotional reactions, too, but that was a trauma dumpster fire. I couldn't go down this early in the morning.

At the front of the small yoga studio, I quickly folded my towel, rolled up the mat, and pulled on a pair of joggers and a hoodie from my gym bag. While I tugged the hoodie over my soaked black T-shirt, the woman manning the front desk asked a question, but her words couldn't pierce through the voices screaming in my mind.

Outside, the cold, early March wind sliced through the overpriced yet utterly soft cotton material. The jolt from one extreme to the other was just what I needed to snap me out of my head, quieting my mind for one glorious second. It wouldn't last, it never did, but that didn't mean I couldn't savor the moment, no matter how brief.

After securing my gear to the back of the bike, I tossed a leg over and lowered onto the seat. Instead of starting her up, I pulled my cell free from the sweats' side pocket. Eyes locked on the blank screen, I debated giving in to the insistent urge that had plagued me since the last time I set eyes on her. It was an obsession, one I fought and failed to smother since I was forced to walk away from the only woman I'd ever loved.

A deep-in-your-soul, imprinted-on-your-heart type of love.

It was fast, unexpected, and forbidden. Well, forbidden from my father's point of view.

Swiping the screen, my thumb hovered over the app that would ease the anxiety thrumming through my veins. Seeing her was an addiction, a drug. All I needed to calm my fears was a simple glimpse to let me know she was still out there, living her best life. Safe.

Far away from me and the danger that came with knowing me.

Because that, unlike anyone else, was what she saw from the very beginning.

Me.

Not the fake-ass playboy I portrayed while at school to keep anyone from looking too closely. No, Millie looked, she saw, and she dug straight into my chest, pulling pieces of me to the surface I didn't even know were there.

Wants.

Dreams.

Things that were mine, so hidden beneath my father's expectations, which always took precedence.

While debating whether to give in to the insistent itch to see her, the phone vibrated in my hand. Grateful for the minor distraction, I tapped the screen, pulling up the new text from my boss, Supervisory Special Agent Rhyan Riggs, team leader extraordinaire over the FBI's Dallas-based Behavioral Sciences Unit.

> Boss Lady: Meeting at 2:00 p.m. Potential new case.

> Me: Potential?

> Boss Lady: Will know more after my 1:00 p.m. meeting with a consultant.

> Boss Lady: Depending on that outcome, we'll discuss the next steps. Could be a long undercover assignment.

> Me: Dangerous?

> Boss Lady: Yes.

> Me: Sounds like a party. Hopefully, it's somewhere fucking warmer than this. Is it too much to ask for serial killers to do their killing somewhere like the Bahamas or Hawaii?

> Boss Lady: You're killing me.

> Me: No, I'm not. You wouldn't see me coming if I were.

I SMIRKED AT MY RESPONSE, knowing she'd get the context. She was the one who helped me escape my previous employer's clutches, after all. I flipped back to the app I was considering before Rhyan interrupted. With an annoyed groan at my zero restraint when it came to anything Millie, I tapped the app.

Immediately, a crystal clear image of her brownstone came into view. Frowning, I zoomed in, noticing the blinds were closed, which was odd for her. The woman loved the sunshine and always kept the blinds open during the day. Tapping the recording controls, I rewound the video, pausing when a black town car appeared on the screen. The whipping March wind flapping my sweats and cutting through the thin material was barely an annoyance as I squinted, studying the screen.

I noted the recording's time stamp and continued watching. At ten, Eastern Standard Time, a generic black town car idled outside her townhouse for a few minutes before the woman who unknowingly haunted me came bounding down the concrete stairs. Wide, excited smile, bundled up in a thick coat, carrying— I sucked in a breath. Was that a fucking overnight bag?

My stomach tightened into knots as I watched her pull open the back door and disappear into the cab. Too many times to count, I rewound the video, watching each time until the town car disappeared from view.

I swallowed down the bile threatening to creep up my throat.

This was it. I knew it would happen again at some point. I just wasn't fucking ready. When she got married, it almost killed me. I lost months of my life, drinking to forget the grief slowly suffocating me.

And now it looked like she had someone new in her life.

Someone taking her on an overnight stay.

My breath turned choppy, and my heart hammered in my chest. With a frustrated roar, I threw my phone to the pavement, watching as it shattered on impact. Yet it did nothing to calm the mounting grief and anger filling my chest.

Slamming my heel down on the clutch, my bike roared to life. With a growl, I picked up the ruined device from the pavement and shoved it into my pocket, not giving two shits about the glass splinters and bits of sharp metal digging into my fingers.

Nothing mattered. Millie wasn't mine and never would be.

But try telling my heart that because it was hers and had been since the first time we met.

I survived being shot, stabbed, and tortured, but losing Millie to another man again might be the one thing that killed me.

4

MILLIE

10 YEARS AGO

"Velma." Bright red and yellow leaves crunched beneath my feet as I slowed, a smile tugging at my lips as I looked over my shoulder toward the man calling out for me. Killian picked up his pace, jogging to cut the distance between us. At my side, he placed both hands on his knees, taking in exaggerated breaths. "Damn, you walk fast for a tiny thing. If I didn't know any better, I'd take it as a personal slight that you basically sprinted out of class after you turned in your test."

I arched a brow and shrugged. Maybe I had left in a rush, but not because of him. I didn't plan to tell him the real reason, either. It felt inappropriate to tell your only friend that the professor's insistent pressure to be his teaching assistant next semester felt... off. Add in that he continued to offer a chance for extra credit if I would stop by during his office hours, and it made me feel uncomfortable around the professor even in the crowded classroom.

"What did you think of the test?" I asked instead of voicing the concerns filling my thoughts and started the walk toward the parking lot.

His hand wrapped around my bicep, slowing me to a stop once again. Exotic eyes scanned my face, lips dipping at the corners.

"What aren't you telling me?" My lips parted, ready to lie, but he cut me off before I could. "Don't lie to me, please. I see it." He pointed a finger between my brows. "It's there, circling in your thoughts."

"Are you a mind reader or something?" I scoffed, hating that he read me like an open book. Was that normal? We'd only known each other for a few weeks. His being able to understand and read my body language at this stage of our friendship was odd.

That finger pressed between my brows. "You get this little line between your eyebrows when you're stuck on something you can't solve. So, out with it, Millie."

"It's nothing, Killian." I adjusted the straps of my stuffed backpack, drawing his attention to the heavy weight. "Hey, what are you doing?"

I grappled for my backpack, but he moved too fast, stripping it off my shoulder and draping it over his own, shooting me a cocky smile. "Nope, it's mine. I'm holding it hostage until you tell me what's bothering you. I know it's not how you did on the test. You could've passed that with your eyes closed."

"Why would I take a test with my eyes closed?" A strong, cool breeze sent the leaves rustling around us, cutting through my thin sweater. Like everything else, Killian noticed my slight shiver, even though I tried to keep it hidden, not wanting this moment with him to end.

Strangely enough, I liked his company, enjoying the confusing conversations and not being alone to figure out so much. Before he sat in that seat, which he demanded I save for him the rest of the semester, I was okay with my solitary life. Now I looked forward to the days I would see him. I even searched the campus grounds between classes, hoping to run into him.

Which never happened. It was like he was here for classes only, then vanished to wherever he went off campus. It was odd and concerning. I'd noticed a few times he appeared exhausted, with deep purple bags beneath his eyes, and after fall break, he returned injured, even though he denied it.

"Come on. You're cold, and I won't stop bothering you until you explain why you ran out of class like your ass was on fire." My whole body tensed when he draped an arm over my shoulders and tugged me to his side. "I'm buying you the best coffee on campus."

My feet followed as he directed me toward the small coffee shop that operated on campus. "But I don't like coffee." My nose wrinkled, thinking about that one time I tried to drink it to stay up and finish a book. "And it's really nothing, Killian." His hand tightened around my shoulder, and I shot him a confused look. "Why do you always do that?"

"Do what?"

"Flinch or react strangely when I say your name. Am I saying it wrong or something?" In my mind, I ran through the various ways it could be pronounced but came up blank.

"No, it's just"—he ran a hand through his shaggy dirty-blond hair—"you're the only one who calls me that, and it just catches me off guard every time."

"I can stop—"

"No," he practically shouted before clearing his throat. "I like it." I remained silent, hoping he'd give me a little more insight. "It's what my mom called me."

"Called? Do you not talk to her anymore?"

His smile was forced as he shot me a wink. "Only on Friday the thirteenth through my Ouija board."

I knew that game and quickly realized what he hinted at in his very Killian way.

"Oh. I'm sorry." His eyes turned sad before he looked away. That expression made my stomach cramp oddly, hating seeing him upset when his smile was what I looked forward to every Monday, Wednesday, and Friday. "I don't like coffee, but I drink tea."

My heart leapt when his smile returned at my words.

Damn. I was in so much trouble with this guy.

At the glass door, Killian grabbed the handle and yanked it open, gesturing for me to enter first. The overpowering scents of coffee, steamed milk, and something spicy engulfed me as I crossed the threshold, the walls offering a welcome reprieve from the crisp breeze.

After ordering our drinks, we settled into a pair of comfortable chairs tucked into the corner. Rapping my fingers along my thigh, I slowly scanned the small space, loving the quaint feel. It was a perfect place to come if I wanted people's interaction without actually having to talk to anyone. My gaze snagged on two girls across the sitting area, who kept eyeing Killian before whispering to each other.

I shifted in the seat, realizing quickly how odd Killian and I looked. He was this preppy, all-American god, with his surfer body, messy blond hair, and chiseled features, and I was, who most would probably assume, his charity case. I ran a hand down my straight dark hair, tucking a few strands behind my ear.

Maybe I should try harder to fit in. I never really cared until Killian, but now I found myself self-conscious about my baggy clothes and lack of style. Makeup would be a good start, maybe some hair products so it didn't just hang limply at my shoulders.

"You're doing it again," Killian said after taking our drinks from the server. She hovered around for a second before realizing his attention wouldn't stray from me. With a quick once-over my way, she huffed and whirled around, hurrying back behind the counter.

"Doing what?" I grumbled. Taking the to-go cup from his outstretched hand, I carefully set it on the side table, giving the leaves a second to steep in the steaming water.

"Trying to solve a problem in that brilliant mind of yours."

I scoffed. "Not so brilliant; that would be you." That was the truth. I could read anything and remember it, but Killian could hear anything and have it memorized immediately. It was insane.

Insanely hot.

"True," he said around the lip of his coffee cup. "Tell me what's bothering you now, then we'll go back to the other issue."

I shrugged, chewing on my lip, and glanced at the window. "What are you doing, Killian?"

When he didn't immediately respond, I dared a look back his way. A shocked expression crossed his handsome features before he schooled them into the aloof mask he wore for everyone else. The one I hated because it was fake as shit. He didn't look at me that way when we talked.

That mask was the Cooper version of Killian that everyone got but me.

"Drinking the best coffee on campus with my friend. What are you doing, Velma?"

"Wondering why in the hell you're doing this. Why are you even here, trying to get me to tell you what's bothering me? Why do you care? What's in it for you? Tell me that, answer that question, and I might just tell you what bothered me earlier."

If he gave me a typical bullshit 'Cooper' answer, then I'd forget the yummy-smelling Earl Grey tea and walk out. I didn't want to tarnish my view of Killian because of this one instance we hung out outside the classroom.

"Nothing is in it for me, and that's why," he said, features falling as he stared at his fingers wrapped around the cup. His aqua eyes looked up through light lashes. "You want nothing from me—" He cut himself off with a scoff. "Well, except for the expectation that I drop the bullshit persona I play."

"Why do you?" I leaned in closer, our knees brushing. His gaze flicked down to the contact. Instead of pulling away, he shifted to keep the minuscule touch.

"My life is... complicated, so much so not even the great Velma or you could figure out a way for me to avoid my future." He took a thick swallow of his coffee. "It's easier to be the person everyone wants to be around than let them see the real me. It keeps them from asking too many questions."

"But not me?"

His lip quirked at the side. "No, Millie, not you. And it's a mind fuck, let me tell you. I've pretended for so long, then I met this tiny thing in class that can actually tell the difference between my bullshit and the real person beneath. Most people don't look that hard. They just take the good times and wait around, expecting more."

"That sounds exhausting," I whispered. "What do you mean, *too many questions*?"

That full lower lip rolled inward as his teeth bit down. "There are expectations for me, ones that my father won't see derailed. Relationships can do that, so he's very... observant to make sure I don't mess up his plans."

I processed his words for a few moments before responding. "And since we're so different, you don't think your father will see me as a threat to that future, so you're okay with being the real you around me."

I didn't like that at all.

"No." I jumped at the conviction in his loud voice. His throat bobbed as he swallowed. "It's not that. Now, I answered your question, so you owe me an answer to my earlier one." His eyes searched my face before they narrowed. "Does it have something to do with the way Professor Daniels watches you?"

I leaned back, lips parted in surprise. "You noticed that, too?" He nodded, lips in a tight line. "He hasn't done anything," I muttered.

"Doesn't mean he won't. That's a shit response, Millie, and you know it. You cannot base someone's future actions based solely on their previous ones. If he makes you feel uncomfortable, then add that to the equation."

My head cocked to the side as I stared at him, unseeing. "You're right."

"Of course I am. I'm brilliant."

I smiled. "So am I, and I didn't come up with that reasoning."

"Let's chalk it up to my street smarts." I rolled my eyes, making him laugh. It was a running joke between us that I didn't pick up on things like he did. I was either more socially inept than I realized, or he was just more observant than I gave him credit for. "Besides looking your way every eleven minutes"—I blinked at that. Had he timed it? And why didn't I think of that?—"what else has he done to make you feel uncomfortable?"

With a resigned sigh, I told him about the extra credit conversation, where Professor Daniels practically begged me to be his TA next semester.

A small squeak escaped, and I flew back in my chair to avoid the spray of hot coffee as it exploded from the now-crushed cup in Killian's hand. He glared at me, though deep down I knew his obvious anger wasn't aimed at me. My heart raced as a cruel smirk curved his lips. Without a word, Killian stood from his seat and weaved through the various tables, grabbing a stack of napkins and whispering something to the girl behind the counter before coming back to the table.

Stopping in front of me, he wiped down the few drops that landed on my hand and shoes before tossing the used napkins away. Still in a bit of shock, I took his offered hand in a daze, allowing him to pull me out of the chair. Fingers wrapping around mine, he led me out of the café, not uttering a word as we walked toward the parking lot.

"Killian?" I whispered, jogging to keep up with his long strides.

"We're all good, Millie. I just remembered I have somewhere I need to be." At my car, he tossed my backpack onto the back seat, slamming the door shut before leaning against it with both arms crossed. "Go home, finish that book you told me about, start another, and don't think twice about that fuck nugget professor." I opened my mouth to ask a question, but his slow headshake kept me quiet. "You're safe with me, Millie, always."

"Okay." The metal key ring bit into my palm as I tightened my fist. "Killian?"

"Yeah."

"Just tell me one thing."

He eyed me warily. "Depends on the question."

"You'd tell me if you needed help, right?" His arms dropped to his side, lips parted. "Your father, his expectations. I'm not much, but I can help you if—" A grunt escaped when his thick, muscular arms wrapped around me and crushed me to his chest. Tears welled in my lower lids as I snaked my arms around his lean waist.

One minute, maybe twenty... I wasn't sure how long we stood in the nearly empty parking lot embraced in the first true hug I'd ever received.

"Thank you," he whispered in my hair.

"For what?"

"For being unapologetically you. For being open to take on an unknown threat, all for me." When he pulled back, instead of seeing contentment like I felt, sadness was written all over his face. "Listen, I gotta go handle something. See you Monday, Velma."

Before I could utter a response, Killian turned and walked away, both hands curled into fists at his side. Warmth grew in my chest as I watched until he disappeared around a corner. He was angry on my behalf, and that was... unexpected.

Amazing, but unexpected.

With a lovesick sigh, I collapsed into the driver's seat of my small Lexus SUV. The luxury car wasn't love and support like most parents offered their kids, but it and unending funds while in school were gracious gestures from Mom and Dad.

Leaning against the steering wheel, I didn't smother the slow smile that crept across my face.

This felt real, the friendship with Killian, and it was magical. Today proved he wasn't talking to me for some agenda but that he actually cared about me. How deep that care went, I couldn't gauge. And that was okay. I'd take whatever I could get from my only friend.

So what if every time I saw him, another little piece of my heart fell for him?

It wasn't his god-like good looks or his incredible brain that had me falling for him. It was the easy conversations that made me feel as close to normal as I ever felt in my life. The way he made me feel special in a crowded room, singling me out to focus all his energetic attention. There were others who wanted it, who did their best to pull his focus to them, but he ignored them every time.

For me.

When, for my whole life, I was the one ignored, brushed off, and not important enough for others to acknowledge.

Not Killian.

I bit my lip and pushed the start button, ready to get home and daydream about one man.

Move over, book boyfriends, a new, real-life fantasy had taken over.

It would never happen, Killian and me, but it didn't hurt to dream.

5

MILLIE

TODAY

With my focus on reviewing the data, it felt like only a minute had passed before we started our descent into the Dallas area. After landing, I was once again whisked away, this time in a blacked-out SUV instead of an unmarked town car. Now I stood outside an inconspicuous building, wondering how in the hell a few hours ago I woke up expecting another monotonous day.

That obviously did not happen.

My grip tightened around the overnight bag strap, a sudden swell of nervousness constricting my lungs. Steeling my spine, shoving down the feeling of inadequacy, I marched through the glass doors.

After checking in with security, I followed his directions to the elevator bank and stepped inside the first one to arrive. A rush of excited energy thrummed through my veins as the elevator rose toward the seventh floor. With the low whirl in the background, I studied my reflection in the shiny doors. Dropping the bag, I smoothed both hands down my cropped black pants and adjusted the collar of my tailored jacket. At a little over five feet, and curvy, my clothes were now tailored to fit my unique figure. Gone were the days of oversized jeans and sweatshirts, hiding what magazines labeled an hourglass figure. These days, I put effort into how I looked, from my clothes to the sleek, sharp bob and all the products that helped it have some semblance of volume. I liked the way I looked now and didn't cringe when I caught my reflection. Plus, the more professional and put-together appearance helped others take me seriously.

My age constantly worked against me at the university and in my field of study. Which meant I had to put more effort into making a positive first impression. Was it fair? No, but life wasn't fair.

The sharp ding as the elevator leveled off made me jerk, my excitement making me more jumpy than normal.

Hell, nothing about this day was normal.

The opportunity was an enormous deal for many reasons. The most important being the urgency to convince this Supervisory Special Agent Riggs that The Union of Blessed Souls was a dangerous organization that needed immediate consideration to investigate and disassemble. Their website, social media, and tax documents all claimed it was a religious, non-denominational community. But if you looked deeper, past the shiny side they presented to potential followers, a power-hungry beast sat at the core.

And that beast had a name.

Gary Paul, AKA Pastor Paul.

Though he was the creator and frontman of the organization, there were several on the leadership and teaching team who seemed as vile as him. The group preyed on those looking for help with their marriage and the lost searching for a community to help them through a tough time. It all needed to stop before they siphoned more money from their 'followers' and others died.

Yes, died.

Murdered.

Except Pastor Paul nor anyone inside The Union of Blessed Souls were questioned about those deaths despite the high body count and all being followers of the group.

The whoosh of the door parting had me grabbing the dropped bag and tightening my fingers around the laptop satchel strap over my shoulder. Soft murmurs from the few agents sitting behind desks, talking to each other or on the phone, reached me as I stepped into the open concept space. A few curious stares flicked from their screens to study the new arrival for a moment before dismissing me.

I glanced down a hall, shifting my weight as I leaned forward, hoping to find a directory that would help point out SSA Riggs's office. A man and a woman standing a couple feet away paused their conversation, both offering me a quick once-over. The man nodded and smiled, while the woman seemed less than impressed by my interruption.

"Are you lost?" the woman asked, flicking her bleached-blonde hair over a slim shoulder, the ends almost smacking the man in the face.

"Not that I'm aware of." I turned to check the elevator to ensure I stepped off on the correct floor.

"I'm Special Agent Herrington. Can I—"

"This floor is restricted," the woman snapped, cutting off Agent Herrington. "Go back down and meet up with whatever college brought you here for a tour and let the profilers work in peace."

I felt a line form between my brows as I focused on the rude woman. The badge hanging from the clip on her skirt said she worked for the FBI, but the writing was too small beneath to read the title.

Holding up the guest badge the security guard loaned

me, I tilted my head toward the small key card. "Yes, I know it's restricted because the front desk security told me I couldn't access this floor without using this card. Also, I am not here on a tour with a college, considering I went to Harvard, Stanford, and Yale for my undergrad, graduate, and Ph.D., and none of those three institutions are within driving distance of this FBI location. Now, if you're done trying to belittle me to make yourself look better in front of SA Herrington, I'd really like for someone to direct me toward Supervisory Special Agent Riggs's office."

The woman's red lips pressed into a thin line, face flushed, but Herrington had a fist pressed to his lips, attempting to hide a growing grin. When she stepped toward me, the man's smile fell, and he moved between us. With the woman at his back, he extended a hand between us.

"Nice to meet you, Ms...." He arched a dark brown brow in a silent request for me to fill in my name.

I tipped my face up to meet his searching gaze and placed my palm in his, giving it a firm handshake. "Dr. Anderson." With a huff, the woman moved around Agent Herrington, glaring at me as her heels clacked against the floor all the way to the elevator. "I'm here to meet an Agent Riggs." I flicked my wrist, activating my watch. "Though I am a little early, I had the car drop me here before going to the hotel."

"I'll show you to her office, and we can see if she's available now." Turning on the heels of his brown dress shoes, he started down a hallway. "You mentioned a hotel, and it seems you're carrying what we consider a go bag. Are you not from the Dallas area?"

"No, the Northeast. I flew in for this meeting with Agent Riggs."

At a plain wooden door, he rapped a single knuckle against the surface and waited until a voice called out for him to come in. After shooting me a warm smile, he turned the knob and pushed the door open, his tall, lean frame blocking me from seeing inside.

"Hey, sorry," said a tense female voice. "I'm crazy busy getting ready for a consultant to help me sort out—"

"You mean this consultant?" Agent Herrington said with a laugh as he opened the door wide and stepped to the side.

I blinked at the beautiful woman sitting behind the large desk, at a sudden loss for words. Not sure why I expected a male agent, but I did. A very wrong assumption, it appeared. By the way she blinked at me, lips parted, it seemed she assumed the same.

A smile curled at the corner of my lips, as did hers.

"Dr. Anderson?" Agent Riggs hedged as she stood.

I tilted my chin up to maintain her stare and nodded. "Nice to meet you, Agent Riggs." I stepped deeper into the office and took her offered hand, giving it a firm shake before setting my overnight bag beside the chair in front of her large desk.

When the door softly clicked behind me, I twisted, finding the other agent had left without a word. When I turned back to Agent Riggs, I found her studying me with a questioning expression on her face.

"Yes, I'm old enough to drink. Yes, I'm over five feet tall, if only by an inch or two. Yes, all my degrees are valid. I graduated from undergrad, grad school, and my Ph.D. program with perfect GPAs."

Agent Riggs's smile grew. "Good to know. Thank you for coming to meet with me on short notice." With a heavy sigh, she fell into her chair, twisting side to side as she studied me. "I was assigned this case, and your information was tagged on the file as an expert to reach out to if I had questions."

With a nod, I sat in the wide leather chair, pulling out my iPad before setting that bag on the floor beside me. "Because of personal reasons, I began investigating various cults and high control groups after I graduated with my undergrad and have stayed on top of those organizations since. I also teach a graduate-level course at Harvard on the subject every other semester. While on the plane, I reviewed the data I collected since identifying The Union of Blessed Souls as a potential mind control group. I'm all set to answer any of your questions."

Pitching forward, Agent Riggs set both clasped hands on her desk and held my stare.

"What we discuss in this room must stay between us. The information we received is highly confidential and, if leaked, could derail any plans of shutting the organization down. Do you understand?" I gave a clipped nod. "Great. Before we dive into that shit show, let's ditch the titles if that's okay with you. I'm Rhyan." She raised a hand and waved.

My tense muscles relaxed, and my back molded further against the chair. "Nice to meet you, Rhyan. I'm Millie."

Her brows furrowed at my name. I tilted my head, attempting to understand what had her confused about my name.

"Where have I heard that name before?" she muttered to herself. With a firm headshake, she schooled her furrowed expression back into that pleasant smile. "Now that we're past the confidentiality notice and formalities, we can dive into why you're here." I scooted forward along the seat, eager to hear what she had to say. "Two days ago, a friend of a friend of the FBI's deputy director claimed her sister and brother-in-law were murdered in their home just before Christmas, and her niece was taken and is now being held against her will by a cult."

"The Union of Blessed Souls," I mumbled under my breath. Tapping the screen, I pulled up my list of known members. "What were their names? The claimant's sister, brother-in-law, and niece."

"Last name, Parker. Dan, Lacey, and their daughter, Karigan."

A breath froze in my lungs as I stared unseeing at the screen. Did she know? Was that why I was really here?

I shook off the uneasy feeling and nodded, knowing exactly where to find their names on my list. "Dan Parker is, or was, a teacher within the group. He moved his family to Georgia from Texas a little over two years ago after he and his wife attended their quarterly two-week on-site marriage seminar."

"And their daughter?" Rhyan asked.

"I have little on her, but she wasn't integrated into the group like other children of those rising in the ranks. That much I know. She attended the local high school instead of the one in the compound." Maybe now was when I should tell Rhyan I knew exactly where Karigan went to school and had spoken to her after waiting outside the school's gates one afternoon. Not that I learned much from the brief conversation with Karigan, who refused to talk to me about her parents' involvement with the organization and what she witnessed behind the massive gates and walls of their compound. "I'm sure I could find out more," I mumbled instead of voicing my connection with the potential victim.

Instead, I swiped the screen to pull up a picture of Pastor Paul and the leadership team and turned it to Rhyan. "The man in the middle is Pastor Paul, and the others are part of his leadership team, along with high-ranking teachers."

"All men, I see." Annoyance hung in her tone.

"They are extremely backward in how they view marriage and antiquated gender roles. Very old-school, dominant and submissive views." I shifted in the seat and set the iPad on my lap. "What makes the caller assume the two adults were murdered? Though before you respond to that question, I'll admit I wouldn't be surprised if they were." That got Rhyan's full attention. She leaned against the edge of the desk and motioned for me to continue. "There have been others, which is why I consider this group so dangerous. There are five cases that I found through my research that seemed suspicious. From murder-suicides, to being found in their home after a suspected break-in, which are still unsolved, or the fact that one leadership member is currently on wife number four; the previous three all died of 'natural causes' despite their young age."

"What? How is that not suspicious to the local authorities? That's a lot of death all revolving around the group." Rhyan flicked open the thick manila folder on her desk and ran a finger along the typed words. My fingers twitched to get my hands on those papers, to dig deeper and learn what they knew. "And why were they not listed in the case file I was given?"

"From what I've uncovered, the whole town is mixed in with the group. Either they are followers themselves or are being paid off. The local medical examiner and police chief have labeled none of the deaths as connected to or even suspecting the church. The biggest difference here is the other potential murder victims didn't have any family left to be concerned about their untimely deaths, unlike the Parkers, who do."

Which was odd. There was something we were missing.

"None of them had family left?"

"It's cult leader 101 to get their members fully reliant on them, forcing distance between them and their family. It's easy once those followers trust the leaders; they believe the most ridiculous things. Believe me, I've seen it all." I released a heavy sigh. "So, in a literal sense, sure, they might have living relatives, but they might not even know the family member inside the cult is dead." I paused, eyes flicking one way, then the other, as I mentally shuffled through all the data I'd gathered on the group. "None of them left behind a child, only their wealth, which was already dwindled because of their 'offerings' to the pastor or were given to the group, which was written in their wills." I nodded at Rhyan's incredulous expression. "Recently changed wills. But Pastor Paul is smart and never cashed in on the life insurance claims, despite the thousands of dollars sitting out there unclaimed."

Rhyan's head bobbed as I spoke, her stare fixed just over my shoulder. "The insurance companies would have investigated the deaths, too, and the group wouldn't want that scrutiny."

"Exactly," I said brightly, excited that she connected it quickly. "A child left behind is an anomaly, which makes me wonder why. What exactly did the caller say happened to her sister and brother-in-law?"

"That's the odd thing. She couldn't give us any specifics, just that it all felt off. Her sister had reached out a few days prior, stating they were leaving the group, but she mentioned having to keep their plans quiet. When the caller reached out to the local police to find out more information, they wouldn't release the details of what happened. All she has is a faxed copy of the parents' will, which stated that their daughter's guardianship would transfer to Gary Paul if something were to happen to them."

"Fuck," I whispered.

"Which makes me wonder," Rhyan added, suspicion in her tone. "How do *you* know the details of those cases you suspect are murders, not accidents or whatever the medical examiner claimed?"

I swallowed hard, knowing I needed to come clean about the dangerous adventure I took down to Georgia during Thanksgiving break. It was definitely the single most idiotic, riskiest thing I'd ever done.

And it was 100 percent exhilarating.

"I might have taken a trip to Bowen, Georgia," I admitted and rubbed at my temples, the beginnings of a migraine sparking from all the stress. Rhyan's lips parted, but I held up a hand, cutting her off. "Yes, I knew what I was doing was dangerous. Yes, it was risky, considering I suspected this group is very comfortable killing people to get what they want...." It hit me like a punch to the gut. All the air rushed from my lungs. I unfolded from the chair and stood, unable to sit still. "That's it. That has to be why."

"Care to fill me in on the revelation you clearly just had?"

"They take matters into their own hands when they think someone will betray their secrets or *have* something they want. In the other cases, it was money, the massive funds the victims left behind, that immediately went to the church. So if they killed this couple, leaving behind a daughter..."

"Then *that's* what they wanted. She was who they wanted and took out her parents before they could leave, just as the victim had told her sister. They must have caught on to their plans and killed them."

"But they didn't kill the one they wanted. Now why, I have no clue. I met Karigan and—"

Rhyan stood. "What did you just say?"

I grimaced and paced from one side of her office to the other. "When I went down there, I talked to the locals, knowing I'd never get inside the compound, nor would I get any of those living outside the walls to talk. It was then that I realized Karigan went to the local high school, so I waited for her one day. She didn't tell me anything, but the way she avoided me and the fear on her face told me enough."

Rhyan's nostrils flared as she inhaled deeply, a hard stare locked on me. "That was dangerous. You're not trained for that."

"I understand, and as I stated before, I have personal reasons to look into these organizations. I hoped to find what I've searched ten years for while I was there, but I didn't."

Yet another dead end. With each one that popped up in my search, slivers of hope of finding Killian again faded.

"If you have proof of the group orchestrating and covering up murders, why didn't you take it to an FBI field office with all the other information you have on them?"

"Suspicions, yes, actual proof, no. When I went to Georgia, I did some snooping around, and that's how I heard about the deaths possibly being murders orchestrated by The Union of Blessed Souls. All rumors and speculations from the few locals who hate the group and would actually talk to me, nothing that the FBI could use to arrest the leaders or even get a warrant issued for a raid. These men, the pastor in particular, are smart. They cover their asses from every angle. So as much as I'd like to help you shut the group down so more people don't get sucked into their evil web of lies, I can't."

"Unless we get proof."

"That's admissible in court. Not suspicions or rumors. We need concrete evidence or someone on the inside who will flip and give us firsthand accounts of their true inner workings."

Rhyan smirked. "Admissible in court? Concrete evidence? Either you watch a lot of *Law and Order* or...."

"I went to law school at night during graduate school to keep myself busy."

"Holy hell," she said, choking on a laugh. "I went to law school all on its own. It was tough as hell. I can't imagine doing it as a boredom filler." Shaking her head, locks of dark red hair fell forward to frame her face. "The girl, Karigan, is who is important right now. The deputy director asked me to look into the situation. We need to know if she is there against her will, then go from there."

I nodded, fingers wrapping around the back of the chair as I leaned forward. "We need to review the parents' will to see how the guardianship is worded. Then we can determine if there is a legal way to send someone to Georgia to poke around." As I spoke, Rhyan flipped through the stack of papers and tugged one free. She slid it across the desk, and I readily picked it up, immediately scanning the legal jargon. "I'd love to see the original document, which I suspect one of their high-dollar attorneys has on file, but this reads concrete. Gary Paul is her guardian until her eighteenth birthday." Noticing a copy of Karigan's driver's license on top of the stack of papers Rhyan thumbed through, I turned it around to scan the birth date listed. "Which is in eleven months and four days. That's a long-ass time to be there if she doesn't want to be."

"You remind me of another agent," Rhyan said with a soft smile. "He's just as quick, mind always working.

Speaking of which..." She glanced at the clock on the wall. "I have a meeting with him and the agent who walked you in shortly. What else can you tell me about the group in the next fifteen minutes?"

I stared at her for a moment, mentally filtering through all the information and quickly determining what was priority, considering the circumstances.

"I could tell you about each member of the leadership team, Pastor Paul's background and rise to leadership, but I don't think that's what you need to know right now."

"What is?" she asked, considering me.

"If Karigan is our focus, if we believe she is truly being held captive inside the group's compound, then you need to focus on getting her out of that fucked-up situation. I don't even want to think about the mental games that girl has gone through in the few months she's been with Pastor Paul. There is no doubt in my mind he's spinning all kinds of lies to get her reliant on him."

"Asshole," Rhyan muttered.

"It won't be easy. Legally, you can't just send agents in and pull her away from the pastor, considering the will; plus, there is the possibility she *wants* to be there. You also can't storm their gates, flashing your badges and demanding you talk to her. This type of group would immediately threaten her to lie her ass off or be harmed if she spoke the truth. If they know a federal agency is on-site, everything will be locked down tight, and all you'll see is what they want you to see. The only way to truly know what is going on with Karigan is to—"

"Send an agent undercover to infiltrate the group from the inside."

"That's the only way I can see it working, to truly get a feel for the girl's situation and potentially uncover the truth about the organization and their involvement in the murders."

"As I reviewed the information in the file, which is a lot less than what you know, I considered that might be needed and put an agent on alert for a long-term assignment." Rhyan tapped a finger against her lips and arched a brow my way. "Any suggestions on how we get our agent into the group quickly without risking being caught?"

I bit my lower lip to stop the growing smile. "I have an idea that might work. But you'll need to keep an open mind."

Both brows slid up her forehead. "If it can help the girl and potentially shut down that shit show, then I'll be whatever you need me to be."

Perfect.

This was it. My chance to actually do something in my life. Not just hide behind a book or teach others who would go out into the world.

I just hoped Rhyan was as open-minded as she suggested.

6

KILLIAN

TODAY

"Hey, Cooper," a sultry voice called out the second I stepped into the lobby, the door that led to the IT department softly shutting behind me. The aggravating high pitch sent a shiver of revulsion slithering along my spine, but instead of rolling my eyes at Jessica, I forced an easygoing smile. My steps slowed when she didn't hurry over to cling to my side like normal. The woman loved trapping me in the elevator, no doubt hoping I'd finally give in to her advances. Instead, Jessica shifted her attention back to the female agent at her side and leaned in close, clearly gossiping about something she didn't want others to overhear.

Curiosity piqued, I changed course from the elevator bank and, for the first time since Jessica joined our team, approached the woman instead of the other way around. Sliding the phone I just acquired after half an hour of promising to not shatter another one, I paused a couple of feet away, still within hearing distance, acting engrossed with whatever was on the screen.

"I don't know who that kid thinks she is," Jessica huffed.

"And Hunter didn't even stand up for me when that bitch got sassy." I held back a chuckle. Knowing Herrington, he was more amused by someone talking back to Jessica than offended on her behalf. "I was just on my way to the security desk to get some information on the... child when I ran into you."

"What is someone that young doing here?" the other agent whispered back. "Maybe you should go easy on her. She could be here needing help."

"No, she's some"—Jessica waved her hand—"consultant."

Interesting. Must be the consultant Rhyan's text mentioned. This day just got slightly better. I loved a good mystery to uncover. To find all the pieces, placing them in the right order to solve the puzzle was thrilling. That, plus my ability to remember everything I hear, was what made me a valuable asset in the CIA, until I left and joined the FBI.

Did I enjoy being an asset? No.

Was it expected of me? Yes.

Did I still resent those who forced me to take on that career and leave the tiny slice of happiness I forged in college behind? Hell fucking yes.

I could've had a normal life. Maybe even been married by now, with high IQ kids running around, making me and Millie crazy with their inquisitive minds and lack of social skills, both qualities from their mother.

Just thinking about Millie had the deep weight of loneliness settling into my gut. That life would never happen, and I knew for a fact I'd never find pure acceptance and happiness again like I did in those months I had with Millie.

Two semesters was all I had with an amazing woman who forever changed me.

Having heard enough of the petty gossip, I turned on my heel and strode to the elevator bank. Just as I tapped the call button, Jessica's high-pitched voice called out my name, her stilettos rapidly clicking against the slate tile floor.

"Hey," she said, leaning her weight against my arm. "You going up?" You didn't need to have my training to hear the excitement and hope in her voice.

"Yep," I said, rocking back on my heels to break the small contact. "Finished with the latest gossip?" I inclined my head back the way she came from. "Seemed juicy."

She waved me off with a fake giggle. "Not as juicy as you."

"Like a ripe peach," I responded with a wink. A sliver of my soul always withered and died with the fake flirting. When she ran a finger along my bicep. Swallowing down the bile rising in my throat from the contact, I forced a fake chuckle.

"I'd take a bite of you any day," she purred, pressing her fake tits against me.

Sweat slicked my forehead. Focusing on my breaths, I counted to ten before starting over, hoping to calm myself down. Any type of contact brought unwanted memories to the forefront of my mind where they absolutely did not belong.

The second the sharp ding of the elevator echoed through the empty lobby, I extracted myself from her grip and stepped onto the elevator. Unfortunately, being one of our three admins on the floor, she followed me to ride up to our floor, and there wasn't a damn thing I could do about it. Her sticky sweet perfume clogged my nose and coated my throat, making the mounting nausea worse.

"Rhyan wants me to sit in on the meeting," she stated, edging even closer until I was backed into the corner, nowhere left to escape her red-painted claws. "Maybe after we could go get a drink and—"

"I already have plans," I said with a cocky grin that had her eyes rolling. "Maybe next time."

"You always say that." Her lower lip jutted out in an exaggerated pout.

I did and would continue to make up nonexistent plans. The thought of someone like Jessica touching me, using me.... Clearing my throat, I grasped her slim shoulder and urged her back a few steps, offering enough room to breathe without choking on the rising disgust and fear.

"Do you know what this meeting is about?" I asked instead of answering her question. Not telling her I already knew the basics would hopefully get me more information. Normally, walking into a case meeting with zero clue about what we would discuss wasn't an issue, but for some reason, I was antsy about this unknown.

Her response filtered through one ear and out the other as I pressed a hand to my flat stomach when another wave of nerves had it twisting.

Maybe those seven tacos I ate from the rundown gas station before coming to the office were a terrible decision.

I was an emotional eater. Sue me.

When the elevator leveled off on our floor and the doors opened, I stepped around Jessica and bolted into the bullpen like the devil was on my heels. Hunter glanced up from his desk with a furrowed brow, no doubt confused about my strange speed walking before his gaze snagged on the woman following me. Understanding flashed over his features. He stood, gathering some papers and a notepad as I strode toward his desk. I kept the fast clip as I passed, and he fell into stride beside me.

"Your shadow seems to be extra clingy today," he muttered under his breath.

Gritting my teeth, I nodded. "If she wasn't so damn good at her job, I'd ask Rhyan to fire her ass for sexual harassment. She needs to keep her hands to herself."

Hunter shot me a look out of the corner of his eye. "You're in a fun mood."

"Bad day," I grumbled and ran a hand through my shoulder-length, dirty-blond hair before securing it into a knot at the base of my skull. "Bad life."

Hunter mouthed the word *wow*, making me chuff. Making sure to only grasp the material of my Henley at the elbow, he pulled me to a stop. Brows dipped, he scanned my face as if trying to uncover the real reason for my shit mood.

"Stop profiling me," I hissed.

"You're my friend, Coop, and I don't want to see you slip into that place you were last year. It took months for us to dig you out of those empty bottles and mile-long bar tabs."

I ground my molars to keep from lashing out. The fucker was one of my only friends, minus the one I recently made in LA, and I didn't want to hurt him with my words. Since I observed everything down to minuscule details, I could cut almost anyone down to their core. Not a quality trait, but one I had nonetheless.

"I'm fine." Leaning forward, I blew my breath into his face. He leapt back with a curse and waved a hand in front of his face. "See? No alcohol."

"What the fuck did you eat for lunch?" He gave an exaggerated gag. "Holy hell, Coop, your breath smells like—"

"Gas station tacos?" I filled in with a snicker.

"Ass. I was going to go with your breath smells like ass, but now that you mention it, both have the same stench, so it could go either way."

Faking another gag, he shook his head and moved down the hall toward the meeting room. I smelled Jessica before she brushed past.

"See you in there, Coop," she said with a wink. At the door to the meeting room, she came to an abrupt halt. "Oh, great, you're here."

Unable to see inside the conference room, I shook my head at Jessica's rude behavior. Again, it was damn lucky that she was good at her job, or she would've been fired shortly after being hired for how uncomfortable she made the male agents in our office. But alas, she was detail-oriented, organized, and fast when we needed her to get something booked or moved around. It would make life a little easier if she did all that without groping us.

A response came from inside the room that made Jessica huff and step inside, grumbling about the consultant she didn't know but didn't like, disappearing as she did. Closing my lids, I inhaled for five beats before blowing it out slowly, hoping that would settle my mind.

Only it didn't. Everything kept going back to Millie, flashing from memories of the video of her moving on today. I needed to give it up and stop watching over her and protecting her from afar, but she was my obsession.

Head angled one way, then the other, to stretch out the tension in my neck, I shook out my hands and settled the happy-go-lucky, easy-going Cooper mask into place. Time to work, and hopefully, this long assignment would get me away from this place for a while.

Forcing my feet forward, I moved toward the conference room where everyone waited when an incoming text pulled my attention to the phone clenched tight in my hand. Full focus on the screen, I almost didn't catch the soft gasp that filled the room as I stepped inside.

"Killian?"

My heart froze, and my lungs forgot how to function as the sweet voice filled my ears. The usual rage that blazed in my chest when someone said my first name didn't come. Unable to move, I peeked up through my lashes toward the familiar voice, slightly terrified of what I would find.

When my gaze landed on her, a black hole appeared beneath my feet and swallowed me whole. Nothing made sense. For the first time in my life, I couldn't process the situation happening in front of me fast enough.

A hard jolt and my heart restarted, slamming against my chest with forceful beats.

"Millie?" Her name was barely a whisper as I stood immobile, completely dumbfounded.

Through my pulse thrumming in my ears, Rhyan's muttered curse seeped through. Breaking off Millie's just-as-shocked stare, I glanced at my boss, whose hand hovered over her gaping mouth.

Why did she look like she knew who this woman was to me? I swallowed a groan when a fuzzy memory reminded me of why Rhyan knew. Fuck my life. My chatty drunk self might have mentioned Millie a time or a thousand after too many drinks.

The clack of chair wheels rolling along the stained concrete floor whipped my attention back to where Millie now stood. Each thunderous beat of my heart felt like it would pound right out of my chest as I took her in. Just as perfect as ever. A little older, a hard glint in her dark eyes, but still the same girl I knew all those years ago. Short dark hair grazed just below her chin that accentuated her soft jaw, tiny nose, and almond-shaped dark eyes.

Damn, she was even more beautiful in person than

through the camera. Nothing could've prepared me for this, to see her within arm's distance.

Fucking hell. I swallowed, mouth and throat desert dry as I continued to stare, no words coming to mind. Despite my training and years of effortlessly sliding into that fake persona, I couldn't. All I could do was watch like a dazed idiot as she took a hesitant step closer.

"Wait, Cooper, you actually know this... this child?"

Jessica's words and haughty tone snapped something inside me. Rage scorched through the shock of finding Millie in the BSU conference room. How fucking dare she. My narrowed-eyed gaze slid to Jessica, who didn't notice my death glare as she continued to scowl at my girl.

No, not my girl.

Not anymore.

"You," I snapped the word like a whip through the room. "Get the fuck out." Lip curled in a snarl, I barely held the tight grip controlling my temper.

"You should listen to him," Jessica preened, a snarky smile directed at Millie. "You don't belong here."

"Not her. You." Jessica blanched at my harsh tone but still didn't move. "I said get the fuck out." One menacing step in her direction had the woman jerking out of her chair and skirting around the table. "You do not get to disrespect her like that in front of me. Ever."

"Rhyan," Jessica whined, turning to our boss. "Did you hear the way he—"

"I suggest you stop talking and read the room, Miss Snapps. Clearly, the woman you were intent on embarrassing despite her being our guest means something to Agent Cooper."

"But—"

"If you don't leave this office right now, I'll make you," I said through clenched teeth. Fuck, I was about to lose it. Feeling the weight of her attention on me, I flicked a weary glimpse at Millie to gauge her reaction to this side of me. "Millie, you stay right where you are."

Two dark brows rose along her forehead. Crossing both arms, she gave an unimpressed expression. "Wasn't planning on leaving, but thanks for the permission. I fully intend to stay right here until I get some fucking answers."

A snort caught in my throat at her snarky reply. It was quick and witty while basically telling me to fuck off. I gave this new grown-up Millie another quick once-over, this time noticing the things I couldn't detect through the security feed. The young, insecure, and shy Millie was gone. In front of me stood a sexy-as-hell woman with a brain that worked faster than most computers. It seemed in our years apart, she learned sarcasm and found her backbone.

My lips dipped into a frown, wondering what happened that made her change. If it was a guy or that fucker of an ex-husband that put that suspicious glint in her eyes, I'd kill them.

What were a few more kills to my already long list?

"Actually," Rhyan said with a clap that cut through the tension. "Everyone needs to step out into the hall. Clearly, these two need a few minutes before we dive into the case details."

I refused to break Millie's intense stare, too afraid she'd try to slip out with the rest of them if I looked away.

"Thank you," I said with a respectful nod to my boss as she passed. "I just need, fuck, I just need a minute."

"Figure your shit out, Coop." She sighed. "Dr. Anderson is here to help with the case. There is a seventeen-year-old girl out there who needs our help, and every minute counts.

You have five minutes to clear whatever this is between you two before we get back to work. Use the time wisely."

Behind me, the conference room door softly clicked closed. Some of the tension eased now that we were alone until the reality of this fucked-up situation hit me like a punch to the balls.

Five minutes. That was all I had to explain to the woman I casually stalked—for her safety, of course—and still loved, which she had no clue about, why I vanished all those years ago.

Right.

No pressure.

Fuck my fucked life.

7

MILLIE

10 YEARS AGO

"So it's a date, then?"

I couldn't find the words to respond, instead simply nodded in agreement. In fact, I hadn't said a single word during the odd, one-sided conversation. The moment I sat down in my chair, Chad appeared, smiling like he was in on some inside joke.

Maybe it was me. I was the joke. But if that was the case, why had he woven through the narrow row of chairs to strike up a conversation and ask me out on a date?

A date.

Something I'd yet to go on. Even though I wasn't thrilled about Chad himself, a date was enticing. Maybe then I could finally lose all the V-cards I had stacked against me. Sure, I was brilliant, but inexperienced in so many ways.

I'd yet to even be kissed.

How sad was that?

Chad's grin grew as he rapped a knuckle against the desk, as if that solidified our agreement.

"What the fuck do you think you're doing?" A familiar,

calloused palm pressed to the top of my shoulder as Killian lowered into the seat beside me, glare directed at Chad.

"Finally asking the prettiest girl in class out on a date," he responded, shooting me an exaggerated wink. "You got a problem with that, Cooper?"

When Killian didn't respond, I swiveled in the hard chair, giving him my full attention. The muscle along his jaw popped, and a deep red highlighted his cheeks while his chest rose and fell in quick succession.

Concern had me reaching over and pressing the back of my hand to Killian's forehead. Those aqua eyes slid my way.

"Whatcha doing there, Velma?" Killian asked, laughter lifting his tone.

"You're flushed and seem to be having a difficult time breathing, so I'm checking for a fever. Are you sick?"

A softness settled over his features as he shook his head. Removing my hand, he kept it clasped in his own as he tucked our entangled fingers beneath the desk. With a curious look, he shook his head before turning back to Chad. The gentleness he showed me vanished between blinks.

"When is this date?" Killian asked.

"Friday night?" Chad asked, turning to me with a sharp grin that had me tensing. Despite the uncertain feeling growing in my gut about the guy, I really wanted to go on a date. To check that off my ultra-basic and pathetic 'bucket' list. At my nod, Chad flicked a winning grin to Killian. "Great. I'll pick you up around seven." Turning my notebook around, he jotted down a phone number in the corner. "Text me your address. See you then, Miley."

"It's Millie," Killian hissed, hand tightening around mine. "Mill-ie. Not like Miley Cyrus."

"Right." He chuckled. "That's what I meant. See you Friday."

The moment Chad turned to head back to his seat several rows down, Killian swiveled in his chair, caging me in with one forearm pressed to the desk, the other against the back of my seat. His intense gaze searched my face, slowly scanning every inch with his full lips dipped in a frown.

"You like him, Velma?"

I shook my head and shrugged. Heat slid beneath my skin as Killian leaned even closer. It should freak me out, being trapped, but instead, my stomach fluttered as desire pulsed through my veins. Lips parted, breaths shallow, I swallowed before responding, hoping that would keep my voice from shaking and exposing how much I liked Killian crowding me.

"I don't know him."

A dirty-blond brow arched in question. "Then why say yes?"

I tilted my head. "Isn't that the purpose of a date? To get to know someone and see if you do or don't like them?"

"Why him, then?" he demanded. Up front, the professor took his place behind the podium, but Killian didn't move. Not that Professor Daniels would look our way to notice. Ever since I told Killian about our teacher making me feel uncomfortable, Professor Daniels had backed off completely. In fact, he almost looked terrified anytime he acknowledged me in class when I answered a question or had one for him.

"Because he asked," I whispered.

Not the right response, apparently.

With a scoff, Killian shoved himself back and turned

toward the front of the class, arms folded over his muscular chest. That muscle along his jaw pulsed in rapid succession.

Disappointment and worry churned in my empty stomach, making me nauseous. My fingers trembled as I picked up a pen and adjusted the notepad back in front of my seat, ready to take notes on the lecture I had no hope of hearing with the confusion and unease swirling in my mind.

I swallowed a yelp when a hot palm pressed to the top of my jean-clad thigh, snapping my attention back to the man beside me. Head resting on top of a forearm folded on the desk, his bright eyes were locked on my own.

"I don't like it. Something feels off. Don't do it; don't go out with him."

I furrowed my brows. "But how will I ever mark it off my bucket list if I say no?"

"Mark off what?" he practically growled.

"A date," I whispered. "It will be my first one. Ever."

Killian's long lashes fanned down in slow blinks. For several seconds, he just stared, not saying a word. "Right. I won't take that away from you, even if I'm disappointed that first won't be checked off with me." A mischievous smirk pulled at his lips. "Guess I better make sure Chad understands my expectations on how to treat my *friend* on this date."

"And what are your expectations?"

Killian just hummed a noncommittal response. With a nod, he released my leg and turned his attention to the professor. I studied him out of the corner of my eye, trying to understand what the hell had just happened. What did he mean by expectations? Maybe he was worried about my safety. I agreed to go somewhere alone with a guy I knew nothing about.

Damn. Maybe agreeing to the date was a dangerous

move. What if he was a serial killer or, worse, dumb? I could end up missing, with my picture on every milk carton in America, or bored to death, all because I wanted to experience my first date.

Though this would offer an excellent opportunity to observe a new social situation to further analyze later. Understanding what drove someone, the why behind their behavior, was why I chose the psychology degree path, after all.

I didn't want to go into counseling, helping others unravel their past trauma or issues. It was more so I could hopefully figure out how to fit in one day. If I understood the world, then maybe I could manipulate myself and my personality to fit what the world considered to be normal.

Well. As normal as someone like me could be.

8

MILLIE

TODAY

All ten fingers pressed to the top of the table, knuckles void of color to keep me upright as I studied Killian. My mind could barely believe he was right there. After all this time, he was only three feet away, yet it felt like thousands.

He was more gorgeous than I remembered. Back then, he was built, but adult Killian was model worthy, with broad shoulders and long, lean muscles that were showcased by the ripped jeans hugging his thighs and ass. A long-sleeve, dark gray Henley stretched across his defined chest, leaving nothing to the imagination. And that hair. Holy hell, was that a man bun?

His exposed thick forearms flexed as he tightened both hands into clenched fists before stretching his fingers out wide. Seconds had passed since Rhyan left us alone. Her five-minute timeframe to clear the uncomfortableness in the air that our past manufactured ticked down, yet neither of us had uttered a word.

Knees wobbly, I eased into the rolling chair, too afraid the lightheaded feeling from shock and various conflicting emotions would send me crashing to the floor. Not the strong, sure-of-herself professional I wanted to portray to the man who shattered my heart when he vanished.

"So you're alive." A wince pulled at his handsome face as he dipped his chin. Not knowing how to follow that up, I bit my lower lip and nodded.

What else was there to say?

He was here, an FBI agent and looking great. All that time I spent worried about him was for nothing, and now all I felt was foolish. The one person I thought I could trust turned out to have ditched me like everyone else. It just took longer than normal.

Fool. I was such a damn fool.

"Millie," he whispered and dared a step closer.

"Don't," I croaked. The unshed tears I held back clogged my throat. Wrapping my fingers around my neck, I worked to swallow down the tsunami of mixed emotions swirling inside me. Anger, shock, longing, more anger, and embarrassment all struggled for dominance, suffocating any sliver of happiness at finding my long-lost friend alive and well.

I couldn't be happy, even if seeing him again was exactly what I have wanted since the morning I woke up groggy and alone. This moment was supposed to be filled with happy tears and radiating joy.

Not this... mess going on inside me.

And the way he was looking at me with uncertainty and desperation behind his eyes was too much. Shaking my head, I pressed both palms to the table and shoved back to stand on shaky legs. They might give out, but I couldn't just sit there dying a little more inside with every passing second.

Marching to the door, I moved around him and reached for the handle.

"Millie, please," Killian pleaded at my back. "Let me explain."

I swallowed hard. Watery gaze locked on the dark wood door. I bit the inside of my cheek to keep the tears from spilling over. "What's there to explain, Killian? You left me. We..." My voice cracked. "You don't get my time. I'm glad you're okay. I was worried about you."

Obsessively worried about him daily, if I were honest with myself. All that concern, strangely enough, was what led me to study cults in the first place, which was why we were reunited now. I had assumed his overbearing father held him inside a cult, not living freely, looking too fucking hot to be human, inside the fucking FBI. "But I can see it wasn't warranted. You're clearly not in danger, and you're living your best life."

Fingers wrapped around the lever, I shoved it down and yanked the door open. Or tried to, at least. A massive palm slapped the center of the wood, keeping it closed. Strands of dark hair blew alongside my cheeks with every heavy exhale from the man holding me hostage. A shiver of desire raced down my spine as he stepped even closer, his chest almost brushing my back. Lust and arousal quickly overtook the roaring of anger. My sweaty grip tightened on the metal lever to keep from swaying closer to Killian's radiating heat.

"You don't understand." His breath brushed along the back of my neck.

Goose bumps erupted, and I fought the urge to angle my head, giving him access to my throat, as my desperation to feel his lips on my skin grew almost unbearable.

"I don't need to," I said, swallowing thickly. "You obviously didn't feel the need to explain yourself in the last ten fucking years. Ten years," I whispered. "And you being here, inside the FBI, an agent... you could've found me, but you never did. Not a single word after... everything. You made it very clear, from the loud silence, that explaining your side wasn't a priority."

"I never meant to hurt you, Millie."

"Stop it," I barked. "Stop acting like you fucking care about me." Whirling around, I sealed my back to the door to put as much distance between us as I could and glared up at him with narrowed eyes. "If you did, you would've left a note for me to find, or called in the last ten years. Hell, a fucking smoke signal would've been better than your damn silence."

The corner of his lips twitched despite the torment written on his drawn features. "You can read smoke signals now?"

My hands curled at my side to keep from shoving him away.

Or pulling him closer.

Fuck, this was confusing.

Squeezing my eyes shut, I focused on my words to convey how his actions, or lack thereof, made me feel so damn small.

"You didn't have the decency to let me know you were okay ten years ago when my friend up and vanished, so I don't understand why you feel the need to explain now. It's fine. I'm fine." Well, I would be after a bottle of wine, some cookie dough, and a shit ton of tears. "So, let's just get on with the case so I can go back to my life, and you can keep doing whatever the hell you've been doing in yours."

My chest heaved up and down after my rant, which apparently was hilarious because a smile split his face, chasing away all traces of his earlier distress.

"What?" I growled, tapping my fingers along my thigh, trying to calm my breathing.

"You're cute when you're mad at me. I forgot about that."

Cute.

The man who forced a friendship on me, made me laugh until I cried, and treated me like I was a priceless piece of art that was treasured and protected, who was many of my firsts, including losing my virginity in a night that no other man could ever live up to, and then vanished, was calling my anger cute.

Oh, I'd show him fucking cute.

A pulse of relief flashed over his features when I forced a sweet smile to hide my violent intentions. He visibly shuddered, lids fluttered closed as my hand lightly grasped at his shoulder, not understanding the simple touch was for stability and to line up the perfect shot.

Time to put those two self-defense classes to the test.

The bastard never saw my knee coming, and the amount of joy that brought me was not healthy.

A pained grunt radiated around the room, triggering a genuine smile spreading across my face. Cooper's beautiful eyes widened in agony as he stumbled backward, hands immediately grasping his crotch, like that could ease the pain radiating from his smashed balls. The utter shock on his face and painful wheezing erased a fraction of the anger rolling in my chest.

I hoped I broke his dick like he broke my heart.

"I'm not the same girl you left behind," I said, smoothing a palm along my jacket and tugging at the sides, positioning it back into place. "Maybe you did me a favor by leaving." A flash of something I couldn't read flickered in his aqua eyes. "Teaching me not to trust anyone. It was a hard lesson to learn so fucking young, but here I am, stronger and not susceptible to assholes like you."

Not waiting for a response, I whirled around and jerked

the door open with a forceful tug. Rhyan and Agent Herrington stood up straight, the former eyeing me with apprehension. I strained an all-teeth smile, which only made Agent Herrington wince. Damn, I probably looked rabid. Releasing a slow breath, I relaxed my shoulders from around my ears and stepped back, gesturing to the conference room.

"We're all good in here." My fingers slipped from the cool metal as I moved toward the chair I vacated a few minutes earlier. Sitting down carefully, I adjusted my iPad and papers to give my nervous hands something to do as Rhyan and Herrington stepped into the room.

"Don't mind him," I muttered. "He'll be fine."

Rhyan's alarmed gaze stayed on the hunched asshole who still struggled to get his breathing under control, while Agent Herrington covered a barked laugh with a fake cough before plopping down into the chair opposite me. Still not recovered, Killian waddled over to the chair at the very end of the table, the farthest from me, and collapsed into the seat.

"I'm going to assume he deserved that?" Rhyan asked, arching a brow in my direction.

"Yes," I responded at the same time Killian snarled, "Fuck no."

"Can we move on to discussing the case and plan, please?" I hissed, jaw clenched tight. "This case, investigating the organization, and helping Karigan is more important than the past." I turned a pleading look to Rhyan. Analyzing the data and creating an action plan would be easier to process and work through than the confusing emotions still swirling inside me.

"Sure," she drawled, seeming unsure but willing to move on. Back straight, she directed a pointed look at Killian and

Herrington. "To catch you two up on the case details, the FBI received a call about an underage child suspected to be held captive by the organization known as The Union of Blessed Souls. After that call and reviewing the information provided, I reached out to Dr. Anderson for additional insight. She's an expert in the field and a contracted consultant as needed by the FBI."

I offered a small, awkward wave. Herrington leaned across the table, hand outstretched. "We met earlier but... Hunter Herrington," he said with a wink.

"Millie Anderson."

"Pleasure to meet you." A low growl from the end of the table had Hunter releasing my hand and flopping back into his seat.

"Right, sorry. I forgot introductions earlier. Sorry about that." Rhyan blew a raspberry. I couldn't help but grin. "Regarding the case, we're kneecapped because the victim's parents' will listed her guardian as the leader of the cult, Gary Paul, also known as Pastor Paul. On top of this, it was brought to my attention that there are other suspicious deaths outside of the victim's parents. The entire town seems to be wrapped up in the organization."

"How do you know that?" Agent Herrington mused while flipping through the file Rhyan had placed in the middle of the table, brows furrowed. "There is nothing mentioned about the connected murders or the shady town."

"That information came from me because I witnessed it firsthand." I felt the impact of Cooper's hard gaze when it snapped to me, but I refused to back down beneath the weight. "Last fall, I visited the town where they are based to see if I could find any additional information." And possibly locate my former best friend, who I thought was trapped in the cult after being brainwashed by his father. I cleared my throat to keep from saying those foolish words out loud before continuing. "What I found was the police, the medical examiner, even the public officials are all connected to The Union of Blessed Souls. Whether that's by being an actual follower or taking bribes. This group is extremely dangerous and has ways to cover up the murders I suspect they orchestrated—"

"You went down there alone?" Killian hissed, his anger almost palpable from where he glared from his seat. "What the fuck were you thinking? You just told us they're extremely dangerous, so you just went down there on a fucking vacation?"

I leveled Killian with a flat look, not letting him see what his anger did to me.

Actually, I didn't even know what the fuck his anger did to me. Part of me wanted to soak in the fact that he was worried about me, while the other part was pissed that he assumed he had a right to care.

Maybe I needed therapy.

"As you experienced firsthand, I can take care of myself."

"And that point goes to Millie," Agent Herrington whispered as his curious gaze flicked between me and Killian. "What happened between you two?"

My lips parted, but nothing came out. How did I explain in a single sentence the complexity of everything that was me and Killian? Thankfully, Rhyan spoke up, keeping me from having to answer.

"We need someone on the inside to investigate and see if the caller's niece is truly in danger. If we uncover details about the other suspicions, then that will be a bonus. She's our priority." Leaning back in her chair, she leveled all her attention at me. "You mentioned having a suggestion on getting an agent inside to assess the situation quickly and without being noticed."

My pulse kicked up, and sweat slicked my palms. Tucking both hands beneath the table, my fingers drummed along my thigh as I gathered up the courage to suggest the crazy plan. No, not crazy. It was the only option if we wanted this done before any more damage happened to innocent people and, of course, Karigan.

"Marriage counseling." Three sets of eyes blinked at me before eyeballing each other. "Hear me out. It makes the most sense. One way they draw in new followers is through their marriage classes and seminars. They offer them online year-round, taught by their so-called teachers but also on-site for two weeks once a quarter. This allows them to not only begin the mind games but also assess the more affluent and powerful couples to invite into the inner circle."

Hunter kept his hazel eyes locked on me as he leaned back in the chair, interlacing his fingers behind his head. "So, you're suggesting to send in two undercover agents to this marriage class bullshit, and then what?"

"Watch your damn tone," Cooper snapped.

I eyed him with confusion before turning back to Hunter, who couldn't hold back a knowing smirk.

"Yes, but not two agents," I drawled. "I'm suggesting one agent and, well, me." My focus swung from Hunter to Rhyan to assess her reaction to that tiny detail.

"Absolutely not," Killian barked, slamming a fist on the table. We all reached for the pens before they could roll off the table from the vibrations.

"Not sure we can do that," Rhyan offered, but her tone suggested she might actually consider it as an option.

"I'll play husband with you any day, Millie," Hunter said while using his fingers to make a heart sign.

A giggle escaped at his antic, which was clearly meant to annoy the other man in the room. That apparently was the last straw. Killian jumped from his chair, which flew backward, slamming against the wall, leaving an indentation in the drywall before lunging toward Hunter. He cursed and jerked out of Killian's reach just before his grabbing hands found purchase.

Both palms slapped to the table, I used the leverage to stand. The two idiots froze and turned to me.

"I understand I'm not an agent, but this is our best option." I turned to Rhyan. At least she hadn't shot down the idea yet. "I'm the one with the most knowledge of the group. I know the ins and outs after months of detailed research. Plus my background, training, and education. I teach a class on forensic psychology, for fuck's sake," I said, tossing both hands up. "I can meet with Karigan—who, bonus, knows she can trust me because of that brief encounter last year— talk to her, and assess where we stand. If she's happy there, truly happy and not brainwashed happy, I'll know. With the short timeframe we have to sign up for the on-site marriage classes, which start on Monday, sending me and a male agent to Georgia is our best option."

Rhyan's lips pursed in a tight line as she stared me down, almost as if sizing me up to see if I was up to the challenge.

"There's the legal aspect of all this—"

"You can't be seriously fucking considering this, boss," Killian snapped.

Her hard gaze slid to Killian. "Watch. Your. Tone." To my surprise, Killian deflated at that and dropped back into his seat. "I'm considering all options." She swiveled her seat to face me directly. "You're not an agent."

"But I am a consultant for the FBI. In my agreement, there is a line about possible on-site assessment when necessary. I consider this necessary. Who knows what kind of mental manipulations this poor girl goes through daily? We're already failing her since she's been on her own with these bastards since her parents were murdered. I don't give a fuck about my safety—"

"That's obvious," Killian muttered loud enough for everyone to hear, but I ignored him.

"She's what's important. Finding justice for those families whose lives were cut short because of the group's greed could be a bonus. My personal reason for investigating this group is no longer valid." Without my consent, my gaze flicked to Killian. "My only focus will be assessing the victim's mental state, helping the agent uncover anything they can find on the suspicious deaths, and then getting out."

Rhyan stayed silent while I pleaded my case. "Send me the consulting agreement you signed with us—"

"Boss," Killian said, the word snapping through the room. "Please. Please, don't do this. Not..." He swallowed hard, making his Adam's apple bob. "Not her."

The anger that had dimmed roared back to life as I turned to face him. "You don't think I can do this?"

"It's not that—"

"You know nothing about me," I hissed. "Nothing. I'm not that pathetic girl you befriended—"

"You were never pathetic," he muttered.

"This is our best option. Once you get your head out of your ass, then you'll see I'm right."

Leaning back in the chair, he folded both arms over his chest. "No, I won't, because it's not happening."

"I need to think," Rhyan mused. I twisted back her way, hope blooming in my chest. "We have you booked at a hotel downtown since I wasn't sure how long this would take today and would possibly need some time tomorrow. Why don't you go check in and relax, and after I think through all our options, I'll be in touch."

It wasn't the firm yes I hoped for, but it wasn't a no either.

Nodding in agreement, I picked up my things off the table before grabbing both bags and heading for the door. A soft grip on the edge of my suit jacket sleeve pulled me up short. Looking over my shoulder, I met a pair of steely aqua eyes.

"We're not done with the earlier conversation," he stated, conviction in his tone.

I offered him a slight headshake and ripped out of his hold.

"Yes, we are." Emotions threatened to clog my throat. "Goodbye, Killian."

With those painful words haunting my every step, I hurried out the door before the tears I held at bay fell from the pain swelling in my chest. Out of all the scenarios I imagined over the years of what it would be like when I saw Killian again, what just happened in that room was never one of them.

9

KILLIAN

TODAY

I gripped the edge of the conference room table, knuckles going white, as I fought the urge to follow Millie. The pictures and videos I studied taken from the hidden camera I placed across from her townhome didn't prepare me for how fucking gorgeous she still was. Millie was beautiful ten years ago, but fucking hell, she was drop-dead gorgeous now.

Silky dark hair that teased at the edge of her jaw gave her a sophisticated and classy look, even though I loved her long hair back then, too. Gone were the thick-rimmed glasses that had always seemed to slip down her cute little button nose, which made the punch of her dark eyes staring into my soul that much more powerful.

Then there were her curves. The suit she wore stressed every inch of her tiny frame, making my mouth water and fingers twitch the second she stood from the chair. I wanted my fingers digging into her hips as I fucked that new sass right out of her.

I squeezed both eyes shut to stop the bombarding images from that night, the last night I saw her in person until now. A single day hadn't passed that I didn't crave the feel of her skin beneath my fingertips, to hear her unique bell-like laugh, or to see those dark eyes sparkle with trust and brilliance.

The click of the door closing snapped my lids open, and I turned a pleading look to my boss, finding her curious gaze already locked on me.

"So, that's Millie." I swallowed thickly and nodded. "Wow." Rhyan leaned back in her chair with a sigh, rubbing at her forehead. "And here I thought today would be a calm day."

"I can't believe that's *the* Millie your drunk ass always goes on and on—"

The unamused glare that clearly communicated, *I'll kill you in your sleep with a smile on my face* made Hunter's lips snap shut.

"She can't be a part of this," I pleaded, and would beg if I thought that would work. "It's too dangerous. She's not an agent and—"

"And you want to roll her up in bubble wrap?" Rhyan scoffed. Pulling out her phone, she typed out a message before laying it down on the table. "Not sure if you noticed, but that woman is a firecracker and won't put up with you setting her on a shelf for safekeeping."

Both hands curled into loose fists along the polished wood. "She doesn't understand what she's signing up for." In fact, why would she even suggest this in the first place? The Millie I knew lived for her alone time with a good book and utter silence. When she wasn't with me, of course. "It can't be an option."

The finality in my tone had a smirk tugging at the corner of Rhyan's lips, which just pissed me off even more than I already was.

"Thankfully, you're not the leader of this team, and it's not your decision because I sure as hell won't let someone dictate for that woman what she can and cannot do, even if that someone is you, Cooper." When I started to say something, she slashed a hand through the air, stopping me. "I understand your concern, and it's warranted. She's not an agent, but her points are solid. We need someone who can evaluate the mental state of the suspected victim—"

"Why?" I cut in. "Why not send a male and female agent in, have them locate the girl, and sneak her out? Millie can do her evaluation here, where it's safe."

"And what if the girl doesn't want to come with you? What if she's brainwashed to where she doesn't see that she's a captive? How will you undo the damage that was done and pinpoint the exact things to say to get her to believe that she's actually in danger by staying where she perceives herself as safe? That's why we need someone like Dr. Anderson, someone who can unravel all the shit this poor girl has probably been told to keep her complacent. I'm sorry, Cooper, but her assisting us in this case is a solid plan."

"But—"

The door swinging open cut me off as I whirled around to see who interrupted the meeting. Charlie Bekham, Rhyan's life partner and our technical analyst slash backup profiler, paused just inside the door, taking in the room.

"Why does Cooper look like someone threatened to take his favorite toy?" he hedged as he closed the door behind him. Laptop tucked against his side, he made his way to the chair beside Rhyan. A soft, adoring expression filled his features as he stared down at her, running a single finger along her jaw before plopping down into the seat. With a small shove against the edge of the table, the wheels rolled along the floor, stopping when he was as close as possible to Rhyan.

"Not take, but possibly damage the toy he wants to keep on a pedestal," Hunter offered. "You wouldn't believe the drama that unfolded earlier." Charlie's fingers paused their tapping on the keyboard and arched a dark brow in Hunter's direction. "First, Coop here snapped Jessica's head off, which we all know was warranted." He gave an exaggerated shiver. "I just wish he would've told her to keep those claws to herself while he was at it."

"Wait, you've had issues with her?" Rhyan asked, a frown tugging at her lips. "Why haven't you said anything?"

I shrugged. "She's good at her job."

"Good at her job or not, harassment is harassment." Rhyan's voice rose with every word. Grumbling under her breath, she pulled out her phone and began typing. Seconds later, my phone pinged with an incoming text. "That is the link to file a report with HR. Please be detailed about her actions, and I'll make sure it's handled from there."

The tension thrumming through my muscles eased, and I shot her a gentle smile. "Thanks, boss."

"And then," Hunter continued, making my eyes roll to the ceiling. "The consultant Rhyan brought in to guide us on this cult case turned out to be Coop's Millie."

Bright green eyes locked on me, scanning my face. "*Millie*, Millie?" I dipped my chin and ran a hand down my face. "Well, shit."

"Exactly," I grumbled, hating my loose-lipped drunk ass, who apparently told everyone in listening range about the love of my life that I was forced to leave behind. I rubbed at my stomach. "Does anyone have any snacks?"

Hunter snorted. "Now, Coop here doesn't want Millie

anywhere near this case because he wants to keep her high on the pedestal he deems safe."

I mouthed the word *wow* and flipped him the bird.

"As entertaining as all this is," Charlie drawled, "Rhyan texted saying she needed me to look into a few things." He turned his attention to her and smiled. "What can I help you with, baby?"

A bright pink flush overtook her cheeks as Rhyan stared into Charlie's eyes. "The Union of Blessed Souls," she stated after a second. "Millie said they have a marriage development or counseling class of some kind starting on Monday. What can you find out about it?"

His fingers moved before she finished talking. It only took a few seconds before he shifted the screen for her to see.

"Did they restock the Cheetos in the vending machine?" I asked, already rising from my seat. "Actually, fuck it. I don't care if they did or not. I'll stress eat anything at this point." I cringed. "Except those fucking rice cakes. Who the hell eats those, anyway?"

"Sit your ass down," Charlie said with a laugh. With a grunt, I flopped back into the chair, threading my fingers through my long hair and dislodging the hair tie. "It looks like the on-site class starts this coming Monday and goes for two weeks with daily classes. Days off on the weekend between the two weeks. Ah, here is a list of the different classes, and..." Charlie trailed off, brows pulled in tight. Worry bloomed as his features hardened. "What the fuck kind of place is this? These classes are clearly misogynistic. Fuck, there is a class on guiding your wife to submit and a separate class for the men about finding your dominance."

"It's a cult, and, per Millie, this is one way they select potential couples for their leadership and teachers." Rhyan jotted something down on the file in front of her. "What are the requirements for the class?"

Charlie turned the laptop back to face him. "For the basic-level class, you sign up and pay the stupid high class fee. Oh, how nice of them. There is a payment plan." I snorted at his clear sarcasm. "The on-site 'ultimate marriage seminar' is limited in space and only available to married couples. Looks like there are more requirements for this one, such as submitting a marriage certificate and, of course, paying the ridiculous, exorbitant fee for this level of 'commitment to your marriage', per the website." His eyes went wide. "Ten thousand dollars for a marriage counseling and development course? What the fuck? Who would actually pay for that? Use those funds on an all-inclusive resort and spend the whole time worshiping your girl's body. That's fucking relationship development."

My cock stirred behind my jeans, imagining doing that with Millie. Hours of my face between her thighs, eating her sweet pussy until she grew hoarse from screaming in pleasure. I'd need days alone with that woman to even come close to settling the need for her that built the years we were apart.

But first, I needed her to talk to me.

"We will need one a hell of a cover story," Hunter mused, running a hand through his short brown hair.

"We," I growled.

The fucker just smiled. "You're so against all this, I figured if we moved forward, I'd be the one to go in with Millie, be her fake husband so you don't have to."

"That makes sense. Cooper seems... volatile," Rhyan mused while attempting to smother a smile.

My palm slapped to the table, making everything shake.

Charlie shot a glare down the table as he hugged his laptop like one would protect a child.

"No," I hissed.

If I kept this up, letting them see how much Millie meant to me, they'd never let me take the case. I learned too many times to never show your weak point, and that was what Millie was to me. My weakness. One that dear old Dad used against me for years until...

Nope. Not diving into those dark memories in front of a bunch of profilers. No need to confirm their speculations that I was fucked in the head.

Inhaling deeply, I channeled the training my dad and that shit agency drilled into me. As I exhaled, I shoved any hint of emotion behind my normal mask. Lip curled in a smirk, I chuckled. "You know I'm the best at blending in. You tell me what role you want me to play, and it's done. Like Millie said, we have little time. No one can memorize the detailed backstory and perfect the persona they'll need to play like I can."

"That was scary as shit," Hunter whispered. "I've never seen you just shut down like that."

"Anyone ready for second lunch?" I asked, scanning the faces around the table. "What?"

"Cooper," Rhyan exhaled. "You don't have to do that with us, with me." A sad expression crossed her face. "It's okay to care about her and want to do this assignment to protect her. I won't assign it to someone else just to spite you or to keep you from reconnecting with her."

My back molars ground together. Of course, drunk Cooper also spilled about the shit my father used to pull to keep me in line. Fucking hell, next time I met drunk Coop, I would royally kick his hot ass. Yes, hot, because with the sexy fucker Charlie in the room, I needed the self-esteem boost.

"I should get finger tattoos," I mused, staring at the designs decorating Charlie's fingers, which immediately stilled.

He held up a hand to inspect the dark lines. "Nah. You can't handle the responsibility that comes with them," he said with a smirk.

"We'll need detailed backgrounds, things online that will support whatever we come up with," I offered, snapping back to the issue at hand. "You know they'll do a thorough background check on anyone they view as a possibility for their dumbass leadership spots. We'll need them to want us, woo us if you will, if you want any hope of getting close enough to uncover evidence of those suspicious deaths or getting Millie in the same room with this Karigan so she can work her voodoo magic on the girl's deep thoughts."

"You just love to hear yourself talk." Hunter laughed.

"It's a musical voice, so I've been told, so yes, I like to grace the world with my lyrical tone."

"Fucking hell," Charlie grumbled with zero heat to it. "Okay, I'll start building some profiles for Cooper and—"

"No," Rhyan said slowly, staring at the file folder. "We need Dr. Anderson's input. She'll guide us on the perfect background the group will find most advantageous for them." She flicked her wrist, stealing a glance at her watch. "Plus, I have to run this idea by a few people before I ask you to put in all that work. If I get the go-ahead from the higher-ups, we'll get with Dr. Anderson tonight to come up with solid identities for her and Cooper."

"I still don't like it," I muttered as we all stood. "So many things could go wrong."

"I know you don't, but if I get approval, this is happening

with or without you. I assume you'd rather be a part of the plan than watching from the sidelines with someone else fake married to Millie."

Fuck. That.

If anyone was going to be fake married to my girl, it was me.

This would be the toughest assignment of my life.

Coming from someone who was captured and tortured in the past... that was saying a lot.

———

HANDS IN MY POCKETS, I strolled behind Rhyan and Charlie, who walked hand in hand down the hotel hall. Ever since we parked, I tried to ignore the apprehension at seeing her again, but it only grew the closer we came to Millie's hotel room. She knew I planned to tag along with Rhyan and Charlie. I couldn't stop the heavy ball of dread, wondering how she'd react this time. Pain like a knife to the heart speared through me earlier when I watched her obvious confusion that bled into shock at me walking into the meeting, which quickly switched to pulsing anger.

I understood *why* she was angry. I deserved every ounce of her wrath, but that didn't stop me from wanting her to give me a chance. To hear me out, allowing me to explain why I left with zero warning or contact after walking out of her apartment. Maybe if she knew I walked away to protect her, that it really wasn't a choice for her safety, then that anger would turn to understanding. I wasn't asking for forgiveness, but it would be nice if, for the next two weeks, she could at least stand to be in the same room with me.

We were about to be fake married, after all. I needed her to at least not look at me with hatred in her dark eyes.

The two stopped in front of the correct room. Rhyan double-checked the number before rapping a knuckle against the solid wood. Fist to my sternum to ease the building pressure, I scanned the hall for threats, fortunately coming up empty. Thank fuck the Bureau put her up in an upscale hotel downtown, or I would've lost my shit and demanded they put her somewhere more secure.

As it was, I'd still probably ask Charlie to hack into the hotel security feed tonight so I could watch over her like I always did. Without her knowing. Fuck, that might come back to bite me in the ass, but I wouldn't apologize for wanting to keep her safe.

The door cracked open. Not ready to witness that hate directed my way again, I took the coward's way out and slid my phone free. After tapping the mindless road cross game, I followed Rhyan and Charlie into the room, not glancing up. My heart locked up the moment I was in her space, and I stifled a groan.

Damn.

Strawberries and vanilla. The same scent she wore all those years ago, and fuck if it didn't make my dick twitch. Even the hint I inhaled earlier at the office had my cock standing at attention, very ready to get reacquainted with the woman who smelled and felt like home.

The chair groaned, shifting back a few inches when I flopped down onto the stiff cushion. From the corner of my eye, I studied the details of the room and, of course, Millie. She glanced between the three of us and hesitantly sat across from me on the ugly green couch.

My muscles bunched tight, ready to fight, when Charlie sat beside Millie.

Nope. Not happening.

She was way too fucking close to that sexy beast.

With an annoyed grunt, I stood from the chair and gestured for Charlie to switch places with me, all while keeping my face tilted toward the phone screen. My poor chicken. It had already been run over a dozen times because my focus was not on helping him cross safely. I ground my teeth to keep from smacking that smirk off Charlie's face as we shuffled around the coffee table. Being the adult in the room, I flipped him the bird behind my back where Millie wouldn't catch the gesture.

Damn, the couch was even more uncomfortable than the chair. After adjusting several times, I settled back, my side sealed to the armrest to keep distance between Millie and me. Still pretending to be engrossed with my phone, I tuned into Rhyan as she spoke, explaining the events that had happened after Millie had stormed out of the conference room.

"They weren't thrilled with the idea, but desperate times call for desperate measures. As I explained on the phone, now we move on to building cover stories. I'd love your help to put together a perfect couple that has an ideal background for the group's leadership team. We want them to be drooling over the couple we create."

Damn. The chicken died.

Again.

Poor guy suffered because I wasn't brave enough to set aside the buffer and actually engage. Instead, I held my cowardly eyes on the screen where the animated animal bounced back into traffic, dying immediately with all my focus on listening and assessing the room. It was trained into me, also known as beaten, to sustain a high level of awareness around me at all times. And with Millie sitting at my side, all my protective instincts were on high alert, sharpening those honed senses.

"I can do that for sure. After you called with the good news, I reached out to my school and let them know I needed an extra week after spring break. My teaching assistant will fill in while I'm out." She adjusted on the couch and cleared her throat like simply mentioning the TA made her annoyed. I filed that information to research later. "You didn't mention which agent will play my fake husband."

Keeping my eyes on the repetitive demise of the chicken, I raised my free hand. "That would be me."

Her audible gasp might as well have been a slap to the face.

"I don't think that's such a good idea," Millie stated.

The annoyance in her tone snapped my restraint. Staring across the small space between us, I smirked. "I'm the best, trained by fuckers who think they are the best, so it's me or nothing, Velma."

Those dark eyes narrowed, and I stifled a smile. "Fine. Just don't get us killed while we're there or any ideas that this changes anything between us."

"Right back at you," I said with a salacious wink that made my stomach sour. "And don't worry, I'll be there every step of the way so you don't fuck this up for us or the girl we're attempting to rescue."

"Potentially rescue," Millie grumbled. Sleek dark hair shifted along her soft, fair skin with a slight headshake. "Rich, powerful, yet susceptible, like we need something from the group. Whatever identity you give us, it needs to be credible, too. Social media, online news articles, things like that." Her gaze flicked side to side as if searching through that brilliant brain. I couldn't look away, mesmerized by everything that was Millie. "Three of the senior leadership members and two teachers are trust fund babies, which means the money they contribute will never run out, plus they have ample time to quote 'lead their flock'." She rolled her dark eyes to the ceiling. "Manipulating assholes."

"That's good info. I can work with that. Maybe create a fake distant relative of some big business tycoon," Charlie mused, rubbing a hand along his jaw.

I watched her fingers thrum along her legs, drawing my attention to the snug leggings that hugged her hips. Fuck, how did I miss those and the off-the-shoulder sweater that gave me access to that bitable neck of hers?

Oh, yeah. Chicken game: death, distraction, avoidance.

"Go with a well-known last name like a Vanderbilt, Ford, or Morgan. You can make up a new branch of their family tree easily, and the name recognition will snag their attention immediately."

"Great idea," Charlie commented, fingers flying over the keyboard. "This is easy to create, then I'll get to work on validating the cover stories with a marriage certificate and identification, plus register you two for the marriage seminar under your new identities."

"We'll need to alter her appearance," I stated, while bending to slide my phone into the side pocket of my jeans.

Millie turned to me with a frown. "What's wrong with the way I look?"

"Nothing, you're perfect." I snapped my lips shut and cleared my throat. "But you visited this shit town already. You might think no one noticed you," which was highly unlikely, considering she was drop-dead gorgeous and drew the eye of every male that passed, "but we can't risk it." I gave her a quick, assessing scan from head to toe. "Changing your hair color would be the easiest and maybe heels to alter your height."

A dainty finger wrapped around a dark strand. "Yeah,

that makes sense, but no to the heels. Maybe just change up my overall style? I didn't wear any makeup, so that can add to the slight change. It's crazy what you can change by contouring. I'll just need to watch a few hundred videos." Pulling that twirled lock of hair forward, she stared at the ends. "What color? Blonde or—"

"Or pink," Rhyan chimed in. I arched a brow at my boss. Rhyan shrugged off my confusion. "She gets this one chance to be someone else. Why not go all out? I think pink hair is awesome. But a light pink, like cotton candy, not fluorescent 80s pink."

"You want to dye your hair pink, baby?" Charlie asked, smiling at her. "I'll take you to a salon right fucking now."

She shoved his shoulder, smile wide and dripping with adoration. Out of the corner of my eye, I caught Millie studying them with longing in her eyes.

Right back at you, sweetheart. I want what those two have, too.

But, unfortunately for me, that ship sailed when I left her behind.

To save her life and condemn my own.

10

—————

MILLIE

10 YEARS AGO

A final swipe of the strawberry-flavored ChapStick across my lips, I tossed the only piece of makeup I owned onto the counter. Tonight was the night, my first date ever. I took extra time to actually blow-dry my hair, giving it a little more volume than normal. My palm smoothed down the front of my baby blue sweater.

My dark brown eyes clashed with my reflection and narrowed. I looked okay, but there was something distinctly missing that one should have when preparing for a date.

Butterflies.

Bubbles in my stomach.

Sweaty palms.

Hell, anything that would hint at excitement for the momentous occasion.

But none of those key indicators were there. Sure, I was a bit nervous, but that was more around what the hell we would talk about and how much 'peopling' was in me. More excitement filled me when seeing Killian in class than minutes before an actual date.

That made no sense, but here I was, dressed up and

regretting ever saying yes to Chad. Maybe I should cancel and instead throw on my comfortable clothes and read all night.

A hard knock on the apartment's front door made me jump. My stomach dropped. Too late to back out now. One more quick peek in the mirror, I inhaled a fortifying breath and started for the door, grabbing my purse and keys as I passed the kitchen.

Surely I was worrying for no reason. How bad could a date be?

Three hours later, I had an answer to that question.

Tragic.

Way worse than I could've expected.

If I woke up puking in twelve hours from the under-cooked hamburger that the hole-in-the-wall restaurant claimed was the best in town, I wouldn't be shocked. Even without the horrible food, I would've considered the night a tragedy.

The metal keys to my apartment bit into my skin, where my fingers curled around the ring like a lifeline as Chad walked me to the door, still talking.

He. Never. Stopped.

And it wasn't about anything mind-shattering or even mind-tingling. Nope, all those words were about one sport, football. Apparently, he played for Stanford, and for the last three hours, I learned every detail regarding the sport and his position. So he tossed an inflated ball through the air and some guy caught it. Big deal.

And apparently, that was the wrong response.

After that, Chad passionately defended why being the school's quarterback was an enormous deal and explained his certain future in the NFL. While he went on and on, I discreetly googled beneath the table the average stats of

NFL quarterbacks. Turned out, their average height and weight made Chad seem like a kindergartener. Nothing he could do about genes, so I thought he should cut his losses.

Yet another internal thought I should have kept to myself.

Not sure why he became so offended; I was only trying to prevent his future disappointment when he wasn't selected to go pro—his terminology, not mine. It also wasn't a brilliant idea to mention he should put more focus on his studies, so his so-called backup plan was more of a plan A.

"This is me." I pointed at my door, my tone alluding to how utterly bored I was. Not that Chad noticed.

"Yeah, I picked you up here, remember?" He reached out, tucking a few loose strands of hair behind my ear. I jolted back at the contact and narrowed my eyes. "Aren't you going to invite me in?"

"Why would I?" I tilted my head, not understanding. Why would he want to see inside my apartment? It was basic, safe and clean, but basic, nonetheless.

"I had a good time tonight," Chad stated, instead of responding to my question. The tight smile spreading across his face made my stomach twist. Or maybe it was the E. coli I ingested earlier getting a head start on making this night even worse.

"Seriously?" I fisted the keys even tighter.

Chad closed in, crowding me until my back hit the apartment door. My heart rate kicked up, my pulse racing at the invasive proximity. I peeked down the walkway, hoping a neighbor would appear to save me.

"Seriously. You understand better than anyone else," he rasped, hand coming to my waist. "You're a great listener, and damn, this body." Straight white teeth bit down on his lower lip as he stared at my heaving chest.

Pulse racing, I struggled to rein in my rapid breaths. "I want you to step back, Chad. You're making me uncomfortable."

He gave a slow headshake, eyes darkening. "You should invite me inside. I bought you dinner, after all. You could thank me by offering a drink or... more."

That would be a hell no. "No, I think you need to leave."

Chad's wide smile froze. "I wondered what that asshole saw in you, and now I see it."

"See what?" I asked, before sealing my lips closed. Damn curiosity. I shouldn't play into his delusion of the night going well or that I gave a fuck about what he saw in me.

"You're the girl who says no when she really means yes."

Dread dropped in my gut like a thousand-pound weight. With no escape, I pressed both hands to his chest and shoved. Not that it did anything. Instead, it gave him the opportunity to capture both hands in one of his own.

"You need to leave," I whispered, voice weak from fear pulsing through my veins.

"That's not what you really want," he sneered, stepping closer until his body had me pinned against the door.

Vomit rose along my throat at the feel of him hard against my stomach. The disgust shredded some of the fear keeping me frozen. Chad's cheap cologne filled my lungs as I inhaled deep to scream.

But it turned out, I didn't need to.

Help was already there.

"Everything good here, Velma?" If it weren't for that nickname, I wouldn't have known it was Killian. His voice, the hard frosty tone, was nothing I'd ever heard come from his lips.

"Hey there, Coop," Chad called out, narrowed eyes locked on mine as he sneered. "What are you doing here?"

"Coming to see a friend, and I'm glad I did. Not much of a learner, are you?" Chad's rancid breath brushed across my face with his scoff. "You have five seconds to step away from my Millie, or I'll remove you myself. With more force than necessary, obviously."

Chad didn't get to respond before his pressing frame disappeared. Between blinks, Killian had removed the asshole and restrained both of Chad's wrists in a single handhold while Killian's other arm was wrapped around Chad's neck. I blinked, unable to understand the sudden turn of events.

"I explained my expectations, you fuck nugget. And the consequences you'd receive if you didn't meet them. Seems you need a more physical lesson to understand my basic expectations of how to treat any woman, but especially mine."

My Millie.

Mine.

If it wasn't for the door at my back, I would've stumbled. Killian's words repeated in my mind like a mantra as I tried to make sense of what he implied. Lost in those confusing thoughts, Killian snapping my name brought me back to reality and the current issue, also known as Chad.

"Get inside, Millie, and forget about this asswipe's version of a date." With a snarl, he whipped his focus back to Chad. "I can't believe you took her to Buck's. I don't even eat there, and I'll eat anything that resembles food." After giving the red-faced man a shake, Killian locked his aqua eyes on me, the hardness immediately dimming. "Go inside, lock the door behind you, and I'll make sure Chaddy here gets a thorough lesson on how to respect and treat women."

With a shaky nod, I turned to the door, checking over my shoulder once I slipped the key into the deadbolt, only to find Killian dragging a kicking and twisting Chad down the sidewalk toward the darkened parking lot.

"Killian," I barely whispered, but his head whipped my way, clearly having heard me. "Can you..." I cleared my throat to steady the slight tremble. "Come back after you're... done?"

Done with what, exactly, I wasn't sure I wanted to know.

He cocked his head to the side and smiled. "Sure, Velma. It might be late, though. I have a feeling teaching this idiot the basics will take a while. I mean, have you heard his answers in class? The idiot can barely spell mental health and is obviously shit with self-diagnosis."

A smile crept across my lips as I shook my head. "I don't mind. Just... I want to make sure you're okay." Because deep down, I knew Killian had zero plans to talk through his expectations with Chad. There was a darker side to my friend that I couldn't pinpoint, but it was there, simmering under the surface. And somehow, I also knew that he didn't like that side of himself, almost as if it wasn't natural, but something that was... twisted by someone else.

But I also knew something that Killian didn't.

That dark side didn't scare me. It did the opposite. Like now, I should be appalled at the thought of Killian hurting Chad on my behalf. But I wasn't. Instead, my heart swelled with gratitude, and my panties turned damp.

"Okay, Millie," Killian rasped as he fought to keep the restraining hold on Chad. "I'll come back to you."

As I stepped into the tiny apartment and closed the door behind me, I smiled despite the dramatic and terrifying turn of the night. Because for the first time since I started getting ready for the stupid waste-of-time-and-energy date, excitement hummed through my veins. Killian would come back, because I asked him to. Not for a date or a drink, but because I simply asked.

My sexy-as-hell friend would come back.

Just for me.

Or so I thought.

Sunlight poured through the sliding glass patio doors, burning through my closed lids the following morning. With a groan, I sat up from the awkward angle against the couch arm where I had apparently fallen asleep. Disappointment at waking up alone, which was normal but not what I expected, had my already queasy stomach cramping. Fist pressed into my abdomen, I shifted on the couch to take in the living room. My watery gaze landed on the closed door. Locked up tight, just the way I left it.

Swallowing past the emotions clogging my throat, I stood and stretched both arms high over my head. Discomfort pulsed from the tight muscles along my spine and stiff neck. Mouth open in a wide yawn, I stilled, hands frozen in the air, at the unusual feeling along my cheek. With a careful touch, I brushed a single fingertip along my cheekbone, a dry texture flaking off.

Hurrying to the bathroom, hip-checking the couch and barely staying upright, I flipped on the overhead light. "What the hell?" Both hip bones dug into the vanity as I leaned closer to the mirror, head angling one way, then the other while pressing along the red streak coating the small patch of skin.

Cabinet doors slammed with my frantic search before yanking a clean washcloth from beneath the sink. Wetting a small section, I swiped the soft cotton against the mark before examining the white cloth that was now tinted pink. Inspecting my face again in the mirror, searching for the abrasion that caused the blood, I couldn't uncover a single mark.

Confused on so many levels, I mindlessly shuffled to the kitchen for something that would settle the gurgling in my stomach, only to draw up short, gaze catching on a ripped piece of paper sitting on the Formica countertop. Expecting someone to jump out and attack, I hesitantly inched closer.

The earlier disappointment swelled into something I couldn't quite describe. Hand to my chest, I read the note, tears in my eyes as I swayed on my feet.

> *Velma,*
> *You were zonked out when I stopped by and*
>   *didn't want to wake you. Everything is all*
>   *good. Chad won't bother you again. See you*
>   *in class.*
> *—K*
> *P.S.—You snore.*
> *P.P.S.—I'm lying.*
> *P.P.P.S.—What were you dreaming about? It*
>   *sounded... good.*
> *P.P.P.P.S.—I expect all the details.*
> *P.P.P.P.P.S.—Sorry about the smudge. I didn't*
>   *want to wake you trying to clean it off. My*
>   *bad. I just couldn't resist.*

THE NOTE TREMBLED in my hand. Unseeing gaze staring out into the living room, I felt heat flush my cheeks as I recalled the dirty dream. Killian was right. The dream was good, more of an epic fantasy, if I was honest.

Setting the note aside, brows furrowed, I moved to the door. My fingertips brushed against the hard metal. The deadbolt was turned in the lock position, just like I left it last night before crawling onto the couch to wait for Killian.

So how in the hell did he get into my locked apartment?

And what did that mean, *he couldn't resist*?

Resist what?

11

MILLIE

TODAY

The whirring engine and gentle vibrations didn't lull me to sleep or still my nerves the way they generally did. The typed words blurred on the screen resting on my lap. Reading normally calmed me, but currently, every drop of concentration was centered on not stealing a look at the dangerously handsome man relaxing in the seat across from me.

I could feel his stare. It hadn't left me since the jet took off. It made me hot and jittery, uncomfortable but not.

Gritting my teeth, I blinked several times as a last-ditch effort to focus on the document Charlie sent with the information on our new identities instead of the crazy, magnetic pull Killian had over me. Memorizing came easy; read the information once, and boom, I filed it away, never to be forgotten. But apparently, my photographic memory failed when I was actively avoiding someone whose sheer presence demanded my attention.

"You can't ignore me forever, Millie," he said, humor lacing his haughty tone, though it felt forced. I rolled my eyes. "We are married, after all."

"I want a divorce," I grumbled while toying with the large, insanely real-looking diamond ring Rhyan handed me just before we boarded the jet.

"And that is why we're going to a marriage seminar, honey." I peeked up through dark lashes, finding him smirking, eyes still fixed on me. "At least we won't have to fake a rift between us."

I snorted. "Rift. More like the Grand Canyon."

All humor drained from his features, turning serious. Leaning back in the chair, he folded both arms over his firm chest. "You're the one who volunteered for this. Not sure why you're so pissed about it when you got what you wanted."

"I didn't think I was signing up to spend two weeks with you, asshole," I snapped back.

"Well, too fucking bad, Velma—"

"Stop calling me that," I hissed and jammed my finger in his direction. "That person, those people we were, don't exist anymore, so neither does the nickname."

"You're right about that." His aqua eyes slowly skimmed down my body. "Maybe we're both better versions of ourselves."

My snarky response sat heavy on my tongue. The quick flash of pain in his gaze that he couldn't hide made me want to reach out to him. Too soon, his perfected fake mask slid back into place, hiding any genuine emotion.

"Well, at least *I* am a better version now than back in college. It's the hair." He pointed to the messy man bun. "It's a personality changer, for real. Not sure how since it's just hair, but I feel like the massive amount somehow alters something in the psyche. Like how your much shorter hair has changed yours."

The snark in his tone told me I'd regret asking. "And how is that?"

"Seems the shorter the hair, the longer the stick up your ass." My lips popped open in shock. "Just a general observation." His broad shoulders rose and fell in an uncaring shrug. "I'm still conducting research."

"You're such a fucking asshole."

His smile turned razor sharp. "Never said I wasn't." Eyes scanning my face, he leaned forward, bracing both elbows on top of spread thighs. "Ready to back out, Dr. Anderson? Or are you excited to spend two entire weeks with me, side by side, day and night, working together and, of course, you learning how to be a good, obedient wife?"

My lip curled in a snarl. "You mean their version of a 'good, obedient wife' as in someone who's had her voice cut off, fear infused in their veins to keep from escaping, and a mental state so damaged she actually believes the shit her husband spews?"

The muscle along his jaw popped before he blew out a slow breath, as if to calm himself.

"Exactly. And believe me, wife, it won't be easy for someone like you, so I'd consider backing out of this assignment now. Let the trained agents help this girl. Not someone who plays the part from the sidelines—where you should stay, where it's safe."

I swallowed hard and adverted my eyes, not wanting him to see how much his words cut me to the core. "*Someone like me?*" I rasped, swallowing down the tears I refused to let fall. Staring out the window, I attempted to follow the tree-covered mountain range that looked so tiny below us.

A grumbled curse jerked my gaze back to Killian. Before I could ask what made him go from cocky asshole to looking dejected, one of his many masks slid into place, guarding the real Killian from letting me fully see him.

"Yes, someone like you. Too smart and reckless for her own damn good," he muttered while scrubbing a hand down his face. "If we're doing this, then we need to use the last hour of this flight to go over the fake identities. This assignment is a dangerous shit show where we'll both probably end up dead or held against our will, but who wants to focus on the dark reality when we can hope for the best? Am I right?"

There was something seriously wrong with his chipper tone mixed with those terrifying words. But I saw it for what it was, what all this was. His snarky attitude, asshole demeanor, and mean words were his last attempt to scare me. If he made me hate him more than I already did, I might back down and scurry back to my boring life. Why he wanted that and didn't want me on this assignment, wasn't clear. If it were young Killian, I would say he wanted to keep me safe, out of harm's way. But I didn't know about adult Killian. Maybe he hated me or couldn't stand the idea of being stuck with me for two weeks.

Now, why did that make me want to throat-punch him while simultaneously sobbing until I died of dehydration?

As much as I loathed the man who shattered my heart so well it never worked properly again, I couldn't help but need to be around him, too. The thought of not moving forward with this dangerous task made my stomach twist in painful knots, knowing if I didn't play Killian's wife for this assignment, then someone else would.

Maybe even that Jessica woman with her big boobs, gorgeous face, and awful personality.

"You feeling all right over there, Millie?"

I cleared my throat and shifted in the seat. "Yes, why do you ask?"

"Because you looked like you tasted something sour, or you really need to fart."

Jaw slack, I gaped at the grinning idiot. "I do not need to fart."

He tossed up both hands. "It's a normal bodily function. No need to be embarrassed."

"I wouldn't be embarrassed if I did actually need to pass gas." *Lie, I totally would be.* "But I don't. I was just thinking about…" Fuck, I needed a cover story so he didn't know I was angry at the mere thought of another woman in my place. The trees outside the window thousands of feet below us, gave me an idea. Not a good one, but an idea, nonetheless. "Pine… cones."

"Well, that settles it. We're officially going to die."

"What? Are we going down?" I shouted. The soft gray leather groaned beneath me as I twisted around to see if the wing had fallen off or if the engine had caught fire.

"The plane is fine. I'm talking about you and this assignment. You're a shit liar, Millie. You always have been. Now you're about to walk into a situation where every word you speak will be a lie. So, yeah, I'm placing my bets on us dying within five minutes of us landing in Georgia." Killian scoffed and pinched the bridge of his nose. "Pinecones. Really? Who the fuck thinks about pinecones?" No one. Not even me. He was right. I was a terrible liar. Should've thought about that before suggesting this plan to Rhyan. "Well, besides Rhyan." I turned, collapsing into the seat with a *harrumph.* "She thinks of the most random shit and tosses out all these odd facts. It's funny, and odd, but more funny. Offers a nice break from all the dark shit we study, you know."

I bit my tongue to keep from telling him I didn't know since he was the cool FBI profiler and me the boring professor. "Are you and Rhyan close?" I tried to keep my tone light, hoping he couldn't pick up on the tension.

Taking a sip from the water bottle at his feet, both dirty-blond brows pulled in tight. "Well, yeah, she's my boss. Plus, she's cool as shit, and... wait." A slow, knowing grin curved his lips. "Are you jealous?"

"What?" I said way too quickly and the tone way too high to be believable. "No, I'm not jealous."

Maybe a little, but not in the way he thinks. I'm more jealous that she'd gotten to spend time with him and knows this version of Killian.

"Me thinks you protest too much."

I scoffed. "You butchered it. The quote is 'The lady doth protest too much, methinks.'"

"Only Shakespeare could make up a word like methinks. But me butchering the quote—"

"Which you did on purpose to piss me off. You have a memory better than mine. You knew how the quote went," I sighed. Exhaustion rode me hard after a terrible night's sleep in the lonely hotel room to the constant stress of the morning. Reaching into my laptop bag, I tapped out a preventative migraine pill and swallowed it dry.

"Was that a compliment?" I just rolled my eyes and pretended to study the document. "So, you're jealous of Rhyan." I didn't dare explain why I was jealous. "After last night, seeing her and Charlie together, I thought it was clear those two were it for each other."

"It's amazing," I admitted.

"What is?"

I didn't hide the sappy smile that grew, remembering how

they were utterly obsessed with each other. "It's his devotion to her, as if he'll burn down the world to make her happy. Plus, the way she looks at him. You can sense that he's her rock, that she can trust him unconditionally to be there for her."

"I'm envious of the effortlessness in their relationship," Killian added with longing in his tone. "They just get each other. So consumed with the other person, yet somehow it's not smothering. Rhyan is a fucking badass profiler and an amazing boss." His aqua eyes met mine. "Who I respect and would lay my life down for, but am not attracted to, just so you know."

"Whatever." My stiff, nonchalant shrug exposed my lie. "It's fine."

It totally wasn't. Killian was back in my life, and even though I was pissed, hurt, and a plethora of other negative feelings, the man was mine.

Always was and always would be.

Oh, fuck.

I gaped at my reflection on the black screen. Was I devolving into a delusional sociopath? Maybe all the years and stress of searching for Killian, dreaming up fantasies of a life with him in it, splintered my psyche, making me delusional enough to actually believe Killian was mine.

I turned my horrified stare to Killian. "If I try to kidnap you or tell you about some fantasy world like it's reality, I need you to restrain me and call for help."

"Oh, Millie," he practically purred. I watched, entranced, as his thumb stroked back and forth along his lower lip. "I'll restrain you any day or time. All you have to do is ask. But call for help." He clicked his tongue. "I don't think so. You on display will only be for me."

And that was when I swallowed my tongue. Well, it felt

like it anyway. That was the only explanation because surely I didn't just choke on spit.

"Also, Charlie isn't intimidated by Rhyan's success," Killian continued, wearing a small, knowing smirk as I smacked at my chest, attempting to breathe normally. "And she's not intimidated by the fact that every man and woman who meets Charlie either wants to fuck him, be him, or skin him alive to make a very attractive skin suit." My eyes went wide. Interesting. Maybe I wasn't the only delusional one on this plane. Not sure if that made me feel better or not. "But the latter is reserved for the serial killers he's identified and put away."

"And that's what you do, too, as a profiler?"

A storm brewed behind his eyes. "Yeah. I joined the team when Rhyan created the Dallas-based BSU unit. She helped pull me out of a shitty situation when I didn't have anywhere else to go."

A surge of possessiveness spiked, heating me from the inside out. It should've been me who saved him. I dedicated my career, the last ten years of my life, to looking for him. Every day, following various leads or rumors to find where Killian's father might have hidden him. I didn't know for certain if his father was a cult leader, but the hints Killian let slip led me to believe he was, or at least deeply involved in one.

"And now I'm here." He shook his head. A few long blond pieces fell forward, framing his face. "I help put baddies away and love every minute of it." I studied his features, noting the tightness around his eyes. There was a lie somewhere in his words. "And you're a teacher."

"Professor," I corrected, fighting down the sudden swell of inadequacy. Killian was not only the sexiest man alive but an FBI profiler, a badass with a badge, and I was just me. I shouldn't be surprised. I always felt that way around Killian. I just hadn't felt it in so long I forgot how it stole my breath for a single heartbeat. "But yeah. I teach at Harvard a few classes a semester for the psychology department. It keeps me busy."

And utterly lonely. Not that I would admit it to him.

"And?" he said with a pointed look. "What else have you been up to these past ten years?"

Lips pursed, I shrugged. "Nothing, really. That's it. I teach, study, research, and document various control groups around the US for fun and sometimes help the FBI when they need me."

A throat clearing startled me, making my heart hammer in my chest, and Hunter folded into the seat beside me. "Holy shit, you two. There is so much sexual tension here. Even sitting in the back of the plane, it's distracting." He pointed between me and Killian. "I hate to interrupt whatever this is, but we all need to review the information Charlie sent. You both might have genius-level IQs, but I'm just a muggle over here, no crazy, cool powers."

I nodded sheepishly. How could I have forgotten he was on the plane, too?

"Muggle?" I questioned, head angling to the side. "Is that a new term for someone with—"

"Careful how you finish that sentence, Millie," Killian said, cutting me off. "You don't want to piss off your handler slash bodyguard for this assignment by pointing out his average intelligence." The rustle sounded beside me, followed by a crumpled piece of paper flying toward Killian's head. He caught it one-handed out of the air without looking away from me. "Muggle as in someone without magic, per the bestselling book series, *Harry Potter*."

I twisted to Hunter. "Killian, over there, learns by

listening to the information while I memorize anything I read. What type of learner are you?"

Hunter responded with a strange, almost confused expression. No matter how he learned best, we'd figure it out. He needed to know the information inside and out, down to the very minute detail, like Killian and me.

Having a bodyguard/handler assigned to my lush new identity was a caveat Killian demanded. Since some classes and seminars were broken up between genders, he didn't like the idea of me being anywhere alone.

"When is your hair appointment?" Killian randomly asked before we could start.

"Tomorrow morning." I didn't mask the cheerful smile as it spread across my face. "Cotton candy pink. It's the most daring thing I've ever done, and I can't wait."

"Next up, infiltrating a dangerous cult. Bet you didn't expect that to be on your life bingo card."

I blinked at Killian. "What bingo card?"

He and Hunter exchanged a look I couldn't read before the latter spoke up.

"No more talking unless it's about the case and our new identities. I'd really rather not get us killed because of a slipup."

With a firm nod, I tapped the screen, bringing it back to life.

"Okay, let's start with Killian's family tree and go from there. We'll have this memorized before the plane lands."

We had to.

Our lives depended on it.

12

KILLIAN

TODAY

My steps came to a halt at the initial step that led up to Millie's brownstone. Blowing out a breath through parted lips, I took the moment to study the front door. I knew every detail of it, thanks to the hidden camera I had installed across the street. It was fucking surreal to be in the exact spot where I fantasized about standing too many times to count. Of me knocking on the door, her leaping into my open arms, and me having the courage to explain. Everything.

From the moment Dad fucking kidnapped me back to DC, to my time with the CIA, almost dying, then landing in the Behavioral Science Unit division of the FBI.

And never forgetting her for a second.

What I felt for Millie was beyond the everyday love. She was my obsession, my rock, my everything. Every damn second, day and night, she was on my mind, beneath my skin, and burrowed in my heart. Ever since I sat beside her in class, she'd never left me, even when we were apart.

I didn't tell her the depth of how I felt on our last night together before my soul was ripped in two. I should've expected it, but I was too hopeful for a normal life that I never saw my father coming. The night before graduation, he found out that I planned to leave everything behind for her.

I knew he was driven; I just didn't realize the lengths he'd go to protect his prized project. A deadly combination of an assassin and con artist, perfect for immediate acceptance into the CIA. Since he himself was a retired asset who shifted to a senior position within the agency, it meant I had no voice.

Or an option to live the life I actually wanted.

No hope of a future outside of being who my father groomed me to be. And no one cared or noticed that my life was a sham—a normal, happy-go-lucky guy to those around me, but behind closed doors, a killer whose training never stopped. I spent months convincing Dad of the benefits of my attending college, on campus, for undergrad. A dirty deal with the devil, but for four years, the leash slowly suffocating me loosened.

Then Millie happened.

"Hey, Killian, are you coming inside?" Millie's concerned tone shut down the dark, spiraling thoughts that could pull me under for hours, if not days. I shook my head, internally chastising myself for dropping my guard, putting her safety at risk. After a quick glance up and down the street, I hitched my chin her way after finding the streets clear. With a bemused smirk, she pushed the heavy door open and stepped inside.

Lungs filling with a deep, calming breath, I climbed the stairs and stepped over the threshold. Millie held the door open wide enough for me to pass through without rubbing against her, but I did anyway. Just a brush of my arm against her had my cock swelling. Fuck, what would it be like to finally feel that soft skin again, to have her naked beneath me, to do as I pleased?

Inside, I stopped in the entry to take in the parts of the townhome I hadn't seen. A cozy living room was on the right. A couch and two chairs faced an unlit gas fireplace. The large street-facing bay window filled the room with natural light. A smile pulled at the corners of my lips as I took in the floor-to-ceiling built-in bookshelves lining one wall, stuffed full of books.

My boots spun on the polished mahogany hardwood floor as I took in the rest of the townhome. The formal dining room was on the opposite side of the picture-perfect living room. I arched a brow, shooting Millie a questioning expression, while my head angled toward the six dining chairs that looked out of place without a table.

She sighed while stripping out of her coat and hanging it on an antique coat rack. "My ex took the table, amongst other things," she muttered. "As observant as you are, I'm sure you'll notice the other random items missing around here."

"Like what?"

She pointed to the couch. "You can't see it from here, but he removed the cushions but left the couch. In the kitchen, he took all the handheld appliances, including the can opener, but left all the canned food."

My fingers curled into tight fists at my side. "What the fuck? Who does that, and why the hell did you marry that asshole in the first place?"

Both dark brown brows flew up over her forehead. "How did you know I was married?"

Well, fuck a cactus. She can't know about my... consistent following. That terminology sounded way classier, and less illegal, than stalking.

"You divided up assets. That screams divorce. And based on what he took, it doesn't sound amicable." I shrugged like stress-sweat wasn't slicking my spine. "Is the kitchen through there?" I pointed to the set of swinging doors that led toward the back of the townhome through the dining room. "I need something to eat. I'm starving."

Her mouth opened, then snapped closed. "Yeah, it is, but... didn't you eat on the plane?" she asked, a hint of humor in her tone. "Follow me." Instead of immediately following her, I stepped back to the front door and locked it up tight.

"Snacks," I said after catching up. "I had snacks on the plane, not an actual meal. Millie, why did you leave the front door unlocked?"

She glanced over her shoulder, brows furrowed as she reached into the pantry. "I don't know. Didn't really think about it with you here. Strange." Her lips pinched together. "When I'm here alone, I lock up the second I'm through the door." Pride swelled in my chest. She didn't think about it because she knew I'd keep her safe, no matter what.

Turning, she held out both full hands, a package of peanut butter crackers in one and some kind of Nutella to-go snack cup in the other.

Not able to decide, I grabbed both.

"Didn't expect you to go for Nutella," I remarked while studying the package.

It was like I could feel her defenses rising with my dumb comment. Damnit, and things were finally not tense between us.

"A lot of things have changed since we last saw each other."

Leaning a hip against the center island, I dropped the

food onto the dark brown granite counter, my growling stomach forgotten. "Do you ever think about it?"

"Think about what?" she rasped, hand coming up to gently grasp her throat.

I swallowed the groan that wanted to escape. Fuck, I wanted that to be my hand on her throat, my skin against hers.

"The last night we saw each other." The night I finally took the leap and gave in to the all-consuming need for her that only grew after I had her. Once wasn't enough with Millie; nothing would ever be enough. With my greedy personality, I'd always want more of her, consume everything she would willingly give, and I'd still beg for more.

Her long dark lashes fanned up and down with slow blinks, but to her credit, she didn't look away as a blush bloomed on her cheeks.

"Nope."

Lie.

What a terrible, pretty liar.

Squeezing her lids closed, she whirled around, putting her back to me. "I've moved on, just like you have." That last part was a low grumble under her breath. "You've got your snack, and I'm all set here." Her dark strands fanned out as she spun to face me. "I'll meet you and Hunter at the hotel Sunday night before our flight—"

"That's not how this is going to work. I think you've forgotten an important part of this assignment." I stepped around the island, which she matched, keeping the distance between us.

"And what's that?"

I sent a pointed glance at the massive ring on her finger and dared another step. "You're my wife."

That pretty pink tongue slid along her lower lip. Fucking

hell, she was killing me. Death by blue balls. Bet it wouldn't be the first time. I'd have to ask our team's resident medical examiner, Rain.

"I'm not your wife yet. And even then, it's fake. This isn't real."

"Well, considering our lives depend on us playing the part, I think we need to practice, in my official FBI behavioral analyst opinion."

Her back sealed to the double oven, preventing her from retreating further. "What do you— What? Practice?"

Cheeks pink, lids hooded, pupils blown wide.

Oh, my Millie's body knew exactly who it belonged to. I just had to convince the rest of her that this between us would happen.

I nodded, stopping directly in front of her much shorter frame. Our height difference meant I had to lean down to inhale her unique scent that reminded me of home. My lids fluttered closed as my chest constricted. "Fucking hell, you still smell so damn good."

"It's just shampoo," she whispered, eyes flicking between mine. "What are you doing, Killian?" Her chest rose and fell with every heaving breath.

"Me? I'm losing control, unraveling," I rasped. "Like I always do when you're around."

"Stop," she pleaded, the word more of a pushed breath. "Please stop." Her palm pressed to the center of my chest. Reluctantly, I took a single step back to give her the space she clearly wanted. "We can't. No, I can't act on this," she motioned between us, "whatever this is between us, and act like the vanishing act you pulled or the fact you've been radio silent for the last ten years didn't hurt me like it did. You left me and never came back."

I felt my lips curl into a cocky smile, focusing on the one

positive. "So you admit there is a *this* between us." Slowly raising my hand, giving her the opportunity to stop me, I sealed my palm to her cheek. Those dark lashes fluttered closed as she sucked in a shuddering breath. I closed the space between us, thumb stroking along her cheekbone reassuringly. "I'll tell you everything, Millie. Everything. Just give me a chance to explain what happened and why—"

"It's too late," she whispered, lids still squeezed shut.

"Bullshit," I barked. The loud sound popped both her eyes wide open. "It's never too late for something like this, what we have. You feel it, too. I know you do."

"Had," she sighed. "What we had."

Pieces of my long hair fell around my face with the sharp headshake. "No. It's not over. We're not done."

"It's not that easy. You can't just say—"

"Sure it is. All you have to do is give me a chance; let yourself fall, knowing I'm not going anywhere." The tip of my nose brushed against hers as I leaned down, desperate to erase the gap between us. "Let yourself trust me again."

For several seconds, she stared up at me in silence. I didn't move, hardly breathed, too afraid of shattering the moment and losing her all over again. Her lips parted, ready to give me an answer to the question burning me alive inside, but a violent, insistent pounding on the front door broke the moment.

Between heartbeats, a gun was clasped in my firm grip, and my larger frame was positioned between her and the perceived danger.

"Are you expecting anyone?" I asked calmly over my shoulder.

"Um, not that I'm aware of. Is the gun really necessary?"

I shot her an incredulous look and started toward the noise that grew more frantic.

"A gun is always necessary."

She tugged on the back of my shirt. "Do I get one, then?"

I stopped short, making her run into me from how close she followed. Millie rubbed at her tiny little button nose, scowling like I meant to hurt her.

"Do you know how to shoot?" She shook her head. "Ever even held one before?" Millie scrunched her nose and again shook her head. "Oh, then, yeah, of course, you can have a gun."

"Really?" she said, perking up.

"No," I deadpanned and turned, focusing back on eliminating whoever was on the other side of the fucking door. Not only was the noise making me twitchy, but whoever was there interrupted Millie's response.

The response I'd give my left, and maybe right, nut to hear.

The gun's rough grip bit into my palm with my firm hold. Flipping locks with more force than needed, I twisted the brass knob and yanked the solid wood door open. The barrel of my gun was aimed between the fucker's brows before he even realized he was in imminent danger. Hand still raised to keep knocking, the deep scowl on his ugly mug melted into confusion before turning white, all the blood draining from his face.

"Who the fuck are you?" I growled, not dropping my weapon until I knew if he was friend or foe. Who the hell was I kidding? It was an unknown male banging on Millie's door. He sure as fuck was the enemy.

"Jeremy?" My muscles bunched at Millie's close voice. Her cute little legs tried to step around me, but I shifted, blocking her path. "Oh, for fuck's sake, Killian." The exasperation in her voice quelled a little of the bubbling anger. "Jeremy isn't a threat. He's my teaching assistant."

I slowly lowered my weapon and gave the fucktard an unimpressed once over. "This guy? The wannabe American Eagle influencer?" I cocked my head to the side with a patronizing smile. "You sure he's old enough to work? Child labor laws are—"

"I'm fucking twenty-six," the Jeremy guy snapped, finding his backbone now that there wasn't a gun pointed between his eyes.

Unimpressed look fixed on him, I raised a palm. "Thought you'd want a high-five or something." I dropped the hand and crossed both arms over my chest, still hanging on to the gun just in case he made a move I didn't approve. Like looking at Millie, moving close to Millie, thinking about Millie, saying her name....

Huh. Maybe I'd been around psychopaths too long because the thought of murdering this asshat didn't bother me as much as it should.

"What are you doing here, Jeremy?" Millie sighed. The strain of her voice snagged my attention away from the numb-nut. Her brows were pulled in as she circled two fingertips against both temples.

"What's wrong?"

"It's a migraine, obviously. She gets them when she's stressed. How did you not know that about her?"

I shot a deathly glare at the Jeremy fucker, which wiped the smirk off his face before turning back to Millie. "Is there something I can get you? Want me to kill him since he's the one causing you to be so stressed?" Obviously, it wasn't me. He was the problem here. A muttered *what the fuck* sounded from the idiot at my back. "Would that make you feel better, baby?"

"Baby?" he exclaimed. "Millie, who is this crazy-ass man? I should call the police—"

Hand fisting the popped collar of his preppy-ass polo, I hauled him into the townhouse, slammed the door closed, and shoved his back against it. The rattle of the door hinges brought a smile to my face. His shock-filled, wide eyes pleaded with Millie, which just pissed me off more.

"Don't fucking look at her." Tightening my grip, I lifted him off the floor; the toes of his loafers scraped against the hardwood, trying to find traction. "And why the hell would you throw out that kind of threat? Haven't you learned when dealing with an unstable person, you try to keep them calm, not instigate them further?"

"You're not unstable," Millie stated, tone tight. "Well, I take that back. You might be based on the current situation. Can you please drop him?"

"You are not calling the cops," I snarled. "Everything was just fucking fine until you showed up. I was just protecting my wife and her home from the threat I assumed was beating on her door. For all I knew, before opening the door, you were the unstable one forcefully attempting to enter her house."

The idiot slow blinked. With an exasperated sigh, I glanced over my shoulder at Millie, who attempted to hide a grin behind her tiny hand. Fuck, that big rock looked good on her ring finger.

"He's not that bright, is he? It's like he can't even keep up with this conversation we're having."

"Pretty sure no one can keep up with this conversation but you," she huffed.

I narrowed my eyes. "You did."

She shrugged and nodded, confirming my assumption. "He was the best option for the teaching assistant role out of the few decent applicants."

"See," the idiot said, making me roll my eyes and turn back to him.

"That's not the compliment you think it is, sweet, sweet child." With a smirk, I released my hold without warning. He stumbled to the side, attempting to find his footing, while I stepped to Millie's side and draped an arm over her slim shoulders, having to bend at the knees a little to reach her fairy-like stature. A genuine smile bunched my cheeks as I gazed down at her. "So, that later-in-life growth spurt you wished for didn't happen, I see."

"Don't be an asshole," Millie huffed, crossing both arms across her chest. Which only drew attention to her fantastic tits in her fitted sweater. "You were the one who suggested I make that ridiculous wish list."

"How else was I supposed to uncover the deep, dark wishes you had buried in that mind of yours?"

"Wait, did he say *wife*?"

I rolled my eyes. "See, not bright at all. There had to be better applicants than him, Millie."

"Millie, what the actual fuck—"

"It's *Dr. Anderson*," she practically hissed, shoulders tensing beneath my arm.

"But Millie—"

"*Dr. Anderson*," Millie and I snapped in unison.

I fluttered my lashes down at my beautiful pretend wife. "Aww, look, we're already finishing each other's sentences."

Millie ignored me and blew out a loud, slow breath. "Listen, Jeremy, I appreciate you coming to check on me. The sudden request off was very unlike me. However, as you can see, everything is fine. I just need you to cover my classes for the week after spring break."

"Extended honeymoon," I added, twirling a lock of hair around my middle finger. "The first week is for all fun, the second for recovery. Hopefully, by the time she returns, she'll be able to walk straight and—"

Millie's tight fist connected with my stomach, exploding the air from my lungs with the unexpected blow.

"It's none of his business why I need that week off," she snapped. "And will you please stop pretending this marriage thing is real?" Her words more of a whispered hiss so the jackass couldn't hear.

I shifted, putting myself between her and the asshat. A gentle tug had her body sealed to mine. A smile curved my lips, feeling her full-body shiver. Leaning down, I brushed my lips against her ear.

"From the moment you accepted the case until we're on the plane back to Dallas with Karigan in the seat beside us, I am your husband. For better or for worse and all that, baby-cakes, you're mine." Her chest rose and fell in quick succession, her wide eyes gazing up in wonder. "You like that idea, don't you?" I whispered. "Of me at your side, ready and willing for you to use anytime you want me."

"But I hate you," she murmured, fingers gripping at the center of my T-shirt. The feel of her nails scraping against my stomach through the soft cotton made my cock swell even thicker. The reaction was odd yet welcomed, considering I usually have to fight the urge to kill the person touching me, not my body pulsing with the need for more.

"If you hate me, then we're playing the average married couple," I joked, even though hearing her say those words was like a knife penetrating my bruised and tender heart. "And don't knock hate fucking until you've tried it, babycakes."

Her breath hitched. Leaning back, I locked my heated gaze with hers. Her tongue darted out and licked along her lower lip before she bit down, teeth sinking into the plump flesh. Heat filled my veins, and my dick strained against my jean's zipper.

Fucking hell, I needed her. Wanted to see and feel every inch of her beautiful body. The past twenty-four hours of having her close yet unable to act on the desires pulsing through me was hell. A hate fuck wasn't what I wanted, but I'd pounce on any opportunity to worship Millie.

Without breaking her lust-filled stare, I shouted over my shoulder. "Meet and greet is over. Get the fuck out of here. As you can see, Dr. Anderson is fine, and you'll do what she asked and only that." Turning, I found him glaring with both hands curled into fists at his side. "Get over the delusional fantasy that there is anything between you and my wife. She's fucking mine."

"Fuck you. She's not yours."

"Oh, shit," Millie muttered as I whirled to the soon-to-be-dead man.

In two short strides, I was back in front of him, his polo bunched beneath my fist as I hauled him off the door while the other palm wrapped around the doorknob and pulled.

"I'm playing nice because I don't want her to witness just how dark my unique abilities run, but know this. If I hear that you've approached her for anything non-school related or hassled her about turning your professional relationship into more, I will make you disappear, and it won't be fun. For you, that is. For me, well, let's just say a twisted part of me would find joy in your painful expiration."

Without warning, I shoved him onto the front stoop and released my hold. Unable to find his footing, he stumbled down a single step, collapsed, and rolled down, ending in a motionless blob on the sidewalk. Dramatically dusting off my hands, I waited a moment, ensuring he wasn't dead before slamming the door closed and turning my full focus on Millie.

"Now," I hummed, the anger and tension from dealing with the fool melting into boiling passionate desire. "Where were we, wife?"

I needed her more than the next breath in my lungs.

Wanted to feel her bare skin against mine, reminding me of that amazing night we had together.

Maybe then I'd remember what it was like to actually feel.

Something that hadn't happened in ten long fucking years.

13

KILLIAN

10 YEARS AGO

My lids popped open from a light sleep. Darkness surrounded me, the blackout curtains doing their job to keep the light out of her small bedroom. The press of Millie's soft skin against my side, the slow rise and fall of her chest tempered the bolt of alert awareness that snapped me awake. The sheets rustled, tangling around me as I shifted to seal her even tighter against me, hoping that would calm the unease pumping through my veins, warning me of an unseen threat.

"You played a dangerous game, son."

Without thinking, only reacting to his voice, I sprang from the bed. The silky material of the expensive suits he wore like armor bunched beneath my tightening grip, fighting for a hold to take him to the floor. But like with everything else in my father's orbit, he was one step ahead. Clearly able to see better than me, he shifted, dislodging my hold and turning me to wrap a thick arm around my neck. Despite knowing it was useless, I fought against his controlling grip with everything I had, not giving two shits that I was naked. My dick slapped between my thighs with every frantic kick.

An audible, annoyed sigh brushed past my ear, and the arm around my throat tightened, cutting off my air supply. Not wanting to pass out, leaving Millie unprotected against my asshole father, I forced myself to relax, allowing shallow slivers of air through to keep me conscious. A blinding light cutting through the dark room from the cheap ceiling fan had me squeezing my lids shut against the sudden assault.

When my sight adjusted, my frantic gaze zeroed in on the bed where Millie lay sprawled along the sheets, still out cold. Icy fear froze me from the inside out. The light was on, plus the noise of the earlier struggle, so why was she still out cold?

"What the fuck did you do to her?" I cracked, barely able to get the words out with the pressure on my trachea.

"Just a small sedative," my father huffed, his words brushing past my ear. "We left her unharmed outside of that, though that can change based on you." At a barked command, a man dressed in head-to-toe black with a balaclava concealing his features stepped into the room, gun in hand, and aimed the barrel at Millie's head. "Still want to fight me, son?"

"No," I hissed, willing to do or say anything for freedom from his hold to angle myself between my Millie and the potentially fatal bullet. The second his arm loosened, I flashed to the bed and pulled the draped blankets up to her chin to cover every bare inch of her flawless skin that was on display. Stepping around the bed, I stood between Millie and the asshole still aiming the gun at her, crossing both arms over my chest.

"We're fine. My son now fully grasps the consequences of his actions on others. Isn't that right?" My nod was clipped, and I didn't let my gaze drop from the bastard's soulless eyes who dared to put my girl in danger. "Go finish cleaning, leave nothing behind, including his prints and DNA. Be ready to move out in five."

My back molars ground together as the armed asshole turned and disappeared into Millie's apartment. I knew exactly what else needed to be 'cleaned'. "You had her place bugged," I seethed.

"I knew there was something off the last time you came home, so yes, I needed to find and eliminate the distraction."

I turned to face him, murder in my gaze. "You will not eliminate her."

"That's up to you now, isn't it? Did you really think you two could disappear from me?"

I wanted to punch the cocky-ass smile off his face. Fucker had listened to our plans, had heard me tell Millie I wanted to be with her, escaping the life he orchestrated for me. My gaze shifted to the bed, heart clenching as I traced the curves of her body hidden beneath the blanket. It was foolish to think someone like me could have a normal life. I should have prepared for this, known my father wouldn't go away without a fight.

Now she was in imminent danger, all because I loved her too much to consider letting her go.

I beyond loved Millie. A love that filled my heart so much it felt like it would burst in my chest when I even thought about her. And last night, finally feeling her in my arms the way I wet-dreamed almost every night since I met her, was more than I could've imagined.

This was the ultimate test of my love for her.

True love was about sacrifices, and I was ready to make a big one for her. She'd hate me, no doubt, wondering where I went, because I knew without a doubt this would be the last time I ever saw her. Life as an asset for the CIA didn't allow for personal relationships, per my father, at least. He had nothing in his life besides grooming me to follow in his footsteps after Mom died.

If I loved Millie like I knew deep in the recesses of my soul I did, I had to make the tough choice.

To sacrifice myself, my freedom and life, for her.

"If I go with you—"

"*When* you come with me," he snapped and pulled a gun from behind his back, pointing the silencer right at Millie's head. "Remember who is in charge here, boy."

I swallowed down the rage and nodded.

"When I come with you, leaving her and all this behind, I want you to forget about her. No surveillance, no bugs, nothing. I will walk away, make a clean break, if you will, too."

He studied me, the way he trained me to study body language and tone. With a nod, he tucked the gun away and smiled.

"Agreed. Now, let's get you where you belong. You have an interview with the director in three days, and we have lots to review before then."

"Understood, sir. Give me a minute to say goodbye." It wasn't a request, and thankfully, and a bit surprisingly, he gave me the courtesy of leaving the room. He knew I wouldn't try to escape, not when it would put Millie in danger.

The mattress dipped beneath me when I sat on the edge of the bed beside her. With reverent movements, I brushed the loose locks of dark hair from her face and leaned in, sealing my lips to hers.

"I know you'll be hurt and confused when you wake up,

and I'm sorry. Fuck, I'm so sorry, Millie. I never should've pulled you into my life, put you in danger like I did. But I was selfish, couldn't stay away from you even when I knew we would end. Please know I love you so much, and no one will ever come close to owning my heart and soul like you did. Be happy. Be..." My voice cracked. "Be loved by someone who isn't fucked up and can give you everything you deserve." My next words were selfish, but I couldn't stop. "But don't forget me," I whispered. "I need to know at least one person knows I'm gone."

With a hard, bruising kiss, I forced myself off the bed. As I picked up my discarded clothes from the floor, I worked to shut down every emotion, sealing off everything I felt for Millie and the dreams of a future with her.

With one last look at the love of my life, I turned and walked out of the bedroom. The man she knew as Killian withering away with the growing distance until there was nothing left without her.

14

MILLIE

TODAY

Jaw slack, mouth gaping, I blinked at Killian, struggling to make sense of the events that had just occurred. Did Killian actually throw my exasperating TA out the front door?

And why did it make me want to giggle?

"Now." He flicked the lock back into place and turned. "Where were we, wife?"

My eyes widened, no doubt the size of dinner plates, as he prowled my way, his long legs eating up the space between us faster than I could process his words. Herding me backward, I jolted when my ass connected with the far wall. His muscular forearms sealed to the wall on either side of my head, boxing me in.

I should scream, shove him back, or at the very least feel a trickle of fear. Killian was a giant compared to me in height and clearly strong as hell if he could toss Jeremy around like a rag doll, one-handed.

My pulse raced, yes, but there was no rush of panic to trigger my fight-or-flight response.

Instead, heat slithered through my veins, collecting

between my thighs while my stomach fluttered and my breaths turned shallow. His dominating me, crowding me with no escape, turned me on to the point I could feel the evidence collecting in my already damp panties.

My natural responses were clearly broken for this man.

"No," I rasped. I'd hate myself if I acted on the desire thrumming through me. Too much hurt and anger still brewed inside me to give in to what my body clearly wanted.

Him.

His brows pulled in tight, a deep line forming between them as he studied my face. "No, to what?" I licked my lips, unsure how to answer, but thankfully he said the words for me. "No, to a quick hate fuck?" I nodded slowly, not wanting to make any sudden movements. The intensity radiating off Killian made me think of him like a hungry predator, and me the prey. "Why is that, Mrs. Cooper?"

I squeezed my lids shut, hating how much I loved the sound of that and not wanting him to see the yearning in my eyes. Peeling both eyes open, I gave my head a quick shake, hoping that would rattle some sense loose, and dipped beneath his arms. Moving to the living room, I paused in front of the unlit fireplace. The framed picture sitting on the mantle of me, smiling at the camera, eyes light with laughter and love, taunted me. The man who stood behind the camera then was the same one standing behind me now.

"No, because I don't hate you, Killian," I stated, voice quivering with the swell of emotions.

Swallowing down the bubbling nerves clogging my throat, I turned to face Killian. It was time to clear the air. I needed answers before we walked into this dangerous assignment and before I gave in to the insistent pull toward him. Hands braced along the back of the couch, his aqua eyes were locked on me, face blank, keeping me from reading how he felt about that declaration.

"Well," I corrected, lips curved in a sad smile. "At least I didn't until I walked into the FBI building yesterday and saw you happy and successful, living a perfect life as a profiler like on *Mind Hunters*—"

He huffed. "You watch Netflix now?"

"Yes," I said, rolling my eyes. He arched a brow and looked around the room as if pointing out the absence of a TV. "Okay, fine, just one episode on my laptop because it looked interesting." He started to say something, but I held up a hand. "Stop distracting me while I'm trying to explain. I need to get this out so you know why." My fingers danced along my loose, black joggers as I actively avoided his intense stare. "Why it hurt so much." My voice cracked. "Fucking hell, Killian." I tossed both hands in the air. "I need you to understand why you leaving me naked in my bed, alone, ten years ago broke me."

"Millie." My name was a whispered plea as he stood up straight and ran a hand through his long hair.

"No," I said, swiping my hand through the air to cut him off. "You have to understand, if we're doing this assignment together, you need to understand me, what I've struggled with for years because it all revolves around you." I paused, allowing that declaration to settle in the heavy silence. "I don't hate you, Killian. I was hurt and scared, yes, but more than anything, I was worried about my friend. And have been since that morning I woke up without you. I've looked for you every damn day since. I never gave up, too afraid that you were out there somewhere, needing... well, me."

"What?" His face fell; the emotionless mask cracked, exposing the man I knew and loved beneath.

So this was it, the time I dreaded and hoped for in the

same breath for years. When I laid out everything. This was healthy for both of us. And hopefully, once we cleared the air, and he realized just how much his leaving broke me, but not nearly as much as finding him alive and well did, he'd stop pushing for more. Stop stoking the long dead and cold feeling inside me that only he could spark back to life. My legs trembled, barely holding up my weight as I moved to the only chair in the room that still had a cushion and fell into it.

"Based on the slivers of information you let slip about your dad, I thought he was in a cult or something similar and that he was forcing you to follow in his footsteps."

"You weren't far off," he grumbled before those aqua eyes snapped to me. "That's why you…" His voice took on an awe-like tone. "You were looking for me." His voice broke at the end, exposing the emotions bombarding him.

"Yes, I was looking for you. The only real friend I ever had."

He cleared his throat and looked toward the bay window. "You never forgot about me."

"Forgot about you?" I shook my head in disbelief. "There hasn't been a day that I haven't thought about you, Killian. Wondering where you were, if you were safe and alive." I angrily wiped at the rogue tear that escaped, and I huffed a humorless laugh. "Just ask my ex. Apparently, no one, including the man I willingly married, could live up to your memory. That's why he left me." My gaze dropped to the floor. "He said he couldn't take being compared to someone who didn't exist. But you still did to me, in my memories, plus in the hope of finding you."

I peeked up through damp lashes at the sound of his boots against the hardwood floor. I tracked his cautious movements as he rounded the couch, inching closer and closer until he paused directly in front of where I sat. With more grace than someone his size should have, he knelt to the floor. Gripping my thrumming fingers, he held them tight in his own. The small, encouraging squeeze gave me the courage to keep going.

"So no, Killian, I can't hate fuck you because deep down it's not hate that I feel. I'm hurt, embarrassed, and feel like a damn fool, but hate…" I shook my head. "I never considered that you just left, not caring about the devastation you left behind. Then you stepped into that office yesterday, not trapped in a cult or in danger. It was like a punch to the heart. In front of other agents, I was slapped with the realization that you left me willingly and never even tried to reach out, despite having the resources to find me." I shook my head, sending my dark hair slipping forward to form a dark curtain around my face. With both hands, Killian threaded his fingers through the silky soft strands, holding my head while he stared into my eyes with so much emotion swirling in his own my breath caught. "I spent the last ten years of my life searching for a man who didn't want me to find him."

His aqua eyes bore into mine as if attempting to detect the truth in my words. Sucking in a deep breath, Killian leaned closer until his forehead pressed against mine.

"I didn't want to leave you. Please believe me. I did what I had to do to keep you safe despite what it would cost me. I needed you far away from me, from my father's reach. He was hell-bent on me following in his footsteps, of being even better than him. He threatened to hurt you so that I would comply with his demands. I can't go into detail because it's still dangerous for me if anyone outside of the agency uncovers my past. I've made a lot of enemies over the years who would love to get their hands on me and anyone who they deem my weakness." Pulling back, he searched my face. "Tell me this. Maybe it will help you believe me. That morning, when you woke up, and I wasn't there, do you remember feeling groggy or out of sorts?"

My lips pressed in a tight line, brows furrowed as I thought back to that morning, pushing past the intense heartbreak that immediately set in at finding his side of the bed cold. I gave a slow nod. "Yes, now that you mention it. It took me an entire day to think clearly again, but I just associated it with the emotional whiplash. In twenty-four hours, I went from elated to devastated, in love with a future to ditched and alone."

"Fuck," Killian cursed. "I'm so sorry, Millie. I knew leaving with my father would save your life, but that you'd be confused and hate me. But I still did it, knowing that the light in my life that was you would hate me. I walked away that morning to save you. And circling back to what you think about me, happy and successful, you saw what I want everyone else to see. Because I sure as fuck haven't been happy since the day I left."

I focused on that revelation, not sure if it made me more upset or pleased that he was unhappy during our years apart.

"I'm so confused, Killian." I sat back in the chair and buried my face in both palms. "You say you haven't been happy, and you're clearly free from whatever your father forced you into, considering you're in the FBI now, so why didn't you reach out to me? All you had to do was google my name and know exactly how to find me."

Was it time to tell him I never changed my last name after I got married because I couldn't let go of the hope that one day he'd find me again? Though I never said that out loud; no, I blamed it on the fact that my diplomas and certifications were listed with my maiden name.

"Why didn't I reach out to you, the woman I left without explanation?" His huffed laugh held zero humor. "Because I'm a damn coward, Millie," he rasped. "I knew that you'd hate me or, worse, had forgotten about me. If I reached out and you turned me away or I found you happy, really happy with a life that didn't include me, I wouldn't have survived that level of devastation. And I thought, considering the shit I went through and still deal with, that you were better off without me. I'm a fucking mess and always will be because of what I've done and have gone through." He looked up, unshed tears filling both lower lids. "I'm not that guy anymore, the man you trusted and wanted. I didn't want you to see this version of me, so... broken."

My fingers trembled as I reached out and cupped his scruff-lined jaw. His lids fluttered closed, and he leaned into my hand.

"Are you better now?" I probed.

"Some days, no, but most days, yes. Though memories of those hard, dark days haven't been an issue since yesterday when I saw you."

"Yesterday, when both of our lives turned into this... complicated mess." I snorted.

"I'd take this every fucking day over the all-consuming nothingness I've lived in since I left you sleeping in that bed." Killian inched closer, his lips hovering over mine. "Please let me kiss you, Millie. Remind me what it's like to feel."

My fingers slid into his hair. Using the light hold, I tugged, erasing that small distance and sealing our lips together.

I wasn't a saint, had kissed and slept with others in the

years we were apart, but the moment his lips touched mine, I knew none of them meant anything compared to this. Every nerve ending flickered alive like sparklers dancing beneath my skin while my stomach tightened and loosened with the swell of desire flooding my veins.

Calloused palms cupped my cheek and tilted my head just enough to take control, deepening the kiss. A soft sigh had my lips parting, giving him access to sweep his tongue inside, amping up the pulsing need for him.

I sucked in a deep breath when he pulled back, though he didn't go far, instead brushing his lips along my jaw, tracking down the column of my neck.

"I missed you so fucking much. Every part of you. I dreamed of this, fantasized about what it would be like if I ever grew the balls to approach you, to see if you'd missed me as much as I had you."

Before I could respond, his lips sealed to mine again, this time with a desperation I felt deep in my core. My arms snaked around his neck, fingers diving into his hair to hold tight in case he tried to back away again. Though I didn't need to worry. His hands dropped from around my face to slide beneath my ass, fingers digging into the plump flesh as he stood. My legs wrapped around his waist, sealing my core to his hard stomach.

"Tell me you want this," he mumbled against my lips. "Tell me you want me as much as I need you right now." I nodded, but apparently that wasn't enough. A stinging slap connected with my ass, making me gasp and pull back. His hooded gaze watched me with blatant heat. "Words, baby-cakes. I need words before I lose myself in this tiny little body of yours."

"You spanked me," I said instead of responding because apparently, a spanking short-circuited my brain.

In the best way possible.

"I did, and I'll do it again to get an answer."

My heart thundered against my chest as I sealed my lips shut. A spark of humor passed over his features before another hard slap hit in the same place as the previous. My head fell back as a moan vibrated up my throat. I shifted against Killian, desperate for any kind of friction to ease the uncomfortable pulse between my thighs.

"You like that, don't you, naughty girl?" A breath caught in my throat. "Oh, Millie, just let me in, baby, and I'll show you how being my good, naughty girl can be so fucking amazing." I tipped my head forward, lips parted to accommodate each shallow breath, and met his heated gaze. "Tell me, Millie. Do you want this, want me? If you say yes, I'll make you forget the hurt from my absence and remind you it's always been me who owned this delicious body."

Once again, my brain stopped working as I fought to catch my breath. This was everything I wanted and wished I had in my boring-as-hell sex life. I needed someone to take control, to help me turn off my brain to forget about everything but my partner. I hesitated to ask what I wanted now, considering my ex scoffed at me and rolled over, disgusted the last time I dared to speak up.

Killian's dirty-blond brows pulled in tight, and a thumb pressed between my own brows, smoothing the line that formed there.

"If you have to think that hard, then it's a no, and that's okay, Millie. I'm a patient man when it comes to you and will wait until my last breath for the chance to touch you, to feel you from the inside, all hot and tight around my throbbing cock—"

"Fuck," I moaned and shifted against him, hoping the seam of my joggers would help relieve the insistent throb.

"Yes, I want this." Fingers wrapped around the back of his neck, I gave it a tight squeeze. "I need you, Kill."

He considered me for a second, his delay driving my frustration higher. Without warning, I slammed my lips to his and bit at his lower lip.

"Please don't make me beg," I whispered, allowing some of the vulnerability to seep through my tone.

"Bedroom," he demanded with a growl as he palmed both ass cheeks, no doubt leaving fingerprint bruises.

"Second floor, last door at the end of the hall," I rasped against his lips, while trying to maintain the hot-as-hell kiss.

With each step, the pounding of his feet against the stairs sent a jolt straight to my core. A low moan escaped as I hung on to Killian, face sealed against his neck. This was happening. Not only was I more turned on than I had been in a decade, but I was in his arms.

My Killian.

Even though my heart was still tender, I knew deep in my soul I could trust him, not only with my safety but my body, too. For years, I chased the same blissful high he wrung from me that night we were together. And hopefully, here in my little townhome, in my bed during the middle of the afternoon, I'd finally reach that ecstasy again.

15

KILLIAN

TODAY

Her soft curves molded beneath my tightening grip as I marched down the short hall, my boots stomping on the polished hardwood with every quick step. If I wasn't careful, just the feel of her in my arms, her soft breaths against my neck, and the lingering sting left from her little nip to my lip would have me exploding in my jeans like a teenager at his first introduction to a porno magazine.

Not that I knew from experience.

I prided myself on steely control, but with Millie in my arms, it seemed all that carefully crafted self-control fucking evaporated.

Inside her bedroom, I did a quick sweep, noting the windows and the two doors, which I assumed led to a closet and bathroom while assessing every escape route and various objects around the room that could be used as a weapon if needed. Sure, I had my gun, but the CIA trained you to be prepared for anything, and that included if your gun failed or bullets ran out before your enemies' did.

With a sharp shake of my head, I gently laid my Millie

on the light gray comforter. The fluffy material molded around her tiny frame while her legs dangled off the edge of the king-size bed. Instead of ripping off her clothes, tying her hands, and covering her eyes like I would any other woman—and had with everyone since Millie—I relaxed both hands at my side to memorize everything about the significant moment.

Dark hair splayed around her head, hooded lids almost covering blown pupils that made her dark eyes look almost black, combined with the flush that covered her slender neck to her cheeks, had my cock straining against the zipper of my loose jeans. My teeth sank into my lower lip as I bit hard to keep a desperate groan from escaping while I adjusted myself.

"Fucking hell, Millie," I rasped. "I could come just looking at you, all flushed and desperate for me. I won't be able to hold back once I get these damn clothes off you. If you want me to stop, please have fucking mercy on me and tell me now, or—"

"If you don't do something right the fuck now, Killian, I swear I really will hate you."

A slow smile tugged at the corners of my lips as I nodded and reached for the hem of her sweater. Millie arched her back and wiggled, helping me pull it over her head, and collapsed back against the bed the second it was free. I licked my lips, staring at her full tits that spilled out of lace cups. Unable to keep my hands to myself, I palmed one and gently kneaded the full globe while brushing a thumb over the hard nipple poking through the delicate lace.

"How attached are you to this torture contraption?" I asked, unable to look away from how her flush spread down to her chest and continued lower.

"What?"

Taking that as an answer, I slid my knife free, the one I didn't go anywhere without, and flipped it around in my hand, loving the way Millie's eyes went wide. I flinched, but there wasn't fear in her gaze, more curiosity and a flicker of heat. Careful to not nick her soft, porcelain skin, I slipped the knife beneath the restraining strap between her breasts and slid the sharp edge against the material. It fell apart with little effort, the lace cups dropping to her side.

"I want to fuck your perfect tits one day soon," I muttered under my breath. The slight hitch of her breath jerked my attention to her parted lips. Hmm, seemed she liked that idea as much as me. What other kinky-ass shit was my Millie into these days?

Stepping back, I returned the knife to its sheath and set it on the floor beside my foot, along with the gun and holster. It was too much to leave it somewhere not within reach. The fact I could set both aside was a fucking testament to how comfortable and safe I felt with Millie. If it wasn't because I was more concerned about her safety than myself, I'd probably be able to move both weapons farther away.

But if something were to happen, as unlikely as that was, I needed to be ready. I failed her once already when Dad got the drop on me. She was drugged, for fuck's sake, while I lay there beside her—

"Killian?" I snapped my gaze to hers. Her dainty hand reached up, brushing along my jaw. I trembled at the faint touch, utterly mesmerized by the lack of shame it conjured. "You okay?" Her fingertips stroked along my skin. My lids fluttered closed as a guttural groan vibrated in my chest. "We don't have to—"

"It's not that." I turned all my focus to the feel of her soft touch. "I'm fucked in the head, Millie, more than I ever was when we were together. I've done things, had things done —" My voice cracked as those dark memories threatened to take hold. "This is the first time I've let someone touch me intimately—hell, almost at all—in ten years."

Before she could respond, not wanting to ruin this moment I had fantasized about, I dropped to my knees between her legs and leaned forward. Eyes locked on hers, I flicked the tip of one pebbled nipple with my tongue before sucking it between my lips. Her back arched off the bed, and her fingers dove into my disheveled hair that draped over my shoulders and danced across her skin.

"No therapy session now, babycakes. Now is my time to reacquaint myself with this perfect body, learn every spot that makes you squirm and beg for more." I shifted to her other side, nipping at the tip while twisting and pulling the other nipple between two fingers. Millie's hips shifted against me, and her legs wrapped around my back, holding me even tighter against her. "Are you desperate yet, baby?"

"Yes," she pleaded as her head rolled from side to side along the bed. "Fuck, Killian."

Watching for the smallest of reactions, I pinched both slick tips hard. Lips parted, Millie twisted, but not to get away from the slight pain, but writhed along the bed in desperate need.

With the waistband of her joggers in my tight grip, I pulled them down her thighs, making sure my scarred knuckles brushed against her soft skin, ramping up both of our anticipation for what was to come. I tossed the pants to the side and stared at the tiny square of lace covering her cunt.

I pressed my nose against the soft material and inhaled deeply, filling my lungs with the overwhelming scent of her arousal. Her legs trembled on either side of my head with every soft kiss I placed along her covered slit, tongue lapping at the drenched fabric, not yet diving into her like I wanted but loving the slow build. Instead of ripping the thin straps on either side, I blindly reached for my knife and used it to cut away the fabric that kept me from my fantasy brought to life.

Fuck, how many times had I dreamed of this, woken up with my leaking cock in hand, and was forced to get myself off or risk not walking normally from the resulting blue balls.

Sitting back on my heels, I made quick work of the top button of my jeans and ripped the zipper down. A guttural groan rattled in my chest as my fingers tightened around my throbbing cock and pumped up to the head, squeezing even tighter.

"I will not come outside your cunt," I growled, more to myself than Millie. Unable to stop, I nipped at the inside of her thigh before biting even harder on the other. Her legs squeezed tight, nearly suffocating me with the constricting hold. One-handed, because the other was busy keeping me from embarrassing myself and shooting my load all over her fucking carpet, which I would then have to burn because no DNA left behind—it was an odd CIA motto that maybe I created and had caught on amongst my peers—I spread her thighs apart.

The first real taste of her on my tongue had my balls pulling up tight. The familiar zing of an oncoming orgasm raced up my spine. With a vicious growl against her slick core, I dropped my dick and stood.

"I'm so fucking sorry, Millie." Her eyes widened as I pulled out my wallet and tossed it to the side after retrieving a condom. "I swear I'll eat that perfect pussy until you pass out from too many orgasms by my tongue, but I need to be inside you. Now." The trash fluttered to the floor as I rolled on the condom.

"Killian," she whispered as I leaned over her. "Why are you still dressed?"

"Baby steps, Millie. Baby steps." I knew she didn't understand those words, but now was not the time to discuss the next level of fucked up I'd become.

"Killian?"

"Yeah, baby," I hissed through clenched teeth.

"Don't be gentle." The frown that pulled at my lips must have told her I wasn't sure she could handle my not gentle. "I'm not as fragile as you think. Please, Kill."

Oh, I liked that. Loved hearing the sweet, yet deadly nickname on her lips.

A predatory smile grew as I lined up with her entrance. Reaching between us, I pinched her swollen clit at the same time I thrust inside her until our hips sealed together. Lips to hers, I swallowed her cry as I shifted, making sure every inch of me was inside her. The demanding kiss turned frantic. Blunt nails scraped along my back, driving me fucking crazy in the best way possible.

Pulling my hips back, I snapped them forward, adjusting the angle with every thrust until she clamped around me, signaling I'd hit her perfect spot.

"I dreamed of this," I panted against her lips as I pulled back to kiss along her neck. "Though I never expected to hold you again, to feel you... fucking everywhere."

Keeping up with the quick pace, I bent lower to seal my lips around her peaked tip and sucked hard. Her cries of pleasure echoed around the room. Knowing I couldn't hold back much longer, I snaked a hand between us. Thumb to her swollen nub, I pressed hard while drawing tight circles.

A curse flew from my lips when she clamped down

around me, her tight pussy keeping me locked in place as her orgasm raced through her writhing body. Not wanting to miss a second, I watched her in fascination as she fell apart around me. Too past the point of holding off my own orgasm, I pushed even deeper inside her and came with a string of curses.

The arm holding my weight trembled and gave out. The bed molded beneath my elbow, thankfully catching myself before I squished my tiny woman beneath my larger frame. Thick dark lashes fanned up and down her flushed cheeks as she worked to get her breathing under control. I wasn't much better. My heart hammered against my chest like it wanted to punch through, to get even closer to her.

I worked out a lot to manage the anger and frustration that always simmered through my veins, keeping me on constant edge. But the last few minutes made me feel like I'd just run a fucking marathon. Sweaty palm to her cheek, I swiped away the few strands of hair sticking to her warm skin as I smiled down at my Millie.

"Tell me this is real," I whispered.

"I know exactly how you feel," she said, stroking her fingers through my hair. Those dark eyes shifted to look at the long dirty-blond strands. "I like your hair. It suits you. Don't cut it tomorrow, please. I have this odd urge to play with it."

My chuckle brushed against her skin as I swept my lips against hers. "Whatever you want, baby. I'm all yours." She held my gaze, and a thin line appeared between her brows. I clicked my tongue and pressed a thumb there. "What has that brilliant mind of yours working overtime?"

"How long?" I cocked my head to the side. "How long are you all mine?"

I froze, unsure of my response, but that didn't stop me

from answering with the truth. "For as long as you'll have me, Millie." I sighed and pushed up from the bed, putting some space between us. Slowly, I pulled out of her and tugged off the condom. After tying off the end, I made my way to the bathroom while fastening my jeans and flushed the condom down the toilet. Back in her bedroom, she watched me with hurt and confusion written all over her features. The bed dipped where I sat beside her. Unable to stop, I trailed my fingers up and down her bare stomach, loving the way her muscles jumped and twitched with every barely there touch.

"I'm not the same man I was back then. Before you commit to wanting me—" I stopped and raked my fingers through my hair. "Wait until all my baggage is exposed, and you'll realize just how fucked-up I am." Turning, I lay down beside her, head propped up by my palm. "You're this amazing professor, beautiful and way too good of a person for someone like me. That doesn't mean I'll stop wanting you or wanting your everything, but before you question how long you have with me, let's see if you even want this dark and fucked-up version I've become."

I avoided her gaze, instead following where my fingers circled around her belly button.

"Fuck, even your belly button is cute." I shot her a smile that would convince anyone else that I'd moved on and was back in a good place. But not Millie. Of course, my Millie could see through the mask; she always did.

"Killian, I think you're forgetting something."

My fingers stilled. "What's that?"

"You don't have to fight it alone anymore." I sucked in a shocked breath. "I'm not sure what you're referring to, but baggage is kind of my specialty." Her smile made my gut flip. "And I've just found you, after also dreaming of this moment for ten years, just like you. Don't think so little of me that your trauma or past, the hard work that will be needed to help you, will stop me from finally getting what I want."

"Orgasms?" My smile was forced and fake as shit.

Hers went all soft and sad, making me hate myself a little more. Holding my face between her hands, she pulled me close until our lips barely touched before she responded with the one word that ripped me apart in the best way possible.

"You."

"You've always had me, Millie. I've never stopped being yours."

My lips slid against hers in a slow kiss. Every emotion that I kept bottled up over the years poured from me to her. Holding her face, I deepened the kiss, hoping to relay how much this, her, meant to me. What she'd always meant to me. Those hard days and nights that never seemed to end when I was a hostage. The memories of Millie kept me going and made me fight to survive another day. If it hadn't been for her, for those months together as friends, I wouldn't have wanted to keep going, to keep enduring the pain and mental torture those bastards put me through.

But now she was here.

Offering to help, to fight through my mental shit with me.

Slowly working my way down her throat, I scooted off the bed until I kneeled between her thighs once again. Palms under both cheeks, I lifted her slight weight off the mattress and yanked her core to my face.

"Now, I think I promised you an orgasm marathon." With a whimper, her head fell back to the bed, an arm tossed over her eyes. My chuckle skated along her slick skin as I nipped at her swollen clit with just enough pressure to sting. My guttural groan vibrated against her slick lips when I buried my tongue into her perfect cunt, ready to devour her until she begged me to stop.

And if she never demanded I stop eating her whole, then that was 100 fucking percent okay with me.

16

MILLIE

TODAY

The feeling of being trapped jerked me awake from a deep sleep. Blinking my lids open, I struggled against the thick band around my waist and whatever had my legs pinned to the bed. Panic made my breath catch with every thundering heartbeat.

"Shh." The hair covering my face was moved away, and a lazy kiss was pressed to the side of my head. "It's me, baby-cakes. Just me."

The memory from the last forty-eight hours slammed forward, immediately easing the panic. Killian, that's whose arm was wrapped around me, whose leg draped over my own. The ache between my legs had a fresh wave of desire surging in my gut, making it twist and turn as the memories of Killian destroying me with his cock before his mouth and tongue consumed my core until I passed out played on repeat.

Destroyed might be a slight exaggeration, but the twinge of pain that flared each time I tried to slip out of Killian's hold told me that might not be an overstatement.

"Good morning, my Millie." A smile spread across my

lips. Breaking free just enough, I rolled to my side to face him. Hair disheveled, sleepy smile, and droopy lids, morning Killian was adorable. I reached up and tucked a few crazy strands behind his ear. I had never been a fan of long hair on men, but somehow, it made Killian look more like himself than the shorter hair in college.

My fingertips trailed along his plump lips before skimming his cheekbones and eyebrows, memorizing every detail. He wasn't just handsome; Killian was beautiful. Add in those intense, all-seeing aqua eyes, and it was like he put you in an awestruck trance when you looked at him. But this close, now that the shock of everything had worn off, I saw what he hid from the world.

Exhaustion, fear, anger, and vulnerability, though that last one was probably there just around me.

"Tell me one thing," I whispered. Outside the windows, the sun barely peeked through the blinds, telling me we didn't have to move just yet. And I wanted this sweet moment with him, to learn one new thing about the man I never stopped loving. Even when I was married to another man. "One thing that's new, different about adult you."

"Only if you agree to do the same." My hair rasped along the pillow with a quick nod. Killian groaned and rolled to his back, bringing me with him until my head lay on his chest. If I didn't know any better, I'd think the move was deliberate so he didn't have to look me in the eye as he talked. "There are so fucking many issues and changes, I don't know where to start."

I plucked at the T-shirt he still wore and leaned up just enough to arch a brow in question. "Want to start with why you used to strip off your shirt the moment you entered my apartment, claiming it was too hot for clothes, but now you refuse to take this off?"

Palm to the top of my head, he turned me and laid me back on his chest. "Not sure that's where I want to start our therapy session today, Dr. Anderson."

I rolled my eyes and pinched his side. His high-pitched squeal sounded through the quiet, and he shifted out of reach. Giggling at the ridiculous sound that escaped him, I did it again, hoping for a repeat. His larger hand engulfed mine and tucked it around his side, holding it in place.

"Naughty girl, didn't anyone tell you it wasn't smart to poke the bear?" I shook my head. "Of course not, Dr. I'm-going-on-a-dangerous-assignment-with-the-FBI-even-though-I've-never-even-held-a-gun."

"But I'll have you and Hunter." His hold tightened at the mention of the other agent, making me preen just a little. "Okay, so start somewhere easier."

"Not sure that describes any of my fucked-up issues, but sure." His fingers drummed along my bare spine. "Oh, I've picked up cross-stitching."

I pushed up onto my elbow and stared down at him, but his gaze was firmly on my exposed breasts. He licked his lips slowly and shook his head. Running a single knuckle down over the now-pebbled tip, he smirked as a full-body shiver overtook me.

"Focus," I huffed.

"Oh, you do not know how focused I am, babycakes." His fingers pinched at the tip, eyes flicking up to mine to gauge my reaction. "Is it too much to ask for the rest of our lives that we never leave this bed, and I get to spend every second reminding you whose you are?"

"Yes, because then we'd die of dehydration."

"Especially you, my Millie." His hand snaked lower. A single finger dipped into my slick core, making me hiss.

"Hmm, so no playing with that pretty pussy today if you're that sore. We could always try the tit fucking."

I smacked at his chest with a laugh. "Cross-stitching? That's so random and oddly cute."

"I met this female agent once when I worked with another agency." I stiffened in his arms, all humor gone. His smile, though, grew as if he could sense the jealousy burning through me. "Jealous, baby?"

"What? No."

I totally was. Even if they weren't together, she got to see him when I didn't. It hit me then what he alluded to when he said a different agency. But I didn't dare ask which one, knowing he probably wouldn't or couldn't tell me. Though it added to the overall mystery that surrounded the beautiful man.

"She had a penchant for sharp objects."

"Like you and that knife."

"Exactly," he said, resting his chin on my head. "And she told me it was therapeutic, and you had a weapon handy if ever attacked while cross-stitching. It made so much damn sense that I picked it up, and fuck if she wasn't right. Though I might switch to crochet; that requires a larger weapon set."

"Pretty sure you shouldn't go to the craft store and ask for the *large weapons section*. You might get security called on you." His chest vibrated beneath my cheek with his rumbled laughter.

"Your turn, Velma. Tell me something no one else knows. Give me a piece of you that is just mine."

I sighed. This was Killian. Too damn insightful and all-consuming. He made me feel like I was the only important thing in the world to him and was obsessed with knowing every thought, every dream... everything that made me me.

"I got married because I was lonely, not because I actually saw a bright future with my ex-husband." His muscular arms tightened as if trying to protect me from my ugly and humiliating truth. "And it worked for a little while. It was nice to have someone to come home to, but then it wasn't."

"Why?"

"It felt like more of an obligation than a relationship, especially on the physical side. We started fighting a lot."

"If he hurt you—"

My fingers tightened, bunching the soft cotton of his shirt at the anger in his tone. It was oddly comforting. "Not in the way you're thinking. It was more arguing. He thought we should have more sex than we were, but he wasn't doing anything to... I don't know, make me want to, if that makes sense."

"I really want you to keep going, but not sure how much I can take hearing about you with that fucker," he grumbled.

My smile grew. "He blamed my disinterest in sex on the books I like to read, which, I mean maybe, but he was also to blame regarding that part of our relationship."

He hummed a noncommittal response while stroking long, lazy swipes up and down my back. "In what way?"

"It was boring when we were..." I pursed my lips, trying to think of the right word. "I would say intimate, but there was no intimacy between us, so sex. When we had sex, it was so damn monotonous. I wanted to try new things, like in the books I read, and he shut it down. If it wasn't gentle and in a certain spot on the bed, he—"

A calloused palm covered my lips. "That's enough sharing for today, babycakes. There is only so much I can handle." My tongue snaked out and flicked across his palm. Instead of pulling away like I expected, his hand shifted enough so a single, thick finger speared through my parted lips and slid in and out. "You are my perfect, naughty Millie, aren't you? Tell me what you want, baby, and I'll make all those dirty fantasies of yours come true. I won't stifle you. I'll help you fucking fly." His lips pressed against my hair. "Over and over and over again."

My thighs squeezed together to ease the throbbing, only to wince when the pressure reminded me of his rough treatment the night before. Which I loved. Holy hell, I loved it. Every man I'd been with, especially my ex-husband, treated me like I was this fragile creature. All gentle hands and sweet words when that wasn't what I wanted at all.

I wanted passion, intensity, the thrill of exploring something new with someone you trusted.

"We have a few hours until your hair appointment. Want to try—"

The shrill of an incoming call cut him off. With a groan, he slid out from under me and reached toward the floor. Discarded jeans in one hand, he dug through the side pocket and pulled out the still-ringing phone. His brows furrowed at the name on the screen and swiped a thumb across the smooth glass.

"It's too fucking early, Hunter. What the hell could you need—" He stopped talking at whatever Hunter said on the other end of the line. Killian stiffened, his muscles no longer soft and relaxed. Brows pulled in tight as he nodded along with whatever Hunter communicated on the other end of the call. "Yeah, okay, that makes sense. It's a good sign that Charlie's identities are cult-nip but fucking hell, maybe it was too much if they reached out directly."

My heart leapt up my throat, making it hard to breathe. Scooting to lie back on the pillows, I pulled up the sheet to cover my bare chest and stared at the ceiling. The pressure of what was to come was all but forgotten until now. In

Killian's arms, the reason we were together wasn't important. With that ill-timed call, now it was.

Tomorrow, we would step into the lion's den, and the hard work started. Not only faking being Killian's lush and wayward wife, but searching for Karigan and the other truths. Those families who lost their lives, all because they were sucked into Pastor Paul's orbit, deserved to have the truth of their deaths exposed.

The mattress shifted, drawing my gaze to where Killian lay back on the pillows beside me, arm tossed over his face.

"It's too late to ask you not to do this," he murmured. "But I really fucking hate the idea of you doing this, Millie." His arm fell to the side, and he turned to face me. "I just connected with you again." Not sure why it sounded like he stumbled over the word connected or why it seemed like a strange choice of verbiage. "I don't want you anywhere near these fuckers. After reading everything you found on them, I think they're more dangerous than anyone realizes."

"Except me."

His lips tugged up at the corners. "Except my brilliant, curious, insightful Millie." His hand palmed my cheek, thumb brushing along my skin in soothing strokes. "But asking you not to go through with this isn't an option now." My brows tugged in, not understanding. "Apparently, my hot friend Charlie is way too fucking good at his job. He did everything you suggested for those fuckers to want us for their so-called leadership team, and it worked."

"Really?"

He shot me an unamused look at the excitement in my tone. "Yes, really. Instead of starting tomorrow at the welcome lunch like everyone else, Pastor Paul himself has invited us to a private dinner with him and several of his sidekicks."

I pursed my lips to silence the giggle. "I wouldn't call them sidekicks when we're there."

"Mind-controlling assholes?"

I shook my head. "And you thought I was going to be the problem."

His smile fell, and he swallowed hard. "Tonight. The dinner is tonight."

Well, fuck.

There went my extra time to overanalyze and prepare for the undercover assignment. Time to prove to everyone, including myself, that I could do this. And I would because if I fucked this up, it wasn't just my life on the line.

And I refused to let that happen.

KILLIAN

TODAY

Any tell of nerves or stress was trained out of me years ago by my father and then reinforced with the CIA. Or I thought it was, at least. Apparently, when Millie was involved, everything I assumed was second nature wasn't even a thought. Because here I was, sitting in the butter-soft leather seat of the jet, leg bouncing in quick repetition and palms so sweaty you'd think I just washed my fucking hands.

For the first time, I was so fucking nervous about an assignment I couldn't sit still or really focus.

"I've never seen you like this, Coop," Hunter said beside me as he flipped through the few papers sitting on the table between us. His gaze flicked up and landed on Millie. "It seems you two made up. Thank fuck."

"Yeah, something like that," I grumbled and shifted to watch Millie walk from the small service area back to our grouping of seats. Her soft pink hair threw me off every time it caught my eye. It was fucking hot as hell, but it was not my Millie. Though she seemed to love it, so maybe it was Millie, the one she kept hidden away from everyone but me. "Nothing can happen to her."

"That's why I'm here," he said, hitching his chin in acknowledgment as she settled into the seat beside me. "I won't leave her side."

"How are we spinning the extra security?" Millie asked after getting comfortable, taking a sip of the steaming tea in her hand.

"They actually didn't question it, per Charlie, when he filled out the information for the classes. But if anyone asks, I'll tell them Hunter here is more of a handler than anything. He's there to make sure you stay out of trouble."

Her lips twitched in a smile around the rim of the disposable cup. "Because I've been known to do so much of that."

"As Marla Morgan, yes. You've been in and out of rehab for alcohol and prescription drug abuse, been caught with your panties down more than once with a man who wasn't me, had a minor scandal with the law that we kept out of the media—"

"Because it never happened," Millie interjected, cutting me off.

"It did now. It's on the internet about you, so it must be true." I shot her a wink, making her chuckle.

"Why do you get to be the trust fund guy who also has a successful business, and I'm the problem of our rocky marriage?" Setting the cup down on the table, she pulled one paper free from the stack in front of Hunter. "Also, why in the hell did Charlie choose a multimillion-dollar vegan meal delivery service as your business?"

Instead of responding, Hunter just waved his hand toward my long hair that I had tied back in a sloppy knot and then to her cotton-candy pink hair.

"Example A." I snorted and shook my head at Hunter's smirk. "You two look the part of a socially conscious and wealthy couple. It's a little stereotypical, but it's not like we had a shit ton of time to come up with something better."

I shifted and gave Millie a slow once-over. Ankle length, multi-color hemp skirt, soft cotton T-shirt, with an array of long necklaces with various pendants, she looked the part we were trying for her identity; a free spirit that got caught up in the money and fame of her husband's successful company.

"I think I like the sexy-as-fuck professor look more," I teased.

Millie looked more ready to visit a farmer's market after she made a dozen soy candles in her craft cabin while I looked like I just stepped out of a *GQ* magazine. Apparently, my fake identity, Kurt Morgan, only made his wife dress in the all-natural fabrics while he wore fine Italian suits. But that was the backwards way the fucked-up group we were infiltrating thought. She needed to play the soft, submissive one with me, the dominant, arrogant asshole who sought the classes to keep his wife in line.

It made my stomach churn every time I thought about the person I needed to play once the plane touched down. Reaching over, I grabbed her hand and threaded my fingers through hers. Big brown eyes met mine, flicking between the two as if reading my thoughts.

"I'll be fine. I promise. Nothing you say while playing Kurt Morgan will change how I see you, Killian. I know what they expect from you, what they will expect from me."

Hunter cleared his throat, breaking the moment. "Looks like you're booked in a couple's cabin somewhere on their massive property while I'm bunking with their full-time staff."

"That's perfect," Millie stated with conviction. "Only followers make up the staff, including their security team. Maybe that extra time will help them open up to you." She paused and frowned. "I'm not sure if they'll let you attend the wives-only classes with me."

"I don't give a fuck if they push back. He will stay with you no matter what," I snapped before inhaling deep to calm down. "I don't want you going anywhere without me or Hunter attached to your hip."

"We'll see," she muttered.

My fingers gripped her chin in a firm but gentle hold. "No 'we'll see.' This is a hard rule, Millie. If you can't agree to that, then I'll tell the pilot to turn this fucking jet around." Her brown eyes seemed to darken more at my dominant tone. The tip of her tongue popped out and ran along her lower lip. A groan escaped as I leaned in close, desperate to seal my lips to hers.

Hunter's pointed cough stopped me. I shot him a glare, ready to punch the fucker out for interrupting.

"Don't forget, you two are going to these classes and seminars because your marriage is not great, so I'd lay off the eye fucking and intense obvious attraction that's going on here."

Before I could say anything, Millie tugged her chin from my hold.

"I will try to stay with Hunter, but if I see an opportunity to sneak away to do a little snooping, I'm taking it. I promise I'll stay safe, but we're here for a reason, and I won't waste an opportunity because you're hell-bent on keeping me in this safe little bubble."

"She has a point." I snarled at my friend, who only smiled back. "There will be places she can go that we can't. They won't see her as a threat because she's a woman."

The plane dipped as we started our descent. I stared at Millie, stomach flipping with unfamiliar nerves. Nothing about our plan felt right, but it was too late to back out now. We'd get in, get the information we needed and the girl, and then get out.

Fuck, if only it were really that simple.

A SHIFT in the air was the first indication we crossed onto The Union of Blessed Souls property. I'd been to enough places around the world to know it was never a good sign when the evil soaked into the atmosphere surrounding a place to where those perceptive enough could feel the impact. We knew going in that this group was corrupt, but the shiver down my spine, as we traveled along the long drive headed toward the massive mansion in the distance, said we didn't have a fucking clue how deeply depraved this place and these people really were.

Millie was slouched in the seat beside me, gaze locked out the window, taking in everything we passed and no doubt cataloging it away in case we needed that information later. Schooling my features to a bored look, I slid my hand across the gap between us and stroked my pinkie finger along hers in soft, reassuring strokes.

She didn't turn, keeping with the annoyed wife persona, instead, wrapped her bite-size finger around mine in silent support. I eyed the driver, making sure his attention was out on the road ahead and not focused on us, only to meet his gaze in the rearview.

"Almost there, sir."

I nodded and shifted to pull out my phone, which had advanced level security protection. Everything I sent to

Rhyan and Charlie was encrypted to look like business emails required for my company. Every time I read the dumb marketing slogan Charlie made up for the vegan meal service business, I had to stifle a laugh. But what pissed me off the most was the food rule. Even though my clothes were not in line with the fake company's mission statement, I was told to fall in line with the stance around the food.

Fuck. My. Life.

I wasn't even allowed to smuggle jerky sticks in my bag. Just thinking about food had my stomach grumbling, threatening to eat itself before the sun came up tomorrow if I didn't find some meat. I was a growing boy, plus these new, inconvenient nerves made me even more ravenous for unhealthy snacks. On top of only bringing plant-based snacks, I couldn't bring my normal stash of weapons. Apparently, a duffle full of guns, ammo, and knives would've raised some red flags. So here I sat, about to meet the leader of this fucking group, starving and with only a small hunting knife strapped to my calf.

Again.

Fuck. My. Life.

Hunter turned to look over his shoulder as the car rolled to a stop in front of the historic mansion. Two stories, tall white columns along the front with a long porch, it gave off a rich yet homey feel. Hunter gave a subtle nod before shoving open the passenger door and stepping out into the crisp, early evening air. When he adjusted his sidearm, I eyed the weapon with envy. The small, sharp-as-hell blade pressed against my calf wasn't as great as the Glock Hunter was allowed, but it offered some comfort. Neither he nor Millie knew I snuck it past them while they went over the plan a final time on the plane, but what they didn't know wouldn't hurt anyone.

I hoped. Because there was no way I'd walk into this fucked-up compound with my Millie and not be armed.

My door swung open at the same time Millie's did. With a curt nod to the driver, I folded out of the Mercedes. My fingers worked to button my jacket as I took in the crisp white mansion with a bored expression secured over my features.

Even knowing Hunter had Millie's safety covered, it still took effort to turn my back on them both. Without thanking or acknowledging the driver, I moved around where he stood, still holding the door open. The heels of my thousand-dollar shoes clicked along the wide set of marble steps that led to the double, blood-red doors. All senses on alert, I tracked Millie's soft steps and Hunter's heavier ones without turning. To the right, in the thick grouping of trees that surrounded the house, slight movement caught my eyes, warning me of the security moving along the perimeter.

Before I reached the massive set of doors, both opened with a flourish. A man dressed in a navy suit, almost as nice as mine, and a crisp white dress shirt strode out, smiling like he was in on a big secret. I immediately recognized him from the information Millie had gathered on the leadership team. He slowed to a stop and raised a hand between us.

"Simon Chase. It's a pleasure to meet you, Kurt." I took the bastard's hand and squeezed hard, which he returned. Fuck my life and this subtle pissing contest. We could save time if we just whipped out our dicks and measured. Then he'd know mine was bigger.

Obviously.

But sadly, unzipping the pressed slacks and whipping out my elephant trunk-like cock wasn't an option. Instead,

I'd have to play nice in the cult sandbox and let this fucker think he was the alpha male between the two of us.

I was benevolent like that, letting others believe in their crazy little fantasies.

"Welcome, come on in. Pastor had to step out for a few minutes just before you arrived, so dinner will wait until his return." With a smile that didn't reach his dark, beady eyes, he gestured into the house.

Not letting on I was seconds from snapping his neck, I followed him into the mansion's foyer, resisting the insistent urge to check on Millie and Hunter. I knew without a doubt my friend would take care of her. And if he didn't, if anything happened to her, then I'd kill him. Hunter understood my expectations that I explicitly lined out when I asked him to help with this assignment.

It was simple: Keep her safe and live.

Don't and die.

Easy peasy.

The Simon fucker led us down the pristine hall, past the expensive artwork hanging on the walls, and into a massive library. I had to school the smile that wanted to appear, knowing Millie was no doubt swooning at the floor-to-ceiling built-in bookcases stuffed full of various books. This was her paradise, minus it being inside a murderous cult.

To my right was a wall of tall windows that allowed natural light to stream through the spotless glass, while to the left was a massive fireplace surrounded by a comfortable-looking leather couch and several leather club-style chairs.

Cozy. Wonder if that was where they plotted out their world domination goals.

A tall, blonde woman gracefully stood from the couch and smiled, clasping both hands in front of her skintight pencil skirt. Her high heels barely made a sound on the expensive Oriental rug as she made her way to stand just behind Simon.

"Hello, welcome."

I had the sudden urge to poke her in the cheek to see if she was real or just real-looking AI. Though like with the dick measuring, poking a woman I didn't know would probably be frowned upon. Though by the way the Simon guy watched me study the woman... maybe not.

"This is my wife, Georgiana." He gestured to her but kept his gaze locked on mine.

Well, well, well. Wasn't this a fun, also known as fucked-up, turn of events. I expected murder and evil from this place, maybe some soul snatching and virgin sacrifices, not captain douche-nozzle acting like he wanted me to find his wife attractive. It was the dark and lustful glint in the fucker's eyes that filled in important gaps Millie's research unknowingly had.

Holy fuck.

This assignment just became more complicated than any of us expected.

18

MILLIE

TODAY

My fingers twisted in the loose fabric of my skirt, giving away the crazy high nerves riding me. I believed I could do this with ease, that it would be a fun new adventure. How damn wrong was I. This wasn't an adventure; it was dangerous for someone untrained. Killian tried to talk me out of coming, to tell me the dangers involved, but my stubborn ass pushed back, thinking this would be easy, considering everything I already compiled about the cult.

Wrong. I was so damn wrong.

Not that I could do anything about it now except hope no one here could see behind the aloof mask I attempted to hold in place despite the churning in my gut. When the woman stood from the small couch and moved gracefully to her husband's side, a jolt of insecurity rocked through me. She was gorgeous. Tall, long blonde hair, and skin that seemed to glow, but when I looked closer, there was something off about her eyes.

Before I could unravel what was off about her, Killian, or Kurt rather, glanced over his shoulder. The look he sent me and then Hunter clearly tried to communicate something, but I did not know what. Apparently, Hunter did, because before Killian turned back to face our two hosts, Hunter stepped even closer to my side.

"My wife, Mrs. Morgan." I wanted to roll my eyes at that show of proprietorship. When he introduced me as Mrs. Morgan instead of my first name, like the other man had with his wife, it subtly gave insight to what my so-called husband thought of me. Not important enough to be addressed by anything other than his last name, which he obviously held in high regard. "Have anything good to drink around here?"

The other man, Simon, chuckled and gestured toward the gold bar cart along the wall of windows. "Of course, though I highly doubt the ladies would like to join us."

Georgiana started toward me with a wide, face-splitting smile on her face. "So true. Mrs. Morgan, let's leave the men to their whiskey or bourbon while we get to know each other." Before I could respond, she snaked an arm through mine and was tugging me toward the doors we came through.

I knew better than to look at Killian, knowing he'd see every ounce of panic that I fought to keep hidden. Though at the doors, Georgiana paused and glanced over her slim shoulder, that wide smile dropping for just a moment.

"Does your bodyguard need to come? You're safe with me, I assure you."

"Her handler," Killian called from deeper in the room. "And yes, he stays with her. My wife is a fucking train wreck," I heard him mutter to Simon, who laughed as he poured amber liquid into a highball glass. "If it were legal, I'd put a leash on her instead."

My heart constricted at the disdain and loathing in

Killian's tone, even though I knew it was all for show. His glare cut through me like I wasn't even standing there. With a wave of his hand, he dismissed us—no, dismissed *me*. Even though I'd prepared myself to be treated this way, it still stoked a blazing fire of anger and disgust in my gut. I hated it, hated feeling like I didn't have a voice all because of my gender.

Back out in the hall, Georgiana led me along the sparkling marble floor toward an ornately carved, gilded door. With that same plastic smile, she pushed it open and pulled me in behind her. Moving swiftly, she shoved at the door the moment we were inside to keep Hunter on the other side. The toe of his shoe wedged between the door and frame before it could close. His pointed scowl at Georgiana silently communicated his annoyance when he shoved the door back open and stepped just inside the small sitting room.

It wasn't nearly as grand as the other room where we left the husbands. This one was more intimate, decorated in calming colors with comfortable-looking upholstered chairs and couches set in a small grouping. Massive vases filled with fresh flowers stood on various side tables, filling the room with their sweet aroma. The setting sun blazed through the windows that overlooked a sparkling pool.

"Would you like some tea?" Georgiana asked after patting my arm and stepping to a Victorian era-looking tea set. "One of the staff delivered it just for us."

Remembering the personality I was told to portray, I shook my head and flopped down onto a couch. I bounced against the stiff cushion that looked way more comfortable than it actually was. "Have anything stronger than tea in that cart?"

"Marla," Hunter growled from where he stood like a statue, back against the wall just to the right of the door.

"Oh, come on, he's not even in here," I complained. "Stop being so uptight."

Georgiana held up a finger in a 'hold that thought' gesture and bent low, opening the double doors and exposing an array of wines. "Red or white?" She gestured to the bottles. Two, one white and one a pinkish color, sat in a bucket of ice already chilling while three bottles of red stood beside it already opened.

"All of them?" I said with a smirk. "It was a long-ass plane ride with that man."

"White, then, so they don't see the evidence on our teeth when we reconvene for dinner."

"I like the way you think," I said with a smile. My fingers drummed along my thigh, catching on the flowy skirt. I eyed the woman as she poured one very full glass of white wine, ensuring she didn't slip anything into the drink. I hated doubting the woman, but we were in the heart of a dangerous cult. One couldn't be too careful. "I like your outfit," I blurted, not sure how to get the conversation going between us. I needed to use every second I could to gain information on anything and everything.

I swear Hunter's eye roll was audible.

Sorry, I was new at this whole subtle interrogation thing. I read a book on covert operations, but reading and applying the information were two different things. My shoulders slumped. Maybe all I would ever be good at was being a professor. Those who can't do, teach, or whatever that saying was clearly applied to me.

"Thank you, though my clothes don't look nearly as comfortable as yours." I listened for a haughty or judgmental tone, considering her outfit was snug and pressed to perfection, but there was none. I relaxed a little further against the couch's stiff back after taking the offered glass of wine. "I apologize. I know little about you or your husband. Why don't you tell me about yourself?"

I took a small sip of the crisp wine, the flavors exploding on my tongue. "There isn't much to tell these days. I live the same day over and over again, under his thumb."

"That must be difficult." The cushion barely even shifted beneath me when Georgiana sat at my side and rested a hand along my knee, giving it a comforting squeeze. "I understand how easy it is to blend into the background, to allow life to just pass you by." I nodded, fully engrossed in her words. Her clear, cheerful tone, the soft look in her eyes, and her serene smile drew me in like a moth to a flame. They trained the recruiters well here, it seemed. "That was me before... well, all of this." She gestured around the room, that smile of hers growing.

"That's great for you, but—"

"I get if you're skeptical about the classes and what we do here for couples. There are those who claim our views and methods are dated, but Pastor Paul created these classes carefully after years of research. His only goal is for couples to walk away stronger in themselves and their marriage."

I took another sip, which Georgiana tracked with a smirk. "So, you and Simon... you two seem to have it all together now." That was a lie. I saw the evil glint in Simon's eyes and the way he studied Killian, then me. There was a predator-type quality in his gaze as it trailed over every inch of my trembling frame.

"Oh, yes, we fought like cats and dogs." She laughed and patted my leg, hand moving a little higher up my thigh. I gulped down another large swallow. Holy fuck, this was getting awkward. "He dragged me here, our last-ditch effort before divorce. I thought he was crazy, but I should've known to trust him. This is where we are meant to be, where we belong. I'm happy and cannot wait for you to feel the love and see the light, too. Now we help others like us, like you and Kurt. Which, oh my goodness, he's a sexy beast, isn't he?"

"Simon?" I squeaked.

"No, your husband. He's all man, if you know what I mean." I couldn't verbally respond without hissing, so I ended up nodding. "Pastor Paul helped us one on one, taught us how to strengthen ourselves first, which would then lead to a stronger partnership. He really is amazing." I blinked, eyes wide at the awe in her tone while speaking about the controlling man. "He is beyond understanding, listens to anyone who reaches out, even when he has so many things going on—oh, and utterly brilliant. The man is so smart and kind. Just wait until you meet him." She fanned her face and shot me a shy smile. "You'll be begging for a few minutes alone with him once you meet him in person. There is something so captivating about a powerful man, isn't there?" I opened my mouth, but she cut me off. "Though you know that or you would've already left your husband. Powerful men are our flames and us the fluttering moths."

Another cold sip slid over my tongue and down my throat. Her words processed fast but still kept snagging on her last statement. Was that how they identified families to bring deeper into the fold? That would make them more vulnerable to someone like Gary Paul and the other men on the leadership team, while also identifying arrogant, narcissistic men to continue building their inner circle.

But why?

What was in it for them? That was something I could

never figure out about this group. They hid everything well behind the marriage classes, sermons, retreats, and religion. I had a feeling once we uncovered what kept the core group of followers circling Pastor Paul, everything else would make sense.

"I guess," I mumbled.

"The power that radiates from Pastor Paul is..." She shivered, fingers digging into my inner thigh. "So alluring." I blinked at the woman. Did she have a crush on that bastard? "He created this safe place for those of us who want to live, love, and learn. The freedom from everything else society labels as important is what drives us all. We want to spread the love and knowledge to others like yourself so everyone can feel this." She grabbed my hand and held it to her chest, right over her heart, which scraped my knuckles against her hard, fake breasts. "He's bigger than life, more than you can imagine. I promise, you'll have to hold yourself back from attacking him. Everyone wants to be the chosen one when he needs help to fuel his visions."

My stomach dropped, and I carefully extracted my hand out of her grasp. The empty wine glass rattled along the side table when I set it down before it slipped from my tightening grip. "Visions?"

Her cheeks flamed pink, and she shook her head, standing quickly. "I'm getting ahead of myself. I guess I just feel a kinship with you." Her smile was soft as she moved to the cart with my empty glass in hand. "I can feel the pain and worry tangled inside you, keeping you from truly living life to the absolute fullest." After filling the glass again to the brim, she returned and sat beside me. "We can help you," she whispered, leaning in closer. "You don't need the alcohol to escape when you're overjoyed with your life. There is nothing you'll want to fade away from."

I leaned back into the couch to put distance between me and the zero-personal-space woman. "That sounds..." Fake. Illogical. Unbelievable. "Magical."

"And it is." Wine sloshed over the rim of the glass when I jerked upright to face the unexpected male voice. Softly, he closed the door behind him, smiling at me and Georgiana, who practically vibrated with excitement beside me. That smile turned sharp when he glanced Hunter's way, but only for a fraction of a second. "Thank you so much for keeping these two beautiful ladies safe while I had to step out." He marched over to Hunter, hand outstretched. "Your courage and strength will be rewarded while here with us."

After dropping Hunter's hand, Pastor Paul strode closer. My skin crawled as if a thousand spiders ghosted along my arms and down my spine. There was violence in his smile, anger behind his bright eyes, and something evil in the way he held himself. Arrogance radiated off him like nothing I'd ever felt before.

My stomach churned as my unease and fear grew with every shallow breath.

Georgiana yanked me upright as Pastor Paul came to stand in front of us. Her fingers squeezed mine as he leaned in and kissed one of her cheeks, then the other. He leaned in to do the same to me, but I retreated a step, evading his touch.

His brows pulled in tight, and he sighed. "You've been hurt by this world. I'm so sorry you've had to go through so much." He gestured to the couch where we were sitting before he entered, and Georgiana and I both sat like obedient little followers. "I'm—" He chuckled and laid a massive palm on top of Georgiana's bare knee. "*We* are so happy you're here, Marla. We're here for you every step of the way as you follow your heart to the light, to happiness beyond compare."

"How?" I asked, taking a sip of wine. Stomach empty from not eating on the plane, too nervous to even look at food, and topped with the full glasses of wine, I felt lighter, less panicked than when I first walked in.

Not sure if that was a good thing or not.

"Helping you heal from the inside out, finding true happiness and love for yourself and others. This world tells us we need more and more material things." He shook his head, though not a single slicked-back piece of dark hair shifted. "That's not the way to pure happiness. Here, we can help you find that spark for life again, and then, if you're like so many others, you will want to help pass on the light to those who you used to be."

"But how? How can this place give all that?"

He smiled, that hand on Georgiana's knee sliding high enough to be inappropriate. He caught me tracking the movement and smirked. "I've been blessed with the ability to read others' troubles and core fears. Some come from trauma in their past; others, it's what they've done to themselves, depending on substances to keep them going." He eyed my almost empty glass of wine. "Aren't you ready to live, Marla? Ready to break through that darkness and loneliness that has kept you heavy for so long?"

I blinked at the soft hand that encompassed my knee.

"We can help you so you don't have to hide who you really are. All your wants, desires, and joys can be exposed, allowed to run free. We will find it, excavate it, and then you'll see."

"See what?" My voice shook with the revulsion from his unwanted touch.

"That here, with me, you're truly free."

Georgiana sighed and laid her hand on top of Pastor Paul's. "Yes, that's exactly it. You've freed us from all our baggage so we can be happy, loved."

My gaze flicked between the two as they stared deep into each other's eyes.

"You'll see," Pastor Paul said, turning to me. "Now come, dinner is ready, and I'm eager to meet this husband of yours."

Without thinking, I took his offered hand and allowed him to lead me and Georgiana to the door. I stared at the contact, swallowing down the bile climbing up my throat that his touch invoked. All I had to do was survive dinner, maybe drinks after, then I could curl up in Killian's arms where I was safe.

It sounded easy.

Turned out... it wasn't.

19

KILLIAN

TODAY

My thirst for the bastard's blood started with him smiling, laughing, and fucking touching my Millie when he joined us in the ostentatious dining room. It was like the fucker needed to make sure everyone knew he had a shit ton of money and power. If he only knew I'd seen better as an asset with the agency. The places I infiltrated, powerhouses I friended to gain information put this place and him to shame.

I sipped my drink, watching as he led a slightly wobbly Millie in my direction. Everything in me wanted to slice off the hand that was wrapped around hers, then shove it down his throat until he choked. Instead, I studied the approaching man, like one arrogant fuck would another.

"You must be this stunning woman's husband." I nodded but didn't say a word, which only made his fake smile grow. "Apologies. I need to introduce myself. Sometimes I forget there are some who don't know me." Oh, the eye roll fight was strong. I'm pretty fucking sure I just strained a muscle from keeping my gaze locked on him. Holy fuck, this might be my toughest assignment ever. "I'm Pastor Paul."

He released Millie's hand to clasp mine, doing exactly what I hoped he would. With a harsh gesture to Millie, I beckoned her to my side, only relaxing when her strawberry and vanilla scent wrapped around me.

"Kurt Morgan." I might have squeezed his hand a little tighter than necessary, but it seemed the asshole expected that and did the same.

"I've been telling Kurt all about the amazing things our church does here and around the globe." Simon stepped beside us and traded out my glass with a full one. Seemed they wanted to get both Millie and I in a more accepting state, AKA drunk, to discuss their fucked-up lifestyle and theologies.

Georgiana stepped to my side, opposite Millie, her fingertips just barely skimming along my thigh in what seemed like an accidental touch. I stiffened, hating the feel of the unwanted contact. Millie glanced up at me, almost as if she sensed the burst of anxiety and fear now coursing through my veins, brows furrowed as she studied me.

"Well, let's eat, shall we?" Fucker Paul said, clapping his hands and drawing all our attention his way. Fingers wrapped around the high back of a dining chair, he pulled it out and smiled at Millie. "Marla, why don't you sit beside me tonight?"

Georgiana's smile widened. "Wow," she whispered across me to Millie. "That's an enormous honor to be seated at his right hand."

"I must learn more about you and what you two are hoping to get out of the classes over the next two weeks." He pushed the chair in after Millie sat and moved to the seat at the head of the table, which was almost twice the size of the others, almost like a throne. "And learn about you, Kurt. I'd never heard of your little company until I did some digging."

My drink's thick glass bottom slammed to the table. The bastard was trying to rile me up. Not sure why, though. There had to be a reason, and if I didn't figure it out quickly, then I could walk right into a carefully laid trap he had for us.

"Little if you mean making multimillions a year, sure," I said with a forced chuckle. After sitting beside Millie, I leaned back in the chair like I owned the place. "Now, let's cut the shit. I don't need you to placate me. I want to know how you're going to fix my wife."

Millie glared at me, and I huffed like her anger was a nuisance.

"There are many things you will learn through the classes that will help both of you find a peaceful union within yourselves and each other," Fucker Paul offered with a smirk. He turned his full attention to Millie. "Though she doesn't look like she needs fixing to me."

My hand clenched beneath the table at the flirty wink he shot my Millie.

Mine.

Fucking mine.

"One way we help bring union between couples is to expose the parts of a healthy relationship that society has deemed bad or harsh," Georgiana said as she slipped into the chair across from me while Simon sat across from Millie. "For example, losing yourself in your husband, for him to catch you and guide you, is freeing. The word submissive is like a curse word out there, but in here, it means everything." Simon nodded and reached over, grasping the back of Georgiana's neck in a gentle but controlling hold. "To trust yourself and them is to really live."

Them, not him as in her husband.

"That's right, Georgiana." She preened in her seat at Pastor Idiot's praise. "Not only will the classes help you communicate with each other, but when we separate you two, Kurt will be in a class working to grasp the forgotten strength and dominance needed in the husband's role. It's a two-way street to find the light that becoming one soul intertwined forever can offer. Though there is a catch."

I arched a brow and pretended to take a sip of the drink Simon brought me. I didn't watch the fucker make it, so no way in hell would I actually try a sip. Sure, Hunter stood watch behind us and had my back, but still, I didn't want to risk being drugged with Millie here.

"Your trust," he stated, eyes locked on me. I nearly choked on my spit. Right. Trust this guy who looks like he came from a long line of snake oil salesmen. I bet a distant relative also sold miles of oceanfront property in Arizona to gullible buyers. "That is where this all starts. So I have to ask, do you trust me to help you? To guide you both to a happier tomorrow? To lead you toward the light and help you live the best life possible?"

"Yes," Millie said before I could.

"What's in it for me?" Fucker Paul raised both brows, acting like he didn't understand my question. "Sure, I'll get an obedient, sober wife that won't make an ass out of the notorious fucking name I gave her, but what else? Why should I trust you?"

Bingo.

That fake smile turned into a wide, genuine one. It was malicious and manipulative, exposing all the darkness inside him. I fought the urge to kill him right there, to end the lies he spread all to gain power and money. But pretty sure my boss would get pissed if I killed him with witnesses. Now, later...

"Oh, Kurt." His voice snapped me out of detailing his murder. "Just you wait and see." He chuckled against the rim of the wineglass at his lips. "But before I show you all that The Union of Blessed Souls can offer to you and Marla, I have to trust you. There are those who say they want the light I offer, who say they are ready to believe in true happiness, but they aren't. I have to protect my followers from those who want to tear apart what we've built."

My lips parted to dig deeper into the bullshit he spewed, but a side door swung open, stopping me. A young girl in a short dress appeared holding a silver tray, a wide, delusional smile on her innocent face. Before the door could shut behind her, another young woman stepped through, then another. Soft smiles graced their lips, dressed in the same, almost provocatively short, uniform in various colors as they hurried to the table. After everything was set out, the lids were removed, revealing steaming chicken, vegetables, and potatoes... well, for everyone but me and Millie. Ours looked like something that a rabbit would eat.

I swallowed down the groan that wanted to escape.

Fuck my life. Not only did I have to deal with these arrogant asshats, but I would starve to death right there in the dining room. No meat? I wouldn't survive the hour.

"Is that what all the security out front is for?" I asked, attempting to not look longingly at his plate of meat and potatoes.

The fork full of the food I wanted hesitated in front of his mouth for half a second before pushing past his lips. It was an arrogant stall tactic, or I really surprised him by noticing the guards carefully positioned around the property as we drove down the long drive.

"Yes, and no. There are those who disagree with our way of life, who have not yet accepted what I can offer them.

Without that light, anger grows, and some have hurt our followers through cruel words or physical attacks." He dipped his head like he needed to compose himself. "It's difficult having the illumination and calling that leads others to pure happiness and unity. Some just don't understand what that truly means. So yes, the guards are there and were hand selected by myself from the local followers to help protect those who have come here for the classes and choose to live on the property. Plus, there are children here who need protecting."

My stomach soured at the thought of his depraved interpretation of protection.

"Children?" Millie asked as she nibbled on her salad.

"Oh, yes, we even have a school where they can learn without the bullying and hate that is so rampant everywhere else. I created a full curriculum for our children, ranging from preschool to high school."

I wanted to ask how many of them went off to college after graduating from his so-called school. Or, more importantly, how many women left the compound versus the men after turning eighteen? I had a feeling it was heavily swayed for the men to leave and the women to stay. Careful to keep my attention subtle, I scanned the room, taking in the young girls who waited along the wall with hands clasped in front of their short dresses.

Too fucking short for how young they looked.

My gaze snagged on one girl's knees and the distinct red scrapes marring her tan skin.

"You keep mentioning this light," I said, forcing my stare off the girl to Fucker Paul, whose gaze was already locked on me. A small smirk pulled at his lips as he cut those light eyes from me to the girl and back again. "What is this so-called light that makes this place a utopia for so many?"

That arrogant look turned soft and vulnerable that had no doubt fooled millions.

"Me," he said boldly, arms stretched out wide. His lips parted to add additional crazy bullshit, but the door that we came through swung open, jerking my attention from him to the teenage girl who entered.

My heart slammed against my chest, immediately recognizing her. Holy fuck. There she was. The reason for us being here, and she just fucking walked into the room. Maybe this assignment would be an easy in and out. Guess we were about to find out if the hair color change and contoured makeup helped make Millie unrecognizable from her rogue trip last year.

I still needed to spank that ass of hers for that dangerous visit.

"Ah, there you are, Kari." I waited for him to finish her name, but he didn't. My lips curled down in a frown. Did he fucking change her name? Talk about mind fuck 101. "Come here and meet some of those who are searching for the light." The chandelier light glinted off her glassy eyes as she marched over to his chair and stood at his side. His arm wrapped around her lean waist and tugged her until her hip dug into the armrest, the only thing stopping him from pulling her onto his lap.

Her glassy gaze didn't fully meet mine, instead focused just to the right of my left ear. "Nice to meet you."

"Is she sick?" Millie looked seconds from leaping over the table and kidnapping the teenager. Mimicking Simon's hold on his wife's neck, I wrapped my fingers around Millie's and squeezed as a reminder to not break cover.

His fingers dug into Karigan's waist in an almost possessive hold. I swallowed a curse and forced my disinterested mask to stay in place.

"Not in the physical sense." That hand slid upward, fingertip barely brushing along the side of her chest before gripping around her bicep. "Kari came to us when her parents...." Again that damn dramatic pause, like he was too emotional to go on. Fucker. Lying fucker. "Her parents were part of my most trusted followers, but poison found its way into her mother's heart. When I learned of her changing heart, I raced to their home in town, but we were too late." His gaze leveled on Karigan as if waiting for a reaction. But one never came. "Her mother had killed her husband before turning the gun on herself, leaving my sweet Kari all alone. Thankfully, her father knew of his wife's poison and prepared, naming me as Kari's guardian since she's not quite eighteen."

"Poor thing," Millie said, tension underlying her tone.

"She's dealt with nightmares and other violent responses to that trauma. Keeping her safe and happy is my number one concern, so we're keeping her calm until the worst is behind her."

Calm AKA drugged.

"Are you this concerned with all of your followers' children?"

I bit my tongue to keep from groaning. Damnit, Millie. Her single focus on Karigan was obvious.

"Why do you ask?" Paul said, tone sharp.

I felt Millie stiffen beneath my hold, and I squeezed ever so slightly. "My childhood was not the best, neglect and avoidance, so not as traumatic as Kari's story, but it still left an imprint." Oh, she was good. Now Paul wasn't only diverted from her focus on Karigan, but he saw an opening to exploit her past to make her lean more on him. Smart Millie. My brilliant Millie. "I find myself slightly jealous of her." Okay, maybe laying it on a little thick. "Seeing as she has a community to support her, has you to take care of her when there was no one else."

I swallowed, waiting for Paul's response.

Palm up, he slid a hand across the table, white cloth bunching with the movement. Millie's tiny hand floated over his for a heartbeat before dropping. He squeezed softly, thumb stroking along her soft skin. Every muscle strained as I held myself back from smacking off his touch.

She. Was. Mine.

"I see you, Marla, and I know we can help you, help you find that light inside. Just like we're doing with Kari. I will heal that hurt and pain from the inside out so you two can find peace and happiness within and with us."

Between blinks, the man went from fake soft and happy to sitting straight in his chair, a faraway look overtaking his pointed focus. When his eyes rolled into the back of his head and he flopped back, I tugged Millie's dining chair closer to me and farther from the freak show.

"A vision," Georgiana whispered in awe.

As quickly as the act started, Paul snapped back to himself before slouching forward.

"Pastor?" Simon questioned, genuine concern in his tone. "Are you all right?"

Pastor Paul, ever the terrible actor, nodded and struggled to sit up straight like all the energy from earlier had drained from his body.

"Yes, I saw...." He stopped and shook his head. "Saw our future, but it was foggy, difficult to see clearly." Standing on trembling legs, he leaned against the table, both hands pressed on top as he swayed. Two of the girls who delivered our food gasped and hurried to his side. Adoring faces tilted up to him with worry in their eyes. "I need to rest, fuel myself and the leaders to help me see clearly." His gaze slid to Karigan. "There was a woman in white, holding a child."

My stomach dropped.

Guess what Karigan wore in that exact moment.

All. Fucking. White.

"Sorry to cut this dinner short, but leadership and I need to convene to fuel me so that the vision sent for our future becomes clear." Simon nodded and hurried out of the room, a smirk on his lips instead of worry as he murmured into his cell phone. When he returned, two men in black suits and earpieces followed hot on his heels. "David, please take Kari to her room and ensure she stays safe throughout the night." Locked down and guarded, noted. "And Saul, take our guests to their cabin before showing their guard where he will stay with the others."

Turning, Pastor Paul smiled at Millie. "I'm sorry to leave just when I was learning so much about you and what makes you a potential special addition to our community. Tomorrow, I'll set aside time to meet with you," his gaze flicked to me, "both of you, together, to see how the first day went in the classes. I can sense great things about you two."

Putting both hands together, he bowed to us before stumbling out of the room, the young girls supporting him the whole way. Brows furrowed, I watched them leave. Too consumed by the bombarding questions the dinner and show conjured, I failed to notice Georgiana until her hand slipped over my shoulder.

Instead of saying anything, she lowered to her knees beside my chair, never breaking eye contact.

What the fuck? My heart pounded, and the palm still wrapped around Millie's neck grew slick. I glanced at Simon, who stood just behind his fucking wife, smiling at her like he was fucking proud. Or ensuring she obeyed. I couldn't tell which.

"Give us a chance to show you, to help you believe in the pastor's vision for this church and his followers." Her hand moved from my shoulder, coming to rest on my thigh. I swallowed down the bile swelling in my throat. "We have so much to offer someone as powerful and driven as you. Just let us show you all the ways *everyone* here can make you the happiest you've ever been."

I gritted my teeth when her hand slid up higher, fingertip barely brushing against my currently shriveled-to-the-size-of-a-raisin dick. While on the outside, I raised both brows and allowed interest to fill my gaze.

I hated it.

Hated myself.

Hated the touch.

Hated the fucking memories all this invoked.

Instead of bolting out of the chair and running screaming from the room like I wanted, I simply nodded and ran a knuckle along her jaw. Looking at Simon, he smiled at me and nodded.

"I look forward to seeing everything you offer." With that, I stood and pulled Millie up with me. My gaze locked with Hunter's, who wasn't nearly as good at masking his disgust, and I hitched my chin toward the door. "Let's get this one locked up before she drinks them out of all the wine they own."

Keeping a controlling grip on Millie, I guided her toward Hunter, who turned on his heel and marched out the door, all of us following the cult creep's security. As we marched down the hall, I focused on keeping my breaths even. Soon I would be alone and could melt the fuck down, give in to the memories that battered against my mental barricades.

But not until Millie was safely behind a locked door would I allow myself to be at my weakest. Our steps echoed through the empty hall. A sliver of worry wove its way past my defenses.

What if Millie saw the broken me I hid from everyone, all the darkness that consumed me from my past, and walked away? Would I be strong enough to go on?

Or would that, plus those awful memories and my trauma, finally swallow me whole?

20

MILLIE

TODAY

Something was off about Killian's behavior that had nothing to do with the asshole he needed to portray.

His thick fingers that were still wrapped around the back of my neck had turned clammy, flexing and twitching against my skin like he couldn't relax. In the four-seater golf cart, he'd put as much distance as he could between us before tugging me against him, only to push me away once again. It was as if he fought a battle only he could see and feel.

I'd seen similar reactions before during the clinical hours required for my various degrees. Those with trauma or PTSD fought an internal war only they knew about. Even if two people went through the same incident, they would deal with the aftereffects differently. One thing was certain: My friend needed help, someone to listen and not judge. I would need to balance being his friend and falling into my schooling once we finally had a chance to talk alone.

I'd walk that line, anything to help him, so he wouldn't feel he was alone in that fight. I might not have gone through what he did, but that didn't mean I couldn't stand with him. It would be difficult. Some people even turned violent during sessions because they were so angry at the world and what happened to them. But I trusted Killian, knew no matter how angry or volatile he became, I was safe.

I always was with him.

Killian had always been my protector, even when I didn't realize I needed one.

"I'll be back to collect you tomorrow at noon to drive you both to the welcome lunch." The security guy handed Killian the key to our adorable cottage. "Your luggage was delivered earlier and is waiting for you inside." Turning to Hunter, he hitched his chin toward the cart. "I'll wait." With that, he slid behind the wheel and pulled out his phone, thumbs flying over the screen.

Without a word, Killian shoved open the door and motioned for Hunter to go in first. When I tried to follow, a thick arm wrapped around my shoulders, yanking me against a hard chest.

"Let him clear it first," he whispered into my hair. His arm relaxed its tight hold when I nodded, not fighting him.

A shiver raced down my spine, goose bumps raised along my skin as a powerful gust of chilly wind whipped through the small porch, though it brought the sweet scents of the blooming trees and spring flowers. Taking the moment, I scanned the area, noting the few cottages spread out around us like a tiny little village in the middle of the massive compound. Tall, thick trees swayed in the strong wind, the limbs creaking through the darkness, adding a creepiness factor.

"Clear, sir," Hunter clipped when he appeared at the door. "Do you need anything before I head out?"

Knowing we had someone listening nearby, I kept my mouth shut and waited for Killian to respond for us.

"Be back around eight. I have some work to get done and can't waste my time babysitting this one." With a sharp nod, Hunter moved past us, careful not to touch Killian or me, and hopped into the cart. I watched them drive off into the dark, stomach dipping with worry.

"Will he be okay?" I whispered.

Killian only grunted a response and ushered me inside. The moment the door closed behind us, his touch disappeared. I tracked Killian as he prowled around the small living room, searching the walls, outlets, and air ducts, before getting on his hands and knees to inspect the lower half of the room. With more grace than I could ever attempt, he leapt up and headed into what I assumed was the bedroom. I stood frozen by the front door as he did what he needed to do to ensure we were safe.

A relieved exhale blew past my lips when he reemerged, only to stiffen when those aqua eyes met mine. Even from across the room, his radiating tension was palpable. Not breaking my stare, he struggled out of his suit coat, balling it up and throwing it across the room like it was suddenly poisonous. His tie followed, fluttering to the pile of expensive material.

Killian's chest heaved with every deep breath. Ripping the hair tie free, he raked his fingers through the long strands, fisting at the scalp. Alarm pulsed through me, setting my feet in motion. A foot away, he tossed up a hand, stopping me in my tracks. Eyes wild, he lunged for the remote sitting on the coffee table. The moment the TV flicked on, he jammed his thumb to the volume button until the voices of the show rang in my ears.

The remote clattered to the floor at Killian's feet as he dropped, ass perched on the edge of the coffee table. Bent forward, hands in his hair and face towards the carpet, I couldn't read his emotions, which kept me frozen where I stood. But when he looked up, the panic and brokenness in his normally self-assured and strong features had me dropping to my knees in front of him. The second my palms settled over his thighs, a sharp hiss whistled through his clenched teeth. Immediately, I jerked back, not wanting to add to the panic that was slowly dragging him under.

"Talk to me," I said, hoping he heard me over the blaring voices pouring from the TV. "I'm here. I'm not going anywhere."

His head shook back and forth, but he shot me a pleading look. One I'd seen before and knew exactly what it meant. He wanted my help but wasn't sure how to get there, how to open up that deep, dark chasm of pain that he'd spent so much time and energy keeping locked away.

"Start with what triggered you." Careful to keep my movements slow, I inched closer and pressed up on the wooden table to sit beside him. Palm upturned on my knee, I left it there, giving him the option if he wanted physical contact. "Was it Pastor Paul?" He didn't move. "Did Simon say something while you were alone?" Again, nothing. My mind raced through the events of the night, attempting to pinpoint when I noticed the change from the fake narcissist persona to the bleeding panic.

The woman, her touch, or maybe the way she offered herself in front of him. That was when he changed. And his reaction to my touch just now solidified the theory. It didn't help much, but at least I knew not to force my comforting touch on him. I needed to wait for him to reach out, for that contact to be initiated by him. So I waited. Palm up on my bouncing knee, I waited, giving him all the time he needed to unscramble his thoughts that the panic caused. If he even wanted to do that now.... Maybe he wasn't ready. That was one thing I realized early on: You couldn't force someone to show you the darkest parts of themselves. They had to be ready for that trust to be there between the two parties. It hurt a little, thinking Killian didn't trust me enough to—

"I'm so messed up, Millie." My heart splintered at his defeated tone. Never had I heard that from him, but still, I stayed, not wrapping my arms around him in a massive hug like I wanted. "There is a lot I can't share, not because I don't trust you, but because it would put you in danger." I nodded like I understood, even though I didn't. He shifted just a little, angling his body more toward mine. "The agency I was with before..." Killian trailed off like the memories suddenly swarmed his every thought. He shook his head. "They made me use any tactic necessary to get the information we needed. Important information that, in most cases, had the potential to save thousands of lives."

I swallowed hard. Maybe I read too many spy novels, but it seemed like Killian hinted at him being an asset with the CIA. Which made his disappearance, his controlling father, and me not being able to find anything online about Killian, all of it, make so much more sense. He didn't disappear into a cult like I assumed; he disappeared into a government-run agency who trained valuable spies.

Oh, shit.

My eyes widened.

I sat beside a trained killer. A spy.

It should scare me, but it only made him more alluring. Maybe I had a death wish or no self-preservation skills, but knowing that sliver of information made me want Killian that much more.

"I did things," he rasped. "Things I'm not proud of." His hands curled into tight fists, the color bleeding out of the scarred knuckles. "But the worst was..." In a flash, he was up and bent over the trashcan beside the small desk, emptying what little he ate during the awkward dinner. My knees bounced in rapid succession. The edge of the table bit into my palms as I fought the urge to comfort him. "It's amazing what people will tell you after sex." He fell to the side, leaning back against the wall, and slid down until his ass hit the carpet. "I hated every second of it, but I couldn't let the mask drop. And now... I'm so fucked up that what happened tonight sent me into this. I can kill without a second thought, but the memories of seducing terrible men and women for information reduce me to this pathetic piece of shit."

Forearms on his bent knees, he dropped his chin to his chest, that long blond hair acting like a wall between us. Not wanting to stand over him, I scooted off the table, dropped to my hands and knees, and crawled. An inch separated us when I sat back on my heels, palms sealed to my thighs.

"Was it the way she touched you, or her touch in general?" I asked so softly, worried he didn't hear me over the TV.

"Both." Anger like I never felt before flooded my veins, heating me from the inside out. How fucking dare she. How fucking dare she touch him without his consent. Only for all the anger to evaporate, leaving me hollow.

"I'm so sorry, Killian." My voice cracked. "I've touched you so many times without even—"

His hands lashed out and wrapped around my shoulders, dragging me between his spread thighs. Arms banded around my back, sealing me to him. Face pressed to his neck, I moved with each of his quick, ragged breaths.

"No," he snapped. "Your touch is the only one I can stand, the only one that doesn't immediately make disgust and rage consume me." Even though his words were said with conviction, I remained frozen in his hold, too afraid to touch him. "Please don't." His chest vibrated with what felt like a choked breath.

"Don't what, Killian?" When he didn't respond, I carefully pulled away to stare into those eyes that could see into my soul. "I'm trying to tread carefully to respect your boundaries—"

"I don't want fucking boundaries between us," he growled. "I'm fucking yours, all of me. I've always been yours." Something flashed in his eyes. "And you've always been mine."

A hand slid up the back of my neck and fisted my hair. My lips parted in a gasp as my face tipped to the ceiling. Soft lips ghosted along the sensitive skin of my throat. The skim of his lips and nip of his teeth made my core clench around nothing. Eyes closed, savoring every sensation, a desperate whimper escaped.

"You still want me, babycakes? Want all the fucked-up parts of me?" His hand snaked under the hem of my long skirt and slid up a leg, fingertip brushing along my inner thigh and dipping beneath the soaked scrap of lace covering me. "Your body wants me, but what about you, Millie?" He jerked my head so our gazes clashed. The vulnerability behind his eyes had me melting into him. "Do you still want me?"

"Of course," I whispered, lids falling closed as a single finger teased at my slick entrance. "Nothing has changed. You're still my Killian. Still the man I trust, the man who will keep me safe no matter what, the man I want. Desperately."

His body shuttered beneath me. Lips against my ear, he sucked the lobe before nipping at the tip. "Tell me a dark truth." I squirmed, shifting to push that teasing finger into my needy core, only to groan in frustration when he withdrew his hand. "A dark truth, Millie."

Desire and need swamped my brain, making my thoughts sluggish. Once again, that finger slid along my slick center, this time circling my swollen clit with a barely there touch.

"I don't know." His lips sealed to my throat, tongue flicking against my racing pulse. How many times had I envisioned something like this happening with him? My dark truth hit me so hard it stole my breath. I licked my lips and sealed my eyes shut, hating to admit this out loud, but I knew telling him my ultimate secret would only bring us closer. He was so damn vulnerable right now and needed me to be right there with him. And for Killian, for the amazing man I'd always loved, I would.

"He was too gentle," I rasped. "Too careful and focused on himself." A low growl rattled in Killian's chest, knowing exactly who I spoke about. "There were times when he'd made me feel so bad about us not having sex that I caved, despite despising his touch. Then after he was done and asleep..." I swallowed a moan as that finger pressed harder, the pressure everything but not enough. "I'd roll over and finish myself off."

His hum vibrated along my skin. "Tell me everything. I want all the details, every dirty fucking one." I shivered, my body trembling with the rising need that had nowhere to go. Still, his finger teased, and his lips skimmed along my throat. "What would you think about?"

"You," I breathed. "I imagined you. That my hand and fingers were yours. I remember everything from that night, tried to replicate the way you had touched me."

"But it was never quite right," he said with an almost sinister chuckle. "Because only I can make you feel like this, Millie. Only I know how to make this perfect, tiny body sing. Do you know why?"

I shook my head, causing soft pink strands to stick to my sweaty forehead and cheek.

"Because you're mine."

My lips parted, but not a word escaped, just a sharp breath. That teasing finger slid along my drenched slit and thrust into my needy center. A moan escaped when he added another finger, then another, the full feeling almost too much. I squirmed, knees sliding out wider to give him room to move.

One hand still in my hair, he tugged until my back arched, chest thrusting outward.

"Lift your top," he rasped, and I immediately obeyed. "Now pull those lacy cups down so I can see those fuckable tits." My hands skimmed along the soft curves of my breasts before tugging the demi cups down. The material dug into my skin, but the discomfort only added to the array of sensations inching me higher.

The tip of his tongue circled the pebbled tips over and over. My hips followed the motion, grinding myself down onto his fingers.

"More," I whined, the sound so damn desperate and needy.

"Don't worry, baby," he whispered before nipping at one nipple with enough bite to hurt. My core squeezed around his fingers. "I know exactly what you need."

And he did. Sucking one nipple between his lips, he pressed the heel of his hand down hard on my clit at the same time those three fingers curled, stroking a spot inside me that had stars dancing behind my closed lids. The assault of sensations hit me all at once, shoving me over the edge into pure, pulsing bliss. I tightened around him, lips parted with a silent scream, desperate to squeeze out every drop of pleasure.

With one last shudder, my taut muscles relaxed, my body slumping forward, only held up by Killian's hold on my hair. With more care than I expected, he guided me forward until I pressed against his chest. A soft sigh brushed past my lips as I snuggled against him. The events of the day finally catching up to me.

"Sleep, my Millie," Killian whispered against my hair.

"What about you?" I muttered, already almost asleep.

"We have all the time in the world. Now that I have you, I'll never let you go."

Something tickled in the back of my brain as sleep swallowed me whole.

Why did he say *have* instead of *found*?

21

KILLIAN

TODAY

Hands braced against the edge of the granite vanity top, I studied my reflection, barely visible through the steam coating the surface. It wasn't enough to hide the thick scars decorating my chest. My stomach rolled in disgust and phantom pain as I traced the outline of the most vicious slice that marred my entire stomach. At least I couldn't see my back, which was another roadmap of the torture I endured after my real identity and mission were exposed.

It was a miracle I was even here. The CIA didn't follow the whole *no man left behind* slogan. It was known if you were caught, then you better figure out a way to save yourself or take your own life because no one would come for you.

No one even remembered you existed.

My gaze flicked to the locked bathroom door as if I could see through it to the still-sleeping beauty on the king-sized bed. Except Millie had remembered me. A ghost of a smile pulled at my lips. The insistent flashbacks from those two months of pain and despair were overtaken by memories of her. Not only did Millie remember me, but she thought about me while touching herself with that asshole asleep right beside her.

If I'd known he was such a lousy fucker, I would've taken him out like I wanted to after he proposed. But I didn't because all my research and snooping on the bastard said he was a good guy. Stable. Safe.

Everything I wasn't.

But she still thought of me. A groan rattled up my throat at the memory of her whispered confessions while my fingers were deep inside her tight cunt. My lids fluttered closed, recalling every twitch of her body, the sounds she made as she came, and the sweet scent of her arousal that flooded the room.

"Fuck," I grunted as my cock stirred between my thighs. My gaze flicked to the door again, debating if I should wake Millie up with my tongue inside her, eating her tasty pussy for my breakfast, or slide inside her like I wanted to last night.

I started for the door, only for the movement in the reflection to catch my eye. My steps faltered at the sight of the ugly-ass scars. I didn't want her to see them, to know I failed and almost paid with my life for the mistake. Plus, if I saw pity or disgust, which she had no hope of covering because my girl had a shit poker face, it would break me.

More than I already was.

Grabbing a hair tie off the counter, I wrangled the long, wet strands into a knot and tugged on the sweats and T-shirt I brought in with me after slipping out of the bed. I knew if this were to be forever, Millie would see my scars eventually. But now wasn't the time. We had enough to deal with at the moment. Thankfully, they were easy to cover, and I'd been able to work around past hookups seeing the puckered scars. After I bound their hands to keep them from touching me, I'd cover their eyes if I planned to get fully undressed, which wasn't normal. The 'be ready for anything at any time' motto the agency drilled into me also encompassed times when you were balls deep inside someone.

Just as the shirt fell into place, the faint jostle of the door handle snapped my attention to the chrome metal, and I reached for where my knife normally sat on my hip. Anxiety mounted when my searching fingers brushed along the soft cotton instead of a hilt.

"Kill?"

My shoulders relaxed as I blew out a controlled breath. Millie. It was Millie, not someone here to kill me. Fucking hell, living with someone would be harder to acclimate to than I expected. Though the effort needed to not reach for a gun or knife at every sound would be worth it for Millie.

The lock popped with the quick twist of the handle, and I pulled the door open. My stomach dropped, taking in the adorable woman standing in front of me. Cotton-candy pink hair a mess, lids still heavy with sleep, and a soft smile on her lips. She was absolutely stunning.

My heart stuttered in my chest. This. This was what I missed the last ten years. If I'd known, realized how much I missed out on, of a normal life, maybe I would've said fuck it to the danger that continued to follow me. But instead, like a fucking coward, I only watched from afar, through lenses and social media, never daring to step into her life.

I was afraid she wouldn't remember me or be so angry that she'd take one look and walk away. I was too fragile for that. Sure, I might seem like I had all the confidence in the world, enjoyed being the shiny object that greedy eyes tracked when I walked into a room, but that wasn't the real me.

Only Millie knew that person.

"You okay?" she asked, rubbing at her eyes.

"Yeah, just getting a head start on the day. I need to check in with Rhyan and—" I swallowed my next words when her tiny arms wrapped around me, and her head laid against my chest.

"Next time, wake me up, too, okay?" Chin to my sternum, she looked up at me. "I didn't like waking up to you gone." A flash of fear and vulnerability flickered across her features. "I thought you left me again."

My hand wrapped around the back of her neck while the other grabbed a handful of her plump ass. "Never again. No one will take you away from me ever again, babycakes. And I swear on my life that as long as I'm breathing, I'll be here, right by your side."

"You already showered?" I nodded. A frown tugged the corners of her lips down. "I wanted to shower with you," she whispered.

My cock jerked at her raspy words, visions of us consuming each other beneath the hot spray making me harder by the second. Her gaze widened, no doubt feeling my stirring cock against her stomach. The fingers digging into her ass cheek tightened as a groan escaped, rattling around the room.

"Is that so, babycakes?" I tugged on a soft pink lock of hair. Her breath hitched at the bite of pain, making me grin. "And what would you have done in the shower with me?"

Her throat bobbed with a hard swallow. I tracked the movement. Cock now rock-hard, twitching behind my sweats.

"It's not fair, really," she said as those small fingers traced the waistband of my sweats. "I've had all the fun—"

"I disagree. Watching you come is my definition of fun, but go on," I said in a teasing tone.

Her eyes narrowed in a fake glare. "What if I want to try it?" A dark brown brow arched in question, but I'd somehow swallowed my tongue and couldn't respond. Fuck, this woman rendered me speechless constantly. "What if I wanted a chance to touch you? To taste you like you did me?"

Squeezing my eyes shut, I inhaled the still-humid air from my shower to keep from propping her up on the counter and fucking her senseless.

Wait.

Why was that a bad idea again?

When I opened my eyes, I found her looking up with glassy eyes and pink cheeks.

"Does the idea of me fucking your mouth turn you on, babycakes?" That disheveled pink hair shifted with an eager nod. "Well, I'm here for your pleasure, my Millie." Her breath caught as I trapped her hand in mine and dipped it beneath the sweats' loose waistband. The second her tiny fingers stroked along my shaft, I couldn't stop the jerk of my hips. "Fuck. Just you touching me might make me explode, but holy fuck, why are your hands so cold?"

Her soft giggle echoed around the bathroom, making my heart soar with pure happiness. That laugh. Oh, how I missed that laugh. Her fingers tightened around me, the cold adding a unique and welcome sensation.

"Did you mention something about tasting me?" I rasped.

Instead of responding, she nodded while running the tip of her tongue along her lower lip. My stomach bottomed out as she lowered to her knees, the hand not wrapped around me slowly working the band of my pants down my thick thighs until all of me was exposed to the humid air.

"I don't actually know what I'm doing," she said, staring up at me before looking away as if embarrassed by her words. "I don't think I'm good at it, but I want to be for you."

Her soft hair slid under my palm as I ran a hand over her head in a sweet, comforting gesture.

"Don't do anything you don't want to do, babycakes. I'm perfectly happy with just—shit," I cursed as her lips wrapped around my sensitive head.

"I want to do it, Kill. Don't think I feel obligated or pressured. It was my awkward way of asking for you to help me."

"Help you," I mused. "Pretty sure if I could manipulate my body to help you suck my cock, I'd forever be stuck in that position."

Brown eyes looked at the ceiling with her frustrated huff. "Tell me what you like. Show me." Crimson highlighted her cheeks. "When the man in a book is more... forceful, it turns me on. A lot."

My brows hit my hairline. "Is that right?"

"Yes." Her soft breath brushed along my bobbing cock.

"Hmm, remind me we need to read those books together, out loud sometime, naked in bed, with nowhere to be for days. Oh, and I should send the authors fruit baskets or bouquets of dick straws." All humor vanished when her free hand cupped my balls and rolled them in her palm. "Forceful, hmm?" She nodded eagerly. "Well, okay then, babycakes, your wish is my pleasure."

My fingers dove into her pink strands and curled into a fist at the base of her skull.

"Fuck, I love this hair on you. Maybe I should send that dick straw bouquet to Rhyan for the perfect suggestion." Her lips curled into a small snarl. My chest heated knowing that just mentioning another woman's name made her jealous. "Oh, my Millie, you are all mine, aren't you? Now clasp both hands behind your back." I waited until she obeyed, immediately missing her hands on me. "Open that pretty little mouth and stick out your tongue."

Eyes locked on me, she did exactly as I asked, making my dick twitch, eager to feel the heat of her mouth it was teased with just seconds ago. Instead of thrusting into her mouth like I wanted, I leaned down and, with a single finger, nudged the thin straps of her silky pajama top off both slim shoulders.

A pleased hum rattled in my chest as the material fluttered down to her waist, exposing her tits. Gaze never leaving hers, I guided her mouth closer.

"Use that clever tongue and lick up that drop." The first flick of her tongue was tentative, but the guttural groan that rattled through the bathroom urged her on. Both legs shook, thigh muscles trembling when the little tease dipped her tongue into my slit like she was trying to draw out more for her to swallow. "Holy fuck, I'm going to embarrass myself. I swear on my life, next time, I'll last longer."

Not waiting for her reply, I pushed past her parted lips, cock sliding along her soft, hot tongue. Her eyes widened, but she didn't fight as I pushed even deeper, the head tapping at the back of her throat, engaging her gag reflex. I tossed my head back with a curse.

"Holy fuck, just like that. Keep swallowing, baby. Keep working that throat around my head." Pulling back slightly, I thrust forward again, her tiny nose brushing my stomach as I worked to slip down her throat. My free hand wrapped around her throat, squeezing just a little to add pressure to the amazingness that was my Millie's mouth owning me.

At a faint whimper, my lids popped open, and I pulled

back, a blast of fear cooling my heated blood. My lips parted to ask if I hurt her only for them to seal together when I caught the reason for the sound. Lids hooded, cheeks and bare chest flushed, Millie wiggled on the floor, her thighs pressed firmly together.

She was in pain, but not because of me.

"Unclasp your hands. Slip one down the front of your shorts and the other I want playing with your tits, understood?" I tracked every movement as I slipped my cock past her lips once again. Chest rising and falling in rapid succession, I couldn't catch my breath as her hand dipped beneath her shorts while the other cupped her breast, fingertips pinching at her hard nipple. "Fuck, you do that when you're playing with yourself, don't you? But don't come. If you do..." A strangled chuckle escaped as her throat constricted around me. "You won't like the consequences." Except when her wide eyes met mine, I smiled. "Or maybe you will. Oh, my Millie, we're going to have so much fun finding your limits."

Biting my lower lip, I gave in to the pounding need to fuck her perfect mouth. In and out, I slid past her lips, each time hitting her just a little deeper until she took all my long, thick cock. Head tossed back, I trembled. A bolt of pleasure raced down my spine. Knowing I was seconds from exploding, I held her head still and thrust even faster, chasing my orgasm.

"Fuck, Millie," I rasped, gazing down at her as I came so hard it fucking hurt, like my soul was ripped from my body. "Swallow it all, babycakes. Swallow every fucking drop you begged your husband for."

Her moan vibrated along my still-twitching shaft, making me curse and my hips jerk forward. Blinking past the dark spots dancing in my vision, I dipped my chin to stare down at the most beautiful and unique woman I'd ever met. My cock slipped from between her lips and I swiped a thumb along her skin, cleaning up the spit and cum dripping down her chin.

"Fuck, you're amazing, Millie." My gaze slipped to the hand still moving beneath her shorts. "And all fucking mine." Hands gripped under her arms, I lifted her slight frame with ease and sat her on the vanity, half her perfect ass hanging off. Palm to her sternum, I urged her back onto both elbows, thrusting those fuckable tits into the air.

Yanking at the band of her sleep shorts, I lowered them just enough for my mouth to latch on to her swollen nub. Her unique, sweet taste exploded on my tongue. A grunt escaped when her legs wrapped around me, heels pressed between my shoulders. I smiled against her, loving the way adult Millie wasn't shy about what she wanted, completely uninhibited, unlike the one I knew in college.

Her hips shifted against my face, telling me she was close. Fingers teasing at her entrance, I pushed one, then two, and finally a third finger deep inside before removing one. Eyes on her to monitor for any hesitation, I slid that one slick finger back while keeping the others inside her tight pussy. Millie's lids flew open when I prodded at her back hole, testing the waters to see how much she truly wanted to explore.

Instead of looking appalled or telling me to stop, her lids slammed shut as her cunt tightened around my fingers. A breathy moan filled the bathroom, and her release coated my fingers, leaking down my hand. Not wanting to miss a drop, I tugged her shorts down even further, a few seams snapping with the force, and licked her from entrance to clit over and over until her fingers grasped at my hair, tugging my face back.

Bare chest and cheeks flushed, breaths coming in quick, shallow pants, I froze at how fucking gorgeous she looked in that moment. Everything I had fantasized about, all those daydreams of her, couldn't compare to the real thing.

I stood between her thighs and bent forward to capture her lips with my own.

"Now that's a way to start a day," I muttered against her mouth. "Ready to start our diabolical plan to take over this shit cult and save some souls?"

Her brows rose over her forehead, but a small smile grew as she nodded. "Seems over the top, but yeah, let's do this."

How I would make it through the next two weeks without ripping out the eyes of any fucker in this messed-up place who looked at her, I wasn't sure. But that was something for future Killian to worry about.

Everything would work out fine.

Hopefully.

Maybe.

We'll see.

No one would miss a few cult members.... Right?

22

MILLIE

TODAY

T wo days.

Two long, full days of bullshit classes ranging from how to 'communicate' with your spouse to sessions on how Pastor Paul's light could heal us from the inside out. Every word that spilled out of the so-called teachers' mouths made me want to scream at those around me who sat taking notes and soaking in every word.

How could they not see it?

The class material was a bait-and-switch style where they made the women feel seen and heard, only to flip it all around to be about the men, forgetting about us. It made the women clamor to get their attention back and do anything for their praise and focus. In one class, when we were separated from the men, the teacher made the wives search inside ourselves to uncover why we would want something if it didn't make our husbands happy, then get rid of it. Toss any wants and desires that were your own so that you could make room for your husband's.

Cool water streamed down my hand, jerking me out of the anger-fueled trance I slipped into while filling my water bottle from the bathroom sink. It wasn't ideal, but the conference hall didn't have a single water fountain or refilling station. Seemed odd and made me wonder just what was in the water bottles they thrust into my hand before every class.

Pulling the bottle away, I shut off the water and screwed the cap back on. Ready for another grueling class, I turned for the door. Only the bathroom door swung open, making me back up a few steps to not get hit.

A tall, dark-haired woman, dressed in the same tight skirt and blouse the other leadership wives all wore, stepped inside. She startled at finding me, gaze locking on the excess water dripping from the overfilled plastic bottle in my hand. The polite smile vanished, and she swallowed, fingers releasing the door so it closed softly, cutting off the voices and laughter from the busy hall. "Did you fill that from the faucet?" I eyed her with suspicion and nodded. "Don't let them see you doing that," she whispered, slight panic in her voice. "You should pour it out before they catch you."

I held up the bottle, inspecting the label that read Union Blessed Water. "Doing what? Saving the planet one plastic bottle at a time?"

Dark hair swished with the forceful headshake, frantic eyes flicking back to the door as if worried someone might barge in. "It shows independence from the church and your husband. Everything has to be unified and approved."

"Independence by getting water?" I asked, tone incredulous. Was this woman serious?

"Yes. If you do that, then they'll think you're not fully... committed. They want control over everything, don't you see?"

Committed or brainwashed?

"Committed to the pastor?" She nodded. "But you're not,

if you're warning me. Actually, you seem scared." That last bit wasn't too much of a leap, considering she was jumpy and flinched at every voice and sound that came from the other side of the door. I couldn't recall seeing her around the spacious building, but that meant nothing. The place was packed, various groups and leaders meeting throughout the day in the sectioned-off rooms and conference halls.

Her face paled. "Don't say that out loud. You'll get me killed."

I dared a step closer, pulse racing. This could be it, my chance to pull the curtain back and see exactly what went on behind the scenes of this place. I reached a tentative hand out, giving her the opportunity to move away. The second my hand touched her bare arm, a shiver seemed to shake her to the core.

"What do you mean, *get you killed*? This is a church."

Play dumb. Don't act like you know anything about the true focus of the group.

That was Killian's advice when preparing me for situations like this. We figured most of the women were here under the directive of their husbands, because the men gained far more from being followers than the women. Killian expected I would have more opportunity to get the dirty secrets about the cult from the unhappy or scared women versus him with the men.

Plus, he said I was approachable. My smaller size and the bohemian style my fake persona wore would put others at ease around me. How he knew that, I wasn't sure, and didn't plan on asking for details. There was a lot that Killian held back from me, but he would tell me in time. We just had to get through this fake marriage that felt less fake every day, shut down the cult, find justice for those who were murdered—oh, and save a seventeen-year-old girl.

Easy.

I shook my head and ran a hand over my pink hair. Why did I sign up for this again?

Oh, that's right. I wanted the adventure. Well, nothing said adventure like being deep inside a dangerous cult, fake married to the man you actually loved.

"This place isn't what you think it is." Faster than I could react, both her hands wrapped around my wrists in a bruising grip. "I know who you are." Fear locked down my entire body; a frozen breath burned in my lungs.

"You do?" I rasped, the words barely audible.

"Everyone is talking about you and your husband." That blistering breath expelled past my lips. I teetered to the side with relief. "How much *he*," she spat, "wants you two to join the leadership team because of your husband and his company."

"He as in Pastor Paul?"

She nodded and looked at the door. "I can't explain everything now, but you have to get out of here. Don't listen to anything they say, and most importantly, don't—"

The door flung open, slamming against the wall and cutting her off. I tensed as a lanky older man stepped into the ladies restroom. White dusted the hair at his temples, and wrinkles bracketed his lips. Deep lines marked his forehead, but they disappeared when his gaze landed on us. The woman's grip tightened. Between blinks, her whole demeanor transformed from panicked and afraid to the soft smile that now spread across her face as she turned to the man who I immediately recognized from my research.

High-ranking leadership member, Davis Culler.

"There you are, wife."

I blinked at the man in genuine shock. I chanced a look

back at the woman. Without the fear and panic pinching her features, she appeared far younger than I first assumed.

Far. Younger.

Fucking hell, she had to be over twenty years younger than her so-called husband.

"Apologies. I kept her," I said sheepishly, redirecting his angry glare my way. The instant he took me in, all that anger and hostility slipped away. The sudden change was practiced and natural for him, which was easy to see. "I was asking for..." Fuck, what should I say?

"How to go about changing her hair back to a more natural color," the woman cut in for me.

I wanted to scowl at that. The pale pink had grown on me. No way in hell would I change it back so soon. The time it took to bleach my naturally dark hair to obtain the blonde needed for the pink took too long not to keep the fun color for a while.

"Yes," I said, dropping my gaze to appear more submissive. "My husband wants me to look more like the women here. Sophisticated, classy."

Brainwashed.

Fake.

Same thing.

"Oh, you're Kurt's wife." Apparently, I didn't have a name. My left eye twitched with the urge to correct him. I didn't realize how demeaning it would be to not be an individual person instead of an attachment to the person they deemed as important. "How lovely for my wife to run into you."

Why did the word lovely sound like a threat?

Releasing his white-knuckled grip on the door, it slowly closed before whispering shut. I swallowed hard, hoping that would help keep my heart from leaping out of my throat. My brain worked overtime to come up with a way out of this unexpected meeting.

In the women's restroom.

With a known emotional abuser and his young wife.

I was so out of my depth. Adventure was what I wanted. Instead, I walked into danger at the nuclear level.

"I've heard so much about you through the others." I forced a shaky smile and pulled my hands away from the woman's, not liking them being restrained with him encroaching on my personal space. "He seems to be the type of man we need on our leadership team. Already, he's showing the mindset and vision that aligns with our community."

His wide, creepy, knowing smile had a chill whipping down my spine.

"My wife can tell you all the ways being a part of the leadership team can benefit you, too."

His hand lashed out and grasped at the back of the woman's neck. Her lips parted as if she wanted to cry out, but not a single sound escaped. Instead, that pained expression morphed back to that serene smile that all the female followers seemed to wear.

"Tell her, honey," he said, words forced, but that fake smile of his never dropped. "Tell her how much you enjoy the benefits of being mine."

I gagged. Well, inside, I gagged. On the outside, I smiled and turned to face the woman with what I tried for was a hopeful and expectant look.

"Oh, yes," she whispered, watery gaze locked on mine. I swear I could feel the panic and fear leaching through her wide eyes. "I'm so happy and free now that I've been guided to the light. Pure happiness."

"Tell her about the leadership meetings," he stated as his

gaze slid up and down my short frame and the flowy skirt that hid my curves. "Oh, you would be fun, wouldn't you?"

"The meetings are my favorite." By the green tint that overcame her pale face, I'd bet that was a lie. "We all benefit from the pastor's visions and community we embrace to fuel those prophecies of the future."

I blanched, unable to stop the disgust that raced through my veins at her tight tone.

"That sounds... interesting," I offered.

"Don't worry about your looks," the bastard offered. "During the fueling, we don't take trivial matters into account." Wait. Should I be offended that he was basically calling me ugly? "Your small size might be just what some need to feed the energies."

Eww.

There was too much to unravel in that statement. Even my rapid-firing brain couldn't process the plethora of hidden meanings behind his words. I knew for certain the so-called fueling wasn't anything good or something I planned to be an active participant in.

The door swung open again, and for a second time, a male walked through the door. But this one had relief rushing through my veins. Careful to keep my features calm, I eyed Killian as his gaze swept over the three of us, quickly assessing the situation. It was beyond attractive how quickly his mind worked, seeing and calculating rapidly, unlike mine earlier.

"Didn't realize I was missing out on a party," Killian said with a calm smile. Allowing the door to shut, he leaned back against it, blocking our only exit. "Tell me, Culler, what are you doing in the women's restroom with my wife?" Culler seemed to flounder for a moment, but Killian saved him. "Not that I mind, just want to make sure I'm not missing out on any of the benefits you've all alluded to during the classes."

Those aqua eyes swept up and down Culler's wife's body in a slow perusal before winking at her. Smile wide, he reached out and clapped the man on the shoulder, jerking him forward a step.

"I'm seeing why so many are happy when you have women like that at your disposal." I flinched, and Killian caught the movement. He rolled his eyes like he was annoyed with me for purely existing. "You didn't think I brought you just to fix you for myself, did you? Fuck, you're more pathetic than I realized."

I knew he was playing the part of an asshole husband, that it was all a show, but still tears sprung to my eyes at his harsh words. A flash of panic flittered across Killian's face when he caught my watery gaze, but he quickly schooled his features back into that cocky mask.

"Come on, wife. Our next class is together." He reached out and wrapped a hand around the back of my neck and squeezed. To everyone else, it looked like a possessive hold, but really, it was a silent apology, the touch meant to comfort, not control. "Maybe you'll actually learn something in this one because fuck knows I've been the only one putting in work since we've been here."

"Oh, yes," Davis chuckled. "I've heard about the work you've put in. You're more enlightened than any new attendee we've ever had. Even Pastor Paul has taken notice of your natural ability to... lead."

I wanted to look at Killian but forced my gaze to the floor. What did that even mean? Was that why he'd barely touched me since the welcome lunch on Monday? Two nights of him sleeping beside me, yet not really there. I'd asked him what was wrong, but he just shook his head and continued staring at the TV, even though I knew he wasn't paying attention to the show. Nor had he mentioned much when we debriefed with Hunter.

Speaking of which. My brows furrowed, suddenly remembering my shadow wasn't there. Why didn't he stop Davis from walking into the women's restroom? My stomach soured with the rising worry. Hopefully, he was just outside the door where I left him.

"Is your next class *Finding your spouse's light*?" Davis asked.

"Yeah, why?" Killian responded for us. I bit my lip, wanting to speak up but stayed in this submissive character, even though I hated being overlooked.

Davis released his wife and clapped Killian on the shoulder with as much force as Killian had to him, but Killian didn't stumble forward under the force like Davis had.

"I'm the teacher for that class today."

Killian's calloused hand wrapped around the door handle and pulled it open. "Looking forward to it. Now, if you'll give me a second, I need to talk to my wife in private about the consequences of ditching her handler."

Davis's eyes lit with excitement when they flicked my way. "Maybe I should stay to coach you. I'd be happy to use my wife here to demonstrate how she makes it up to me when I'm displeased with her behavior." Killian froze. It was clear to me he wasn't as relaxed as he seemed when he arched a questioning brow in Davis's direction. "It's not as harsh as it sounds. What you learn through this process and as a follower of Pastor Paul is a woman is happiest when she has set rules and is held accountable. It's for their own good. Keeping them in line brings us happiness, which makes them happy, as well. I'm sure you've heard some of this in the classes you've attended already."

Killian nodded, the movement stiff. "While I appreciate the offer to demonstrate," his aqua eyes locked on Davis's wife—I should really find out her name—then he smiled. "It would be informative and enjoyable, I'm sure. I need to speak with my wife alone to ensure she's not distracted and fully understands my expectations for the rest of the day and our time here."

Davis eyed Killian before smiling. "Of course. It takes time to become comfortable with how open we are with every aspect of our lives and marriages. Though, hopefully, as you proceed in the classes and continue to become enlightened, you'll see the benefits of our lifestyle and how you can prosper from them, as well." His wife's lips parted when those thick fingers dug deeper into the side of her throat as he guided her toward the door. "Our break ends in five minutes. Don't be late." Evil-filled eyes locked on me. "Or you won't have a choice regarding a group demonstration on authority and following our guidelines."

Back ramrod straight, Killian didn't move as the two disappeared out the door. Hunter's frame immediately filled the doorway. His worried gaze locked on me.

"Did I get him in time?" he whispered.

"Give us a minute, will you?" Killian rasped and released the door handle, shutting it in Hunter's face. My lips parted to tell him how rude that was. Hunter was clearly worried about me, but the words vanished when Killian's muscular arms wrapped around me. Face pressed to his chest, thick biceps banded around my back as all the built-up tension dissipated. Inhaling deeply, I slowly released the calming breath, already feeling better after a few seconds in Killian's protective hold.

"He didn't touch you, did he?" he rasped into my hair. I shook my head. "I don't know if I can do this."

Alarm raced through me, and I pushed away from Killian with wide eyes. "What?"

Features tight, he reached out and pulled me back into his arms. "This place is so fucked-up, the way they think and what they're teaching. I've had some tough assignments in the past, but this one.... This one might prove to be the most fucked-up and difficult one I've ever had."

"I know," I whispered. "But it's not forever, and if we do this right, then all this will stop. We can't walk away now." And please don't ask me to, was my silent plea.

"Will you still want me when I mass murder every fucker who has looked at you, thought about touching you, or mentioned how hot you are?"

A relieved smile overtook my face, the first genuine one of the day. "Of course." I inhale, pulling wafts of his expensive cologne into my lungs. "Did you see how young she was?"

"Yeah."

"She had to be at least twenty years younger than him. And he's the one whose previous wives died mysteriously... all that, plus he has a hot young wife? Seems suspect."

"This whole place is suspect," Killian grumbled. After placing a kiss on my forehead, he stepped back, his intense stare scanning my face. "We'll talk tonight, after dinner with the other participants."

I nodded and followed him to the door. Before he swung it open, he turned. "Have you noticed how easily the others taking these classes are believing all this shit? It's basic indoctrination 101, setting the foundation for what they really want."

"What's that, you think?"

"Control. Paul thrives off seeing all these people follow him like blind and fucking dumb sheep, while the leaders in his inner circle salivate at having control over those who look to them for guidance."

I nodded in agreement as we stepped into the hall. Other couples smiled at us as we emerged, no doubt thinking we stepped inside the bathroom for a quickie. At the sudden presence at my back, I glanced over my shoulder, finding Hunter a few paces behind me, eyes darting from one side of the hall to the other.

Safe.

I was safe.

For now, at least.

23

KILLIAN

TODAY

Would a jury believe I tripped over a nonexistent bump in the carpet, with my knife in hand, and stumbled into that Davis fucker, accidentally stabbing him directly in the heart?

It sounded legit to me, and the CIA trained me to be one hell of an actor, so....

The feel of a hand on my thigh had me stiffening. Without looking, I knew it wasn't Millie. Hers never made ants crawl under my skin. There was no control or possessiveness in her hold. Unlike the one now inching higher on my thigh. Swallowing down the guilt and disgust, I turned with a grin at the woman who cornered Millie in the bathroom, Davis's wife.

With her sitting so close, and this time me not focused on restraining my murderous thoughts, the pallor of her skin and the sweat lining her hairline were obvious. There was even a slight tremble in her fingers as they tightened along my thigh. Though her gaze was zeroed in on my shoulder, the fear behind her eyes was unmistakable.

"What did you think of class?" she asked in a monotone voice that sent a pulse of alarm through my system.

"It was great." I leaned back in the uncomfortable chair and stretched both arms out wide, one along the back of the empty seat to my left and the other along hers. A shiver of revulsion spread from the small contact with her hair despite no skin-to-skin contact. That was the only positive to the stuffy fucking suits my arrogant persona wore. "The theory of talking to my wife to ensure she understands my expectations and needs is solid. Though that hasn't really worked in the past. She consistently fails to meet the baseline of what someone of my family's caliber requires."

"And what's that?" she asked.

"How we are viewed is everything. It's why we are here. For her to get her shit figured out and for me to connect with Pastor Paul." Her brows rose a fraction before schooling her features.

"And why is that, Kurt?" I turned at the sound of Davis's voice. His smile widened when his gaze landed on his wife's hand on my thigh.

I stood, enjoying the fact I towered over the slimy fucker. "Pastor Paul has surrounded himself with powerful friends and knows half of DC. After his fight for this place's religious freedom, which he took to Capitol Hill, it proved his power. I want in on that. The company I built is just the first step to where I want to be. At the fucking top, where my family always lands." I cut my gaze to his wife and bit my lower lip. "And the other benefits of this place are becoming more and more enticing."

"You're correct on many points," Davis chuckled. "I don't normally do this, but I'd like for you and your wife to join us tonight for dinner. Our house is in town, not on the church grounds. It would be an honor to talk in depth regarding all the ways Pastor Paul and the leadership team here at The Union of Blessed Souls can help you achieve all your goals."

With a fake-ass smile, I held my hand out and shook his. "Just let me know when and where."

After releasing my hand, he held it out toward his wife and dragged her away. A calming presence paused beside me, and my genuine smile pulled at my lips.

"Dinner. Really?" Millie grumbled behind the bottle of water hovering over her lips.

"You wanted to talk with her," I said under my breath so no one close could hear our conversation. "And maybe we could do a little snooping. You said he's at the top of the food chain here, right?" That pink hair slid forward with her slight nod. "Fuck, I love that hair on you. So damn sexy."

The corners of her lips twitched, only to tug down in a slight frown. "Then why haven't you... why haven't we... you know?"

My stomach tightened, knowing exactly what she meant. Fuck, how could I explain what this place was doing to me, what pretending to be this person made me feel like, and how it affected me on a cellular level? Plus, what I had to do in the classes, the posturing and touching. It was too much, and at the end of the day, safe with her, all I could do was shut down.

"Later," I said, turning to Millie. "Back at the cottage." Her responding nod was hesitant as she stared at a blank spot on the wall instead of flicking those dark brown eyes up to me. "Trust me."

"I do," she whispered. "I always have."

Before I could voice how much that meant to me, one husband in the class came up and started a conversation. Not wanting her soothing presence to vanish, I wrapped an arm around her shoulders and held her close to my side. I didn't give a fuck what it looked like to the teachers and leadership team.

I needed my Millie.

Or I was seconds away from burning the whole place down.

THREE LONG-AS-HELL HOURS LATER, the late afternoon breeze whipped through the open golf cart we rode in together. My loose, long blond strands smacked at my face as I kept my gaze straight ahead. In the last class, they separated us again, and I was not okay.

Not by a fucking long shot.

I eyed the security fucker driving the cart slower than a damn slug, as if he could feel my pulsing urgency for Millie and was being a dick by taking the longest route while barely pressing on the gas pedal.

"Hurry the fuck up," I snapped, unable to take it any longer.

Instead of looking pissed, he smirked over his shoulder. "I can only imagine how it is after all those classes," he chuckled. "I'd be worked up, too."

Blowing out a calming breath, I fixed my cocky smile in place and leaned forward, both forearms pressed to the seat beside the asshole.

"I don't know how you do it. Seeing all the… options… all day every day but not being able to participate." I wasn't sure if that was true or not.

"Oh, we're well compensated." Lead filled my stomach at the way he said the word compensated. "We all believe in Pastor Paul's vision, knowing he's the way to true enlightenment." Oh, poor man, he was simpleminded. I should cut him some slack, but I wouldn't. "During the leadership meetings while they meet and fuel Pastor's visions." There was that phrase again about fueling his visions. I really didn't want to know more about that, but it was my fucking job to understand all aspects of this place, even if it made me want to jump out of this moving cart into a tank of hungry alligators. "We're on point, making sure no one interrupts. If everything goes smoothly, we're taken care of later."

The cabin Millie and I shared came into view as we rounded a bend.

"Everyone here seems on board with everything Pastor Paul says. What happens if they disagree?"

The man's lips tightened into a straight line, the edges turning white. "They won't if they truly understand the light and the sacrifices Pastor Paul makes to ensure we're on the path to being saved."

"But what if they did?"

"Then they leave."

"On their own?"

He said nothing until we stopped in front of the cabin. I shifted to step out but paused when his soft words hit my ears.

"I'll only say this once." Gaze locked on me, he sat up straight and braced a forearm on the steering wheel. "Because I can see you want to find somewhere to belong, to uncover the full potential of your life—"

"And you think my wife is fucking hot?" I hated the huffed words.

He smirked, staring at Millie like he'd done most of the drive. "That helps, too. I sure as hell wouldn't mind those seconds if you ever make it to the leadership team." Well, fuck. I was on such a good roll, not having premeditated murderous thoughts in the last hour, but this asshole had to go and ruin that streak. "But no one is keeping anyone here against their will. Hell, the FBI has been here before, trying to shut us down. But they can't because everything is consensual and between legal adults."

"So, if my tastes are slightly... darker?" I arched a questioning brow. The insinuation in those words made me want to punch myself in the dick. With brass knuckles. Adorned with spikes. That were on fire.

"Then you'll need to find that outside of the church grounds." He didn't say I couldn't participate in said darker kinks, just not here on-site. Made me wonder what the houses off-site might hold. "But take it from me, follow the rules, believe in Pastor Paul, and everything will be good. This, he, is the way to true happiness."

"And you're happy after this light business he's selling?"

His smile grew. "Fuck yeah, I am. I was miserable as shit before taking an online enlightenment class. After that day, I was hooked. Sold all my shit in Nebraska and moved here to be fully immersed into the community. Pastor Paul gave me a job and believed in me. That's more than I ever had in my old life."

I nodded and stepped out of the cart, fingers moving to button my suit jacket. "Good to know. Thanks for the lift."

"Mr. Culler mentioned you two are invited to dinner at their place." I dipped my chin in acknowledgment. "I'll have a cart come get you and a car waiting to take you at seven."

The sputter of the small engine filled the air as he took off down the path. If I had my gun, I could take him out, putting a bullet in the back of his head. Everyone would assume it was just an unfortunate golf cart accident. Surely they wouldn't notice the 9mm bullet lodged in his brain.

"You coming inside or just hanging out there all day like

a weirdo?" Small pebbles crunched beneath the soles of my shoes as I spun around to face Millie. Her dark eyes scanned my face. "You look like you're devising some diabolical plan to take over the world."

"Or kill one motherfucker who dared to acknowledge how fucking attractive my wife is," I offered. Shoving both hands into the pockets of my slacks, I strode to the door. "He's not wrong. I just have this urge to cut out the tongue of anyone who voices it out loud in front of me."

She blinked up at me, slightly shocked at the anger and truth in my words, no doubt.

"Did you kill him?"

My head tilted to the side. "You're smart enough to know if he were dead, he couldn't drive off into the sunset on that dumbass cart he drives like a ninety-year-old with vision problems."

"Pretty sure all ninety-year-olds have vision problems." A smile pulled at her lips, taking my breath away for a single heartbeat. Fuck, she was perfection personified. Everything about her was made for me. "But not the security guy; Chad Parker, from school."

A low growl rumbled in my chest at that name. "Why the fuck are you thinking about that douche?" Worry rushed through me. I gripped her shoulders in a demanding hold. "Did someone hurt you?" My lip curled as I stormed into the cabin, searching for that motherfucker Hunter. "Where was he? Where the hell was that fucker whose only job is to keep you safe while you were—"

A hard tug on my jacket whirled me around.

"Killian," she whispered. "I need you to calm down, okay? Take a deep breath and just... I need rational Killian back, please." My eyes narrowed, which made her laugh. "Forget I mentioned whatever his name was. Come sit down and talk to me. I don't think I've ever seen you on edge like this."

Falling onto the couch, I released the band holding my hair and ran my fingers through the long strands. Millie sat on the opposite end and curled both knees to her chest.

"Talk to me," she said. "Tell me what's going on in that brilliant mind of yours." I snorted and leaned forward, pressing both elbows to the top of my thighs. "If this is too much, then we'll leave."

My head whipped her way. "What?"

"Kill, your mental health is more important than this assignment. Someone else can come in during the next set of marriage classes this fall."

"But it might be too late for her," I muttered, thinking about that poor girl from the other night. "We're here for Karigan."

Millie nodded. "We are, but—and this might make me selfish—I'm more worried about you. I don't like seeing you hurting and on edge. When I suggested we do this, I did not know it would take this kind of toll on you."

"And it's not on you?" I said with a fake laugh. "Don't think I haven't noticed you're not sleeping." She quickly looked away, clearly hiding something. "What?" She shook her head. Reaching across the distance between us, I gripped her ankle and tugged. Her squeal of surprise filled the space, coming to an abrupt halt when I wrapped an arm around her to settle her on my lap. "Tell me."

She worried at her lower lip. "It's not me having the issue sleeping," she whispered.

It took a second for her words to make sense. "You're waking up because of me."

With a sigh, she leaned her head on my shoulder and wrapped an arm around me. A relaxed sigh brushed past my lips. "You don't have to tell me anything you don't want to, but I think you need to let some of your past go. Talking about it is the best way to do that. You know it is, even if you don't want to admit it."

Her soft hair brushed along my cheek. "There are some things better left buried than letting those toxic memories infect your mind, too." She didn't say a word, simply held me as tight as I held her, allowing me a moment to absorb her comfort. Suddenly, the words bubbled out, with me unable to stop them. "I'm terrified." I swallowed hard. I put that out there and had to follow it up with an explanation. "Not only about our current fucked-up situation, that I won't be there when you need me, but that I'll ruin you."

"How would you do that, Kill, when I feel the safest I've ever felt when you're near me? Even when you're not, it feels like you're out there watching over me." I cringed, knowing there was a slight truth to her words that I hadn't admitted to. Soon. Maybe she'd be turned on by my stalkerish tendencies when it came to her safety and my obsessive need to check in on her.

That was a strong and hopeful maybe.

"I've done a lot of horrific shit because of orders. I couldn't question the why or even balk at the way they wanted me to obtain the information needed. What if my past catches up with me and puts you in the crosshairs? What if this inky darkness that taints me from the inside out spreads to you?"

Palm to her cheek, I urged her back enough to look down into her searching gaze.

"I won't be your ruin, Millie, and that's exactly what I'll do. But I can't walk away from you, either. I won't. That makes me a fucking bastard because I should, and I know I should."

"What about what I want?" she asked, heat in her tone. "Did you ever think to ask me what I wanted or explain why you feel the way you feel?"

"You have no idea what lives in my head, Millie."

"Then tell me," she snapped. "Give me a glimpse inside so I can help you, Killian. Let me fucking help you."

My lips pursed, trying to keep the words unspoken, but the determined look in her narrowed eyes cracked my defenses. It was time to tell her, at least let her have a glimpse inside my darkness. What she did from there, how she reacted, was the ultimate test for us as a couple.

"I don't know how it happened, but this group of arms dealers I infiltrated, thirteen months into the assignment, discovered I wasn't who I said I was." My stomach rolled, remembering the utter terror that flowed through my veins when I realized they knew. "I was in Argentina, at their compound, and..." I shook my head to quiet the memories that attempted to swallow me whole. "I was held for two months."

"Killian," she whispered against the skin of my neck. "How did you get out?"

"After everything they did and barely giving me enough food and water to stay alive, they assumed I was too weak to attempt an escape. But do you know what they didn't account for?"

"That you're a determined badass?"

My chest vibrated with a chuckle. "You."

She pulled back. "Me?"

"Every night, when I wanted it to be my last, I prayed that they'd just end it already instead of—" I cleared my throat. She didn't need their unique torture techniques and the resulting blinding pain in her head. "It was the memory of you that kept me going." My palms sealed to her cheeks.

"The hope that one day I'd get to see you again, hold you." I swallowed, the mounting emotions making my voice crack. "You're what got me through the absolute worst time in my life and have ever since. There hasn't been a day that you haven't helped me keep going."

Pulling her closer, I sealed my forehead to hers.

"Thank you for fighting," she whispered, "so we could be here."

"Deep in a sex-crazed cult, trying to liberate a child trapped in its clutches and possibly uncover other dubious acts?"

She huffed a laugh. "With me." Soft lips brushed against my own, sending a shiver down my spine.

"Not all of my scars are internal, Millie. My body is littered with physical reminders of what happened, what I went through."

Cold-ass hands slid along my neck and dove into my hair. "That's why I haven't seen you without a shirt on." I nodded. "Are you embarrassed?"

My shoulders lifted in a shrug. "Maybe. That's why when... in the past, when I needed an outlet, the woman knew upfront about my needs."

"Which were? You haven't said anything to me."

Damn, was that hurt in her tone?

"That goes back to the whole your touch is the only one I want, the only one that doesn't make me hate myself. Your touch is comforting. Even just you being close soothes the jagged edges of my broken soul. In the past, I made sure my partner for the night was restrained, and I never fully undressed, or I blindfolded them if needed. I don't let anyone see my scars unless it's absolutely necessary."

Like a drugged woman lying naked on a rotten mattress in a serial killer's basement. My scars didn't even cross my mind when I whipped the T-shirt off my back and laid it over her. Though considering the circumstances, I doubted Hudson even noticed.

"Show me," Millie demanded. "I won't... it doesn't matter, Killian. Scars or no scars, you're mine."

"Damn right," I practically snarled, before slamming my lips to hers.

Angling her head with a firm grip on her hair, I deepened the kiss, pouring all the worry and stress and pain from the conversation into her. And she took it all. Pulling the broken pieces of my soul back together with her unwavering commitment to me.

A hard knock on the door sounded through the room, but neither Millie nor I paid it any attention. At least not until it continued, shifting from demanding to impatient. Her soft sigh brushed against my lips as she pulled back.

Palms to her cheeks, I slid both back, pushing pink hair away from her face. "Guess our break from the current reality is over."

Her soft smile sent a wave of reassurance through me. "That might be, but we're not. Not ever."

Fuck, I hoped that was true.

Because if there were a point in the future where she wasn't in my life, it wasn't a life I'd want to live.

24

———

MILLIE

TODAY

My fingers thumbed along my thigh as I paced from one side of the cabin to the other before whirling around and taking the same steps all over again. Hunter and Killian continued to talk, their voices an inaudible murmur in the background as my brain worked in hyperdrive to help figure out our next steps.

"I hate to admit it, but that fucker is smart about how he's set this place up." I whirled around to face Killian, unsure where he was going with that statement. "Ensuring that everything on campus, in the main building, the surrounding cabins and homes is consensual—"

"Consensual, my ass. They're brainwashed and don't even realize it," I exclaimed. "They believe following his so-called visions and doing as they are told will help seal their happiness here on earth and for eternity. He's using their hope and desperation for a better life or fear of the unknown after death against them. That's not smart, it's manipulative."

Both of Killian's hands rose in the air in surrender as he shot a cautious glance over at Hunter.

"Cooper understands that and agrees," Hunter stated. "But what I think Coop meant with that comment was regarding how Pastor Paul has kept the FBI off their backs for so long, not how he indoctrinated his followers. He's smart because, unlike other cult leaders, he's not suggesting multiple wives or forcing underage girls to get married like other leaders have done in the past, which resulted in the group being shut down. Everything done here *in* the church's compound is perfectly legal."

A huff of acknowledgment was all I could muster. Leaning against the wall, I crossed both arms over my chest and glared at the carpet.

"You're too cute when you pout," Killian said with a hint of laughter in his voice.

Some of the muscle-tightening, migraine-inducing tension drained as I stared at his soft smile. It seemed his mounting strain and frustration from the last two days had eased a fraction. Hopefully, that meant tonight he'd curl up at my side instead of sleeping with distance between us. He didn't wake me up thrashing when he stayed over back at my townhome or that first night here. It made me think that skin-to-skin contact, him subconsciously knowing he wasn't alone, helped keep the worst of his memories from flooding him while asleep.

"I'm not pouting," I corrected. "I'm frustrated."

His head tilted one way, then the other, weighing my words. "So kind of like... pouting."

Both my hands flew into the air as I groaned. "Fine, maybe a little. I don't know what to do or where we go from here. We're taking the classes, integrating ourselves with the leadership team, and yet"—I stumbled over to the couch and fell onto the cushion beside Killian—"it feels like I'm even farther from finding the truth and helping these people than I was back home. Every day counts. Places like this ruin lives. Thousands are affected by The Union of Blessed Souls's bullshit every day. I guess I'm feeling helpless that we haven't really done anything and have no clue where to go from here."

Killian nodded and dropped an arm over my shoulder before pressing a kiss to the side of my head. "You know what helps me when I feel like I've hit a dead end?"

My shoulders lifted in a halfhearted shrug. "What?"

"I use one of my lifelines."

With a groan, I buried my face into both palms, no doubt smearing the makeup I carefully applied this morning. "Sometimes I don't understand you, Kill. What are you talking about?"

"*Who Wants to Be a Millionaire?*" Hunter stated, focused on his phone.

"I guess we all do?" I responded slowly, confused by his question.

He peeked up through long, dark lashes, a smirk playing at his lips. "Yes, I'm sure we all do, but Cooper is referencing the show, *Who Wants to Be a Millionaire*. It was a popular game show where they asked the contestants questions, and if they didn't know the answer, they could use one of three lifelines. Phoning a friend was one of them."

"You speak Cooper well," Killian praised with a nod. "We can stay friends."

Hunter's barked laugh echoed through the room, followed by his grumbling something under his breath with a smirk as he turned his attention back to his phone. A quick tap on the screen and a loud ringing blared through the speaker.

"Don't tell me you've killed Coop and now need to know

how to dispose of his heavy body," said the familiar, exasperated voice pouring through the phone.

"I'm offended that one, you think he could kill me, and two, that I'd be heavy," Cooper shot back with fake annoyance. "All that yoga makes me light as a damn feather."

"I don't think it works that way," I whispered loudly behind my hand.

"As you just heard, he's still here, Charlie. And surprisingly enough, I haven't had the urge to murder the fucker on this case. I think Dr. Anderson keeps him calm, less..."

"Verbose," Charlie grumbled at the same time Killian responded with, "Awesome."

"We're all here and calling you because," Hunter drawled, reminding everyone to stay on topic, "we keep going back and forth on the next steps, not getting very far. What have you uncovered on your end?"

Charlie's sigh rasped through the speaker. "Not fucking much. Since Millie mentioned the police chief and sheriff were probably members of that damn place or on their payroll, I did some digging after breaking through the station's firewalls. Unfortunately, that was a bust." His gruff tone told us all how pissed that made him. "Which is odd, because I should have at least found the redacted or changed case files of the murders, but there wasn't anything."

"Sounds suspect." Killian leaned back against the couch and rubbed a hand along his jaw. "So if they're not there, then you think the files could be somewhere else? Somewhere the police chief or sheriff consider more secure than the station's servers?"

"That's exactly what I'm thinking," Charlie offered. "Either it's on an external hard drive, flash drive, or maybe this Pastor Paul fuck is kicking it old-school and has the paper files."

"I can't imagine the police chief or sheriff not holding on to some kind of leverage against Gary Paul if either of them helped him cover up the orchestrated murders." Hunter tapped the phone against his knee. "They'd want blackmail material to cover their own asses if the truth was exposed."

"Charlie." I leaned closer toward the phone so he could hear me. "Can you run the county sheriff and everyone on the police roster against the known members list? Then maybe look at the church's donations to see if they 'donated' to the sheriff's election campaign or maybe nonprofits that support local law enforcement."

"I already ran the names against the followers list, but nothing hit. The funding angle is a great idea. I'll do some more digging. The group has several accountants working to keep the church and other lines of business in good graces with the IRS. If he made a charitable donation, the accountant no doubt itemized it somewhere to get the deduction. I'll call when I have more."

After Charlie hung up, Hunter shoved the phone into the side pocket of his slacks. "Dinner tonight. That should be fun."

Killian snorted. "Right, fun. Did you see that Davis fucker? He's hiding something."

"The fact I think he murdered his first three wives and probably already has plans to do it with the current one?" My voice held an inappropriately cheerful pitch. Guess Killian's humor rubbed off on me. "But you're right. He is hiding something else that requires him to live off the compound. Tonight, I still think it's worth a shot for me to convince his wife to tell us what that secret is."

"And I still don't think it's a good idea," Hunter sighed.

"She could be playing you. What if her role is to expose those who aren't there for the right reasons? It could get us kicked out before we've helped Karigan, or worse."

Locks of pink tickled my cheeks with the quick head-shake. We'd discussed this option at length earlier, but I'd hoped to change their minds. I knew I was right about Davis's wife. She was scared earlier. There was doubt she'd help us, but how much I should tell her was the debate.

I thought exposing who I was and how we could help her gain her freedom from this place would encourage her to open up. But Hunter and Killian both disagreed, claiming it was too much of a risk. I saw their point, yet if Davis's wife knew I had the power to help her escape, or more, was with the people who did, maybe she'd be more inclined to help.

"It's worth the risk." I twisted on the couch to face Killian. "You saw her. She doesn't have the same blitzed look in her eyes like the others. She was scared and warned me away. That makes me think if she knows who we are, the hope of escaping will overshadow the fear. We should have Charlie look into her background before we leave to give us insight into how she ended up here. Oh, and I'd love to know the woman's name while we're at it. I'm wondering if my research was dated and Davis is already on to wife number five."

"On it." Hunter's thumbs flew across the screen. "If we're taking that risk, there needs to be a hefty reward for us to expose our real reason for being here."

"Like what?" I questioned.

"An invitation," Killian mused. "To one of the leadership meetings. Or maybe a one-on-one meeting with Gary Paul. Hell, if she knew where those records were stored, that would be worth it for me." He focused an intense stare my way, holding my gaze for several seconds before nodding. "I trust your judgment. Just be certain she wants out before telling her who we are. It could be our lives on the line if she's playing you."

I swallowed hard and dipped my chin in a clipped nod.

Right. No pressure.

AN UNEASY FEELING bloomed in my gut as the car taking us to the Cullers continued to drive, taking us farther and farther away from the compound. When it finally turned down a long, gravel drive that cut through a thick cluster of trees, I shot a worried look across the car. It felt like we were experiencing the first act of a horror film.

Although the house we drove toward wasn't dilapidated or haunted looking. It appeared to be a newer build and well maintained. The single-story, mostly dark red brick with some pristine white siding, gave a cozy and welcoming feel. Blooming flower beds skirted the front of a white-painted wraparound porch, where the town car slowed to a stop.

Our hesitant footsteps hardly made a sound as we walked up toward the front door. Surrounded by the two men, I sensed their tension creep higher as they scanned the dark for threats. Trees surrounded us on all sides. The home sat in a large clearing, which was set so far back we didn't see it from the main road.

"If I were a serial killer," Killian said, his hand flexing against my lower back, "this would be exactly what I'd want for a home. Away from town, lots of raw acreage to dispose of bodies, and most importantly, no one around to hear my victims scream."

"Let's hope that's not the case with the Cullers," I

muttered under my breath. "Maybe he just likes the seclusion and space away from the compound."

"Oh, he's hiding something more sinister than any of us realize." Hunter kept in step beside me, head on a swivel, similar to Killian.

"What is your background?" I asked as my flats toed the edge of the welcome mat.

He shot me a curious look. "Marines. Detective. The FBI. Why?"

"You seem... diligent in how you assess the area for threats. Just made me wonder. Girlfriend?"

Killian's hand at my back tightened into a fist, which Hunter noticed and huffed a laugh.

"No. Can we talk about this when we're not about to walk into a serial killer's lair?"

"See?" Killian whispered as he reached for the doorbell. "He agrees with me. Perfect killing lair. I bet it even comes with a basement for all the—"

The wood door swung open, cutting Killian off. Davis stood on the other side of the threshold with a wide, all-teeth grin that made him look more menacing than inviting. I resisted the urge to take a step back, putting more distance between us, though whole states between me and the creepy asshole might not be enough.

"Welcome. Come inside, please." He gestured into the cozy entryway, the complete opposite of Pastor Paul's massive and opulent mansion. "I see you brought her handler along." Was that an undercurrent of anger in his tone? "Can't control your wife without help, Kurt?"

I don't pick up on sarcasm or subtle hints easily, yet even I heard the jab in his question.

Killian's hand wrapped around my waist and jerked me

to his side. I stumbled, feet tangling together at the unexpected possessive move.

"Just covering my bases. I didn't want to be saddled with keeping her at my side all night. I assumed we'd—just us—discuss my questions regarding the church and Pastor Paul, and how a partnership could be mutually beneficial. Leaving her unattended isn't an option."

Davis eyed Killian before sweeping that dark, assessing gaze to Hunter. After a moment, he nodded, and that wide smile was back.

"You're right, no need for the women to be in those discussions." I bit my tongue to keep from screaming at the arrogant prick. "They can work on the finishing touches for dinner. Though I have to ask her to remove her shoes."

Which was funny because he didn't ask me, instead kept his gaze locked on Killian. It was as if speaking directly to me was beneath him, even though he had before. Which, in his mind, maybe I was.

"Why?" Curiosity lightened Killian's tone.

"I prefer for the women who enter my home to be barefoot. Call me old-school." He laughed, but it held zero humor. "You know the saying, *barefoot and pregnant in the kitchen is the only correct place for a woman.*"

Davis's gaze cut to me as if watching for my reaction, but I angled my face to the floor so he couldn't see the anger and disgust whirling behind my eyes.

"Makes sense. Take them off, Marla. Do as our host asked."

After I slipped off my shoes and set both by the door, Davis offered brief directions to the kitchen as he and Killian moved toward a massive study just to the right of the foyer. My bare feet padded down the hall, the scent of something cooking a better guide than the directions Davis gave.

Each step, Hunter mimicked, keeping close to my back as we maneuvered through the dark together.

Palm pressed to the swinging door, I urged it open, giving myself a chance to assess what I would walk into before stepping into the room. Call me paranoid, but I couldn't shake the foreboding feeling that we were circling closer and closer toward a dangerous trap. The feeling of my stomach twisting in knots while an elephant sat on my chest, preventing me from taking a deep breath, grew worse with every passing minute.

Davis's wife, who I now knew was Carrie Culler, based on the information Charlie found, stood in front of the stove, smiling while she stirred something in a tall pot.

"Oh, hello." She turned to face me, a fake mask frozen in place. "Welcome. Did my husband send you to help me with dinner?" I responded with an uncertain nod and inched forward, each step hesitant. There was something very wrong here. Earlier in the day, she was open, clearly terrified, and okay with telling me to leave while I could. Yet now she looked like all the other women who mingled around the conference center, utterly fake. "Do come in. Let's not anger the men."

The slight tremble in her tone caught my attention. She turned back to what was cooking, the move giving the perfect angle to notice the swelling along her jaw and the super thick makeup that did little to cover the blooming bruise. My gaze slid down to the top of the black turtleneck she wore and the faint purple mark that barely peeked out.

Noticing my stare, she tugged the material higher, but that only drew my attention to the similar purple bruise that circled her dainty wrist.

"What happened?" I whispered, the words barely audible.

Her eyes went wide. The spoon clanged against the side of the pot when she dropped it to hurry over to me. Palms pressed on top of my shoulders, Carrie shot me a wobbly smile.

"So good to see you again." With that, she forced me into a hug, her arms banding around my back. I stiffened in the uncomfortable embrace. "He can see and hear everything in here."

"Good to see you, too," I offered with a light pat on her back before extracting myself. "You have a lovely home."

"Thank you," she rasped and hurried back to the stove. "Where are our husbands?"

"Talking, in the office." I scanned the room. Fuck, if he had this place covered in cameras, how would I get her to open up? The open bottle of red wine on the counter snagged my attention. "Any chance I can have a glass?" I swiveled to Hunter. "Just one, I promise."

His brows dipped, gaze zeroed in on the bottle, making it clear he didn't like that idea, considering the wine could be drugged. But surely they didn't invite us here to drug us all.

Right?

Carrie nodded and wiped both palms on the red-and-white-checkered apron around her waist. "Of course."

As Carrie pulled down a glass, Hunter nudged my side. "You're allowed one of these a night, too, if you want to step outside." I stared at the pack of cigarettes in his hand. It was on the tip of my tongue to tell him I didn't smoke, only to seal my lips shut to keep the comment to myself. "I'm sure they wouldn't mind if you two stepped out for a moment. I'm here and can keep you both safe."

As in, *keep watch and let us know if the men were on their way to find us.* It was a perfect excuse to escape her pretty prison for some privacy.

I met Carrie's wide eyes where she stood frozen, a glass in one hand and the bottle in the other. "Would that be okay? Do you have a back deck or something?"

"The food, it can't burn," she said. The bottle trembled, some of the wine splashing over the rim of the glass.

"I've got it covered," Hunter said. "If this one doesn't get her nightly cigarette, she's more of a handful than normal. Go. But be quick." He looked at me. "You know how angry he can get if you're not where you're told."

The soft pack molded beneath my grip. After taking the offered lighter, I spun on my bare heels and padded across the cold tile floor toward Carrie. Without another word spoken, we headed for the glass-paned french doors that led to the back and slipped out into the cool night air. Goose bumps sprouted along my arms, the light skirt and top not doing much against the wind, but I ignored the discomfort, knowing this might be my only chance to get answers. Though, annoyance helped heat me from the inside out. I wouldn't be so damn cold if my bare feet weren't pressed to the deck's wooden planks.

I took the glass of wine from Carrie and scanned the vast, wooded area. It made me wonder if part of the house rules of *no shoes for women* reduced the likelihood of us running. Only if your life depended on it would someone run into the dense forest without shoes.

"Even out here, we have to keep our voices down." Carrie paused beside me, her shoulder brushing against my own. "The camera out here is at my back, but with the low light, I doubt he could read our lips when he studies the recording later."

"He's done that before?" She just nodded. "Carrie, what—"

Tears filled her lower lids, glimmering in the faint light

pouring through the glass-paned doors from the kitchen. "You.... Say it again. Say my name, please."

The desperation in her voice broke my heart. "I know who you are, Carrie." A soft sob filled the air, swept quickly away by a wind gust. "What I don't know is what's happening here or what happened to you."

Her hands rubbed up and down her arms, the black material of her sweater bunching beneath her palms. "How do you know my name? Once we're married, no one may speak it except for the pastor and our husbands." The way she spat the two names told me everything I needed to know. "And this..." She gestured to her neck and face. "He wasn't happy that I talked to you in the bathroom. Said it set a poor example for others. I shouldn't take that initiative."

"Oh." Multiple degrees, and that was the only response I came up with. "He's bad, then." That response wasn't much better, but it was more than a single syllable, so it would have to work.

"Worse." Her voice broke. "He killed his other wives, and I know..." Carrie paused and looked out over the darkened backyard. "I know I'll be next once he's done playing with me. He's terrible. I'm constantly walking on eggshells, never knowing when the next attack will happen."

"Attack? As in the physical abuse happens often?"

"As in, he enjoys catching me unaware to force me to *take care* of him." Bile rose in my throat. "And then there is..." She drew in a deep breath. Trembling fingers slowly lifted the hem of her sweater, just enough for me to see the shallow slashes along her stomach and side. "He's a monster. They all are. That's why you have to run. Now, before they convince your husband to join the leadership team. Once he does, he won't want to leave, and you'll be stuck here, too."

"Why do you say that?"

"No man would leave what Pastor Paul offers them. When a meeting is called, all the leaders must attend with their wives. Based on the vision, we, the women, are shared amongst the leaders until Pastor Paul has enough strength to see what's to come."

"And you don't believe that?"

"I did, a long time ago, when I didn't know what went on inside the leadership team, before I was forced to marry Davis based on a vision. I didn't want to get married and begged the pastor not to make me. Do you know what he did?"

I shook my head. Remembering the reason for us being outside, I set the glass of wine on a table and pulled out a single cigarette, lighting the end the way I'd seen in movies.

Disgusting smoke filled my lungs with the first puff. "What did he do?" I croaked around a hacking cough. Smoking was officially disgusting.

"He told me it would all be okay, that it was my calling." My stomach roiled at the waver in her soft voice. "The night before the wedding, Pastor Paul came to me, saying I was just nervous about sharing a marital bed, and he was there to fix that problem." She wiped at her leaking eyes. "That was the night I knew he was more evil than divine. The things he said and made me do..." She balled up her fist and pressed it to her lower stomach. "After he left me broken and sobbing in bed with my parents downstairs, I realized everything I believed in was a lie. The truth is, he's a power-hungry predator, just like the rest of them."

I swallowed down the unshed tears clogging my throat. "How old were you?"

"One day after my eighteenth birthday."

"Fuck." I lifted the smoking cigarette to my lips, this time careful to only pretend to take a drag. "Carrie, what would you say if I told you I could help? That you don't have to be stuck here with that man, but I'd need your help in return." Both her dark brows pulled inward. "Any information you have about the leadership team, anything illegal that you know is going on at the church or with Pastor Paul directly. We came here not to join the cult but to shut it down."

Dark eyes searched mine before a determined look filled her features. Rolling both shoulders back, she wiped at her wet cheeks. "I want my freedom. I want a real life away from this bullshit." Leaning in even closer, her lips brushed along my hair. "What if I told you I know Gary Paul and others had a hand in covering up other leaders' and teachers' deaths?" When she pulled back, I caught a sparkle in her eyes, one that screamed *hope*. "And I know who helped them."

Perfect.

"I'd say talk fast."

And she did. Spilling all the dark secrets of The Union of Blessed Souls.

Exactly what we needed.

25

KILLIAN

TODAY

The edge of the fork dug into my palm beneath my white-knuckled grip. Forcing myself to move, I stabbed at the last of my salad and shoved it into my mouth. As I chewed, I glared at the motherfucker still staring at my wife like he'd done through the entire meal. After what he told me in the office, I knew exactly what was going through his head.

He was a sadistic motherfucker.

"Kurt's wife." Millie's gaze slowly rose to the end of the table, where Davis sat. "How are you enjoying the classes?"

Millie's throat worked as she swallowed a mouthful of wine. The glass trembled as she slowly lowered it back to the table. "Very enlightening."

"That they are," Davis praised. "Next week, the classes focus mainly on the wife's purpose in the marriage and will help guide the husbands on your training."

"Training?" she squeaked.

Nostrils flaring, I worked to calm the rage boiling in my veins. "Tell me more about this training," I somehow got out through my clenched teeth. If I didn't crack a molar by the time we left, I'd be shocked.

"Tell?" Davis's smirk made me freeze. "How about a demonstration? Wife," he barked. "Here."

The scrape of chair legs along the floor snapped my attention to Carrie, who now stood and stepped to Davis's side. I masked my shock when she lowered down to her knees and bowed her head. That smirk still firmly in place, Davis patted the top of her head like one would a dog.

"Knowing it makes me happy and understanding the consequences of not obeying, my wife does exactly as I say. I enjoy having her at my feet while I eat, knowing she's within reach if I need her."

A quick glance at Millie, and I almost cursed at her ghostly pale face.

"Kurt, give it a try. Your wife might not be as obedient, but the punishment part is a part of our fun."

Millie's panicked eyes met mine, and I swore I heard her begging me not to make her kneel at my side. My stomach churned with indecision. What the fuck was the best option? Make her do it to keep cover, or kill Davis, eliminating one sick bastard from the world?

I swallowed hard and nodded, lips parted to respond, when the chimes of the doorbell rang through the home. Davis's lips dipped into a frown, face turning toward the front door. After wiping his lips, he tossed the used napkin onto his plate and turned to his wife.

"Don't move." With that, he shoved back from the table and stormed out of the room.

The tension sitting heavy in the room lightened the moment he was gone. I slouched back against the high-back chair and rubbed my eyes. Millie rubbed her temples in tiny circles. I didn't dare look at Carrie, knowing I'd break cover and yank her off the floor to sit in Davis's seat, where she belonged.

Voices filtered down the hall.

I knew exactly who had interrupted dinner, and I wasn't sure if I was thankful or annoyed. The two men appeared in the wide door frame, still talking. I eyed Davis and Pastor Paul, wondering if this was some kind of ambush. Muscles bunched, I shifted in the seat, ready to fight them off with the dull dinner knife, but a small figure shifted from behind Pastor Paul.

What the fuck is Karigan doing here?

THE DOOR SLAMMED SHUT behind me, the force shaking the whole fucking cottage. Stripping out of the suit coat, I tossed it over the back of a chair and pulled the hair tie from my hair. The stiff cushions barely moved beneath my weight when I flopped onto the small couch, arms stretched out wide along the back, taking up the entire thing.

I tracked Millie as she paced back and forth, dainty fingers drumming along her thigh as she worked through the same frustration and disgust that raced through my veins. By the door, Hunter had a green tint to his skin, telling me he was seconds away from losing his dinner. The dinner Davis made him eat in the kitchen, away from us, because he was considered "the help".

Fucking bastard.

Fingers threaded through my hair, I pulled hard, hoping the bite of pain would center me enough to think.

"That's why," Millie muttered to herself. "That's why he

had her parents killed. He wanted her as his wife this whole time." Pausing, she swiveled, her long, loose skirt fanning out with the move. "Karigan's aunt, the one who called the FBI and started all this, said her sister acted strangely, scared even, the month before the murders. Maybe Gary Paul had approached them, hoping they would offer Karigan without a fight." Her groan of frustration filled the room. "But why would they name him as her guardian in their will?"

I nodded as she spoke, also working to unravel how this shit show came about. The moment Pastor Paul walked into the Cullers' house, right at the end of dinner, I tensed, knowing shit was about to go down. And fucking hell, I was right. I was so distracted when he described his now-clear vision, I left the yummy chocolate cake untouched. Per Pastor Paul, Karigan was the future of the church, as his fucking wife.

I rubbed at my grumbling stomach and stood to rummage through the emergency snack stash. The crinkle of the foil bag filled the cottage as I ripped open the veggie chips. Shoving one into my mouth, I settled back on the couch, stilling when I felt eyes on me. Millie's smiling face watched me with a slight headshake at the surprisingly scrumptious treat.

"What? I can't think on an empty stomach."

"We just ate." Her giggle softened the edges of my anger, though my thirst for vengeance still rode me hard. There was a fun, kind of aerobic, way to ease the mounting frustrations, but that couldn't happen until Hunter left.

"It's his thing." Hunter stood straight from where he slouched against the wall. "I don't think we've had a team meeting where he didn't munch on something."

"The documents could've been created and signed, giving Gary Paul guardianship of Karigan before he approached them about marrying their only daughter." I shoved another cardboard-like chip into my mouth. "Or it was forged after the fact." That was my bet.

"If it's a forgery, then it's a hell of a good one. I can't see any flaws or differences in signatures," Millie offered.

"But you haven't seen the original copy," I countered. "We only have the scanned documents. There could be evidence of tampering on the original document that doesn't come through with the copies we have."

"There is always AI, too." I turned my focus from Millie to Hunter. "With how quickly that technology evolves, I bet there is some type of AI that could mimic a signature, which could be the copy we have, while the original documents state the truth in their wishes for their daughter if something happened to them."

The bag crumbled in my hand, and I tossed the small ball into the trash can beside the TV.

"None of that matters, really. That girl was drugged out of her mind tonight." I winced, remembering her glassy eyes and sluggish movements. The manipulator said she was still on medicine to help her through the grieving period, but I called bullshit.

Millie held up a hand, using her fingers to tick off her theories as she spoke. "He's keeping her drugged for one or all of the following: One, so she won't run. Two, to keep her from telling others what really happened that night. Three, to make her more susceptible to his manipulations and lies." Millie rubbed at her temples as if warding off a migraine. "Who knows what kind of brainwashing techniques he uses during those so-called 'therapy sessions' he told us about. She's in a vulnerable state, which makes her more susceptible to believing any well-constructed lie. Hell, they might alter her memories so she doesn't know what's real and what's not."

"But kind of like the will thing, why she's drugged or what's going on behind the scenes, it doesn't change our goal." I leaned back against the couch and motioned for Millie to join me. The insistent pacing added another layer to my tension with every tiny footstep. Plus, I needed to touch her and know that she was safe at my side, despite the dangers surrounding us. "Millie needs a chance to talk with Karigan, one-on-one. That's our priority. What did Carrie tell you?"

I wrapped my arm around her shoulders, sealing her side against mine. Millie's cotton-candy pink head leaned back, resting on my bicep and soothing some of my buzzing worry.

"We didn't have too much time outside." Her head rolled along my arm to look at Hunter. "Great idea on the smoke break to get us out of the house and away from the cameras." He shrugged like the brilliant idea wasn't that big of a deal. Which it was—huge, in fact—if Millie was able to pull information out of Carrie. "When I asked her why she didn't go to the police after everything..." Millie's voice cracked on that word, making my brows pull in as I studied the deep line between her brows. I'd have to find out what she meant by *everything* later. "She said the police chief is on the church's payroll. She wasn't sure how, but the chief not only helped cover up the few suspicious deaths but also the death of Davis's previous wives. When I asked her if the police chief was a member, she said no, which makes me wonder." She looked up into my face. "Maybe the theory of blackmail material hidden away somewhere isn't such a long shot. But I'm not sure how we'd know for sure, considering Charlie couldn't find anything."

A slow smile pulled at my lips, spreading across my entire face.

"I have a brilliant idea." Both she and Hunter shot me skeptical looks. "Don't worry. It will be easy." Whipping out my phone, I tapped on the Amazon app. "We just need to order a few things first." Lips pursed, I studied the size of Millie's head. "What size balaclava do you think you need?"

"*THIS* IS YOUR BRILLIANT IDEA?" Millie hissed as I secured the black beanie over her pink hair.

Amazon's next-day shipping to the off-site hub locker and the wide range of clothing perfect for breaking and entering made tonight easy to prepare for. Instead of responding, I bopped the end of her button nose. She hissed like an angry kitten and tried to swat my hand away.

Fuck, she was adorable.

How I allowed my trauma to push her away while I drowned in the overwhelming shame and guilt of the persona I was forced to play after we arrived was unacceptable. I hurt her and myself by not opening up and explaining. After exposing the dark scars littering my soul, I immediately felt lighter, allowing myself to move past the memories and focus on her. Which I did several times last night and this morning in my desperate attempt to make up for those two dumb days when I didn't seek comfort in her touch or listening ear.

Now we stood a block away from the police chief's home, preparing to do a little snooping. Taking Millie on this crazy outing wasn't my first choice, but I couldn't leave her back at that creepy cult's compound unprotected. At least here she was with me, safe. Sure, the situation was slightly dangerous, but I wouldn't be able to focus on what needed to be done if she were back at the cottage, alone and vulnerable.

Because this also required Hunter's help.

Plus, if we got caught, I could easily hide Millie in a cabinet or similar tight space while I manipulated my way out of trouble. How was I so sure I could sweet talk my way out of being arrested when caught red-handed breaking and entering?

Because I was fucking good and had done it before.

And the police chief was a single woman. I wasn't above using my unnaturally good looks to our advantage. If we were caught—this was my plan, so I highly doubted we would—I'd seduce the granny panties off her if that meant keeping our cover and giving Millie the opportunity to escape. Would I hate myself after? Absolutely. But this was bigger than me. I'd suck it up and do what needed to be done like I had so many times before, all for the greater good.

Greater good.

That was what my father believed in all those years with the CIA and what made him hyperfocused on me following in his footsteps. My mom, the love of his life, was murdered during an overseas trip by a terrorist group the CIA knew about but didn't have enough intel to shut down when they planted a bomb outside her hotel. She wasn't the target, but that didn't change the outcome. I was left without a mother, and Dad became the worst version of himself.

At least until I was held captive for those two months. The blinding fear, wondering where I was, what happened to me, and if he would ever see me again, changed his tune.

When I woke up in a Guatemalan hospital, somehow making it that far barely alive and through the jungle, he was there at my bedside and very different. While I recovered, he did everything in his power to get me out of that fucked-up agency and over to the FBI. After he secured that, he retired and hadn't looked back once.

He was the key driver in my decision not to reach out to Millie after I left the CIA. Even though I was out of my past, everything that I had done for the 'greater good' could come back to haunt me. Which, in his mind, meant never having someone you truly cared about. It left you too vulnerable. That was probably why he'd been married and divorced more times than I changed my sheets.

"Killian?" Millie whisper-shouted as she shoved my arm.

Aww, it was like being pushed by a baby panda.

"We need to get you self-defense training," I muttered.

"Where did you go?"

My head tilted to the side. My black cap kept my hair away from my face despite the wind. "I'm standing right here. Are you having an aneurysm?" I placed the back of my hand against her forehead.

"What? Kill…." Her head fell forward. "First, you cannot tell if someone is having an aneurysm like that, and second, I meant you got this far-off look in your eyes and literally froze." I glanced at my hand that hovered midair. Huh. "I think we need to increase our sessions to daily," she grumbled while tugging on a pair of tight gloves.

"I'd love to work your body daily, sweet cheeks," I practically purred.

"I meant therapy sessions."

"It's physical therapy."

"You're impossible. You know what I meant."

I did, and honestly, I wasn't sure if I was okay with

uncovering every dark part of me to my Millie. Yes, she was trained and probably the only one I would feel comfortable enough to talk to, but I didn't want her to look at me differently. Though the way I felt after our impromptu counseling session earlier was proof that I needed to talk to someone.

"Can you two focus, please?" Hunter snapped beside me. Leaning against a tree, both arms crossed, he glared my way. "Two minutes until Charlie sets off the police station alarm. We better hope that drags the chief out of bed at one in the fucking morning."

"So grumpy," I whispered to Millie, making her giggle. "We're all set here. Now all we can do is wait."

We didn't wait long. Five minutes later, the chief's car flew past our hiding spot in the neighborhood park. Not wasting a second, I gripped Millie's hand in mine. With a curt nod to Hunter, who would be our lookout man for the night's activities, I tugged Millie toward the chief's home, ensuring we stuck to the shadows.

We hurried on silent steps, only pausing to carefully swing the side gate open and slip through the small gap. Tension kept my muscles tight as we approached the back door. Slipping the lock-picking kit—again, thank you, Amazon—from my pocket, I released a steadying breath and got to work on the multiple locks securing the home.

Millie shifted side to side beside me, her nervousness almost palpable. The click of the final lock disengaging felt like a thunderclap in the otherwise silent night. Shooting a hopeful look to Millie that Charlie was able to successfully disengage the home alarm and cameras, I twisted the doorknob and pushed. The wood groaned as it separated from the door frame, but no alarm blared through the night, warning everyone in a five-mile radius of the danger.

Millie's hand in my own, I pulled her behind me as I

stepped into the small kitchen, closing the door softly behind us.

And that's when it happened.

The unexpected.

One step deeper into the kitchen had the entire night going to shit.

26

MILLIE

TODAY

The scream of an alarm seemed to vibrate through the darkened kitchen. Both palms slapped over my ears to dull the…

Wait.

That wasn't an alarm. It sounded like… a cat's pain-filled screech? Squinting as if that would help my vision in the dark, I searched the kitchen. A small shadow darted, nails scratching along the tile, its disgruntled hisses and meows growing quiet as it bolted away.

Hand on my heart to keep it from beating out of my chest, I heaved in deep gulps of air, hoping my lungs would quickly remember how to function. Eyes wide, I stared at Killian, who, with the low light pouring through the windows, looked just as shocked as me.

"Was that a demon?" he whisper-hissed.

I shook my head, the panic suddenly morphing into a hysterical giggle. I pressed a fist against my lips to quiet the unexpected and inappropriately timed laughter.

"Cat." That was all I could manage now that my hysteria completely overtook all common sense. Bending forward, I sealed a palm across my lips to stay silent as tears leaked down my cheeks. "You stepped on her cat."

"So, a demon." Killian's white teeth flashed in the faint light with his exaggerated grimace. "Just kidding, I'm a cat and dog person. Just ask my new bestie out in LA. His animals loved me." He turned in the direction the cat ran, brows pulled in tight. "Pretty sure I stepped on its tail. I should go apologize. Bad juju for this B&E is the last thing we need."

My fingers gripped the soft cotton of his snug, black long-sleeve Henley, keeping him in place. "Focus."

"But I feel bad. What if I broke something?"

"It ran out of here fine. I'm sure it's okay, and you approaching it will only make it even more terrified."

Killian faced the open doorway, lips curved downward. "You sure?"

Oh, my goodness. The genuine worry in his tone melted my heart even more toward the man. He was a deadly spy, went through hell, based on what he's told me, and yet, still had the same heart that made me fall for him all those years ago.

My arm snaked around his waist. "We don't have much time. The chief could come back sooner than we expect. Let's go look for those files we hope are here somewhere. We need that concrete evidence for the FBI to have a reason to investigate and shut that group down."

With a clipped nod, his features shifted, the forlorn look gone and replaced with steely determination.

"You're right." Finding my hand again, he threaded our fingers together and led me toward one of the two doorways. "Let's go snooping."

Light from the streetlamps streamed through the slats of the thin metal blinds, giving enough visibility to move through the living room with ease. After a quick squeeze, Killian released my hand and motioned to the opposite side of the room.

Guess that was my cue to be useful.

After getting past the multiple guards around the compound, we called a ride share, which was when Killian pulled me into his lap to whisper instructions for once we were inside the house. He would do most of the heavy lifting, but he walked me through what to look out for. Wall safe hidden behind pictures, beneath furniture, or even in the floor.

I didn't have the same gut instincts that he did, so I hoped I didn't fail him. Give me a person, a mind to analyze, and I was golden. This. This was beyond my expertise. They didn't teach expert-level snooping in any of the undergraduate, graduate, or doctoral classes I took.

The thrill of what we were doing had my heart racing and my hands shaking at my side. Evening out my rapid breaths, I shuffled around the room to inspect the walls and check behind the few pictures that hung there. A tan upholstered couch that seemed well-used sat in front of a massive TV. End tables sat on either end, and a single La-Z-Boy-type chair was the extent of the furniture. Despite the narrow, rectangular room, everything fit well, but the modern art on the wall clashed drastically with the classic furniture.

After lifting each frame to check for a hidden safe under the furniture and tapping along the floor, I waited for Killian to finish his more detailed search. Hands on his hips, he turned with a headshake.

Nothing.

Well, that made two of us.

This wasn't good. Some of the earlier pulsing excitement bled into nervous energy. If we didn't find what we needed here, then our next stop was more... daring. We needed to find the blackmail material here, so we didn't need to move forward with Plan B: breaking into the police station tomorrow night.

In two strides, Killian was beside me and wrapping those thick, strong fingers through my own. Urging me forward with a gentle pull, we slipped into the almost pitch-black hall.

I swallowed hard.

Hopefully, Killian knew what he was doing.

Because I sure as hell didn't.

27

KILLIAN

TODAY

We had little time, thirty minutes at best, before needing to be long gone. We had to work fast.

Thankfully, Charlie found the building plans for the suburban home, so I knew the basic layout. The modest size made us question if our suspicions were wrong, considering the home was well within her pay grade. Someone accepting bribes or being paid off normally flaunted the extra cash. However, once we checked all her assets, we knew exactly where all that dirty money went. An expensive boat and a condo in Cabo and Florida were a little above her pay grade, plus she paid in cash. It was a major red flag, pointing to her being into something shady.

The squeak from the soles of my boots against the hardwood floor echoed through the dark. Paused outside the first door, I peeked my head in, finding the room set up like a normal guest bedroom. Not what we needed and terribly decorated. The chief had no idea what theme she wanted to go with. Modern, country chic, casual, it all mixed together like a shit stew. Shaking my head, I continued down the hall, tugging Millie behind me.

At the next door, I pushed it open with a single gloved finger. Inside the room sat a large mahogany desk, two club chairs in front, and two three-drawer metal filing cabinets along the wall.

Bingo.

A quick squeeze, and I dropped Millie's hand, stepping into the home office, knowing Millie would be right behind me. Hands on my hips, I turned in a circle, scanning the room to spot anything out of the ordinary. Any small clue that would signal where the chief would hide the files or flash drive with the electronic case files we hoped were here.

Paused in front of one filing cabinet, I clicked on the pin light and stuck the thin metal cylinder between my lips. The top drawer slid smoothly along the track, immediately telling me this unlocked and in plain view drawer wasn't where she'd store the files. Any good blackmailer would know to at least lock the incriminating evidence away from snatching fingers like mine.

Dropped in a crouch, I tugged on the second drawer. Same results. The thin beam of light highlighted paper stuffed inside hanging folders. We didn't have time to go through each one, so I had to trust my gut. Quietly shutting it, I tried the bottom drawer, only to have it roll open with ease.

Fuck.

Quickly shifting to the next filing cabinet, I did the same with the three drawers, only to have the same results as the other. Turning to face the room, my assessing scan paused on Millie. A corner of her lips was turned down as she shifted her weight from one foot to the other.

"What?" I asked, sliding alongside her.

"It feels different," she whispered and repeated the

shifting motion. "Beneath my feet, this one spot gives differ-ently than the rest of the floor. It's solid, almost."

Immediately, I dropped to my knees, the polished planks smooth beneath my palms. Fingers dipped beneath the ugly-as-hell multi-color geometric rug, I carefully rolled it toward the desk, revealing... more hardwood.

Pin light in hand, I leaned closer, pressing where Millie's foot had been. There was a slight difference, firmer, as if covering a solid surface beneath instead of the open crawl space under the older home. Rough fiber scraped along my hands as I rolled the rug back even more, revealing a minus-cule notch in the hardwood.

Needing both hands, I bit the small flashlight's metal handle between my teeth and slid the lock-picking kit free. Tool in hand, I inserted the long, thin metal end into the small opening. The shadows shifted as Millie kneeled beside me. Using the flooring as leverage, I jimmied the square plank enough to wedge my fingers beneath.

Muscles straining to silently maneuver the heavy piece of removable flooring, I moved it to the side, leaning it against the edge of the desk. When I twisted back, the thin beam of light reflected off slate-gray metal. I cut my eyes to Millie and raised a hand for a high-five. She shook her head and pointed to the safe, shrugging her shoulders.

"Is this like charades?" I whispered after removing the light from my mouth. "Two words?"

"How will we get into a locked safe?"

Apparently, she wasn't in a playful mood. Which made sense. She wasn't used to this kind of thing, whereas I thrived in these moments. Excited energy thrummed through my veins, knowing this was an in-and-out mission. Hopefully, at least.

A soft, comforting pat on her ass made her sigh in exasperation. I turned back to the problem at hand. Unfortunately, it was a combination safe instead of one I could easily open with the lock-picking tools. We had little time remaining before the chief came back. Handing off the light to Millie, I slid my phone free and tapped Charlie's contact, sealing the smooth screen to my ear.

"What happened?" I smirked at the worry in his tone.

"Combination safe. We only have ten minutes left in our window. Help."

He cursed under his breath, and the sound of his fingers flying over the keyboard filled the background. While he did whatever a hacker did to uncover information, I shifted toward Millie.

"The chief needs to use some of those funds for an interior decorator. Clearly, she is horrible at it." Sitting up a little, I scanned the top of the desk and pulled a spiral-bound calendar down. Flipping through the pages, I handed it over to Millie, along with the light. "Here, memorize each month's entries." Her lids widened. "Don't give me that look. You can do it with ease, and the information might be helpful later on. I don't want to take it from the office. She would notice that missing and realize someone was in her home."

Taking the offered calendar, she flipped back to January and began scanning the entries.

Charlie cleared his throat. "Try her birthday. Eleven, thirteen, eighty-one."

My fingers made quick work by spinning the dial. I gripped the handle and tugged, but it didn't budge. "Not it. Seven minutes, Charlie."

"Fuck, I know. Hold on, let me check if she has siblings or close parents or—"

"Animal," I mused, thinking back to the kitchen incident. "She has a cat."

"Good thinking," Charlie murmured while typing at a rapid pace. "Son of a bitch. I swear you're a robot or something. She's obsessed with that animal, spending more on its food than her own, plus two monthly cat subscription boxes. Okay, let's check—"

"Try its birthday or maybe when she adopted it." He rattled off both dates from a random veterinary bill he pulled up. I immediately went to work spinning the dial to the first date he listed. The ticking clock inched up my anticipation with every turn. At the final number, I held a shallow breath, shot Millie a hopeful look, and tugged the handle.

The thick metal door groaned, its hinges doing little to help me lift the solid weight.

"I'm in." The phone clattered to the floor. Eyes locked on the inside of the safe, I carefully plucked the light from Millie's tight grip. The thin beam flickered over a tall stack of stuffed manila folders. Twisting one to read the tab, excitement bloomed. Instantly, I recognized the last name as one whom Millie suspected was murdered instead of what was reported in the public files. "Let's go through these and—"

The phone vibrated by my knee, the screen lighting up with a text from Hunter. Thumb to the smooth surface, I swiped it open, a muttered curse escaping after reading the urgent message.

"Time's up, sweet cheeks. We have two minutes to put everything back in its place and get out of here, or we're cooked." I stared at the files. "Let's only take a few files. Hopefully, she won't notice them missing anytime soon. Hold out your arms." Her small arms jutted out, and I went to work, pulling three thick files from the middle of the stack and placing them in her grasp. Shutting the safe, I replaced the square chunk of flooring and unrolled the rug back into place.

Grabbing everything we brought with us, I took the files from Millie and urged her toward the door. Just as we reached the back door, the vibrations and grinding gears from the garage door filled the kitchen. Millie glanced over her shoulder, panic clear in her dark eyes. Hand pressed to the small of her back, I shooed her out the back door, with me right on her heels. The door didn't make a sound as I sealed it closed and picked the deadbolts back into place. Kit back in my pocket, I scooped up the files from the ground and gripped Millie's hand.

"Stick to the shadows," I whispered into her hair. "Pretend it's real-life *Crossy Roads*, and we're the chicken."

Her glare was obvious despite the darkness.

With a shrug, I pointed to the side gate we came through earlier and started that way. Backs pressed to the flimsy stained wood fence, I held up a hand and waited. Each breath clouded in front of my face. Thirty tense seconds later, the light flooded the kitchen, and a shadow danced in the window. With the chief inside, I pushed open the gate and followed Millie out of the backyard, into the neighbor's, before picking up our pace.

As we jogged back to where Hunter waited, a slow smile crept up my cheeks.

What a fun and—bonus—successful fucking night.

28

MILLIE

TODAY

I softly flipped the folder closed and shoved it to the opposite edge of the coffee table. Horror at the injustice and grizzly crime scene photos made my stomach turn. Head back against the couch, both lids fluttered closed but immediately popped back open when the images flickered behind my lids.

We didn't have all the files, but what we brought back from the chief's house was the evidence needed to push the FBI into action. The problem we now faced was how to get the thick files to Rhyan. Which was what Hunter and Killian were currently debating, despite the late hour.

Three in the morning was way past my bedtime, especially for a school night.

Fuck, my life was boring.

My head rolled along the back of the couch, gaze landing on Killian, who sat beside me. Something told me with him, the term *boring* would never describe my life again. The idea of a future with Killian had my stomach fluttering with excited nerves. Tonight was a one-off for sure, but I knew Killian would keep me on my toes no matter the situation.

"It's the best option." Hunter looked utterly exhausted as he dragged a hand over his dark hair. "One more problem we need to address. How will we explain me sneaking back into the staff quarters at four in the damn morning?"

"Tell them we're into threesomes," Killian muttered. "And you're our convenient third when the mood hits us."

I choked on a laugh. "What?"

Killian just shot me a wink before continuing. "It's settled. Tomorrow afternoon, Hunter will take the case files away from this creepy-ass—slightly incestuous, if you ask me—town, and get them to Rhyan. Either mailing them, faxing, scanning—fuck, I don't care if it's by pigeon. They need these files before anything can happen. Hopefully, our team's new resident ME will find enough discrepancies in the autopsy findings to exhume bodies or some shit to reenforce the truth in these files. This"—he tapped the file in front of him—"is the evidence we need to shut this fucking place down."

"And save countless lives from the lies these people spew," I added. "But we still have a plan for Karigan, right? We can't leave her here to suffer. Who knows what will happen while we wait for the FBI to get their shit together. She needs out. Now."

Hunter looked at us. "This all sounds great to us. But you know not everyone here knows they are being mind-fucked by the pastor, right?"

I sat forward. "But in the long run, they will benefit from being told the truth."

"Agreed," he stated slowly. "But just know, when this goes down, lives will be ruined. They don't realize how much control they've given this place, and once it's gone, they will be left with nothing."

"So you're saying we shouldn't do anything?" Killian asked the question that was on the tip of my tongue. "Let them continue to live in this fucked-up bubble? That's some *Truman Show* shit." Killian turned to face me. "Great movie. Jim Carrey was fantastic. We'll add that to the ever-growing list of things you need to watch."

Hunter's brows arched. "Do you live under a rock?"

"In a book is more like it," Killian answered for me. "And she's just a baby."

I shoved at his shoulder. "I am not."

"Wait. How old are you?" Hunter gave me a quick, assessing once-over. "I thought it was just your small size—"

"Petite," I hissed.

"—that just made you look young."

"My birthday was in December, which makes me..." My words trailed off at the mention of my birthday.

The flowers.

Killian admitting to being in the CIA. Him having access to Charlie, a hacker genius at his fingertips.

"You sent the flowers," I whispered, more to myself than to the man sitting beside me. "Every birthday, you found me." My brows furrowed. "Except for the year I was married."

Killian cleared his throat and stood. "Well, I think that's all for tonight." Both arms reached up high toward the ceiling with an exaggerated yawn as he stood. "Damn, I'm tired. I think I'll just go to bed and get my beauty sleep. It's not easy looking this good—"

"Fuck no!" I shouted and stood to face him. "It was you. You sent the flowers. You knew I got married and divorced."

Shoving both hands to his chest, I relished in him stumbling at the unexpected assault.

"Well, shit. So, I'm just going to..." Hunter hooked a thumb to the door and didn't finish before racing out of the cottage like his ass was on fire.

I glared at Killian and crossed both arms over my chest.

He groaned at whatever he saw on my face. "Fine. Fine. We'll have this conversation now." Deflating, he perched on the edge of the couch and stared at his clasped hands hanging between his spread knees. "What do you want to know?"

My heart clenched at the exhaustion in his tone. It almost pushed me to wait for his answer, to talk about it tomorrow after some sleep. But it couldn't wait. I needed answers now. Sleep wouldn't happen until I knew everything.

"Why?" I asked.

"Why what, babycakes?" He rubbed at his eyes, refusing to look at me.

"Let's start with my birthday. Why send me anonymous flowers? Why not leave a note to let me know you were okay? Why stop that year I was married?"

"That's three questions."

"Killian," I groaned. "Just tell me."

"Fine." He slapped the top of his thighs and stood, turning to face me straight on. I tipped my head back to hold his gaze as he stepped closer. "You told me about your parents. I knew how lonely you were, even though they were still technically in your life. I wanted you to not feel so alone on your birthday, even if I wasn't there with you. Every year I found your address and sent the flowers anonymously. That year you were married...." He blew out a breath and squeezed his eyes shut. "You getting married gutted me. I barely remember the months after, lost in my grief and way too much booze." He cleared his throat and shifted his gaze to the other side of the room. "And while I'm confessing all my crazy, I'll admit to running a background check on him." My mouth gaped, jaw completely slack. "I needed to make sure he was a good guy and not some abuser or scammer. You're too trusting, Velma."

My lips opened and shut several times, but no words came out.

"Oh, and I might have slightly stalked you from a camera I had installed across the street." He cringed. "Nothing inside your townhouse, though, so there's that. I wanted to make sure you were safe and—"

I held up a hand, cutting him off. "You watched over me. You did all that to keep me safe?" His chin dipped in a hesitant nod. "Sent me flowers, no matter where I was, so I wouldn't feel alone on my birthday." Awe instead of anger leaked from my tone.

"It was all I could do, especially while on assignments. I couldn't let my father or others at the agency know how important you were—*are*—to me. My father thought I cut all ties. It's how I kept you safe from him for all those years. It was all I could do, even if it wasn't much."

I chuffed a humorless laugh. "Not much? *Not much?*" My voice rose with every word. "Those flowers meant everything to me, Killian. Everything. At first, it creeped me out, sure, but you were right. They made me feel less alone on a day that no one else acknowledged. It made the day easier knowing someone out there was thinking about me." I blinked, lashes wet from the unshed tears rimming my eyes. "I wanted it to be you so badly. I daydreamed that they were from you and that you were out there thinking about me but unable to come yourself. It further validated in my mind that you were somewhere that you couldn't leave."

"Like a cult," he rasped. Those aqua eyes scanned my face. "It wasn't just your birthday. I thought about you every fucking day we were apart. I never stopped loving you, my Millie."

I felt my eyes go wide. Those unshed tears rolled down my cheeks and dripped off my jaw. Calloused palms cupped my face, careful thumbs swiping away the tears with gentle strokes.

"You love me?" I rasped, the overflowing emotions making it hard to talk.

He nodded, watching my reaction with laser focus. "Like I said, I never stopped."

"Say it, please," I begged.

The worry lines along his face faded as a knowing smile curled his lips. "I love you, Millie."

A sob broke free, shaking my small frame. Closing both lids, I took a minute to let those words seep into my soul. For so long, I felt unwanted. By my parents, by other students or coworkers, by society because I didn't fit a certain mold. Yet here he was, saying he didn't only want me or love me, but he'd never stopped.

Which was good because neither did I.

And I was done holding back.

I launched myself at him. He grunted from the impact, and two strong, protective arms grabbed me beneath my ass to hold me steady as my legs wrapped around his hips and my arms circled his neck. Nose to nose, I gazed into those soulful aqua eyes and said the words I'd held in for so long.

"I've always loved you, too. I still do."

His lips crashed against mine, desperation from both sides seeping through the kiss. One hand slid up my back, dipped beneath my hair, and encircled the back of my neck, angling my head to deepen the kiss. The world swayed when he whirled around, each step toward the bedroom causing my core to grind against him.

"I hope you know," Killian said, pulling back slightly, "you'll never be rid of me now, my Millie."

"Good." I curled around him tighter, my face nearly suctioned to his neck. Reality tried to weasel its way into the moment, taking my focus from the amazing man holding me to the logistics of his words.

Where would we live?

Would he still work for the FBI in Dallas?

If I moved, was I really okay with giving up teaching at an Ivy League school?

"I can feel you thinking." Killian nipped at my ear. "It will all work out, Millie. We'll figure it out." He bent forward, patting my thigh when my back hit the bed, a silent request to release my tight hold. A soft chuckle escaped the gorgeous man at my exaggerated fake pout, but I did as requested. "How about I help distract you from everything going on in that brilliant mind of yours?"

My hair slid along the soft duvet with my eager nod. Killian chuckled while taking a step back. An unsure expression flashed across his features before he gripped the hem of his long-sleeve shirt. My heart pounded against my chest as he slowly stripped it off his toned body. Careful to keep my features neutral, I took in every beautiful inch of his abs and chest. Jagged, puffy scars littered his torso while straight slices left white marks along his pecs.

I felt his gaze, and I swear his chest didn't move while he waited for my reaction to his scarred body. The mattress dipped beneath my hands as I pushed up. Hooking a finger into the belt loop of his black tactical pants, I pulled him close. Peeking up through my lashes, I found his intense stare locked on me.

Without breaking his gaze, I brushed two fingertips along his abs. The bed shifted beneath me as I adjusted to sit up straighter. With a delicate touch, I kissed each scar, standing from the bed to reach the ones marking his chest. With every press of my lips, his heart raced faster, his chest rising and falling with quick, shallow breaths.

At the one right below his shoulder, I dared to suck on the skin, flicking my tongue along the mark. A grunted curse filled the room before hands gripped my shoulders and gently pushed me back to the bed.

"Fuck, Millie," he rasped, fingers working at his belt. "You couldn't be more perfect for me." His teeth sank into that plump lower lip as he swept a heat-filled gaze up and down my body. "Take off your top, babycakes, and let me see those perfect tits."

The black cotton brushed along my oversensitive skin as I tugged it over my head and tossed it and the basic black sports bra to the floor. Gaze fixed on Killian, I fought to swallow a desperate whimper. Pants hanging precariously on muscular thighs, his hand worked his thick length while staring down at me.

Arching a brow in challenge, I leaned back on both elbows, teeth sinking into my lower lip as I watched his hand. A low groan rattled past Killian's parted lips as he toed off his boots and allowed his pants to puddle to the floor before kicking them aside.

My jaw hung open. No words formed as I stared at his hot-as-hell naked body. Thick muscles bunched and strained as he bent over me.

"Keep that mouth open and I'll find something to fill it with, babycakes." An embarrassing whimper escaped.

"Hmm, sounds like you like the sound of my dick down your throat." I could only respond with an eager nod. "Later, I'll let you swallow my cock like a good naughty girl. Right now, though, I need to feel your cunt wrapped around my cock while I fuck the woman I love."

My heart stuttered in my chest, skipping a beat as he tore off my shoes and pants, leaving me naked on the bed, panting in anticipation. Palms to both inner thighs, he spread me wide, licking his lips while staring at my dripping center. One hand slid up my inner thigh to cup my core while the other moved up and down his long cock.

A single thick digit prodded at my entrance, sliding easily inside my drenched pussy. My lids fluttered closed, everything focused on the bursts of pleasure as he dipped in and out of me.

"Your cunt is absolutely soaked for me, babycakes. Is this greedy pussy weeping for me, begging for my cock to stretch it wide?" He added another finger, teasingly pumping them in and out. "Can I take you bare, Millie?"

My lids snapped open. "Yes." I moved against his hand, desperate for more. "Just, please," I begged. "I need you, Kill. I need you now."

Head tipped back, Killian released a guttural groan to the ceiling. "Fuck, that deadly pet name does it for me every fucking time." Releasing his dick and pulling the two fingers free from my core, Killian stepped out of my spread thighs and fell back onto the bed beside me. Confusion barely registered before his arm snaked beneath my shoulders and pulled me on top of him.

With only his upper half on the bed, feet still firmly planted on the rug, he helped swing my leg over his torso to straddle him. A thundering beat pulsed beneath my palms, which were pressed to his chest. Realizing my slick center slid along his taut abs, embarrassment warmed my cheeks.

The sound of Killian's hands connecting with my ass pulsed through the room at the same moment a bite of pain spiked from the hard spank.

"I showed you my scars, Millie. Literally." Killian reached up and raked his fingers through my hair. "You have nothing to be embarrassed about. I love every inch of this perfect, tiny body. From your brilliant mind to your child-sized feet." Running his hands down my chest, he cupped both breasts and pinched my pebbled nipples. "I want you to have all the control. Ride me, babycakes."

With a hesitant nod, my mind too fogged with lust to overanalyze the situation, I shifted back until his cock slid against my soaked center. The first tap of his tip against my clit had me tossing my head back, pink hair brushing between my shoulder blades. Back and forth I slid against him, working my desire higher with each pass.

The hands gripping my hips tightened, no doubt leaving bruises, but he didn't rush me, allowing me all the control in the moment. Maybe he wanted it, too, already feeling so vulnerable about showing his scars that he needed someone else to be in control. While I loved it when he directed our intimate moments, making each one more mind-blowing than the previous, this was special.

To him and to me.

"Try getting yourself off just like this," he rasped, gaze trained at where I moved against him.

Closing my eyes, I focused on every sensation that burst through me with each pass. I gasped, almost choking on my breath, when he pinched and tugged hard on both nipples, shooting me right over the edge. I ground against him, working myself through the tiny orgasm as it blasted a shiver across my whole body.

My arms trembled, fingers curled against his chest, no doubt leaving nail marks on his skin.

Desperate to feel him, for that bite of pain that came with stretching around his thick cock, I rose on shaky knees and positioned his drenched dick right at my entrance. My jaw went slack as I worked myself down, sliding inch by inch. Taking him halfway, I shifted my hips, forcing my body to take all of him. A stinging flash of pain quickly turned to burning pleasure as my body stretched to accommodate his large size.

Head tossed back, I circled my hips, breathing out a content sigh when my hips touched his.

"Fucking hell, Millie." His guttural tone had me popping my head forward to stare down at him. The hands on my hips tightened, shifting me side to side, causing sparks of pleasure to shoot through me. "This tight cunt takes my cock so well. Feeling your hot, wet pussy on my bare cock is fucking heaven. But I need you to move, my good naughty girl."

"Help," I moaned, too lost in the full feeling as I continued to shift forward and back. "I can't... I need you."

"My pleasure, sweet cheeks. My fucking pleasure." Fingers digging into my cheeks, he slid me off his cock until just the thick head remained inside before he slammed me down hard.

My scream bounced around the room, mixed with his barked curse.

Over and over again, he pulled me up before slamming me back onto his cock while flexing his hips to ensure every inch made its way inside. Soft flutters in my lower belly turned frantic. Balancing on the edge, I cupped both breasts and pinched my nipples hard.

My body locked around him as a soul-shattering orgasm blasted through me.

"Fuck. Shit." Killian pumped into me, using his feet on the floor as leverage until he shook, holding me tight as he followed me over the edge. His cock twitched, sending another aftershock through me.

"Damn." I slumped forward, forehead pressing to his pec. "That was amazing. I had no idea this could be so life altering."

His chuckle made his chest vibrate beneath me. "Same, sweet cheeks. Fucking same. Now, I know it's late, but...."

Peeling off his chest, I sat back with a smirk, shivering at the feel of him still inside me.

"You want to do that again?" I finished for him.

"Fuck yeah, I do." He ran a finger down my sternum, eyes locked on my chest. "I'll never get enough of you, my Millie. Never."

"Same, Kill. Fucking same."

He arched a brow. "I'll show you fucking."

I didn't hold back my wide smile. "I was hoping you would."

And he did, until the sun peeked through the blinds, and I was 100 percent certain I'd walk bowlegged for days.

29

KILLIAN

TODAY

I tracked Millie around the small meeting room during the brief break.

As did others.

A familiar deadly calm, the sudden need for bloodshed, rose in my chest. Not that I could do anything about it. Most of the people in this room were innocent, only here hoping to strengthen their marriage, and were none the wiser about the dirty deeds that went on behind the fake mask of The Union of Blessed Souls.

A firm grip on my bicep jerked my attention away from Millie to the woman at my side. Fuck, how old was she? Platinum blonde hair, fair skin with freckles over her nose, and almost the same height as Millie, the girl didn't look more than sixteen years old.

"What?" I barked, making her flinch. Swallowing down my annoyance at her hand on me, I forced my normal mask back in place. "Did you need something?"

Eyes wide, she gestured to the door that led out to the hallway. "There is a mandatory meeting for the leadership team, teachers, followers, and those interested in joining the church."

With a clipped nod, I carefully extracted myself out of her light hold and strode to where Millie stood with the other wives attending the classes. Her eyes lit up as they followed me weaving through the chairs and other attendees.

How was I so damn lucky?

I didn't allow myself to think this was an actual possibility, a life with her in it. Once we were out of the shithole cult, this assignment far behind us, we could start a life together. Where that would be, I didn't give a fuck, as long as I was with her. If she wanted to keep her job at Harvard, I'd just tell Rhyan I needed to work remotely or maybe even transfer to the BSU team at Quantico.

We had time to figure it all out.

Together.

My fingers wrapped around the back of her neck, the possessive hold one expected of me by the leaders and teachers of this damn place. Tugging her close, I pressed my lips against her ear, feeling the eyes of the four women around us zeroing in on the small contact.

"There is a meeting in the main conference hall. Let's go." I deeply inhaled, allowing her soul-comforting scent to embed in my lungs before pulling back.

Using the hold, I guided her toward the door and out into the packed hallway. The noise level was higher than normal, and many faces I hadn't seen before filled the space. Everyone moved in the same direction.

"How many people live in the compound?" I whispered under my breath. "This is a lot of fucking people."

"Anywhere from seventy to one hundred and fifty. The main housing for members who want to live at the compound is located in the back of the property. Apartment-style setup, unlike our cushy cottage."

I hummed, acknowledging her whispered response. This whole thing was so fucked up. I thought I had seen everything while working as an asset, but this place was just plain creepy. The bad guys pretending to be good and wholesome always made me angry and sick to my stomach.

Gary Paul preyed on those hoping for happiness in their lives, all for money.

Evil, greedy fucker.

Releasing a calming breath, I focused on the voices and whispers. Most talked excitedly about the upcoming announcement, speaking in hushed tones, guessing what it was all about.

Oh, I knew what it was about. After Gary Paul's visit to the Cullers' house, I had no doubt he called this mandatory meeting to tell his whole congregation, AKA cult followers, that he intended to marry Karigan the day after she turned eighteen.

Inside the large auditorium-style space, I continued forward while others darted down various rows to find an open seat. Millie tensed beneath my palm as I debated the best place to sit. I brushed calming strokes with my thumb along the column of her throat, hoping to reassure her that she was safe with me. Sitting in the front row wasn't ideal, but we had to make sure Gary Paul saw us, so farther in the back was out.

Not that there were any available seats closer to the front. I swallowed down a surge of disgust at finding the first row filled with young women, each wearing a similar type of dress but in various colors.

What in the hell was that all about?

Movement down another aisle jerked my attention to

the Simon fuck waving at me. He pointed at Millie, then gestured to a few rows behind him, where Georgiana and the other women sat, before motioning to an empty seat beside him.

"Fuck this day so hard," I grumbled with a chin hitch and smirked at Simon. "You'll be okay back there without me."

Or Hunter, considering he left before class to deliver the files to an Atlanta-based agent. Charlie nor Rhyan could get here for the drop, so Rhyan called in a favor to the closest FBI office. Hopefully, everything would go smoothly, and he'd be back before anyone noticed he wasn't with us.

"I know," she whispered.

My heart gave a solid beat at that response. My Millie didn't need me to hover or offer a protective bubble around her at all times. She lived ten years on her own without me. Sure, none of those years were deep inside a misogynistic cult, but still, she survived just the same on her own. With a supportive squeeze, I released my hold and gestured toward the women before stepping beside Simon and folding down into the chair he clearly saved for me.

I eyed the other men down the row, noticing they all wore similar suits to Simon's, expensive and tailored to fit. Craning my neck, I glanced over my shoulder, seeking out Millie. She was easy to spot, the only pink-haired, bohemian-dressed woman in a sea of skirt suits. The bottom of their red-soled heels gleamed in the bright overhead light.

"Making sure she behaves?" Simon questioned, with a slight chuckle beside me. "Don't worry. Georgiana will help keep her in line." When I turned back around, I caught the confused look that flashed. "Where is that handler guy?"

Well, fuck.

Time to think fast.

"We had a rowdy night." I shrugged and brushed some lint off my pants. "Apparently, I'm a little too enthusiastic, and the bastard can't walk normally today."

That frown deepened. "You fuck men—worse, the help?"

Whoa. Hunter should be offended that this asshole didn't see him as a catch. Hunter was a hot guy, not as panty-melting as Charlie, but he still pulled looks from men and women wherever he went. I calmed the rage his repulsed tone stirred in my veins. But clearly, that was the wrong made-up story. I needed to redirect to pull myself out of the hole I dug.

"No. My wife likes to be watched. The bastard's dick is rubbed raw from how much hand action it saw while he watched me fuck her."

My stomach rolled at the interest that now gleamed in Simon's gaze. "Oh, really? Likes being watched... interesting." The soft chuckle that sounded as he turned to stare up at the women had my muscles stiffening. "I might have to join in. I, too, enjoy watching, though I prefer to not waste a good orgasm on my hand, if you know what I mean."

My forced smirk stayed in place. "Yeah, I know what you mean."

"How about—"

Before he could finish the thought, the lights dimmed above us while the ones around the main stage brightened, which was good because if he asked what I assumed he was going to, I would've cut out his tongue. Deafening applause erupted from those sitting around the auditorium as Pastor Paul walked onto the stage.

The bastard's wide, all-white-teeth smile as he waved and faked graciousness by bowing to the crowd was full of malice and superiority. He no doubt got off on his adoring fans who sat here and those who watched him online, all viewing him as a god.

"Thank you so much for gathering so quickly, my beautiful followers," Pastor Paul said, once the noise died down. "You being here, surrounding me with your light, energizes me beyond measure." Again, he did that fake-ass half bow. "I won't take up much of your time. I know you all are working hard to spread the light to others with the classes here and facilitating the many meetings online." My stomach soured remembering just how far this bastard's reach was, not only in the US but globally. "I couldn't wait another moment to share some exciting news with all of you. After many vision-fueling sessions..." Eww. Just fucking eww. "The vision that will change the course of this church has become clear."

Turning from the crowd, he looked offstage and extended a hand. One careful step at a time, Karigan made her way onto the stage, grasping Paul's outstretched hand. Somehow, his smile was even wider when he turned back to the audience.

"The vision that was delivered from above showed that this beautiful woman would be my wife and bear the future heir to this church." Whispers erupted around me, along with frantic, excited clapping. "I know what you're thinking because I thought it, too. There is a blessed hand in this vision since Kari came to me as my ward after her parents' death. And now she will give me the future of this church." Punctuating the statement, he raised their combined hands high in the air. "We will stay for a while to chat with those who would like to congratulate myself and Kari on our future union. Blessings and light to all."

The lights around the meeting space brightened above

us, a signal that the announcement was done. Time to move on to our next activity or move forward to where he and Karigan stood.

"I heard the announcement doesn't come as a surprise to you," Simon said as we stood. "Davis mentioned this morning in a meeting that you were at his home when the pastor came by to tell him of the good news." I nodded, not trusting myself to speak because what I really wanted to say about this fucked-up place might spill out. "Tonight, Pastor is having a small leadership gathering, a celebration of sorts for their engagement, and I was told to extend a rare invite to you and your wife." My brows flew up my forehead. "I was surprised, too, since you're not one of us just yet, but Pastor has faith in you." And the fake bank account that he wants to raid, and business connections to use for his own gain. "He wants you to see how enlightening the meetings can be if you join the leadership team and move close by."

I nodded along while going against the flow of idiots headed up front toward Karigan and Paul.

"And her handler's current... predicament works out well since he is not on the invite list."

My steps faltered, head whipping to glare at Simon. "Why not?"

The slow smile that spread made my fingers itch to wrap around the fucker's throat and squeeze until I heard a distinctive snap.

"He's not the one Pastor Paul sees as a beneficial addition, only you and, of course, your wife by proxy. See, everyone who joins must be married to a woman that others also find appealing. Her handler," Fucker didn't even know Hunter's fake identity's name, "clearly can't afford the sizable donation required to join but also doesn't have a female partner to bring with him."

My nod was clipped, neck snapping with the sharp movement.

"Right," I ground out. "Just let us know when, and we will be at the celebration."

"I almost forgot." He paused, hand landing on my shoulder. "Make sure your wife wears something more appropriate. Skirts are required for the women, just classier than the ones she tends to wear. If she doesn't have anything, I'm sure Georgiana could lend her an outfit. And one more thing." I glared at the contact before shifting it to Simon. "This is just a preview for you, the benefits of being on the leadership team. You can actively participate only *after* you've made the life-altering choice to follow Pastor Paul's enlightened path, have taken all the classes to absorb our truths, and, of course, donated to the church. Tonight might be a little"—he smirked—"wilder than the normal leadership meetings, but you will get the idea of what we do to support Pastor Paul's visions and enlightenment."

Teeth clenched, I stormed through the crowd, shoving people out of my way if they didn't veer around me on their own. Finally at the cluster of women, I grabbed Millie's shoulder in a tight hold and spun her to face me. Those dark eyes scanned my face, brows furrowing, no doubt seeing the anger and stress there.

"Let's go," I hissed and pulled her away from the women. Georgiana called out to me, but I ignored her and stepped back into the wide aisle. "We need to say congratulations to the happy couple, wife."

Millie nodded, fully understanding the amazing opportunity we were just afforded. While I spoke with Pastor Douche, hopefully, she could get Karigan aside to conduct a quick mental health evaluation and decode the lies and possible brainwashing that she's been subject to. I relaxed a fraction at finding a large crowd around Pastor Paul while a couple of young women clustered around Karigan.

With a quick squeeze, I dropped my hold and moved toward Gary Paul while Millie weaved her way toward her target.

Good girl.

Now it was on me to keep the manipulating bastard distracted while Millie evaluated Karigan, putting us one step closer to ending this assignment and getting out of this hell hole.

And off to start our real lives. Together.

30

MILLIE

TODAY

Sometimes being short had its advantages. Like now. No one even noticed me as I moved around the crowd surrounding Pastor Paul on my way to Karigan. She stood off to the side, from her soon-to-be husband, who was well within hearing distance, but I couldn't pass up the opportunity to really evaluate Karigan.

And possibly, depending on how the conversation went, reveal that I was the crazy person who stopped her outside the school last fall. That was my proof that I was someone who could help and was not integrated into the cult, like the others she was surrounded by. I just hoped it didn't all backfire and she would tell Pastor Paul everything.

We assumed, based on her dazed-out expression, that she was drugged or slightly sedated. Now was my chance to see if our suspicions were true about her being a captive, not knowing that freedom awaited just outside the compound. One thing all the leaders like Gary Paul did was alienate you from your family and make you put all your hope and support system on the leader. Once trust was gained, it was easy for them to convince you that outsiders were bad, hurting you, or even stunting your enlightened growth.

Two girls about Karigan's age hung around her but seemed relieved when they all caught my approach. After a quick wave, they merged with the group around Pastor Paul.

"Hi." I paused beside her, purposefully putting Pastor Paul at my back and using a tall man as cover on the chance he looked this way. "Kari, right?"

A glassy gaze slowly slid from the dispersing crowd to meet mine. My heart sank like lead at the emptiness behind them as she nodded.

"Or is it Karigan?" Her lids opened a fraction, giving away the shock or recognition of her real name. I waved a hand like it didn't matter when it absolutely did. Every reaction I could pull from her, big or small, mattered. "I'm Marla. It's nice to meet you." I held a breath, waiting to see if she recognized me.

"Nice to meet you, too," she whispered.

I loosed that burning breath in a heavy sigh. Guess the pink hair and makeup made me look just different enough for her not to remember. Or her memories were altered by the drugs they clearly had her on.

"It sounds like congratulations are in order on the engagement." If possible, the girl curled in on herself even more. "Are you excited?"

A pause. One very long pause that spoke volumes despite her quiet answer that followed.

"Yes."

"You're so young. How old are you?" Fuck, this was more difficult than I expected.

"Seventeen."

"And your parents are excited?" Was that a low blow to mention her dead parents? Maybe. But I needed a reaction from her. Something that would help me understand how deep Gary Paul's manipulation went.

"I don't have any parents." Somehow, her voice took on an even more bland, almost dead tone.

"Where are they? What happened?"

Her gaze lifted to mine again, eyes searching. "They gave me to him." My stomach dropped as her lower lip wobbled. "This is what they wanted for me before..." With zero emotion on her face, a lone tear dribbled out of the corner of her eye, followed by several more. It was unnerving to see someone crying without showing any emotion. "They are gone, but they believed in Pastor Paul and his visions. This is what they wanted for me before they died."

My hand lifted, the tips of my fingers barely brushing down her bare arm in a comforting stroke I hoped no one else witnessed.

"What happened that night?" I glanced around quickly and released a relieved breath at finding Killian now talking to Pastor Paul, the two deep in conversation. "What happened the night your parents were killed?"

Her dark brows pulled in tight, but that dead gaze didn't leave my face. "They planned it. All of it. That is what I remember. They left me to him." The bite in her tone at those last words made me want to jump with joy.

I stepped even closer so she could hear my whispered words. "But what if they didn't?" I wrapped my pinky finger around hers. "What if it's all a lie?"

Long, dark lashes fluttered up and down. "A lie?"

"Are you happy here, Karigan?"

"Happy?"

"Are you taken care of, looked after... hurt?" I rasped that last word.

"I'm loved. Everything I need is here with Pastor Paul. He is my only family left."

I bit my lip to keep from turning and screaming at the bastard behind me. That motherfucker. I hoped I got the chance to punch him in the nuts after all this was over.

"That's not true, Karigan. You have family out there looking for you. Your aunt—"

"Looks like our women get along well." I tensed, spine snapping ramrod straight at the menacing presence at my back and fake-ass jovial tone. My hair stood on the back of my neck when a heavy hand dropped to my shoulder. "What are you two ladies deep in conversation about?"

"Wedding plans," I blurted. My pleading gaze locked on Karigan, hoping she understood our conversation was not to be shared with him. Damnit. Sweat beaded along my forehead and palms from the building nervousness. "I asked if she wanted help with the wedding plans." Swallowing hard, I carefully removed myself from Pastor Paul's hold and stepped to Killian's side. "I enjoyed planning ours."

That was a lie, even if our marriage was fake. Planning any event was not on my list of things I enjoyed. Hell, my wedding with the ex was tiny, with only about fifty people attending, and even that felt too large.

"She just loves spending my money." Killian snaked a hand around my waist, gripped my hip, and tugged, sealing me against his side. "Tell me more about tonight. I hope I'm able to witness all the benefits of being on the leadership team that the others have mentioned." He leveled Pastor Paul a bored look. "It will need to be compelling to warrant the sizable donation you suggested."

Pastor Paul's eyes brightened, smile wide. "Of course, Kurt. Of course. It's why I invited you and the wife to attend tonight. The engagement celebration will be one to remember, I have no doubt." He shot a look to Karigan that I couldn't read, but she did. The next second, she was at his side, smiling up at him like he was her world.

But when he turned his attention back to Killian, I saw a flicker of something that made my heart race. Ever so slightly, her fake smile slipped, the corners of her lips curling into a frown as she stared at her soon-to-be husband.

Maybe, just maybe, the brief conversation was enough to worm through the lies and drugs. If she began to question the lies now, it would make convincing her to leave easier.

And with the unexpected invitation to the engagement party, our chance to tell Karigan the truth about her parents' murders and break her free of this place could be tonight.

"THIS OUTFIT ACTUALLY MAKES ME feel more like me rather than the long, flowy skirts and tops do." I adjusted the soft silk top, smoothing out nonexistent wrinkles. It didn't fit me as well as it would Georgiana, but my goal wasn't to draw attention but to blend in. I studied my reflection and gave a soft pink lock a tug. "Well, I feel like Dr. Anderson, minus the pink hair."

Killian's strong arms wrapped around me from behind, sealing my back to his chest. Nose in my hair, he inhaled deep. "I love it."

"Me, too, but I'm not sure the university will." His forearm twitched beneath my fingers as I caressed his soft, golden skin. "What are we doing, Kill? What will we do?" I turned in his hold. Chin pressed to his bare sternum where the dress shirt hung open, I stared up into his handsome face.

"We will be together, that's what." Calloused hands cupped my face. "If you want me with you, I'll figure it out. Or if you're ready for a career change, then we can look into that, too."

"A change?" I wrinkled my nose. "What do you mean? I love my job."

Didn't I?

"How close are you to becoming a licensed criminal psychologist?"

"A few observation hours short. Why?"

Those aqua eyes scanned my face. "You threw yourself into this case, forced Rhyan to bend the rules for you. Those are not the actions of a professor who is content with sitting behind a desk and teaching. You seem to want more. Tell me I'm wrong and I won't say another word, but I think you're bored."

I shifted my stare to his chest, fingers absentmindedly tracing the defined muscles along his shoulders and arms. My mind wandered to the last year, how bored I had become in my role and increasingly annoyed with the students' lazy attitudes. Maybe what I felt wasn't just missing Killian in my life, but maybe I was meant for a bigger purpose. Something more.

"It wouldn't be much of a leap for you to consult with the BSU team on a more consistent basis. Just think about it. But remember what I said. We're in this together, you and me."

"Okay," I whispered. A sudden swell of emotions and a heady mix of gratitude and pride had my voice cracking.

"Now. Let's finish getting ready." His palm came down hard on my skirt-covered ass. I squealed, pushing my chest against his in a half attempt to avoid the next spank and the next. "Fuck, okay, I need to stop or all those clothes are going to come right off, and I'm going to fuck you from behind, watching your face in the mirror as you come around my cock."

Lip between my teeth, I nodded, totally down with that plan.

A genuine, full-face smile pulled at Killian's lips before he bopped me on the nose. "Don't give me that look."

"Then don't tease me with a good time."

His groan rumbled through the small bathroom. "Fuck, you were made for me, babycakes. So fucking perfect." His hands slid down my arms to weave our fingers together. "Now, come on, we have some baddies to hoodwink while we steal their virginal bride."

My eyes rolled to the ceiling. "You're so dramatic."

"But you love me."

Bare toes pressed to the cold tile, I lifted to kiss his soft lips. "I do love you."

"What if we get married sooner rather than later?" My lips brushed against his as my grin grew. "What are your feelings toward saying fuck it to a big party and eloping off into the sunset?"

My contented sigh brushed along his skin. "That sounds absolutely perfect."

Fingers gripping my chin, he held me in place while he devoured my mouth. "Something to look forward to. Which is good. I have a feeling tonight will suck the worst out of all the nights we've been here."

Lead dropped into my stomach at the reminder of what we had to do, but I held the smile so he wouldn't see my rising worry.

What if tonight didn't go as planned and our future together never even had a chance to start?

31

KILLIAN

TODAY

E ven from the front steps with the door closed, the noise poured into the night. With an encouraging squeeze to Millie's dainty fingers, I shoved the solid wood open and guided her into the evil lion's den. Couples and groups mingled in the foyer and along the hall, spilling into various open doorways. Familiar faces smiled our way as we weaved through the crowd. Almost to the study, a server appeared at my side, two full champagne flutes resting on top. I took one and motioned for him to leave before Millie could grab the other, keeping up the charade of her character.

"None for you, wife," I said in a low voice as I hitched my chin, acknowledging the fucker in the corner eyeing Millie like she was a piece of meat.

"I love that title," she whispered back. "Fake or not."

"Soon, it won't be, my Millie. Soon." Securing my arrogant mask, I scanned the study as we walked inside the less crowded room. Simon lounged in the deep leather club chair in front of the gas fireplace, highball glass in one hand while the other lazily stroked up and down the lean thigh of the woman sitting on the armrest beside him.

My eyelid twitched, but I forced a cocky smirk and hitched my chin his way, fake approving of the scene. If people wanted to swing, switch partners, or have multiples in a solid unit, that was their prerogative. We had Jameson on our team, who lived with the medical examiner and a former Santa Coasta detective. The three were together and on their way to having a litter of kids. I was happy for them and didn't care what society thought about their unique relationship, just that they made each other happy, but that wasn't what this was in front of me.

These women were coerced by their husbands to participate to keep their spot on the leadership team. The few moving around the room tipped glass after glass of champagne back as if desperate to feel the effects of the alcohol. Though some, like Georgiana, were predators just like their husbands. The sooner we shut this place down and exposed the twisted and fucked-up brainwashing, the better. Lives would be ruined, sure; Hunter was right about that. But leaving them in this false reality wasn't an option either.

"You must be Kurt." A tall, burly man I hadn't met yet paused in front of us. "And the wife." Dark eyes swept a predatory look up and down her small frame. My nostrils flared, the only outward sign of the burning rage rolling through my veins.

She was mine.

Only mine.

"That's me, and you are?" He introduced himself as he continued to stare at Millie like she was on the dinner menu.

"What's the deal with tonight?"

The bastard's dark beard shifted as he smirked. "Our

only direction was to have fun, all together." Reaching out, he ran a single finger down Millie's bicep. I glared at the contact, debating the repercussions of snapping his finger off and feeding it to him, forcefully. "We can all enjoy the benefits of Pastor's engagement."

"I need to pee," Millie blurted. A few heads turned our way at the unusual and panicked outburst. Crimson bloomed along her cheeks before she ducked her head, hiding the evidence of her embarrassment. If we weren't in a room full of predators, I'd chuckle at how damn cute she was. But we were, and I needed to take the out Millie gave us before I maimed and killed the bastard.

"I told you to go before we left the house," I fake chastised as I led her from the room with a firm grip on her elbow. Back out in the buzzing foyer, I guided her toward the powder bath I used that first night we were here. The mahogany door slammed shut behind us, my hold immediately dropping now that we were out of the spotlight. "Fucking fuck."

Both sweaty palms pressed to the white marble vanity. Dropping my head forward, I focused on inhaling through my nose and exhaling through my mouth until my entire body didn't tremble with anger. I tensed out of habit at the sudden pressure against my lower back, only for it to immediately ease. This was Millie, my Millie, not one of the random women out there. I swear their eye fucking could get someone pregnant with the way they followed me around the room.

"Sorry, I just..." I inhaled deeply. "Needed a second. I don't like when someone touches you."

"It's okay, Kill." My heart hammered in my chest. We were so close. Only a few more hours of pretending to be this arrogant fuckstick, of her having to put up with the assholes desperate for a taste of what was mine. "Take all the time you need."

Knowing what would cure the jealousy and anger, I whirled around and engulfed her smaller frame in a desperate hug. Lean arms snaked around my waist and squeezed, holding me even tighter than I was to her. Which said a lot, since I was clinging to her like the lifeline she was to me.

"We can do this," she whispered. "Only a few more hours and we're done. We'll take her somewhere safe where they can't hurt her."

We had to see this through; find the girl and get her free. The FBI had more damn red tape than Santa's workshop, so who knew when they would actually coordinate a raid on the compound and the police chief's house to gather the remaining files. Hell, I'd be shocked if they made a move before summer. With Karigan's birthday approaching and no firm date on the raid, that meant we were having some kidnapping fun tonight.

"I'm good." Leaning down, I placed a kiss on top of her head. "Thank fuck Simon and Gary Paul said we could only watch and not participate until we were official members of the leadership team. We can put up with all this shit until everyone is good and drunk. With the way they are tossing back their drinks, I'd bet we only have a couple of hours before we can sneak away to find where they have Karigan locked away."

While we mixed and mingled, I needed to subtly feel out where the main bedrooms were in this damn mansion. A shiver of revulsion slid through me thinking about all the unwanted touches I would need to put up with to get that information, but it was worth it.

Saving Karigan meant a lot to Millie.

And that was all I needed to know.

Well, that and it was kind of my job.

So, yeah, off to be sexually harassed, all for the sake of saving a young girl.

Yay.

32

MILLIE

TODAY

I'd never been a big drinker. I didn't enjoy the taste, but I also wasn't a fan of not being in complete control. Hell, when I was sick, mind foggy from the sinus pressure or medicine, I hated not being my normal sharp self. Though, after tonight, I planned to cut even that small amount of alcohol from my life.

The couples laughing and shouting around me were basically one drink away from being sloppy drunk. Oh, wait, spoke too soon. A woman that just exposed both her breasts in the corner, allowing a man to suck on them while she was fucked from behind... she was for sure sloppy drunk. Though no one seemed to mind but me. Probably because I'd sipped the same glass of water that was made to look like a cocktail—thank you, Killian—for the last two hours.

A high-pitched scream reverberated through the room, where we watched from our perch along the wall, making me tense. I watched in frozen shock as a man tossed the woman over his shoulder and marched toward the powder bath Killian and I used earlier. Her smile was wide as she playfully slapped at his back and demanded to be put down.

What in the hell was this place?

Thankfully, the women seemed to enjoy themselves, not forced, but how much was out of coercion versus what they actually wanted? That wasn't something I could dive into now. This was the perfect moment to slip away. Dinner was done, and everyone around us was either too drunk or engaged in other activities to notice our absence. Grabbing Killian's hand in my own, I gave two hard squeezes, hoping it was enough to detach him from the woman who was basically dry-humping his thigh.

With a fake chuckle, Killian pulled himself away from the woman, muttering something about his wife needing some alone time. She offered to join, but Killian just laughed and reminded her we were there to observe only. It was irrational of me to be mad at the way she pawed at him. He didn't want her or any of the others touching him, which was clear by the tension pulsing off him. Or maybe it was just clear to me.

Because he was mine.

Fucking mine.

I fought the urge to bare my teeth at the woman. Killian had told me enough about his particular trauma that I knew he didn't want that woman touching him, no matter how beautiful she was.

Maybe I was wrong about the no-alcohol thing and a glass of champagne would help settle some of the anger boiling beneath my skin. My fingers stretched out, ready to wrap around the long stem of a glass as a waiter passed, but Killian gripped my hand midair. The waiter passed, none the wiser of my desperate need to dull the growing irritation.

"Stop," I hissed over my shoulder. "I can have a drink."

His chuckle skirted along my skin, heating me from the

inside out. A gasp escaped at the pulse of need between my thighs. After watching the many live porno performances tonight, I was turned on and irritable. It was wrong, but I couldn't help that watching what was happening right in front of me made me needy. It was human nature, biology, and psychology, damnit.

Killian's hand wrapped around the back of my neck in a firm hold and guided us around the couples who were barely dressed at this point. Sure, clothes were on, but the more important parts were fully exposed. Out in the hall, Killian's grip tightened as Pastor Paul approached. Only wearing a pair of white linen pants, he smiled our way.

Before turning my gaze down to the floor, I flicked curious glances at the two women on his arms. Wasn't this his engagement party?

"Ah, there you two are, my most special guests." Gary Paul shook Killian's hand before taking mine and planting a kiss on the back. "Very special indeed," he murmured against my skin. "I do hope tonight was enough to entice you to consider joining The Union of Blessed Souls. I see so much potential in you two. I know together we can bring light and happiness to your lives, your marriage, and into eternity."

I bit my tongue to keep from snapping at the idiot.

"It has been... enlightening for sure," Killian said. "A little too much, considering we weren't able to participate."

Gary Paul's haughty laugh sent a shiver of revulsion down my spine. "Ah, well, only after you've pledged your souls and future, plus taken the required classes for ultimate enlightenment, does one access the full benefits of the leadership role. Though, I'm sure we can discuss other ways to speed up the process."

Yeah, like adding a few zeros to the donation amount he'd already mentioned to Killian.

"Tomorrow," Killian snapped. "Now, I need to go relieve some of this... enlightenment."

Pastor Paul chuckled. "Of course. Though no one would mind if you gave us a glimpse into other ways you two could benefit the leadership team."

I felt all the blood drain from my face. My mind spun, and I swayed on my feet. Did he want us to.... No. No. No. Killian wouldn't agree to that, would he? I peeked a look up into his face, finding him already looking down at me with a smirk.

"She does love to be watched," he murmured while running a knuckle down my cheek. "But maybe next time. Let her get used to the idea of such a large audience." Pastor Paul nodded slowly. "I do want to stay and continue watching.... But..." He adjusted himself and huffed. "I have to take care of this, or I'll break all your rules and fuck every person in this room before the night is over."

"That's the spirit." He slapped Killian's back. "But don't worry, we have private rooms for those who want to participate but are not as adventurous."

"Where?" Killian snapped.

Leaning to the side, Pastor Paul whispered something to the woman on his right. She smiled and nodded before stepping out of his hold. Hand held out to me, she inclined her head further down the hall.

"Come. Pastor has asked me to show you to a private room." My clammy palm pressed into hers, and she guided me down the hall, Killian hot on my heels.

"I... we haven't been down this way before," I said softly. "Is this where all the bedrooms are?" Our guide looked over her shoulder and nodded. "Wait, is this where Pastor Paul sleeps?" I injected a bit of breath into my words, hoping it sounded like excitement.

"Not in this hall. His and the future of our church's rooms are upstairs."

I wanted to vomit. So now she didn't even have a name? With the announcement, Karigan, or Kari rather, just ceased to exist and was now only known as *the church's future*.

"That makes sense," Killian said behind me. "Need to keep them safe. They are both the future of all of this."

"Oh, yes," she said as we slowed in front of a closed door. "Also, that way, security doesn't get distracted by what happens on the first level." Her hand wrapped around the knob and twisted at the same time she urged the door open.

Heart in my throat, unsure what to expect, I stepped into the room. A relieved breath blew past my parted lips. Normal. A normal, though just as opulent as the rest of the house, room with a four-poster bed, side tables—I did not want to know what was in those drawers—and a chair situated in the corner.

"It's perfect. Leave." Killian pulled me toward the bed. "Now," he barked over his shoulder.

The girl just giggled and quietly closed the door behind her. Killian stood frozen for a few seconds, staring at me, though somehow I knew his attention was on the room. It looked normal to me, the untrained eye, but if there was something off, Killian would no doubt find it. His shoulders visibly relaxed, and he leaned against the bedpost, staring down at where I sat on the edge of the bed.

"You ready for this?" he asked with a smirk. Stepping in front of me, he ran a single finger along my jaw and bent low. His lips brushed against my ear. "So now we know to go up a level, and the security we assumed would guard her door was just confirmed."

"How?" I whispered. The single word spoke to so many questions.

How will we get up there?

How will we get around the security?

How will we get Karigan out of here, all of us, without being seen?

How in the hell did I get myself into this?

I knew the answer to the last one, but it didn't stop me from questioning my decision-making skills, considering I put myself in this messy situation.

"Based on the plans Charlie pulled, there is a staircase at the end of the hall. It's hidden since it's meant for the staff. We can make our way down there and then go up to the second level. I'm not sure what to expect as far as the security goes. Could be multiple armed men, could only be one."

"That doesn't sound promising for success."

"Do you trust me?" And being a tease, he sucked my lobe between his lips and nipped.

A moan slipped out, and I swayed toward him. "You know I do."

"Then don't worry. We've got this." Pulling back, he studied my face. "Flushed cheeks, hooded lids—why, Dr. Anderson, did seeing all those couples out there fucking turn you on?" My reluctant nod made his smile grow. "Oh, we will have so much fun together, my Millie. So many dirty, dirty sides of you for us to explore together."

"I—"

The door swung open, cutting me off. Both our heads whipped toward the familiar frame stepping into our room and quietly closing the door behind him. Killian's hold on my shoulders tightened as he glared at the smirking Simon.

"This is a private room," Killian hissed, tracking Simon's every step like a predator hunting its prey. "Get out."

Ignoring Killian's order, Simon moved toward the single upholstered chair in the corner of the room and folded into the seat. "Don't worry," he said, gaze locked on me. "I won't touch, but you did mention she loves an audience." My wide eyes flicked to Killian, who winced. What the hell was this guy talking about? "And I do love to watch." His fingers worked at his belt, the clang of the metal resounding through the otherwise silent room. "Please, continue. I'm looking forward to this show."

I watched in awe as Killian's entire demeanor shifted from rigid to relaxed between blinks. With a cocky-ass smile, he leaned down and planted a kiss on my lips. "Be right back," he whispered so low I almost missed the words.

Stepping back, Killian tucked both hands into the side pockets of his slacks and casually ambled over to where Simon sat, fingers hovering over his partially undone pants. When Killian stood in front of the now-confused Simon, he huffed a humorless laugh.

"I've wanted to do this since that first time you eye fucked my wife."

"What—"

Simon didn't get a chance to finish his question. The look of confusion morphed into utter fear as Killian's solid fist swung toward his head. The man didn't even have time to duck, too caught off guard and not nearly as fast as my husband.

I flinched, palms flying up to cover my ears, when the distinct sound of Killian's fist connecting with Simon's temple sounded through the room. But I couldn't stop watching. Again and again, Killian beat his tightly clenched fist into Simon's face and head, even after the man slumped unconscious out of the chair and onto the floor.

After a swift kick to Simon's back, Killian stood tall and

shook out his blood-splattered hand. I purposefully avoided looking at the crimson droplets, knowing I'd likely pass out. Me and blood were not friends. Checking over his shoulder, he caught me watching and smiled.

"I feel a shit ton better. Fuck, I needed that. Now, if I could only do that to every other asshole who has dared to look at you, maybe I won't need therapy after all." His wide grin held an edge to it that warned me he wasn't nearly as relaxed as he wanted me to think.

Slowly standing from the edge of the bed, I made my way to him and paused at his side. I nudged the unconscious body with the toe of my black patent leather high-heel shoe, carefully avoiding looking at the blood. Peeking up through my lashes, I offered Killian a hesitant smile.

"Does it make me a bad person for not being upset that you just beat a man to death?"

"Nope, it makes you even more perfect to be mine. And he's not dead. I held back."

My lips parted, and my jaw went slack. "That was you holding back?"

"Oh, babycakes," he said with a huff. "You have no idea what I'm capable of. If I wanted the asshole dead, he would be."

My shoulders shook with the pulse of desire his dark words sent down my spine.

"Now what?" I asked, instead of questioning my sanity. Who got turned on by violence? Me, apparently. Guess all those dark romance books I'd read over the years prepared me for this moment.

"Now I tie him up with his own tie, stuff one of those awful throw pillows into his mouth and lock him in that closet. Then we go upstairs, and the real fun begins."

"Right," I muttered. Eyeing Simon, I sighed. "Want some help?"

A genuine smile spread across Killian's lips. "Really?" I nodded. "Best. Date. Ever."

My hair shifted as I shook my head in exasperation, and I bit down on my lower lip to hide my smile.

What the hell had I gotten myself into?

And why wasn't I worried?

33

KILLIAN

TODAY

There was no fear, disgust, or annoyance in those dark eyes after I KO'ed the asshole with a single hit to the head. The additional hits after he was out were all for my enjoyment rather than ensuring he stayed unconscious. If he didn't want to almost die, he shouldn't have looked at what was mine. Wiping the blood from my knuckles on my dark pants, I stepped out of the small closet and closed the door with a soft click.

When I spun around, ready to put the new plan into action, I found Millie perched on the edge of the bed, both high heels dangling from one hand, just like I instructed. For two reasons: One, if we needed to run, there was no way she could in those three-inch heels. Two, well, call me a caveman, but I loved our height difference. Loved how her tiny frame fit perfectly against mine, how she had to tip her face up to meet my gaze.

It spoke to the protector in me.

And the fucked-up side, too. I couldn't wait to see all the different ways that tiny body could bend for me.

"Ready for scene two?" I asked, waggling my brows,

hoping to lessen the seriousness of the situation. "Spoiler alert: we win."

A cute snort escaped as she stood. "You don't know that."

"Sure I do."

"How?"

"Because you have me, chameleon extraordinaire, and I have you, the smartest person I've ever met."

Her teeth sank into the lower lip I loved to suck between my own, hiding a grin. Interlacing our fingers, I tugged her toward the closed door and slipped my cell free to check for any missed messages or alerts from Hunter.

Nothing. No texts, calls, or alerts from anyone.

Unease churned in my gut. He should've made the drop hours ago and sent an ETA of when he would be back, but there was complete radio silence from his end. In fact, I hadn't received any messages or calls since the moment we stepped foot in the mansion hours ago. As I stared at the darkened screen, it hit me as to why.

A hissed curse escaped between my clenched teeth, making Millie curl tighter against my side.

"They must have a jammer," I muttered. "Probably so no one can live stream while they get their fuck on." Worry flickered over Millie's features. "Don't worry. It's fine. We're still good to go. Now I know why Hunter hasn't reached out. I was getting worried. Once we're out of range, my phone will work again, and we can call in reinforcements."

It really was fine. We didn't need my cell for the next step of the plan, but it sure as hell would be nice on the off chance things went sideways. I didn't care what happened to me, more about Millie. Wait. As I thought those words, I realized they were a lie.

Sometime between when I saw Millie again and now, I began to care about my safety. With her in my life, I wanted to make it out unscathed, to fight harder and be smarter. For too many years, I was reckless with my life, taking unnecessary risks.

Now I had a life to look forward to with Millie. So it was settled. We would both make it out of this shithole alive and unharmed. Failure was not an option. Rolling both shoulders, I stretched my neck to one side and then to the other, relieving some of the tension from the tight muscles.

"Remember the plan."

"What plan?" she hissed as I opened the door.

I paused and looked down at her with a frown. Shit, did I forget to tell her what I came up with while I hog-tied the fucker in the closet? Seemed I was too used to working alone.

"Right, just act drunk and horny. Since you're already one of those, it should be easy." I shot her a salacious wink and pulled the door open wide enough to poke my head through the gap. Head on a swivel, I checked up and down the hall, relaxing slightly at finding it empty. Only the distant sounds of laughter and voices came from the direction of the ongoing fuckfest back in the main part of the house.

One foot out in the hall, then another, I led Millie towards the staff's stairwell, each step silent and cautious. My heart raced, and sweat slicked my spine, but it wasn't out of fear or worry. Anticipation and excitement thrummed through my veins. My body reacted this way in high-pressure situations like this. My dad was right about one thing early on: I was born for this kind of work. My ability to remember anything I heard only added to my value as an asset for the CIA. I loved the thrill, the thrumming anticipation that kept all your senses on high alert.

A heavy thump and vibrations shaking the wall on my

right had me whirling to the sound, instantly searching and prepared to snap the neck of anyone close. A loud, muffled moan followed by another solid thump came from the other side of the wall.

Right. Clearly not a threat to tonight's mission.

Seemed someone was having fun in there.

Shaking my head, I continued down the long hallway, my fingers constantly tightening around Millie's, reassuring myself that she was close behind me without needing to turn around. I couldn't afford to be distracted, not when so much was at stake.

Pausing at the plain, white-painted door at the end, I turned the bronze knob, careful not to leave any prints on the shiny metal, and inched the door open, ensuring the staff stairwell was empty before guiding Millie in behind me. The soft click as the door shut behind us echoed through the quiet space. Step by step, we eased up the stairs. Thanks to the thin carpet, each careful step was silent and cushioned the bottom of Millie's bare feet.

Paused at the second-floor landing, I tugged Millie close and pressed my lips against her ear.

"Act drunk and idiotic, like you have no sense that we're doing something wrong." She nodded. "And no matter what, let me handle the security. If there is a... disagreement between me and them, I'll handle it."

"Disagreement meaning a potential fight to the death?"

I smirked. "Exactly. Ready to act?"

At her hesitant nod, I opened the door wide like I had no care in the world or knowledge that we were entering a restricted area. Instantly, I identified two fuckers in suits that stood outside a door. Both their heads whipped our way as we stumbled from the stairwell.

"Oh, this is pretty," Millie giggled, pitch high and filled

with excitement. "Look, honey, we have extras." Dropping my hand and her shoes, she clapped and bounced on her toes. "Can they join us, please?"

I huffed a humorless laugh and wrapped an arm around her shoulders, moving us both toward the frowning security.

Both wore nine millimeters on their hips, but neither reached for the sidearms. Instead, they watched us meander closer, one with curiosity, the other with suspicion. The latter was the one I needed to take out first. No way in hell would I give either time to radio for backup or alert others we were here.

"This is a restricted area," the suspicious one said, though he couldn't stop watching the way Millie swayed to some unknown beat in her head. If our lives weren't on the line, I'd watch her, too. She jerked like a person possessed, nothing that anyone would consider labeling dancing. Somehow, it all made her even more adorable and perfect in my eyes. "The available private rooms are downstairs—"

"That's where we were, but"—I angled my head toward Millie—"she wanted to go find some company, though it seems we got turned around."

"Babe," Millie whined, tugging at my shirt sleeve. "I'm super horny. I need you." Her head lolled to the side, and she eyed the two men with hooded lids. "Or them. I'm not picky."

"Neither am I," said the curious one. Welp, seemed Mr. Suspicious was now second on my kill list because Mr. Curious thought it was okay to eye fuck my wife like she was a piece of meat.

How dare he.

Only I could do that.

Again, Millie clapped excitedly as she skipped down the hall with me hot on her heels.

"Ma'am, you need to go back downstairs where you're allowed." Mr. Suspicious eyed me. "Who are you two? This is a private event, and I don't recognize you from the leadership team."

Right, no time to waste, then. I needed to deal with the two immediately.

Noting the height differences between Millie and the two men, I placed a palm to her lower back and urged her between them. She shot a questioning look over her shoulder, but I just smiled and nodded.

"It's okay, baby, I don't mind sharing. These two men look like they could use a break."

"Fuck yeah, we could," Mr. Curious huffed, hand going to Millie's waist. I bit down on my lip so hard I tasted blood, but I kept my mouth shut.

"Carl, we can't—"

"Yes, we can," Millie rasped, voice breathy and oh so fake. Damn, she was good. Wonder if she took acting lessons since college. "It won't take me long, I promise."

"Ben, for fuck's sake, relax. The pastor isn't even up here. Let's have some fun with this—"

And just like that, the two idiots died because they thought with their dicks.

Okay, fine, they didn't die, but I was tempted to add a little more power when I palmed the back of both heads and slammed their foreheads together. The crunch of their skulls connecting made me wince as I snagged Millie's elbow and pulled her from between the men before they crumbled to the floor.

Mr. Serious was out while Mr. Curious blinked up at me, clearly seeing stars.

"What the fuck?" he groaned, hand flopping at his side where the radio hung off his belt.

"Nope, sorry, bucko, can't let you radio for help. That would ruin our plans. Nighty-night."

Pulling my already bruised and split fist back, I slammed my knuckles against his temple. Once to knock him out, the second time because he touched Millie.

It made me feel better. Way more than what was probably considered healthy.

"Maybe I should pick up boxing instead of going to therapy. I really feel lighter already."

"Focus, please." Millie sighed. "Think this is her room?"

"I don't know, Margo," I said in my best snooty voice. "Get it?"

"What..." She tossed her hands up in the air. "A movie quote?"

I nodded. "A movie quote. We have serious work to do if you can't identify that quote from *Christmas Vacation*. There are a solid ten to fifteen iconic lines from that movie." With a dramatic, defeated sigh, I hitched my chin toward the door. "See if it's locked."

Reaching out, Millie tried the handle. It rattled in her hand instead of turning. Kneeling between the two unconscious idiots, I patted their pockets, removing their guns and radios, securing all to my belt as I went, until I felt the sharp outline of metal keys inside Mr. Serious's pants.

"Try these." As she pulled the keys from my outstretched hand, a sense of urgency sent a bolt of trepidation through me. "And hurry, they probably have cameras out here in the hall. We need to pull Tweedledee and Tweedledum into the room so it's not obvious Karigan is in trouble."

The multiple metal keys rattled, jingling together as she tried one key, then another. The third and last on the small ring smoothly slid into the keyhole and turned the knob, twisting with it. Millie flashed a victorious grin over her shoulder and pushed the door open wide for me to see inside.

I did a quick scan of the room, only pausing for a moment on the girl staring out the window from her perch on the bed. I gestured for Millie to continue inside and turned back to the two unconscious idiots. With no time to waste, I gripped under their arms and stepped back, grunting through the effort needed to drag their heavy-as-hell bodies into the room. Deadweight was always a bitch to move.

Millie spoke in a soft, comforting tone as she carefully approached Karigan, her words barely audible over my heavy breaths as I strained to pull the bodies deep enough into the room to allow the door to shut.

A male voice crackled through the room. Both women's heads whipped my way, eyes wide at the loud sound. One stolen gun already in hand, I scanned the room, moving to clear the adjoining bathroom and small walk-in closet.

When the voice came again, I froze, only to relax when realization wormed its way through the kill fog.

The radio.

The voice came through the radio on my hip. The clip snapped against the plastic back as I ripped one from my waistband. Fingers on the dial, I upped the volume and set it on the dresser beside me.

"Hurry, Millie," I ordered. "I'll try to keep up with the chatter, but we're on borrowed time. When these two don't report in, someone will come check on them."

With a clipped nod, she closed the distance between her and Karigan, slowly sinking onto the bed beside her.

Pulling the other gun free, I double-checked both clips

and engaged each slide. One in each hand, I pointed the barrels toward the door and widened my stance, gaze locked on the only way in and out of the room. Now it was up to Millie to convince Karigan of the danger she was in and the freedom that waited beyond the compound's walls, hopefully, before the rest of the security team noticed Tweedledee and Tweedledum missed their check-in.

I smiled and shifted my weight, keeping my muscles tensed and ready for anything.

That pastor fucker's ragtag security team had nothing on me. If they tried to hurt my Millie or the innocent girl we were here to save, then they'd quickly find out that I wasn't here to play games and they would be dead before they even realized they were in my crosshairs.

34

MILLIE

TODAY

The bed dipped beneath me as I hesitantly perched beside Karigan, who had returned to staring out the large, darkened window. My heart raced as I worked through what to say. This moment was the whole reason I fought to be here on this assignment. I had planned out what I would say, the best way to help her remember her past, and that there was a future away from this place, but under this kind of pressure, with Killian armed at our backs, ready for war, I couldn't seem to remember any of my carefully planned words.

"Hey." I cleared my throat, hoping that would stop the slight tremble. "Remember me from earlier today?" Instead of responding, she continued to stare out the darkened window. "Karigan, it's me. Millie Anderson, the crazy person who stopped you outside of school last fall." She blinked, head slowly turning my way. "Hi."

Her gaze slid to Killian and down to the two men unconscious on the floor before looking at me.

"Ugh, yeah, they didn't want us to come in. You're locked in here every night, aren't you?"

Karigan's throat worked as she swallowed and gave a hesitant nod.

Careful to keep my movement slow, I reached between us and gently pressed two fingers to her upturned wrist. The slow and steady beat made my stomach turn. Fuck, what the hell were they giving this poor girl? Two people just broke into her room and her pulse wasn't even raised.

"Karigan," I whispered. "We work with the FBI." I was more of a consultant, but we did not have time for those minuscule details. I studied her features, releasing a relieved sigh when her brows raised a fraction. Good, at least they hadn't brainwashed her to be afraid of government agencies.

"FBI," she whispered.

I nodded and slid my fingers to interlace with hers.

"You're a prisoner here, Karigan." I hoped that continuing to say her real name would help break through the drugs and whatever mind manipulation they'd achieved in the last few months. "You don't belong here. It's not what your parents wanted."

Her head fell forward, long dark hair acting like a curtain, keeping me from seeing her face.

"I don't belong anywhere."

My fingers flexed around hers. "Yes, you do. You have an aunt, an aunt that demanded someone from the FBI come find and rescue you." That got her attention. Slowly sitting up straight, Karigan's full focus returned to me, eyes wide and searching. "You're not alone, Karigan, and from what I've learned about these people and what they are capable of, I don't think this is what your parents wanted."

Her dark brows furrowed. "This is my home," she whispered, tone unsure.

"Do you remember your parents?" I asked, instead of arguing with her.

"Millie," Killian said, drawing my attention. "We don't have much time."

I nodded and repeated the question to Karigan, hoping triggering the good memories of her parents would help her see that this wasn't where she was meant to be.

"Yes, I remember them."

"They loved you, right?" She nodded. "Didn't make you go to school here but wanted you to be in a public school away from this place." If possible, those brows pulled in even tighter. Hope bloomed in my chest. "They didn't want this for you. I don't think so, and neither does your aunt, your mom's sister."

"Why?" A single tear trickled from the corner of her eye.

"Your mom called her sister before their murder—"

"Murder?" she breathed.

I nodded. "Your mom was scared, Karigan, and I think it was for you."

She licked her lips, eyes flicking back and forth as if searching her memories. "Why?"

I swallowed. "I think they knew Pastor Paul wanted you. Either he told them or they figured it out on their own—that, I'm not sure. I think... I think he had your parents killed so he could have you without a fight."

Her gaze slid to the window. "He killed them. For me?"

"Yes. We need to get you out of here, Karigan. You're not safe. This place, these people, it's not right. None of what goes on here is the way the rest of the world works, and I think you know that. Remember what it was like, living with your parents, going to school with your friends, living outside of this place?"

Karigan slowly stood and walked to the window, fingertips pressing to the glass pane.

"He said my friends didn't want me anymore, that they

didn't understand the light we had." The words were mumbled, as if reciting lines she was told as she worked through her memories. "My parents abandoned me.... They...."

"Millie, we need to go. Now," Killian barked. "They've called for these two twice with no response, since they're... well." He gestured to the two still-unconscious men with the end of a gun. "They'll send backup. Soon."

Popping off the bed, I stepped to Karigan and grabbed her hand.

"Please believe me," I begged. "You've been manipulated, lied to, and so many, many other terrible things, I'm sure."

She finally turned to face me, tears leaking down her sweet face.

"He comes to me at night," she whispered. Her free hand rose and pointed to the chair in the corner. "Sits there and tells me all the things he can't wait to do to me." Her shoulders shook as a sob broke free. "I don't want to marry him," she begged. "I don't want him touching me, doing... that."

I squeezed her hand even harder. "That's why we're here, Karigan. We're here for you. You don't have to marry him or live here." Stepping back, I tugged her toward Killian, whose aqua eyes flicked between us and the door in rapid succession. "Come with us now. We can help you—"

The scream of an alarm cut off my words. The shrieking vibrated through my ears, jumbling my thoughts with the loud, penetrating sound. Killian's lips moved, but his words were eaten up by the noise.

I pointed to the ceiling where the ear-piercing noise blared. "I can't hear you."

With a frustrated look, he slid one gun back into the holster and hurried to the window. Face plastered to the glass pane, his lips moved like he cursed and stepped back.

Grabbing my hand, he led me and Karigan, since she had a death grip on my other hand, toward the door. I swallowed down the protest when his fingers slipped away from mine to wrap around the doorknob, the borrowed gun clutched tight in the opposite hand.

The screaming alarm continued to blast through the room, making it hard to think about anything other than the noise. I watched Killian like a hawk, and my stomach dropped when he eased the door open, only to slam it back shut.

The moment our eyes met, the fear and worry that blared from his gaze, I knew we were in trouble.

I watched his lips move, desperate to understand the words he attempted to convey.

My stomach revolted when understanding hit me like a sucker punch to the gut.

Trapped.

We were trapped.

35

KILLIAN

TODAY

Well, fuck.

A wince pulled at my features as I took in the two fear-stricken faces depending on me to get them out of this alive. Good thing I was positive I could make that happen. Rolling both shoulders, I scanned the room, searching for something to give me a little more time, pausing on a large, heavy dresser.

Perfect makeshift barricade that should hold until I got the two settled somewhere safer than standing frozen in the middle of the damn room.

Fingers gripped around the white-painted wood edges, a grunt escaped as I shoved it hard, the balls of my feet sliding on the soft carpet with every push. Once the heavy piece of furniture's broad back was pressed against the door and the lock engaged, I whirled with both hands on my hips. Karigan stood sealed against Millie's side, trembling in fear or maybe anger, based on the firm set of her lips and red cheeks. If it were me, I'd be pissed as fuck. The girl was just told the man who played her guardian for the last few months might have murdered her parents and lied to her about, well, everything.

Hell yeah, I'd be angry.

Pissed enough to kill the bastard with zero remorse.

Though maybe that was a me thing.

Just as suddenly as it pierced the air, the screaming alarm and flashing lights cut off. Relieved, I stretched my jaw, mouth opening and closing to ease the tickling sensation as my hearing slowly adjusted. In the quiet, a pain-filled, incoherent groan snapped my attention to the floor where the two men were slowly coming to. Remembering the handy-dandy zip ties dangling from Mr. Curious's belt, I stretched over Mr. Serious to snag a handful. One man grunted something unintelligible as the thin plastic dug into the thick flesh around his wrists before I made quick work of securing his ankles, too.

With both restrained, I pulled a borrowed gun free and slammed the butt against one bastard's head, followed by the other. Pausing a moment, I waited to make sure both were out again before turning on the balls of my feet to face Millie and Karigan.

"Get to the bathroom and into the tub—"

"Kill, we're trapped and—"

My hand wrapped around Millie's, and I gave it a firm squeeze. "You said you trusted me, right?" Her responding nod was slow, but still a nod. "Great. Then go to the bathroom, both of you, get into the tub, and keep your heads down." The large clawfoot tub I caught sight of when I cleared that room earlier was the best protection against stray bullets once the fun started. "Don't come out. Don't make a sound until I come to get you."

"Kill—"

A quick tug on her hand had her stumbling against me.

My lips slammed to hers, cutting off her words. Despite the danger around us, I held her close, allowing myself the brief distraction. When I pulled back, her slightly swollen lips and hooded eyes told me she needed the quick kiss break, too.

"Go, do what I asked, wife. You said you trusted me. Now it's time to prove it. What waits on the other side of that door is child's play." Standing, my fingers still wrapped around hers, I guided Millie to the bathroom and pointed the gun barrel at the deep tub. "Don't worry. Everything will be okay, and I'll more than likely have a shit ton of fun doing it."

Light pressure against the small of her back had her moving deeper into the bathroom. I waited patiently while actively ignoring the thumping against the bedroom door until both were settled in the tub, their heads dipped beneath the cast-iron lip.

Perfect.

Closing the door behind me as another level of protection, I marched back into the bedroom, where the dresser fought valiantly to keep the door shut under the slamming force from the other side. The gun's rough grip dug into my palm as I raised it high and fired off a few rounds in rapid succession. Shattering glass filled the room as the window I put five strategic holes through came crashing down. With a proud smirk and nod, I tossed both guns onto the bed and pulled the knife secured around my calf free.

Soul-soothing calm folded me into its embrace the moment my palm wrapped around the hilt. It wasn't my favorite knife, but it was sharp as hell and would do what I needed to get out of this alive and without putting the two in the bathroom in danger with showering bullets. A sharp crack reverberated around the room as the wooden doorframe snapped. One more push from the other side of the door and the lock broke free from the frame.

A deep inhale to center the excitement pulsing through me, I rotated the blade so it lay carefully against my forearm and raised both hands in the air. The dresser groaned as it slowly dragged along the carpet from the door slowly working open. A battle cry sounded from the hallway, and the dresser toppled over, slamming to the floor.

Gap wide enough to slip through, one security idiot wedged his way inside the room. The moment he saw me, the barrel of the gun in his hand aimed at my chest.

"She's gone." I angled my head toward the shattered window. "Hopefully halfway across the property by now and on her way to sweet, sweet freedom."

"Damnit!" he shouted, while fumbling with the radio on his belt. Gun still aimed at my chest, he eased further into the room before striding to the open window and scanning the dark. "Confirmed breach. Suspect down." A scoff almost escaped. I was not fucking down. I was waiting for the perfect moment to take him, and what sounded like three to four additional security asshats waiting in the hall, out. "Send backup to sweep the grounds for the female. Secure her, unharmed." He tossed the radio onto the bed and bent down, pressing two fingers to the throat of one hog-tied asshole, then the other. "Who sent you?"

I pressed my lips shut, knowing I needed to bide my time and give the others a chance to enter the room so it could be an all-participants party. Snorting like an angry bull, the bastard stormed forward, free hand curled into a tight fist that swung toward my face. Spit flew and my teeth rattled with the solid hit across my jaw.

Fucking hell, that hurt. The bastard didn't hold back.

Mouth open, I stretched out my jaw to ease the steady

throb and glared at the asshat. When he cocked his fist back a second time, ready to hit me again, I braced for the punch, but he faltered at the commotion of the others pouring into the room.

"Two of you, check the closet," he barked over his shoulder, not looking away from me. "The other two, clear the bathroom. I'll finish this asshole off, and then we'll join the grounds search."

Well, fuck. Thought I had more time to play, but it seemed this one was actually good at his job. Time to get the party started. Flipping the blade around, giving it a few twists to stretch out my wrist, I shot the bastard a wicked smile. Confusion quickly turned to anger as he shifted to reposition the gun from the floor back toward me.

Exactly what I hoped he would do.

Time to fall back on all that fucked-up CIA training.

Chaos erupted around the room. Their shouts of alarm vibrated through the air, but it was all too late. For them, anyway.

I lashed a hand out, wrapping my fingers around the bastard's wrist. A quick half twist had the gun barrel pointed toward his buddies instead of my gut. Using the bastard's own finger, I pulled the trigger, quickly firing off four shots, each hitting exactly where I intended. With the boom of the gunshots still pulsing in the room, I stepped behind the security guy's back and slid the razor-sharp edge of the knife along his throat.

And then it was done. For now, at least. If anyone saw me, they'd have no idea I just took the lives of five men. The haze of the moment, filled with the thrill of the life-or-death situation, always kept my heart rate slow and breathing even despite the chaos.

The man dying at my feet writhed on the floor. I stared

down at him with zero remorse, zero... anything. Glorious blank numbness filled my veins during times like these, whether from all the training I went through or just normal self-preservation.

Though that numbness never lasted long, and too soon, I knew heavy guilt would fill my chest, weighing me down until it felt like I was drowning on dry land.

Later. Right now, I had precious cargo to escort out of the mansion and across the property.

Carefully stepping over the growing puddle of blood at my feet and over another body with a perfect hole between his brows, I swung open the bathroom door. Peeking my head in, I scanned the room, relieved to find the two stayed hunkered down in the tub like I asked.

"All right, ladies, let's blow this joint." I couldn't help but smile when Millie's pink head popped above the rim, dark eyes locking on me and widening to the size of saucers.

"Is that blood?" Uh-oh. That high pitch sounded a little hysterical, and when did she become so pale?

The smile turned into a confused frown as I checked my dress shirt. A few crimson spots dotted my white dress shirt, but it wasn't like I was soaked in the stuff. Not like the puddles they would both have to walk over on their way out. I cringed, thinking about the massacre at my back. Shit, maybe I should've moved the bodies. No time for that now.

"All good—"

"All good," she screeched as she clambered out of the tub, which was difficult in the pencil skirt and her short legs. A trembling finger pointed to my right hand. "There is blood dripping on the floor."

I held up the drenched knife and flicked it to the side, splattering the wall. "There, better?"

Millie swayed on her feet, face now completely void of

color. Karigan was there before I was, already out of the safety of the tub, and had an arm wrapped around Millie. My head tilted as I studied the girl, whose eyes seemed clearer than earlier in the day, with features set in determination.

"I think it's the blood," Karigan said, noticing my confusion.

"But not you?" Suspicion slowly crept in, making me stand a little straighter as I assessed the girl holding my Millie. What if she was too far gone or wanted to be here, and I'd let the enemy close to my ultimate vulnerability?

Slowly, I raised the knife and pointed the bloody tip at her face, a snarl curling my lip. Instead of crying or screaming, Karigan just rolled her eyes in that dramatic way only teenagers could manage. "Guy. I'm from Texas." I held her stare, waiting for an explanation of why that bit of information was important. "I grew up hunting at a managed game preserve with my dad before we moved here. Blood, guns, cleaning the kill to eat later... I'm used to it. Her? Not so much."

With a hesitant nod, I adjusted my grip on the knife and turned for the door. "We need to get the fuck out of here. Now. No way they won't send more security to investigate the gunshots."

With a firm nod, she guided the dazed and wobbling Millie to the door.

"Close your eyes, babycakes. You don't want to see this." Arm wrapped around her narrow waist, I hauled her against my body, her face immediately tucked against my throat. A sharp inhale at my back as we weaved through the bodies had me whirling the knife around, ready to sink into anyone who dared get close. Karigan's eyes were wide, a hand covering her gaping mouth.

I winced. "Oh, yeah. Um, sorry?"

"Sorry?" she whispered, face slightly green. "These bastards kept me locked in here. They knew what he was doing and didn't help me. They let him in here every night, not giving two shits if he would just stay in that damn chair or act on his fucked-up fantasies."

A slew of curses filled my thoughts. We so didn't have time for this therapy session. "Wish it were that simple, kiddo. These men were manipulated, too, though not innocent by any means. Hence why I don't feel bad that I'm the one who pulled the trigger and took their lives."

At least for right now.

Later, I'd wallow in the guilt. Though this time, unlike any other, I'd have my personal therapist at my side, so maybe I wouldn't sink so deep.

"Come on. We need to get out of here." My plan centered on us getting out of the house of horrors and far enough away from the cell jammer to message Hunter for backup. "You good?"

Karigan arched a dark brow and leveled me with an annoyed look. "No, but do I have a choice if I want out of here?"

"That's the spirit." With Millie still pressed against me, I swiped the two guns off the bed, holstering one while gripping the other, and started for the door. My fingers flexed around the weapon as I edged around the door frame, checking both directions before stepping into the hallway. All clear for now, though it wouldn't stay that way for long. When Karigan didn't immediately follow, I twisted to look behind me. Still in the room, she leaned over one body, but with her back to me, I couldn't see what she was doing.

Brows furrowed, I started to ask her why the fuck she stopped to play with a corpse when the pounding of several sets of boots from the direction of the main stairs vibrated down the hall. Whirling around, I aimed the gun toward the sound and fired off two warning shots in hopes they would hunker down so I didn't have to add their deaths to the growing tally mark on my soul.

"Let's go, now," I snapped at Karigan. She stood quickly and hurried to my side. "Stay at my side. I need to know where you are." Gun still aimed at the unseen threats, I backed down the hall all the way to the staff stairwell. The boom of a gun firing sounded just as a vase exploded on a side table to my right.

"Fuck," I hissed, holding Millie even tighter against me, careful to keep the knife still clutched in the hand around her back, away from her delicate skin. After firing off two more warning shots, I turned and bolted for the stairs, Karigan keeping up like I asked. There were too many questions around the girl, who looked alert and pissed. What happened to her drugged-out expressions or the almost unresponsiveness from earlier?

But those answers would have to come later. They didn't matter in the moment, and I wasn't willing to pause to ask them.

The staff stairwell door slammed open beneath my foot, almost ripping off the hinges from the force. My boots hit the stairwell landing just as multiple rounds of shots were fired from the other end of the hall. Karigan's bare feet and the leather soles of my shoes pounded against the stairs as we flew down the steps, almost making it to the first floor before the door slammed open. I took the shot the moment I confirmed he was armed, though this time, I put one in each thigh instead of between his brows.

His scream filled my ears. Not that I gave a shit.

Stepping over his writhing body and ignoring Millie's

complaints to let her walk—like that would happen with us in the middle of a near war zone—I bolted to a different door than the one we had come through earlier. The toxic stench of bleach and laundry detergent filled the air as we stepped into the laundry room and headed for the door on the other side. Rapid gunfire erupted behind us but not close, meaning we still had a small lead. Thank fuck Charlie had helped me map out multiple escape routes just in case shit went down.

And this was exactly what I would define as shit going down.

I sensed Karigan hovering near my back as I shoved the side door open that faced the east side of the property. Cool, damp air wrapped around me in a false sense of security as I flew outside. Millie wiggled against me, fighting my hold as I hopped the three concrete steps that led to the laundry room's side door, my boots slamming onto the soft grass.

"Put me down. I'm good now. I think." Her pink hair fluttered with my incredulous huff. "Killian."

The clear warning in her tone had my hold loosening, allowing her smaller frame to slide down my body. Wishing we had time for me to check her over and make sure she was okay, I opted for a quick scan of her face before nodding.

Needing a free hand to help guide the two through the dark, I flicked the knife to the side, the blade burying itself into the damp soil several feet away. Millie's fingers wrapped around my own, and I hitched my chin for her to grab Karigan's. The moment their fingers interlocked, I took off toward the trees for cover. Just as we slipped into the concealing shadows, just outside the mansion's security floodlights' reach, men poured from the laundry room. Their heads whipping one way, then the other.

I swallowed an inappropriately timed laugh as I led us deeper through the tall trees that surrounded the property. Minutes passed, but none of us said a word or made a sound. Even with the pace slower than my normal fast clip, the angry shouts at our backs faded. Barely winded, ready to keep going until we reached the fence that edged the property line, I failed to notice the two behind me struggling until Millie yanked on my hand, urging me to stop.

Their combined heavy breathing hit me when I turned, and I wanted to smack myself in the face.

"Sorry, forgot not everyone is..." I paused at the scowl on Millie's face. "As exceptional as me?"

She huffed and turned to Karigan. "You good?" Karigan just nodded, but now that my attention was on her, I zeroed in on the hand tucked behind her back. Fuck, was she injured?

"I know you two are tired, but we need to keep moving. They won't stop looking until they find us."

I felt like an ass saying that, but it was true. We could fix up their bare feet, and they could have a nice rest once we were on the other side of the fence. A silent prayer that we were far enough from the house, I pulled out my cell, thankful that it was still there. Hope and relief swelled in my chest at the messages and voicemail notifications popping up on the screen in rapid succession. "Thank fuck," I muttered to myself.

Before I could swipe to Hunter's contact information, the screen lit up, brightening the dark that helped conceal us. Thumb to the screen, I quickly swiped to answer the phone and pressed the smooth surface to my ear to minimize the beacon that could give away our position to anyone close by.

"Where the fuck have you been?" Charlie yelled.

"Dude, chill the fuck out. My ears are still sensitive from

that damn alarm." Plus, it hurt my feelings when he yelled at me.

"Oh, you mean the alarm I triggered because I caught you trapped with five guards trying to storm the room?"

"Aww, you hacked into their cameras. You love me."

"Shut the fuck up and tell me where you are. Rhyan is freaking out."

"They had a jammer, so I couldn't reach out at the initial check-in." There was a lot I needed to tell him, but not now when I was a sitting fucking duck with two little chicks to keep safe.

Wait.

"Are baby ducks chicks like chickens or something else?"

My lips quirked at the exaggerated loud exhale Charlie took on the other end of the line. "I'm tracking your phone now," he grumbled instead of answering my very pertinent question. "I'm sending it to Hunter, who—"

The soft crunch of leaves had me turning to the sound, dropping the phone, and aiming the gun all within a single heartbeat.

"Get behind me," I snapped to Millie and Karigan. Eyes narrowed, I scanned the dark, hoping to catch movement with help from the full moon's light pouring through the trees. It wasn't much, but I'd take it over nothing any day.

A flash of a white shirt had me zeroing in on the person stepping from behind a wide tree, empty hands raised. It took a second for the light to hit just right to make out the person's features.

A low growl escaped as my lip curled the moment I realized who stood between us and freedom.

Fucking Pastor Paul.

36

MILLIE

TODAY

Already lightheaded, foggy confusion kept me from instantly moving to Killian's side the moment Pastor Paul's profile became clear. My stomach dropped like a hundred-pound lead weight, and a shallow gasp caught in my throat.

I stood, frozen and trembling, completely unable to make my feet work.

The night's events, the blood, and just everything over the last several days had finally caught up to me, and now here I was, completely immobile while a known manipulating narcissist crept closer. Hands raised, steps cautious, he didn't appear harmful, but I knew the truth. He might not be lethal like Killian, trained to kill a million different ways, but Gary Paul was still deadly.

"I'm not here to hurt you, Kurt. Unlike what you did to my security team." Paul added a fake hitch to his voice in faux emotion over his men. "Those men had families, people who counted on them. Did you not think about the lives you ruined when you pulled that trigger?"

I chanced a quick look at Killian to make sure he wasn't

buying that bullshit. The man had ordered the murder of Karigan's parents. I couldn't prove it, yet anyway, but I knew it was his doing.

"Shut the fuck up and stop moving closer, or I swear I'll drop you where you stand." Killian's white teeth flashed in the moonlight with his menacing smile. When we first stepped out of the house, the darkness was blinding, but after my eyes adjusted, plus the full moon, seeing wasn't that challenging. "As you just stated, I have zero remorse about taking a life, so I suggest you stop where you fucking are and keep those hands in the air."

"All I wanted was to make sure my darling, sweet, and innocent Kari was okay," Paul pleaded. "You don't understand the depth of the trauma she has been through. She needs my help, needs to be with us so we can help her heal." The light shifted on his face as he turned his attention to the woman standing a few feet away, full focus on him.

My lungs stopped working, a restricted breath burned in my lungs.

She couldn't really believe his lies, could she?

"You were safe and cared for with me. These two outsiders, those without our shared light, want to ruin you, snuff out the light I know is buried deep inside you, Kari."

"Karigan." I prayed her whispered name reached her ears.

"You were safe and loved with me, remember? No one wanted you after your parents died, only me. Even your so-called friends abandoned you when you needed them most. But I didn't. The community surrounded you. Loved you. Provided for your every need. This is where you belong, where you can heal and be free for eternity." His hands were no longer high in surrender but stretched out wide. "They can't take you from me, Kari, not legally. This is your home, your life, and your future. It's all with me. Together, we will conquer the world. Just look at the danger they've already put you in; look at the violence they've brought to our doorstep."

"Oh, please, just shut the fuck up." Killian's voice echoed in the dark.

"Pastor." Karigan's soft, trembling voice cut through me like a knife.

"Yes, my darling Kari. My future bride, I'm here. I'll always be here for you. Come to me, child. Come to the light that I know you are desperate to feel so it can spread through you, too."

I pressed a hand to my stomach to keep the bit of water I drank earlier from exploding up my throat. Fuck, the man was a monster. He knew all the right buttons to push.

"She's not going anywhere—" My words cut off when Karigan took a single step closer to Pastor Paul. "No," I begged. "Please, Karigan. He's a liar and—"

"I need to know why," Karigan rasped, voice cracking. "I need to know why you killed them."

Huh. By the slow blink Pastor Paul gave, he didn't expect that question. He quickly recovered, that fake, confused, and innocent mask back in place. "What lies have they filled your head with, Kari? I didn't hurt them. They hurt each other. They lost the light—"

"Shut the fuck up." I stilled as Karigan's firm voice rang out, echoing through the trees.

"Oh, hell," Killian muttered under his breath and stepped closer to where I still hadn't moved.

"What?" The word had barely left my lips when the moonlight glinted off metal.

A gun.

A raised gun.

In Karigan's hand.

Pointed right at Pastor Paul.

"Ah, that makes sense now." I blinked up at Killian's tight features, hoping he'd fill in the gaps. "She paused inside her room. Guess she wanted a weapon, too. Smart girl." Killian's back brushed against my chest as he angled himself between me and Karigan. "Hey, Karigan, let's not—"

"He murdered my parents. I know he did," she said with a sob. "I know he did. They wouldn't have left me with him. They knew. They knew I didn't want anything to do with this place."

"That's not true. They loved you so much they wanted you to be free here with me—"

"I suggest you shut right the fuck up, you motherfucking idiot," Killian muttered to Gary Paul, but his focus was locked on Karigan's hand that held the gun. "Karigan, you don't want to do that."

"You don't know what they've done, what they do here." Her voice cracked. "Why?" she pleaded. "Why would you take them from me? We were happy. They were everything to me."

Silence filtered through the clearing, sounding like a bomb. Pastor Paul was clearly as smart as most cult leaders and knew when to keep his mouth shut. Whatever lies he spun were clearly unraveling. He was fucked.

He knew it.

Karigan knew it.

I knew it.

"Karigan, I need you to put the gun down," Killian said so softly, with so much emotion that tears flooded my lower lids. "You don't want to do this."

"He killed my parents. I'm all alone now. I'm—" Her voice broke. "He deserves to die just like they did."

"Oh, yeah, I totally, 100 percent agree—"

"Killian," I hissed.

He waved me off as he stepped closer to Karigan, tucking his gun into his waistband. "But not by you, not at your hand, sweet girl. That shit fucks with your mind more than the shit they've put you through the last few months. Believe me, I know."

The weight in that admission had my heart dropping.

My sweet, sweet Killian no doubt carried so much guilt and weight from the things he'd been forced to do throughout his career.

"No." Karigan sniffed and wiped at her eyes with her free hand. "No. Eye for an eye. Isn't that right, *Pastor*?" His fake title was more of a hiss than an actual word. "He deserves to die out here. No trial, no excuses."

"Then let me do it," Killian offered while taking another step. My eyes widened in horror when I realized what he planned to do.

"Killian, no," I pleaded, stumbling forward to stop him from putting himself between Karigan and Pastor Paul.

As if he didn't even hear me, Killian took the last step, placing his body almost directly in front of the trembling gun in Karigan's hand. Both hands slapped over my gaping mouth to quiet the soul-rattling sob that shook my body.

"Give me the gun, sweetheart. You don't need to do this. Don't let them take that piece of your soul. They've taken enough, yeah?" He reached out slowly, as if his hand moved through mud. Karigan's gut-wrenching sob broke through the night. Shoulders rounded, the barrel lowered to the ground, right into Killian's waiting palm. The moment he had control of the weapon, he tossed it away and yanked her tightly to his chest.

Lashes wet, a watery smile pulled at my lips at the sweet yet totally fucked-up scene.

I would for sure need hours of my own therapy after this. Stepping closer to the two, movement out of the corner of my eye snagged my attention. Between blinks, the wash of relief and joy vanished, terror taking hold as Gary Paul's hand withdrew something from behind his back.

Metal glinted as it raised high.

"No," I screamed, though not a single sound escaped because of the fear clogging my throat and constricting my words.

Without thinking, not even considering the multitude of consequences for my actions, I lunged toward Killian and Karigan. My shoulder slammed into Killian's side, shoving him and the girl still wrapped in his comforting arms away.

Just as a booming crack echoed through the night.

Fiery pain erupted from my side as I free-fell to the ground, both hands stretched out to catch myself. I winced, bracing for the impact. Twigs and leaves bit into my palms as they slammed into the damp soil. Teeth rattled as my face bounced off an exposed root. Stars lit behind my squeezed eyelids from the impact that jarred everything from my brain all the way down my spine.

Killian's roar sounded so far away, barely audible over the rapid thump of my heartbeat pounding in my ears. Dirt embedded beneath my nails as my fingers curled, the all-consuming pain contracting my muscles made me twitch along the ground.

A blazing inferno filled my lungs, the need for oxygen to breathe even a sliver of life-saving air turning desperate. But I couldn't, my entire body no longer under my control as I writhed along the ground.

Strong hands gripped my shoulders and flipped me

back, slamming into the dirt. My spine arched as pain like I never experienced coursed through.

"Millie." Whoever spoke felt like they were far away, underwater, attempting to talk to me though hot breath fanned over my chilled skin.

Everything faded, the pain, the fear, all feeling. I welcomed it, wanted that peaceful oblivion that beckoned me closer. Until something searing hot pressed to my lips, forcing them open and blowing unwanted air down my throat. I choked and coughed as my lungs kick-started. Razor blades sliced along my throat with every gasping, choking breath my body forced me to take.

Slowly the darkness receded, but with it came the blinding pain.

My teeth clenched, jaw tight, as I screamed through the pulsing agony. I couldn't pinpoint where it hurt. Every part of me seemed to pulse.

Through the blood rushing in my ears, shouts and loud cries sounded, but I couldn't focus on anything besides the pain and desperate need for more air. Another pain-filled scream sliced up my throat as I was lifted, my limp body held tight as I floated in the air.

At the first jostle, the pain pulsed even higher.

Too much.

Slowly, all the sounds, all the pain, everything, faded away.

37

KILLIAN

TODAY

Was that fucker Gary Paul dead? Fuck if I knew. I didn't stick around long enough to find out, not with my Millie shot and bleeding in my arms. Hunter was there, considering he was the one who shot Gary Paul half a second after the pastor fired his gun. He'd take care of everything while I ran like my life fucking depended on it. Over and over, I pleaded with any deity listening that Millie would be okay as I sprinted through the trees, with her unconscious body tucked tight against my chest. Unconscious or...

I gave my head a hard shake. Millie was simply unconscious from the shock of the night and being shot and her head slamming hard against a fucking tree root. It had nothing to do with the hot, sticky blood soaking my shirt and dripping onto the leaf-covered ground with every pounding footstep.

She would be okay.

This wasn't our end. Not when we'd just found each other again.

A flicker of light up ahead signaled I was near the fence

that spanned the perimeter of the compound. With a grunt, I increased my speed, knowing every damn second counted for the love of my life in my arms.

Millie would be okay.

I could get her to the hospital and demand that every person there save her.

Skidding to a stop, breaths fogging in front of my face with every heavy pant, I scanned the wire fence for the hole Hunter was supposed to cut out for our escape—though I never imagined the escape would be with a bleeding Millie in my arms.

There.

Jogging, I attempted to keep each step soft, so as not to jostle my precious cargo, and squeezed through the opening, not caring that the cut sharp ends sliced into my back as I ensured not a single one touched Millie. A single car waited along the curb, headlights off. Praying I didn't have to shift my girl to pull the gun from my waistband, I moved toward the vehicle. A tight breath released at finding it empty and the keys waiting in the driver's seat.

I needed to remember to kiss Hunter the next time I saw him for thinking ahead.

"Hold on, my Millie," I whispered as I jerked open the passenger door and slowly lowered her into the sedan. "You'll be okay." After buckling her in, worry flooding my mind when she didn't wake, I stepped back and slammed the door. Behind the wheel, I shoved the key into the ignition and slammed the gearshift into drive.

"You'll be okay, Millie," I repeated. "You have to be."

HAND WRAPPED around Millie's dainty fingers, I pressed the back of hers to my bowed forehead. A steady beep from the heart monitor was the only sound in the private hospital room. Her skin against mine triggered the night's events two days ago to replay over and over in my mind as a reminder of how I failed her.

I was too damn focused on making sure Karigan didn't end up like me, her soul splattered with dark stains, that I took my focus off the real threat. It was all I could do in the moment to not let my fear and emotions take control as I cradled Millie against my chest, running through the thick trees toward the gate. Thank fuck Hunter and Karigan were hot on my heels because with Millie hurt, she was all I could focus on.

My hold tightened around Millie's hand as hot tears leaked down my cheeks and splashed onto the thin white blanket wrapped around her still body.

The bullet wound to her side was technically a graze—though a little more to the left, and it would've been a through and through that would've been a hell of a lot worse. It was the head injury that the doctors needed to monitor, which was why they kept her sedated. Once the scans came back showing the slight brain swelling had gone down, they'd bring her back to me.

If she'd even have me.

I fucked up, bad.

The one woman I wanted to keep safe almost died because of me. Hell, she wasn't out of the woods yet. The doctors didn't know if there would be any lasting damage from the head injury.

If I couldn't protect her, then what in the hell did she need me for? She didn't. And there was no way in hell I could stick around and watch those dark eyes fill with disappointment and disgust once she woke up and realized how badly I had failed her.

This was why I had stayed away, why my father forced me to leave her behind. The woman he loved was hurt, killed, and he never recovered. That wasn't even his fault, like this situation was mine. I just knew she would never forgive me.

The chair legs scraped along the cheap flooring as I stood. Arched over the bedrail, I sealed my lips to her forehead, a few tears falling to her too pale skin. "I'm so sorry, Millie. I'm so fucking sorry."

Turning, I started for the door, stilling when it swung open and Hunter stepped through, a steaming to-go cup in each hand. He froze, just like me, eyes searching my face while his frown deepened.

"What are you doing, Coop?" Using the toe of his shoe, Hunter closed the door and leaned back against it. "You look like shit."

"Good." I ran a hand through my hair, and as if to prove his point, my fingers caught and pulled at the tangled mess. "That's exactly how I feel."

Lips pressed in a tight line, Hunter inclined his head toward the hospital bed I'd stayed vigil over since they wheeled her into the room. "Still sedated?" I nodded. "Damn, Cooper. Tell me what's going on. Talk to me. This look on your face is sheer devastation." Palm on my scruff-covered jaw, I pressed on the bruise, hoping the burst of pain would distract me from my heart fucking breaking. "You look like the families of victims we talk to. As if you've already lost her."

Hand dropping, I swallowed hard, refusing to look at the bed. If I looked at her now, I'd go right back to her bedside instead of leaving like she deserved. "Haven't I, though?"

"She's right there, Coop. A little banged up, but she's still here. But that look in your eye, the way you're acting, makes me wonder, will you be here when she wakes up?"

Both hands slid into the side pockets of my slacks, and I raised both shoulders in a noncommittal shrug.

"Nope." The bite of irritation in Hunter's tone had me snapping my focus to his anger-lined face. "Fucking hard nope."

"Nope? What do you mean, *nope*? This shit right here is none of your concern—"

"Not my concern? Oh, you motherfucker," he whisper-shouted. Coffee sloshed over the side of the disposable cup onto the floor when he jerked a finger to point at himself. "I'm your damn friend. The one who watched you go from hiding who you really are behind this dumbass persona to..." He sighed, some of the fight leaving him. "To being damn happy. I saw it all this past week, Cooper. Millie is it for you. She's your person. I know it, you know it, and she knows it."

Guilt rolled in my gut when I finally allowed myself to glance at the bed.

"I failed her," I whispered. "She's here in the hospital, fighting for her life, because of me. Her fucking brain is bruised." My finger jammed into my sternum. "Because of me."

"Really?" Sarcasm dripped from the single word. "I guess I saw the whole thing go down wrong. You were the one who shot her?"

"No," I growled, hands balling into fists.

"You tripped her and angled her body so that her head would perfectly hit the edge of a tree root?"

"You know what I meant," I growled, taking a menacing step closer. "Stop talking sense."

A wicked smirk played on his lips as he eyed my balled-up fists and defensive stance. "Okay, okay, you want to go right here, right now?" Stooping over, he set both cups on the floor and rolled his shoulders. The tight black T-shirt that stretched to the max over his arms and chest with the movement reminded me he was the only one on our team who could kick my ass in hand to hand. "Come at me, Cooper, because if you will not fight for you and her, then I will."

My jaw dropped. He stared me down for a few seconds before relaxing.

"Special Agent Cooper, speechless. That's something new. I should document that somewhere."

With an exhausted sigh, my shoulders dropped. "What good am I to her if I can't keep her safe? She doesn't want me."

"Did she tell you that in her sleep?" I flipped him the bird. "Just asking because you seem really damn sure that the woman who looks at you like you're her entire world will just walk away because of what happened. It wasn't your fault. If anything, it was mine."

An incredulous bark escaped. "What the hell? No, it's not. You're the one who took down the bastard, who got there in time—"

"Not before he pulled the trigger and hurt Millie." The door rattled as he leaned back against it. Easing to the floor, he balanced both forearms on his bent knees. "I feel responsible for it all. It was my fault, and I'm so damn sorry. I owe her an apology, too, but that will have to wait until she's awake."

"What the hell are you talking about right now, Hunter?"

"If I would've gotten there a second sooner, taken a different route or ran a little faster, he wouldn't have had time to pull the trigger. She wouldn't be in the hospital, and you wouldn't be considering walking out on the best thing that has ever happened to you."

With a resigned sigh, I moved to sit beside him. We sat in comfortable silence for several minutes, both lost in our own grief and guilt.

"I don't know what to do," I admitted.

Hunter's head hit the door, and he rolled it until he faced me. "You stay here with her. Pretty sure that's all she wants."

"And if she doesn't?"

His smile turned mischievous. "Then kidnap her and use that damn chemistry between you two until she does."

A huffed laugh escaped. As crazy as that suggestion sounded, it made sense to me. "Enough about my shit-show love life. Everything wrapped up in the case?" My phone wouldn't stop blinking and rattling with incoming calls and messages that I continued to ignore. Rhyan understood why I couldn't leave Millie to head back to the scene, but that didn't mean she stopped checking in. "Sorry I can't be there to help clean up the mess I made."

His shoulder knocked against mine. "All good. Though the paperwork to explain the eight dead bodies is all yours once you're back."

My brows furrowed as I calculated how many I took down. "I only took out five. Well, and the one I put two bullets in the thigh. Oh, and the guy I beat to shit and left tied up in the closet."

He actively avoided my gaze as he hid a knowing grin behind the coffee cup. "I couldn't let you have all the fun." The sparkle in his eyes dimmed. "I saw some messed-up stuff while I bunked with the security team. Several of them didn't deserve to continue breathing, so I made sure that happened."

I raised a tight fist until he tapped his against it. "The followers, leadership team, sheriff? I feel like all you're focusing on is the pile of bodies we left behind."

Hunter smirked. "Followers? Well, most are fucking pissed that a government employee killed their precious pastor. He wove so many lies and promises that they're confused, angry, and left with nothing. The FBI sent counselors over, but most are refusing help. Hell, they won't even leave the compound. That fucker Davis is stepping up, trying to calm everyone's fears while quietly replacing Gary Paul as the lead of the church."

"His wife?" Fuck, I was an asshole. I hadn't even thought about her since that night at their place.

"She's safe. Traumatized but safe. The FBI moved her out of state and will hold off on making her relive everything she's gone through until she's ready. As for the leadership team, some stayed, but most bailed, not wanting to get wrapped up in an FBI raid. You should've seen how fast that Simon guy bolted after we found him hog-tied in that closet."

"You're welcome for that, by the way. I hope you got a few hits in yourself."

"He might have tripped a few times and landed on my fist. The sheriff... no one knows where the hell she is. We had a team raid her house, and, of course, the files are gone. Not sure how she was tipped off, but she's on the run. We'll find her, though. It's a shit show, which we knew it would be."

I nodded and looked back at the hospital bed. "Now what do I do?"

"Now, you wait, and the second she wakes up, you marry

that woman." With a groan, he stood. "Because if you don't, I for sure fucking will."

He was right. Millie was mine, now and forever. Time to make her title as my wife an official one.

Leaning to the side, I pulled out my phone, ignoring the missed calls and messages, and tapped on my contacts, scrolling until I found the one I wanted. Phone pressed to my ear, I held a nervous, shallow breath, waiting for the call to connect.

"Son." Dad's voice boomed through the line.

"Dad," I choked, suddenly terrified and way too damn emotional. "I need to tell you something, and then I have a favor to ask." His silence was all I needed to continue.

I just hoped he had changed as much as I believed, and admitting the future I wanted with Millie didn't put her in more danger than she was in the last week. But if he came for her to tie up loose ends, or sent someone to do it for him, I'd be ready.

She'd never be in the line of danger again.

Not on my watch.

38

MILLIE

TODAY

Damn, I hated the zombie fog after a long nap. I always woke up more tired and groggy than when I had lain down. Lips in a frown, I shifted on the uncomfortable bed, the stiff sheets scraping against my skin.

Wait. I stilled. Something wasn't right. Pinpointing what felt off, I narrowed it down to the stiff cotton against my bare ass.

I never slept naked, so why in the hell did it feel like I was?

Getting my eyelids to cooperate was more difficult than I expected. The thick lashes almost refused to separate, like they were glued together. Damn, how long a nap did I take? A bolt of panic spiked through me. Damn, what if I slept through a class? Movements frantic, I jerked and writhed on the bed, utterly confused and slightly scared.

"Millie." I stilled at the voice seeming to hover over me. Breaths shallow, I focused on using my other senses. A steady beeping, muffled voices that sounded far away or behind thick walls. Then the smells hit me. Antiseptic, bleach, and something else I couldn't name.

The high-pitched beeping increased as I again struggled on the bed. The urgency to force my eyes open made heat build beneath my skin and sweat to bead along my upper lip.

"Easy, babycakes. Easy." A held breath rushed from my lungs, and I relaxed against the uncomfortable mattress.

Killian. He was here. And if he was here, then I was safe.

Blowing out a controlled breath, I licked my cracked lips. "Where am I?"

"Hospital. You're okay, baby. You're safe."

"Well, yeah, because you're right here." I could've sworn I heard his breath catch. "Kill, why can't I open my eyes?"

"Because you've been out for three days, Millie. Do you remember what happened? Why you're here?"

I felt my brows furrow despite the ache that slight movement caused as I searched the dark recesses of my mind. Everything was blurry, my memories unclear, but the feelings weren't. Fear, panic, and love all flickered in and out as I tried to piece together what emotion went where.

My hair rasped along the pillow as I turned toward Killian's voice. Millimeter by millimeter, I forced my eyes open, only a little at a time, until finally, Killian's blurry face filled my vision. His hand smoothed down the side of my head, coming to rest on my cheek.

"You don't remember, do you?" he asked.

"Not really."

"Do you want to?"

"Yes," I rasped. "Tell me."

Killian's lips parted, but the door swinging open had him snapping them shut at the same moment he was out of the chair, and—wait. Was that a knife?

"Sir, you cannot have a knife in here." I followed the

trembling voice to a man in a white lab coat, with both hands raised in the air, one holding a clipboard.

"I dare you to try and take it from me. It's been a while since I've—"

"Kill," I rasped, cutting him off.

His aqua eyes softened as he looked down at me. "Yeah, babycakes."

"I think we should let the doctor do his thing." I paused and licked my cracked lips, which reminded me of how long Killian said I'd been in the hospital. "You'll be here. I'll be safe."

Slowly, the knife lowered and disappeared back to wherever Killian had it hidden. He nodded and motioned the very pale doctor deeper into the room.

"Sorry, Doc. I'm just a little on edge. You do your thing, and make sure my girl here is all good, now that she's awake. But"—the doctor froze halfway to my bed—"if you do anything I don't like, I will kill you. Slowly."

The doctor's Adam's apple bobbed with a thick swallow.

A heavy weight settled over me, making my lids flutter closed.

Safe. I was safe.

Because I knew Killian wouldn't allow any other outcome.

"ARE YOU SURE YOU'RE READY?" I shot Killian a glare, making him toss his hands up in surrender. "You only woke up twelve hours ago and have been in and out since. Sorry for making sure you're up to hearing all this."

"I need to know, Kill. Please."

After releasing a slow breath, Killian walked me through

everything I didn't remember from the night we kidnapped Karigan and I was shot. Some of what he said triggered a memory, others not so much. When he got to the part where I saved his life and possibly Karigan's, his voice trembled, and the hand cupping my jaw tightened.

"I thought I lost you. I'm so sorry, Millie, so fucking sorry."

Maybe it was the effects of the meds or the brain bruise, but I couldn't figure out what he was actually apologizing for. Instead of asking, I twisted to kiss the inside of his palm.

"How is she?" I asked, hoping to erase the devastation from his face. I hated him looking so... not my Killian.

"She's doing okay. The doctors cleared her fairly quickly. They ran bloodwork the second she got to the hospital, and they found remnants of light sedatives in her system. I asked her why she was so coherent that night instead of blitzed out, and she said you talking with her that day made her question everything. That night, she pretended to swallow the so-called vitamins they forced her to take with dinner and spit them out in the toilet."

"Smart girl," I murmured.

"Her aunt came and picked her up yesterday. Karigan wanted to say goodbye, but..."

I nodded, wincing at the movement. "I understand. I'm sure she was ready to get as far away from this place as possible. What else?"

"Carrie Culler got out and is somewhere safe from that asshole Davis. It only took a few hours after the chaos we caused for the Atlanta FBI office to send a handful of agents to the compound to start an official investigation and clean up our mess. Unfortunately, that gave the sheriff time to get away with the files. When they showed up at her place, it was empty, but the agency froze her assets and have the entire country searching for her."

My fingers picked at a loose thread. "And Gary Paul?" I hated the way his name struck fear through me.

"Dead. Shot almost the same second you were."

"Were you the one who did it?" My heart sank for Killian. Another guilt mark that I knew he would wear.

"Hunter, actually. He was half a second too late to prevent you from getting shot, which he feels terrible about. Don't worry, I told him you liked black roses and bouquets of penis straws." My huffed laugh turned into a groan. "The gunshot wound was just a graze. It was the head injury that caused all the issues. The doctors don't believe there will be lasting damage but want you to take it easy for a while. No stress, no heroics."

A corner of my lips pulled up in a half smile. "I'm not the hero, you are."

Killian leaned in close, brushing his nose against mine. "You are to me, to Karigan, to all those people who are free from Pastor Paul's reach. Now," sitting up straight, he shot me a hesitant look. "Do you need a nap, getting a little sleepy-peepy after story time, or are you up for another visitor?"

I checked in with myself before responding. Sure, my thoughts were slower, my memory spotty, and my body ached in places I didn't know could ache, but overall, I was okay. As I shimmied up the bed, Killian stuffed a few pillows behind my back for support.

"Don't freak out," he said, walking to the door. "Everything is going to be okay."

"All right," I drawled and pulled the scratchy white blanket until it tucked under my armpits.

After sticking his head out into the hall, Killian stepped

back, allowing an older man, who looked eerily similar to Killian, into the room. I did a double-take. The same dirty-blond hair, though the older man's hair was sprinkled with gray streaks. Square jaw, an inch taller than Killian, but there was no denying the resemblance.

"Dr. Anderson." His deep voice rolled through the room, making me want to sit up a little straighter. "Danny Cooper." At the end of my bed, he paused and shoved both hands into the side pockets of his slacks.

My gaze flicked to Killian, who waggled his brows. "My dad."

A sharp breath hissed through my teeth, and I shrank into the bed, hoping it would swallow me whole while a flicker of anger burned in my chest, knowing this man was the reason Killian went into the CIA, why we were ripped apart.

"Ah, I see your wheels turning. Smart, just like he said." He nodded over his shoulder to his son. "I know you need your rest, but after being berated by my son, I knew I needed to get my ass to Georgia to apologize to you in person."

My jaw dropped. "Apologize?"

He nodded and ran a hand through his hair, the movement so familiar I couldn't help but grin.

"I made a decision, a lot of poor decisions, regarding my son. What I thought was best for him actually wasn't. I realize now the devastating grief I felt over losing my wife," he cleared his throat and glanced at the ceiling, "twisted me into a man I didn't recognize. I've worked the past few years trying to make it up to my son, but now I need to do the same with you."

"Sir, you don't—"

He held up a hand, cutting me off. "I do. Which is why I'm here. I knew how my son felt about you, and I still forced him into a career, a life, he never wanted but what I thought was best for him. As an employee for a certain agency, you're alone, never in one place long enough to settle down. Never able to build a life that might cripple you if it were ripped away. It's also a known fact that anyone close to us is a weakness that will be exploited to keep us in line by our own government or revenge for our many enemies. Even though my son is out of that line of work, he was very good at what he did. Disabling trafficking rings, shutting down drug cartels, hell, even upending governments are only a few of his successes."

Jaw still slack, I turned my gaping face to Killian, who winked.

"What he's done won't go away. There will always be those who want revenge. We've done our best to hide him in plain sight, cover his tracks so no one knows exactly who our best asset was. So far, nothing has happened, but that doesn't mean it can't or won't, which was why I urged him not to reach out to you, even after he left that agency. Two days ago, he called to tell me everything that happened and that he had zero plans to let you go again."

The breath I held whooshed from my lungs with a relieved sigh. "Good. Because I'm not letting him."

"Damn, you're perfect," Killian muttered. In two long strides, he was at my bedside, brushing hair off my forehead in sweet, reassuring strokes.

"I will continue to do what I can from the sidelines, since I also left that agency. But I still have connections to ensure your safety and his. It's the least I can do for what I put you both through, taking him away that night."

The guilt written on his face had me holding out my

hand to him. A look of shock flicked across his features as his palm met mine.

"I forgive you," I rasped. "And thank you for coming and apologizing in person."

He cleared his throat and wiped at his eyes. "I had another reason for coming." Light blue eyes flicked to the other side of my bed. I followed his stare, only to gasp at the small, pale blue box resting in Killian's open palm.

"Kill?" My voice trembled. "What's going on?"

He lowered onto one knee beside the bed. Tears rimmed his aqua eyes and slowly leaked out of the corners.

"I love you, my Millie. I've always loved you. From the time you were my Velma to now, not a day has gone by when I haven't thought about you, wanted to see you, to hear your laugh, and to see your smile. There has never been anyone else for me, and there never will be. The last week, pretending to be your husband, made me realize just how badly I wanted to make it true. Be my wife. Be mine forever."

I blinked past my own tears. Out of the corner of my eye, I saw a tissue dangling in the air, and I gratefully took it to wipe my running nose. The creak of the box as it opened sounded like a jet engine. My eyes widened, and a gasp escaped as I took in the sparkling ring that sat on the tiny pillow, a massive round diamond surrounded by tiny sapphires. It was beautiful and perfect.

"It was my mother's," Killian rasped and glanced at his father before looking back at me. "I know she would've wanted you to have it. Say yes, my Millie. Please, please be mine."

So many questions filled through my mind, whirling to where I felt dizzy.

Where would we live?

What would he do for work?

What would I do for work?

Did he want kids?

Did I want kids?

Could we get a dog?

But as I stared into Killian's patient aqua eyes, I knew none of those questions or answers mattered as long as I had him. Together, we'd figure it all out. It would be difficult, but all the best things in life were worth fighting and working for.

Sucking in a deep breath, I bit my lower lip to stop it from trembling.

"Yes," I rasped. Killian's eyes widened. "Nothing could stop me from being yours. I always have been."

A giggle escaped when he leapt off the floor and folded over the bedrail, wrapping his arms around me. Despite the discomfort, I relaxed into his hold and wrapped my own arms around his back, squeezing him even tighter.

Mine.

This amazing, slightly broken, brilliant man was mine. Forever. No matter what came for us, we'd be ready, together.

For ten years, I'd dreamed of this moment.

Somehow, it was even more perfect than I ever imagined.

EPILOGUE
KILLIAN

"I now pronounce you husband and wife."

Cheers erupted around the small chapel, though I didn't take my eyes off my beautiful bride to acknowledge our friends. Wrapping a hand around the back of her neck, I tugged her closer and lowered my lips to hers. Whoops and whistles met my ears as I kissed my Millie like she was the air I needed to continue living.

Which wasn't a far-off analogy, considering she was my sole reason for living and had been since we met.

"You're mine now, wife," I murmured.

"I already was, husband."

The corners of my lips kicked up, and I brushed my nose against hers before straightening to my full height. Turning to the small gathered crowd, I finally acknowledged our friends and my family who had either flown or driven to Vegas for our intimate wedding. Dad smiled at us with pride and joy in his watery gaze from the front row, clapping as he stood with the rest of the guests.

Behind him was my team.

Our team technically, now that she had accepted the

newly created forensic psychologist role with the Dallas-based BSU team. The dean wasn't happy that she didn't commit to another year of teaching, but once I explained he'd end up a missing person if he made her feel bad about her decision, he changed his tune and even gave her a parting bonus.

Crazy how a little bodily harm threat can turn anyone's frown upside down.

After selling her townhome and most of her belongings, she moved down to Dallas and into the townhome we now co-own in the bustling uptown area. We'd barely had time to get settled, between the move and tying up loose ends from our joint assignment, taking down The Union of Blessed Souls, before jetting off to Vegas to get married.

And now, we were.

Holy fuck, how did I get so damn lucky?

Charlie and Rhyan waved and cheered as we walked up the aisle, the latter stepping out from the chairs to wrap Millie in a tight hug. While they whispered in each other's ears, Charlie slapped me on the back and nodded.

"Best decision you ever made, Cooper." I nodded, unable to look away from Millie. She was glowing with happiness, and I knew if I caught my reflection, it would be the same. "Did she see the additional guests you flew in last minute?"

At the mention of my surprise, I glanced to the very back row and raised a hand, beckoning the two closer.

"Congrats, Coop." A grunt escaped, and I staggered forward at the hard slap between my shoulder blades. I turned with an annoyed look and flipped off Slade, our resident medical examiner's boyfriend, before shooting a smile at Jameson, her husband and another profiler on our Dallas BSU team. Yes, she was with both, and none of us cared. She was amazing, and they made her happy. That was all I needed to know.

"Happy for you two, man," Jameson said as he shook my hand. "I really never thought I'd see this day for you. I was almost certain, with your crazy-ass antics and lack of self-preservation, that you wouldn't even see your next birthday."

"Thanks for the confidence. Bastard," I grumbled at the end. I looked over his shoulder and shifted. "Where is Hunter?" At his wince, I straightened. "What?"

"He wanted to be here, Coop, but a case came up that one of us needed to take immediately. I tried to go in his place so he could be here, but..." He ran a hand over his head. "The location was only a few miles from his home-town in North Carolina, so he wanted to be the one to go."

"A bad one?" I asked, suddenly nervous for my friend.

"Yeah. A bad one. Multiple young women and the local police have no clue how to handle it."

Before I could ask for details, the two guests I flew in just for Millie approached. Smiling, I laced my fingers through Millie's and squeezed to pull her focus away from Rhyan. When she whirled around, that wide smile faltered as she took in the two women. My stomach sank. Fuck, was this the wrong wedding present?

"Karigan?" Millie whispered, fingers at her wobbling lip. I glanced at the young woman, who looked just as emotional as my wife. "What are you doing here? How did you...?" Those dark eyes snapped to me. "You invited them?"

"Invited, planned, and paid for all our travel. Even left us a goodie basket in our hotel room," Karigan's aunt said. She extended a hand to Millie. "Thank you for all that you did, all that you risked for my niece." After dropping Millie's hand, she wrapped an arm around Karigan's shoulders.

"She's doing amazing, considering everything that she went through."

In a flash, Karigan surged forward and wrapped her arms around Millie's shoulders, pulling her in for a tight hug. Tears collected in my lower lids, but I refused to let them fall as I watched the two.

Karigan was safe.

Millie was officially mine.

And me...

I finally had it all.

ALSO BY KENNEDY L. MITCHELL

In Clear Sight: A Small Town, WITSEC Interconnected Standalone Series

Safe Haven - FREE Prequel

Guarded by the Marshal*

Cherished by the Agent*

Saved by the Officers *

Hidden by the Doctor *

*Now available in Audio!

Protection Series: A Dark Romantic Thriller Interconnected Standalone Series

Mine to Protect *

Mine to Save *

Mine to Guard *

Mine to Keep *

Mine to Hold *

Mine to Love *

Mine to Share

Mine to Shelter

Mine to Shield

*Now available in audio!

SEALs and CIA Series: A Navy SEAL Interconnected Standalone Series

Covert Affair

Covert Vengeance

More Than a Threat Series: A Connected Bodyguard Romantic Suspense Series

More Than a Threat

More Than a Risk

More Than a Hope

More Than a Threat Series Boxset: Complete Series

Power Play Series: A Protector Romantic Suspense Connected Series

Power Games

Power Twist

Power Switch

Power Surge

Power Term

Standalones:

Finding Fate - Dark, Captive Romantic Suspense

Memories of Us - Contemporary, Small Town Romance

ACKNOWLEDGMENTS

The first people I'd like to thank are my alpha readers. You four are amazing and I cannot thank you enough for all that you do. From encouraging messages, to begging for more, and of course pushing me to finish the book right instead of just blowing everyone up so I could write 'the end'. You four make all this fun and I wouldn't want to do it without you in my corner.

My editor and proofreader are so fantastic. I cannot thank them enough for turning my mess of words into something readable.

Thank you to my beta readers, ARC team and everyone who has helped me share this story. You guys are amazing and I cannot thank you enough for all that you do.

And of course, thank YOU! You amazing reader you are who I write these stories for. All the stress, late nights, and worry is worth it when I get your email or message about how much you loved the book. Whether it be one reader or millions I'm so very very thankful that you gave me a chance.

ABOUT THE AUTHOR

Kennedy L. Mitchell lives outside Dallas with her husband, son and two very large goldendoodles. She began writing in 2016 and has no plans of stopping.

She would love to hear from you via any of the platforms below or her website www.kennedylmitchell.com You can also stay up to date on future releases through her newsletter or by joining her Facebook readers group - Kennedy's Book Boyfriend Support Group.

Thank you for reading.

www.ingramcontent.com/pod-product-compliance
Lightning Source LLC
Chambersburg PA
CBHW022300310726
48973CB00001B/150